my LITTLE PONY
Friendship is Magic

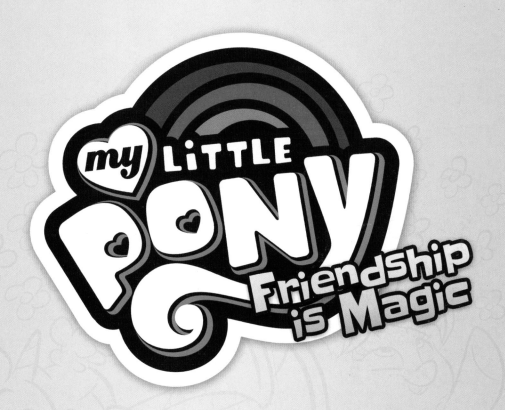

COLLECTION EDITS BY
Justin Eisinger and Alonzo Simon

COLLECTION DESIGN BY
Neil Uyetake

PUBLISHER
Ted Adams

Special thanks to Meghan McCarthy, Eliza Hart, Ed Lane, Beth Artale, and Michael Kelly.

For international rights, contact licensing@idwpublishing.com

ISBN: 978-1-63140-903-5

20 19 18 17   1 2 3 4

Ted Adams, CEO & Publisher • Greg Goldstein, President & COO • Robbie Robbins, EVP/Sr. Graphic Artist • Chris Ryall, Chief Creative Officer • David Hedgecock, Editor-in-Chief • Laurie Windrow, Senior Vice President of Sales & Marketing • Matthew Ruzicka, CPA, Chief Financial Officer • Lorelei Bunjes, VP of Digital Services • Jerry Bennington, VP of New Product Development

Facebook: facebook.com/idwpublishing • Twitter: @idwpublishing • YouTube: youtube.com/idwpublishing
Tumblr: tumblr.idwpublishing.com • Instagram: instagram.com/idwpublishing

www.IDWPUBLISHING.com

Accord

WRITTEN BY
Ted Anderson

ART BY
Andy Price

For The Pony
Who Has Everything

WRITTEN BY
Jeremy Whitley

ART BY
Jay Fosgitt

From The Shadows

WRITTEN BY
James Asmus

ART BY
Tony Fleecs

COLORS BY
Heather Breckel

LETTERS BY
Neil Uyetake

SERIES EDITS BY
Bobby Curnow

COVER BY
Andy Price

art by Andy Price

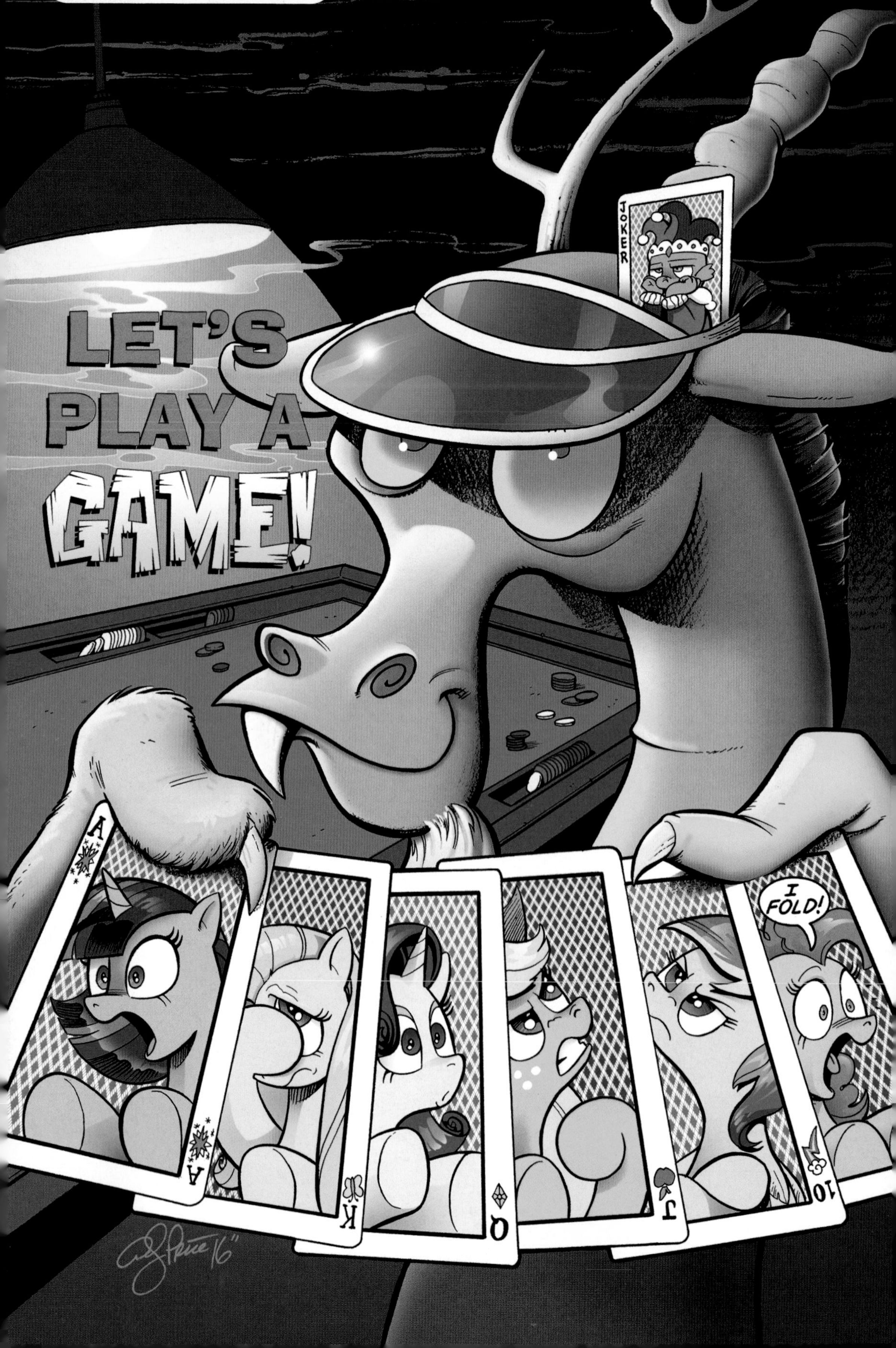
LET'S PLAY A GAME!
JOKER
I FOLD!
A
K
Q
J
10

ACCORD

PART THE FIRST: FROM CHAOS COMES ORDER

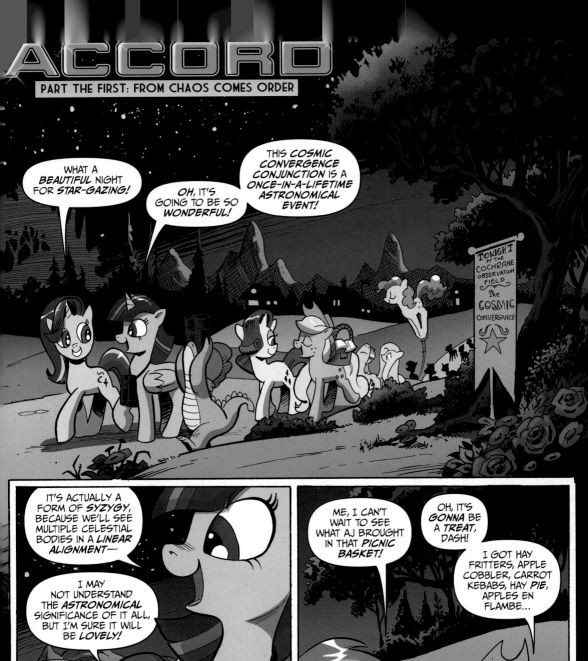

WHAT A *BEAUTIFUL* NIGHT FOR *STAR-GAZING!*

OH, IT'S GOING TO BE SO *WONDERFUL!*

THIS *COSMIC CONVERGENCE CONJUNCTION* IS A *ONCE-IN-A-LIFETIME ASTRONOMICAL EVENT!*

TONIGHT AT THE COCHRANE OBSERVATION FIELD — The COSMIC CONVERGANCE

IT'S ACTUALLY A FORM OF *SYZYGY*, BECAUSE WE'LL SEE MULTIPLE CELESTIAL BODIES IN A *LINEAR ALIGNMENT—*

I MAY NOT UNDERSTAND THE *ASTRONOMICAL* SIGNIFICANCE OF IT ALL, BUT I'M SURE IT WILL BE *LOVELY!*

OH, YES!

ME, I CAN'T WAIT TO SEE WHAT AJ BROUGHT IN THAT *PICNIC BASKET!*

OH, IT'S *GONNA* BE A *TREAT,* DASH!

I GOT HAY FRITTERS, APPLE COBBLER, CARROT KEBABS, HAY *PIE,* APPLES EN FLAMBE...

MATTER O' FACT, I MIGHT JUST NEED TO GRAB A LI'L SOMETHING RIGHT—

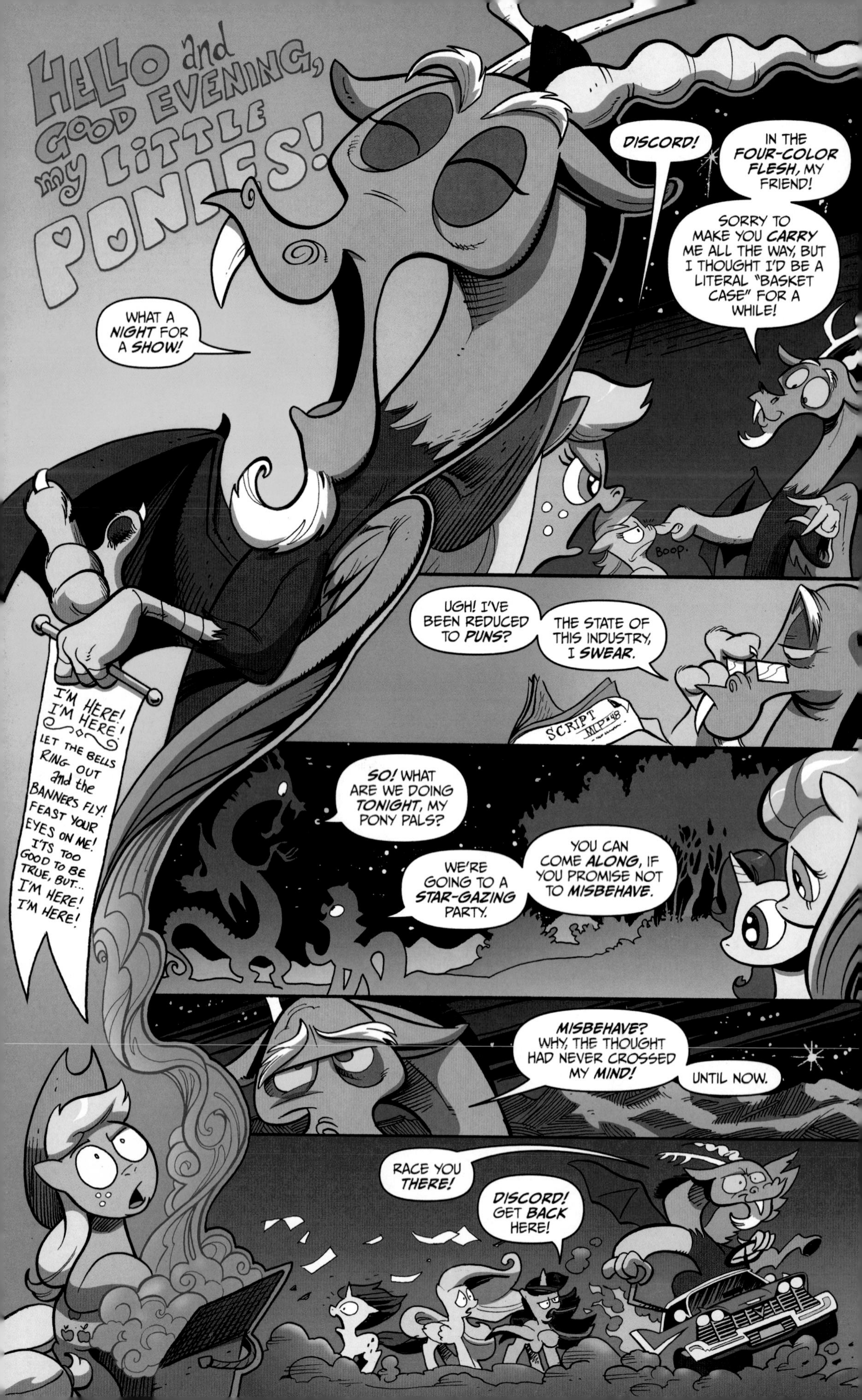
HELLO and GOOD EVENING, my LITTLE PONIES!
WHAT A NIGHT FOR A SHOW!
I'M HERE! I'M HERE! LET THE BELLS RING OUT and the BANNERS FLY! FEAST YOUR EYES ON ME! IT'S TOO GOOD TO BE TRUE, BUT... I'M HERE! I'M HERE!
DISCORD!
IN THE FOUR-COLOR FLESH, MY FRIEND!
SORRY TO MAKE YOU CARRY ME ALL THE WAY, BUT I THOUGHT I'D BE A LITERAL "BASKET CASE" FOR A WHILE!
BOOP.
UGH! I'VE BEEN REDUCED TO PUNS?
THE STATE OF THIS INDUSTRY, I SWEAR.
SCRIPT
SO! WHAT ARE WE DOING TONIGHT, MY PONY PALS?
WE'RE GOING TO A STAR-GAZING PARTY.
YOU CAN COME ALONG, IF YOU PROMISE NOT TO MISBEHAVE.
MISBEHAVE? WHY, THE THOUGHT HAD NEVER CROSSED MY MIND!
UNTIL NOW.
RACE YOU THERE!
DISCORD! GET BACK HERE!

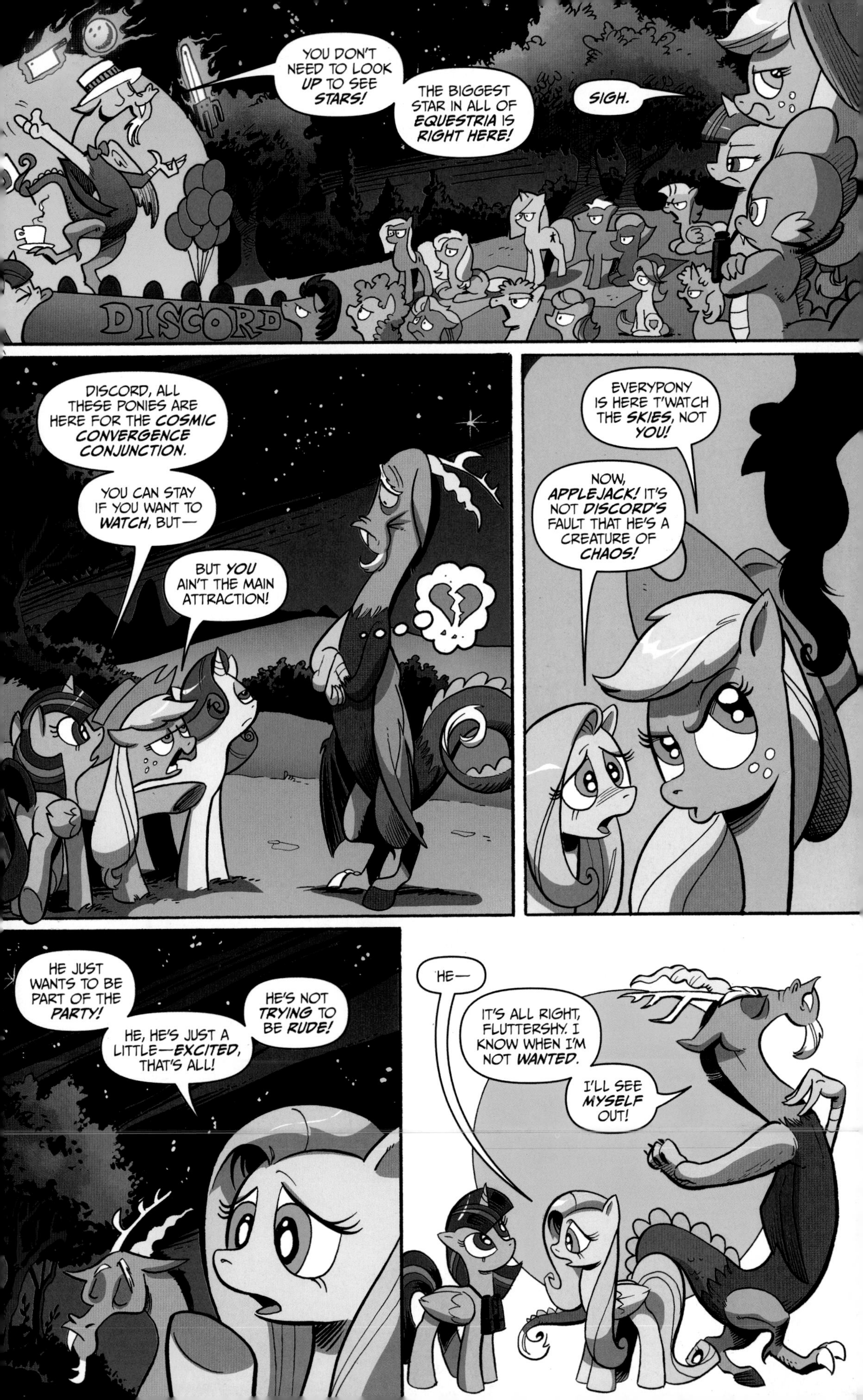
DISCORD
YOU DON'T NEED TO LOOK UP TO SEE STARS!
THE BIGGEST STAR IN ALL OF EQUESTRIA IS RIGHT HERE!
SIGH.
DISCORD, ALL THESE PONIES ARE HERE FOR THE COSMIC CONVERGENCE CONJUNCTION.
YOU CAN STAY IF YOU WANT TO WATCH, BUT—
BUT YOU AIN'T THE MAIN ATTRACTION!
EVERYPONY IS HERE T'WATCH THE SKIES, NOT YOU!
NOW, APPLEJACK! IT'S NOT DISCORD'S FAULT THAT HE'S A CREATURE OF CHAOS!
HE JUST WANTS TO BE PART OF THE PARTY!
HE, HE'S JUST A LITTLE—EXCITED, THAT'S ALL!
HE'S NOT TRYING TO BE RUDE!
HE—
IT'S ALL RIGHT, FLUTTERSHY. I KNOW WHEN I'M NOT WANTED.
I'LL SEE MYSELF OUT!

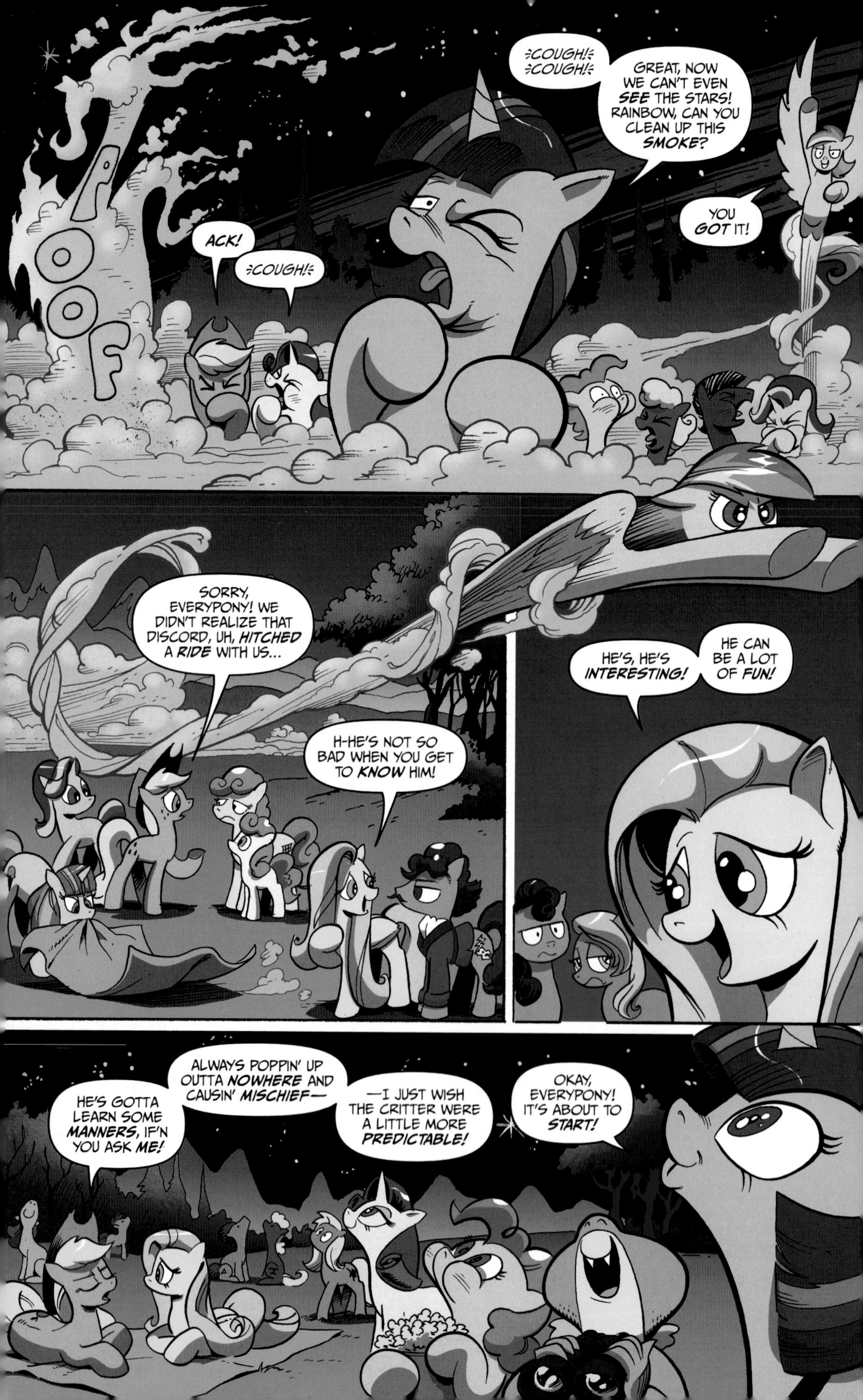

FOOF
ACK!
COUGH!
COUGH! COUGH!
GREAT, NOW WE CAN'T EVEN SEE THE STARS! RAINBOW, CAN YOU CLEAN UP THIS SMOKE?
YOU GOT IT!
SORRY, EVERYPONY! WE DIDN'T REALIZE THAT DISCORD, UH, HITCHED A RIDE WITH US...
H-HE'S NOT SO BAD WHEN YOU GET TO KNOW HIM!
HE'S, HE'S INTERESTING!
HE CAN BE A LOT OF FUN!
HE'S GOTTA LEARN SOME MANNERS, IF'N YOU ASK ME!
ALWAYS POPPIN' UP OUTTA NOWHERE AND CAUSIN' MISCHIEF—
—I JUST WISH THE CRITTER WERE A LITTLE MORE PREDICTABLE!
OKAY, EVERYPONY! IT'S ABOUT TO START!

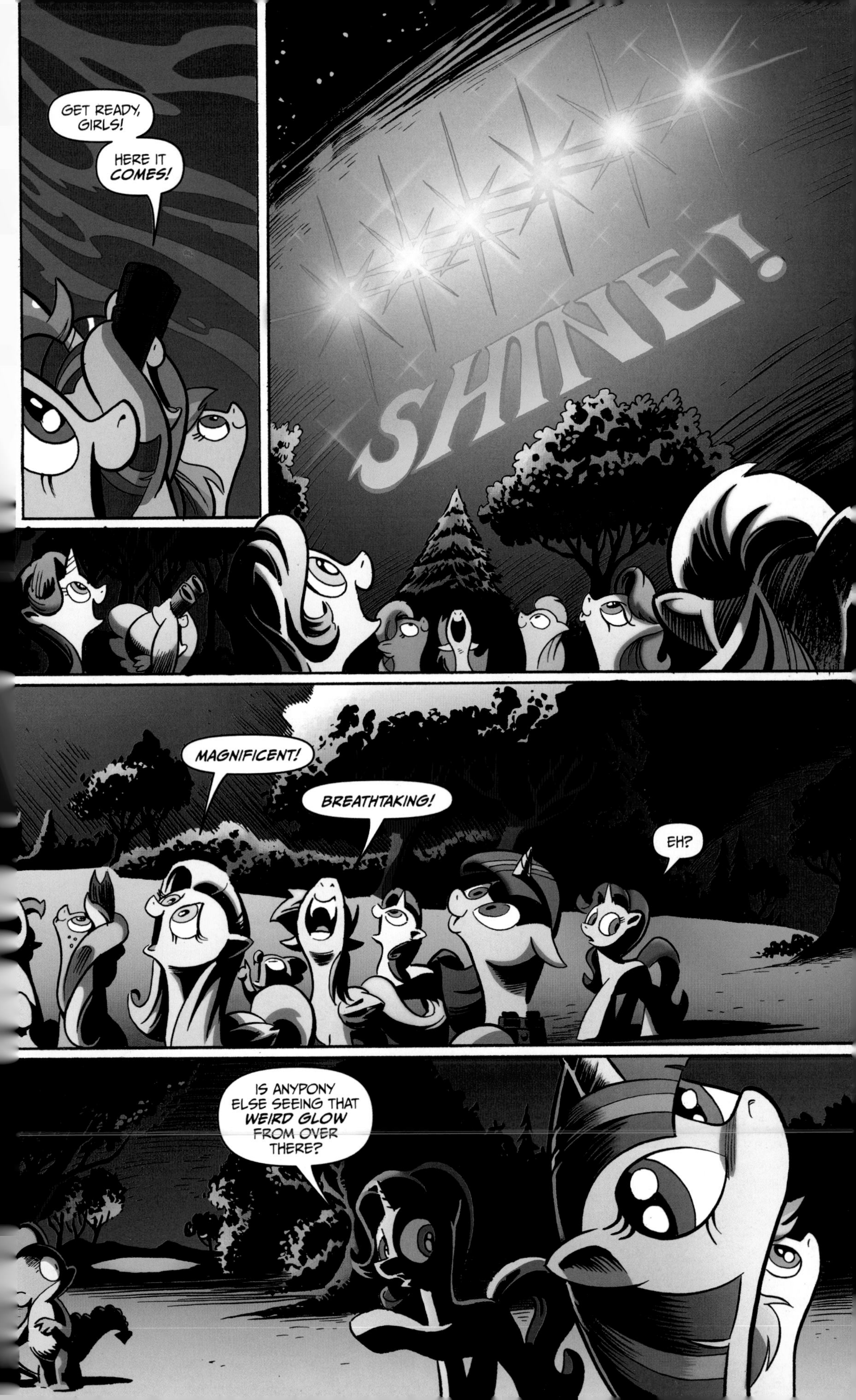
GET READY, GIRLS!
HERE IT COMES!
SHINE!
MAGNIFICENT!
BREATHTAKING!
EH?
IS ANYPONY ELSE SEEING THAT WEIRD GLOW FROM OVER THERE?

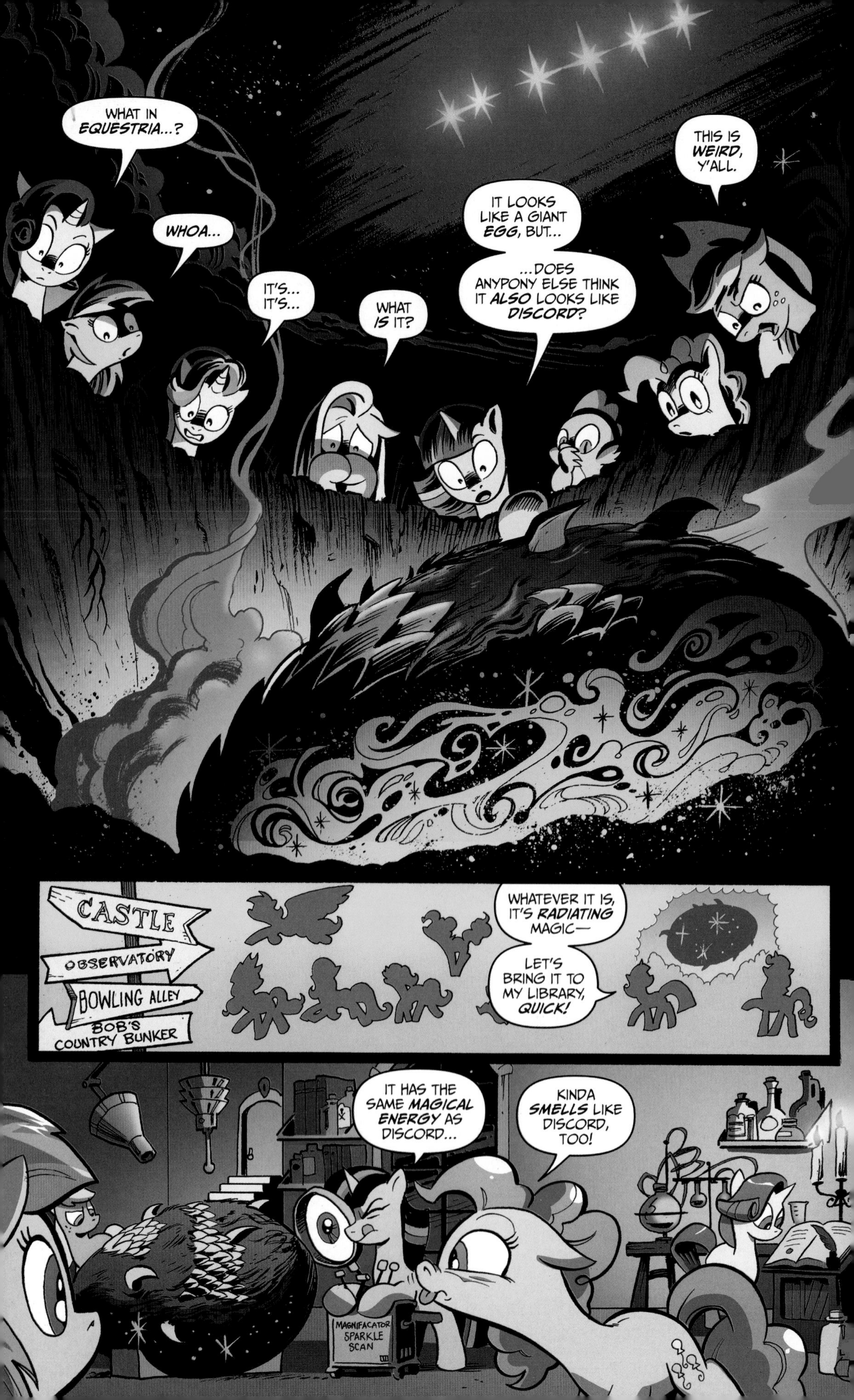
WHAT IN EQUESTRIA...?
WHOA...
IT'S... IT'S...
WHAT IS IT?
IT LOOKS LIKE A GIANT EGG, BUT...
...DOES ANYPONY ELSE THINK IT ALSO LOOKS LIKE DISCORD?
THIS IS WEIRD, Y'ALL.
CASTLE
OBSERVATORY
BOWLING ALLEY
BOB'S COUNTRY BUNKER
WHATEVER IT IS, IT'S RADIATING MAGIC—
LET'S BRING IT TO MY LIBRARY, QUICK!
IT HAS THE SAME MAGICAL ENERGY AS DISCORD...
KINDA SMELLS LIKE DISCORD, TOO!
MAGNIFACATOR SPARKLE SCAN

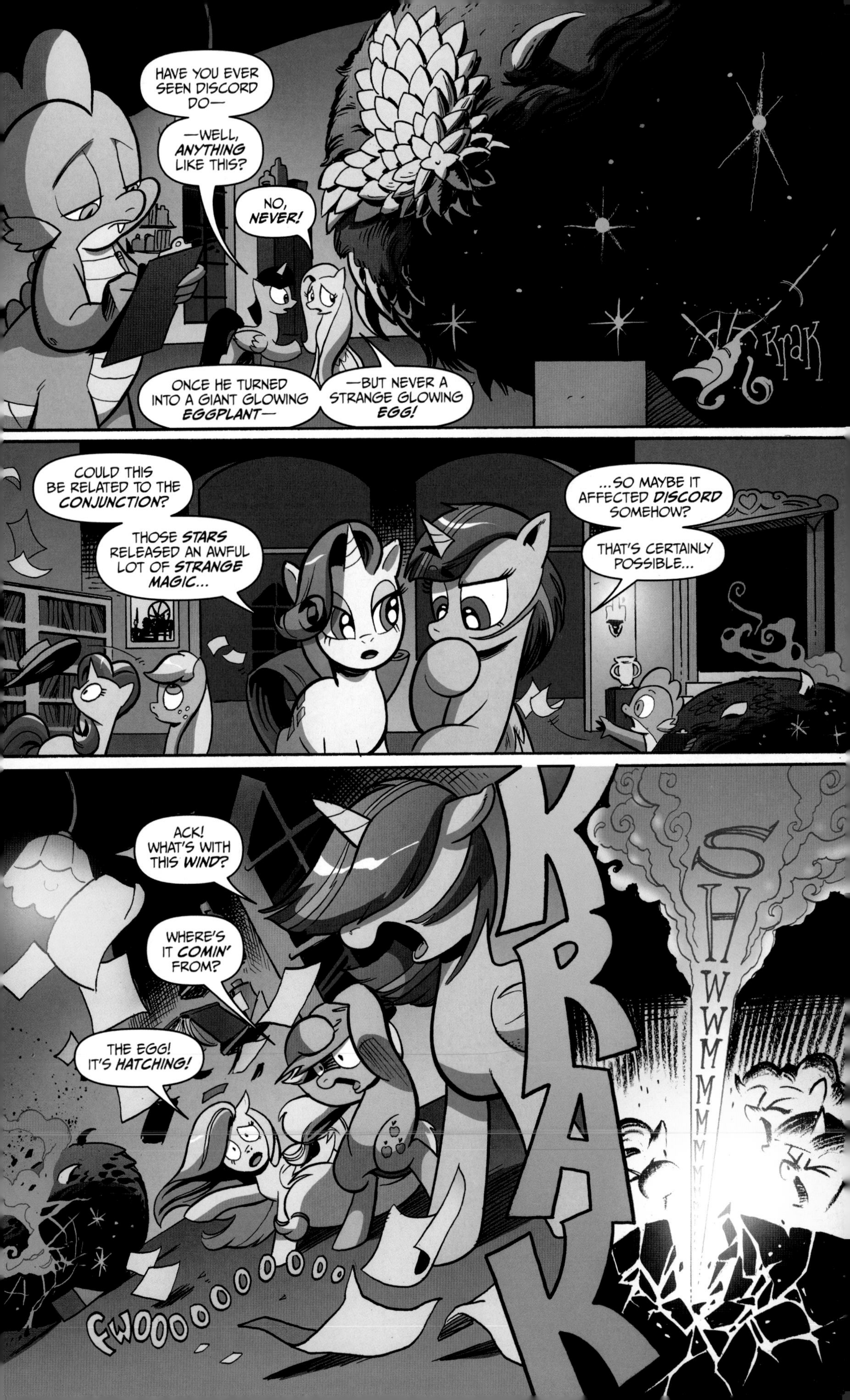
HAVE YOU EVER SEEN DISCORD DO—
—WELL, ANYTHING LIKE THIS?
NO, NEVER!
ONCE HE TURNED INTO A GIANT GLOWING EGGPLANT—
—BUT NEVER A STRANGE GLOWING EGG!
KRAK
COULD THIS BE RELATED TO THE CONJUNCTION?
THOSE STARS RELEASED AN AWFUL LOT OF STRANGE MAGIC...
...SO MAYBE IT AFFECTED DISCORD SOMEHOW?
THAT'S CERTAINLY POSSIBLE...
ACK! WHAT'S WITH THIS WIND?
WHERE'S IT COMIN' FROM?
THE EGG! IT'S HATCHING!
FWOOOOOOOOOOO...
KRAK
SHHWWWMMMMM

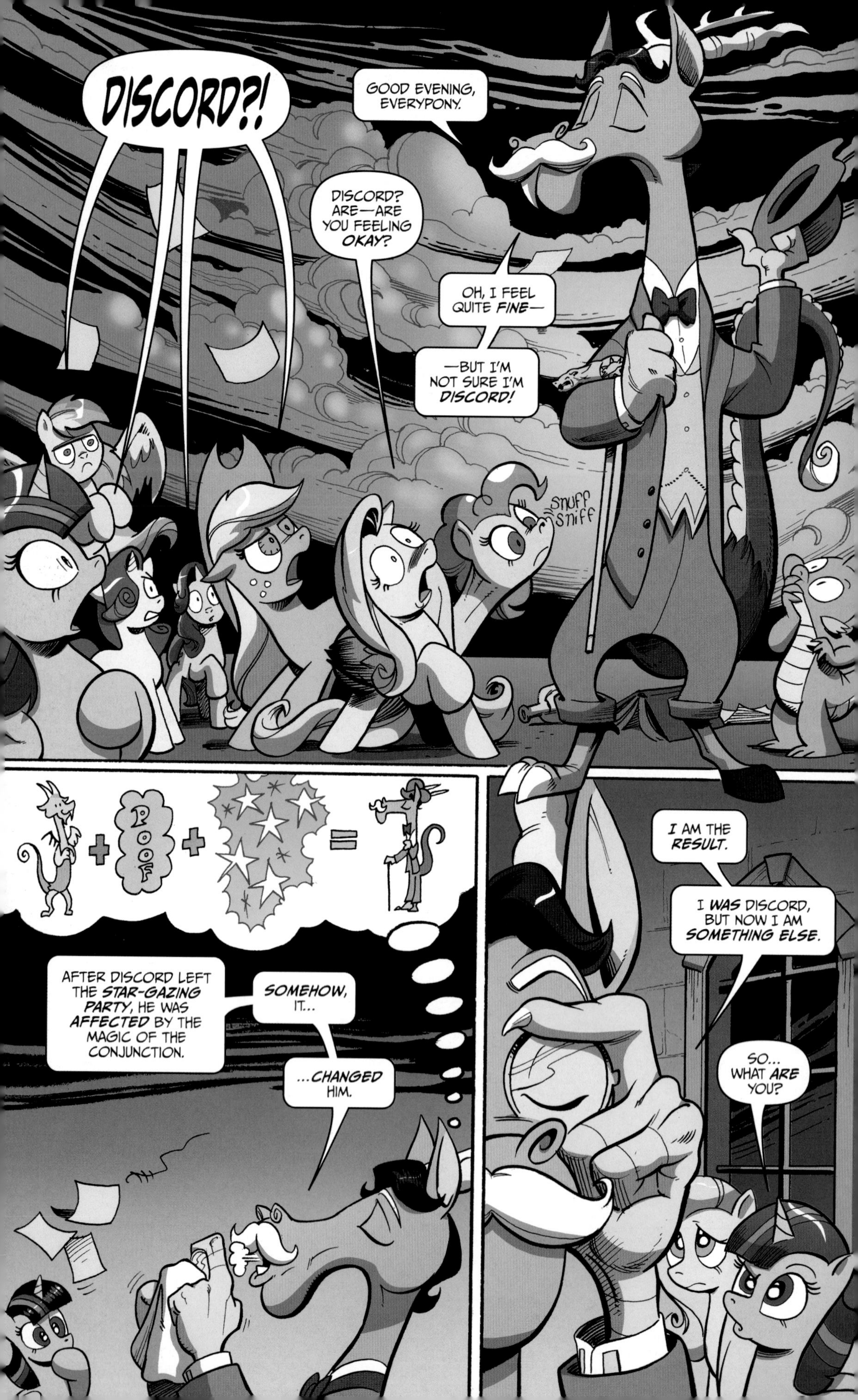
DISCORD?!
GOOD EVENING, EVERYPONY.
DISCORD? ARE—ARE YOU FEELING OKAY?
OH, I FEEL QUITE FINE—
—BUT I'M NOT SURE I'M DISCORD!
SNUFF SNIFF
POOF
AFTER DISCORD LEFT THE STAR-GAZING PARTY, HE WAS AFFECTED BY THE MAGIC OF THE CONJUNCTION.
SOMEHOW, IT...
...CHANGED HIM.
I AM THE RESULT.
I WAS DISCORD, BUT NOW I AM SOMETHING ELSE.
SO... WHAT ARE YOU?

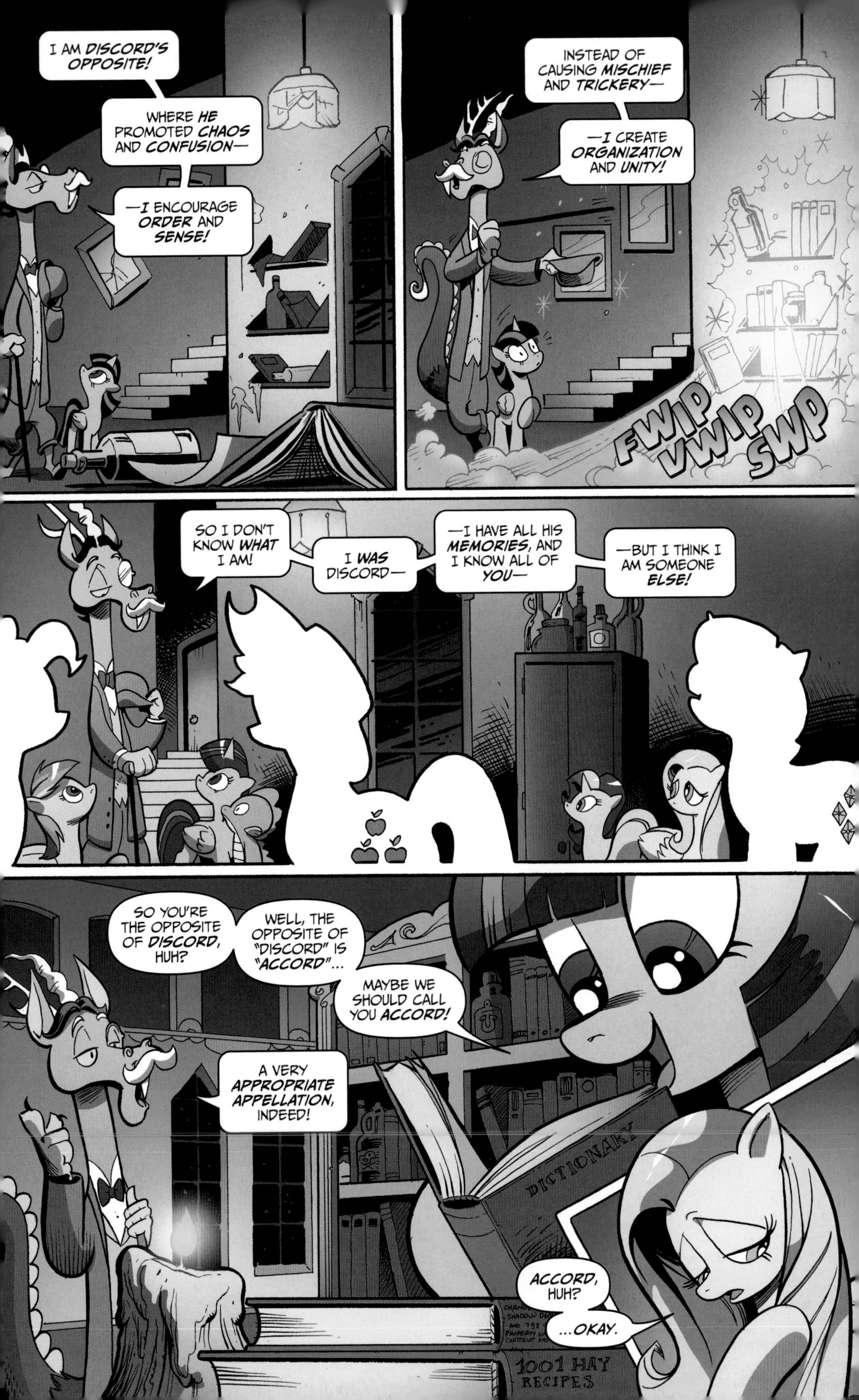
I AM DISCORD'S OPPOSITE!
WHERE HE PROMOTED CHAOS AND CONFUSION—
—I ENCOURAGE ORDER AND SENSE!
INSTEAD OF CAUSING MISCHIEF AND TRICKERY—
—I CREATE ORGANIZATION AND UNITY!
FWIP VWIP SWP
SO I DON'T KNOW WHAT I AM!
I WAS DISCORD—
—I HAVE ALL HIS MEMORIES, AND I KNOW ALL OF YOU—
—BUT I THINK I AM SOMEONE ELSE!
SO YOU'RE THE OPPOSITE OF DISCORD, HUH?
WELL, THE OPPOSITE OF "DISCORD" IS "ACCORD"...
MAYBE WE SHOULD CALL YOU ACCORD!
A VERY APPROPRIATE APPELLATION, INDEED!
DICTIONARY
ACCORD, HUH?
...OKAY.
1001 HAY RECIPES

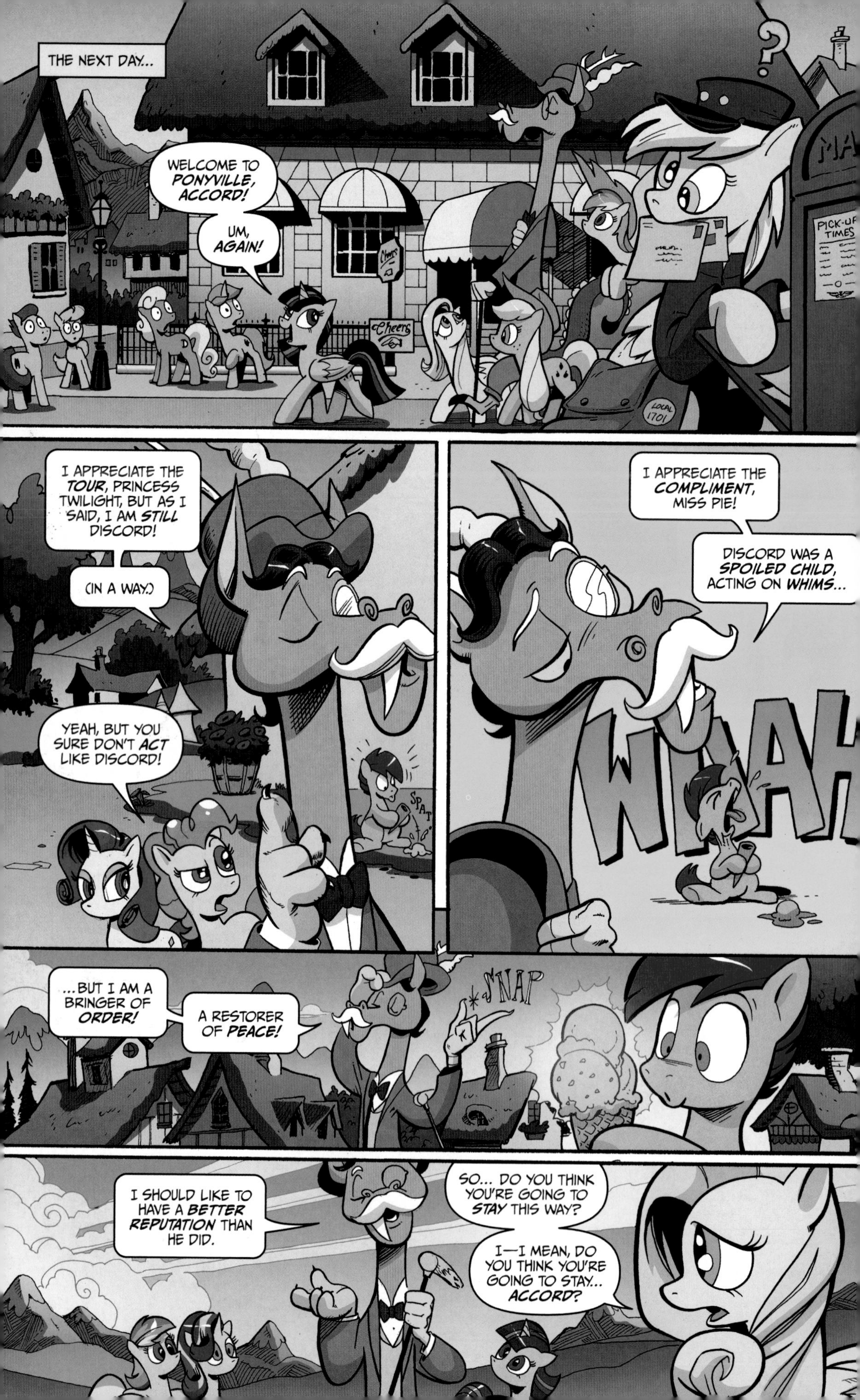
THE NEXT DAY...
WELCOME TO PONYVILLE, ACCORD!
UM, AGAIN!
I APPRECIATE THE TOUR, PRINCESS TWILIGHT, BUT AS I SAID, I AM STILL DISCORD!
(IN A WAY.)
YEAH, BUT YOU SURE DON'T ACT LIKE DISCORD!
SPAT
I APPRECIATE THE COMPLIMENT, MISS PIE!
DISCORD WAS A SPOILED CHILD, ACTING ON WHIMS...
...BUT I AM A BRINGER OF ORDER!
A RESTORER OF PEACE!
SNAP
I SHOULD LIKE TO HAVE A BETTER REPUTATION THAN HE DID.
SO... DO YOU THINK YOU'RE GOING TO STAY THIS WAY?
I—I MEAN, DO YOU THINK YOU'RE GOING TO STAY... ACCORD?

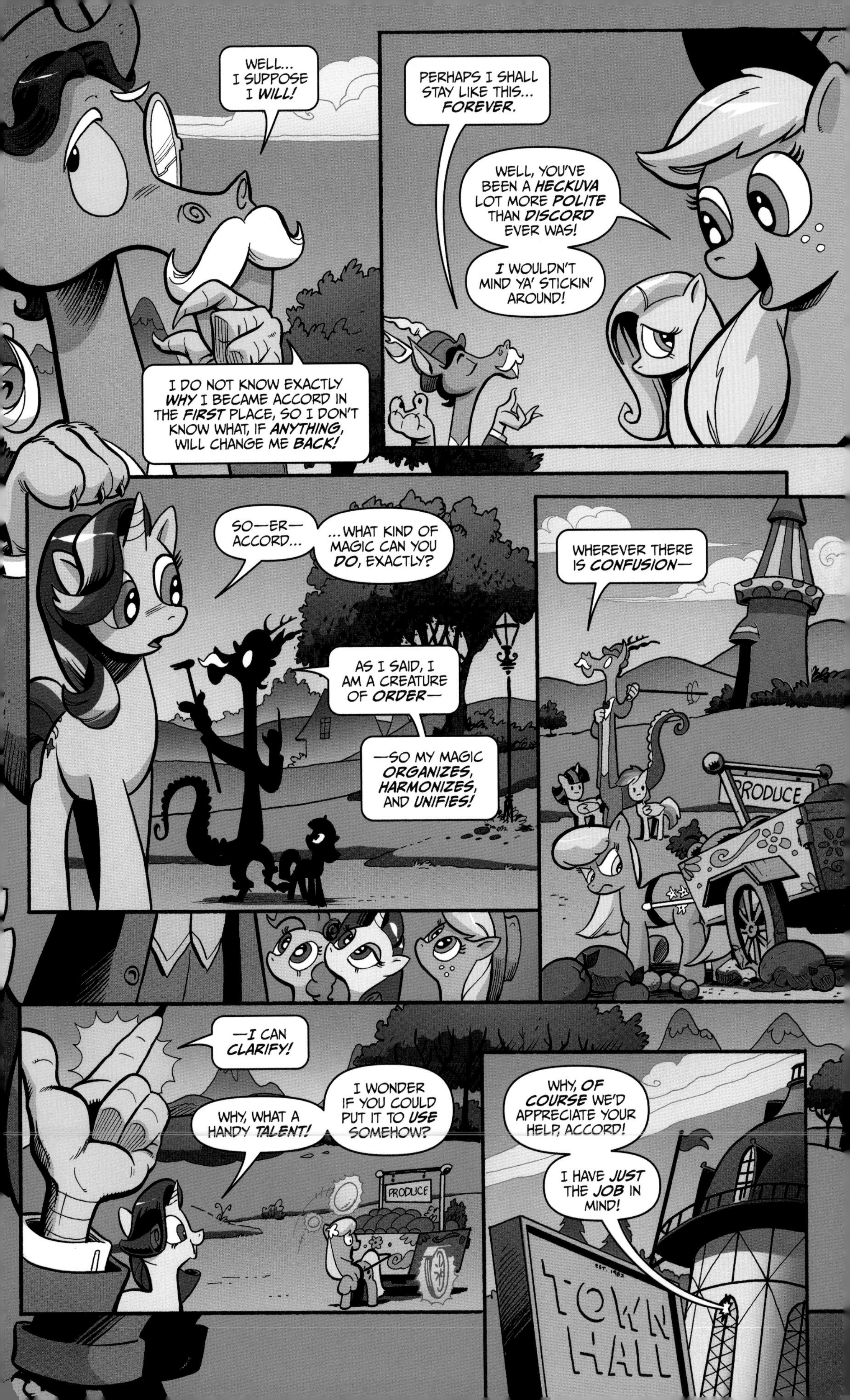
WELL... I SUPPOSE I WILL!
I DO NOT KNOW EXACTLY WHY I BECAME ACCORD IN THE FIRST PLACE, SO I DON'T KNOW WHAT, IF ANYTHING, WILL CHANGE ME BACK!
PERHAPS I SHALL STAY LIKE THIS... FOREVER.
WELL, YOU'VE BEEN A HECKUVA LOT MORE POLITE THAN DISCORD EVER WAS!
I WOULDN'T MIND YA' STICKIN' AROUND!
SO—ER—ACCORD...
...WHAT KIND OF MAGIC CAN YOU DO, EXACTLY?
AS I SAID, I AM A CREATURE OF ORDER—
—SO MY MAGIC ORGANIZES, HARMONIZES, AND UNIFIES!
WHEREVER THERE IS CONFUSION—
PRODUCE
—I CAN CLARIFY!
WHY, WHAT A HANDY TALENT!
I WONDER IF YOU COULD PUT IT TO USE SOMEHOW?
PRODUCE
WHY, OF COURSE WE'D APPRECIATE YOUR HELP, ACCORD!
I HAVE JUST THE JOB IN MIND!
EST. 1982
TOWN HALL

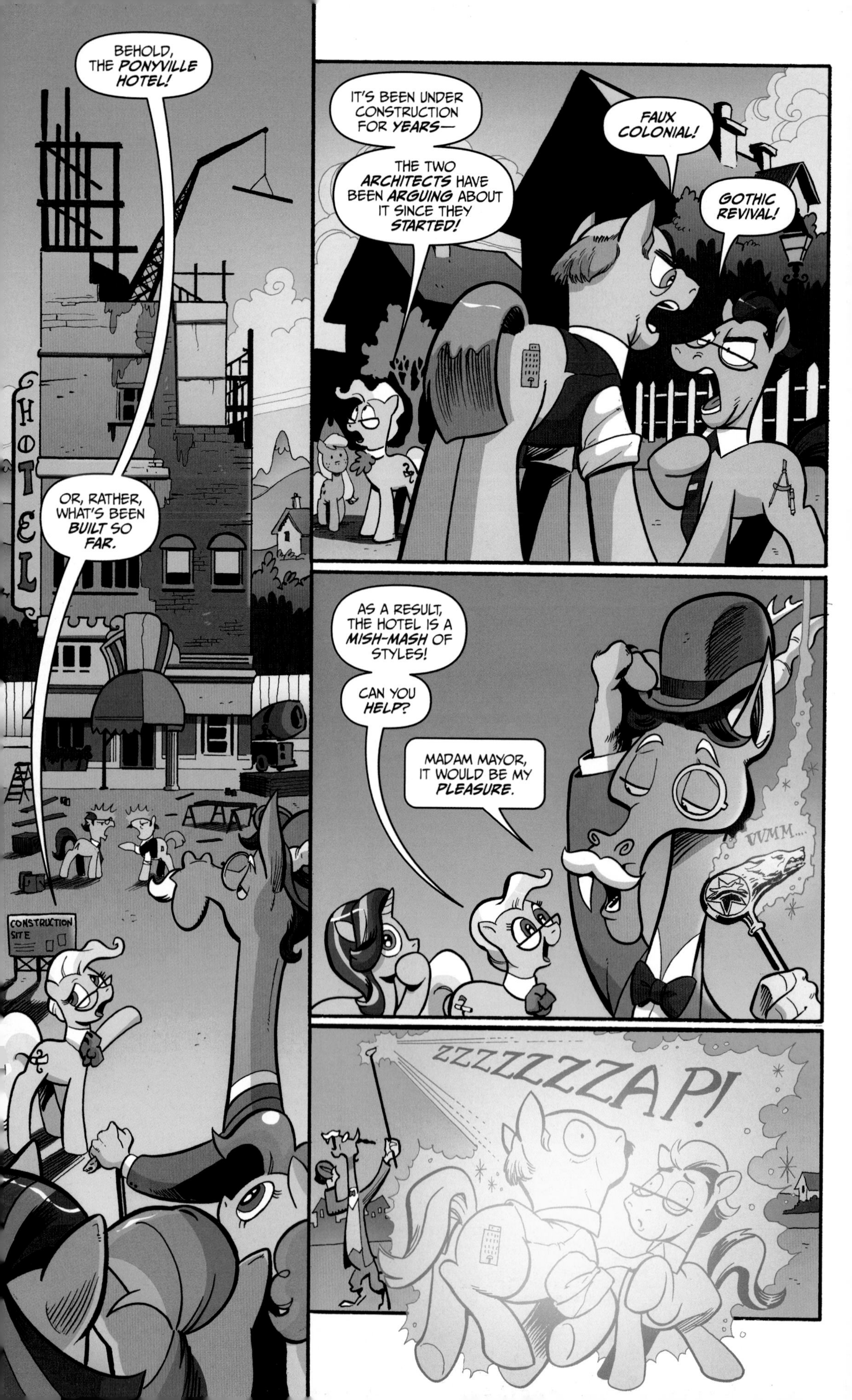
BEHOLD, THE PONYVILLE HOTEL!
HOTEL
OR, RATHER, WHAT'S BEEN BUILT SO FAR.
CONSTRUCTION SITE
IT'S BEEN UNDER CONSTRUCTION FOR YEARS—
THE TWO ARCHITECTS HAVE BEEN ARGUING ABOUT IT SINCE THEY STARTED!
FAUX COLONIAL!
GOTHIC REVIVAL!
AS A RESULT, THE HOTEL IS A MISH-MASH OF STYLES!
CAN YOU HELP?
MADAM MAYOR, IT WOULD BE MY PLEASURE.
VVMM....
ZZZZZZZZAP!

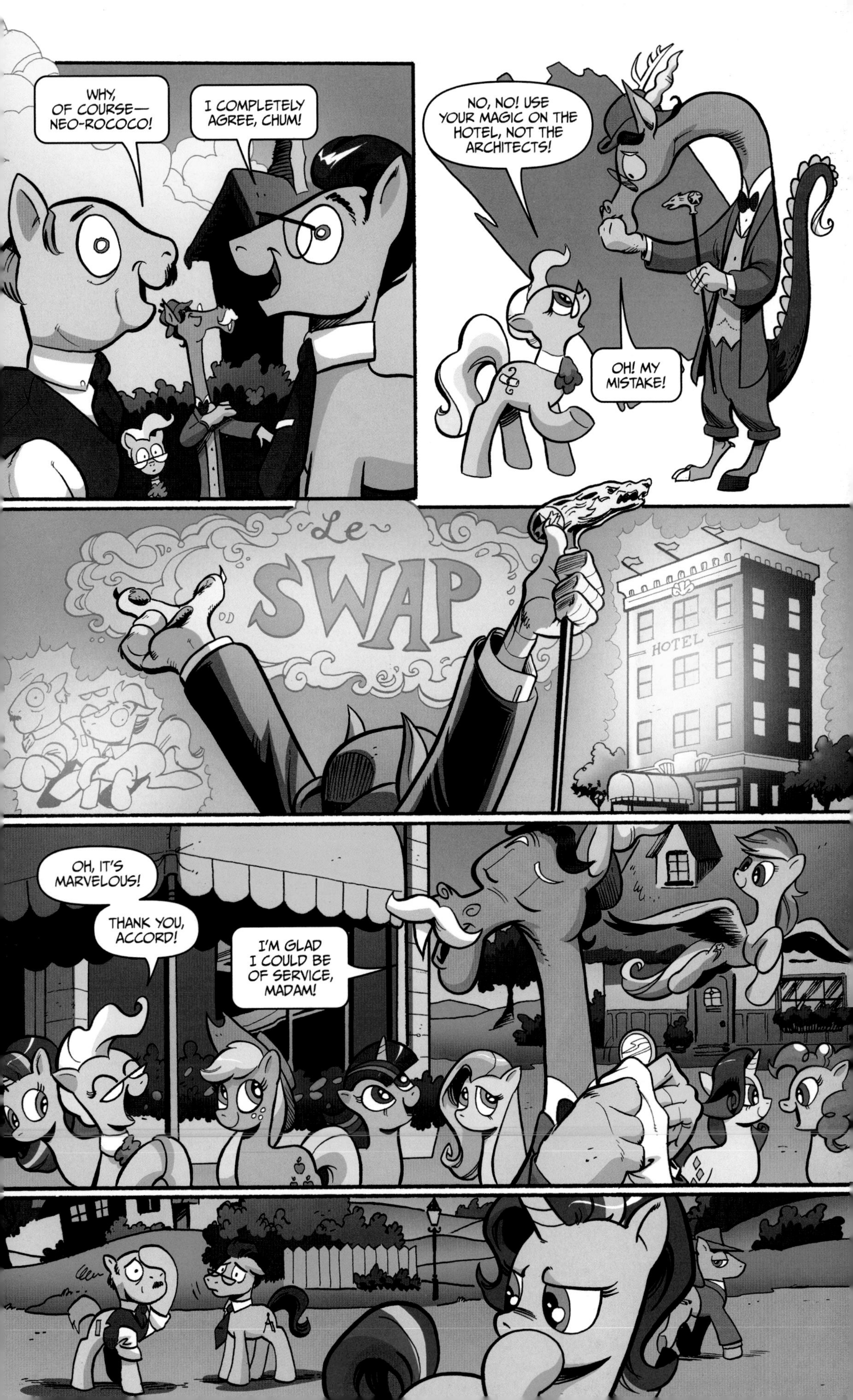
WHY, OF COURSE— NEO-ROCOCO!
I COMPLETELY AGREE, CHUM!
NO, NO! USE YOUR MAGIC ON THE HOTEL, NOT THE ARCHITECTS!
OH! MY MISTAKE!
Le SWAP
HOTEL
OH, IT'S MARVELOUS!
THANK YOU, ACCORD!
I'M GLAD I COULD BE OF SERVICE, MADAM!

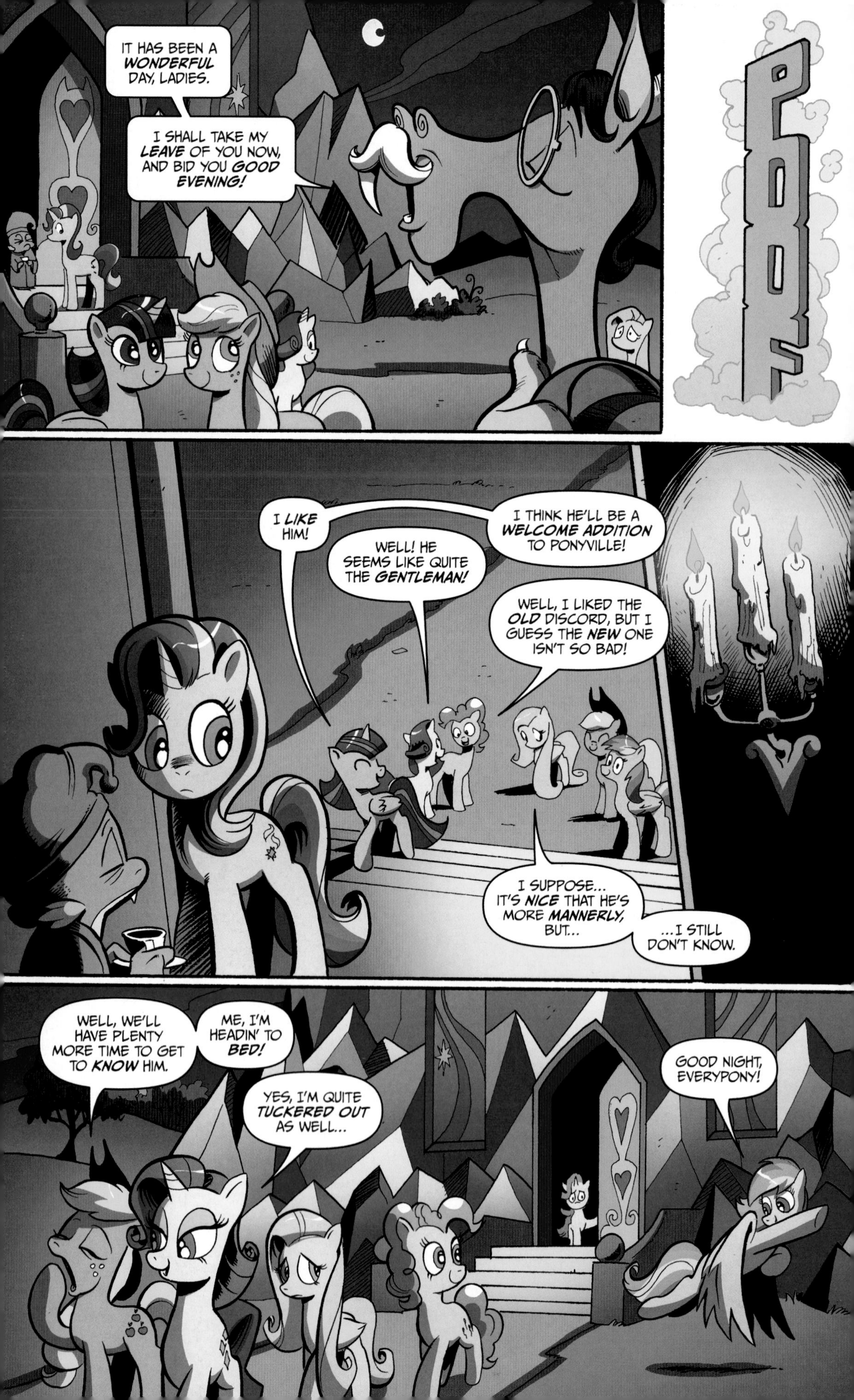
IT HAS BEEN A WONDERFUL DAY, LADIES.
I SHALL TAKE MY LEAVE OF YOU NOW, AND BID YOU GOOD EVENING!
POOF
I LIKE HIM!
I THINK HE'LL BE A WELCOME ADDITION TO PONYVILLE!
WELL! HE SEEMS LIKE QUITE THE GENTLEMAN!
WELL, I LIKED THE OLD DISCORD, BUT I GUESS THE NEW ONE ISN'T SO BAD!
I SUPPOSE... IT'S NICE THAT HE'S MORE MANNERLY, BUT...
...I STILL DON'T KNOW.
WELL, WE'LL HAVE PLENTY MORE TIME TO GET TO KNOW HIM.
ME, I'M HEADIN' TO BED!
YES, I'M QUITE TUCKERED OUT AS WELL...
GOOD NIGHT, EVERYPONY!

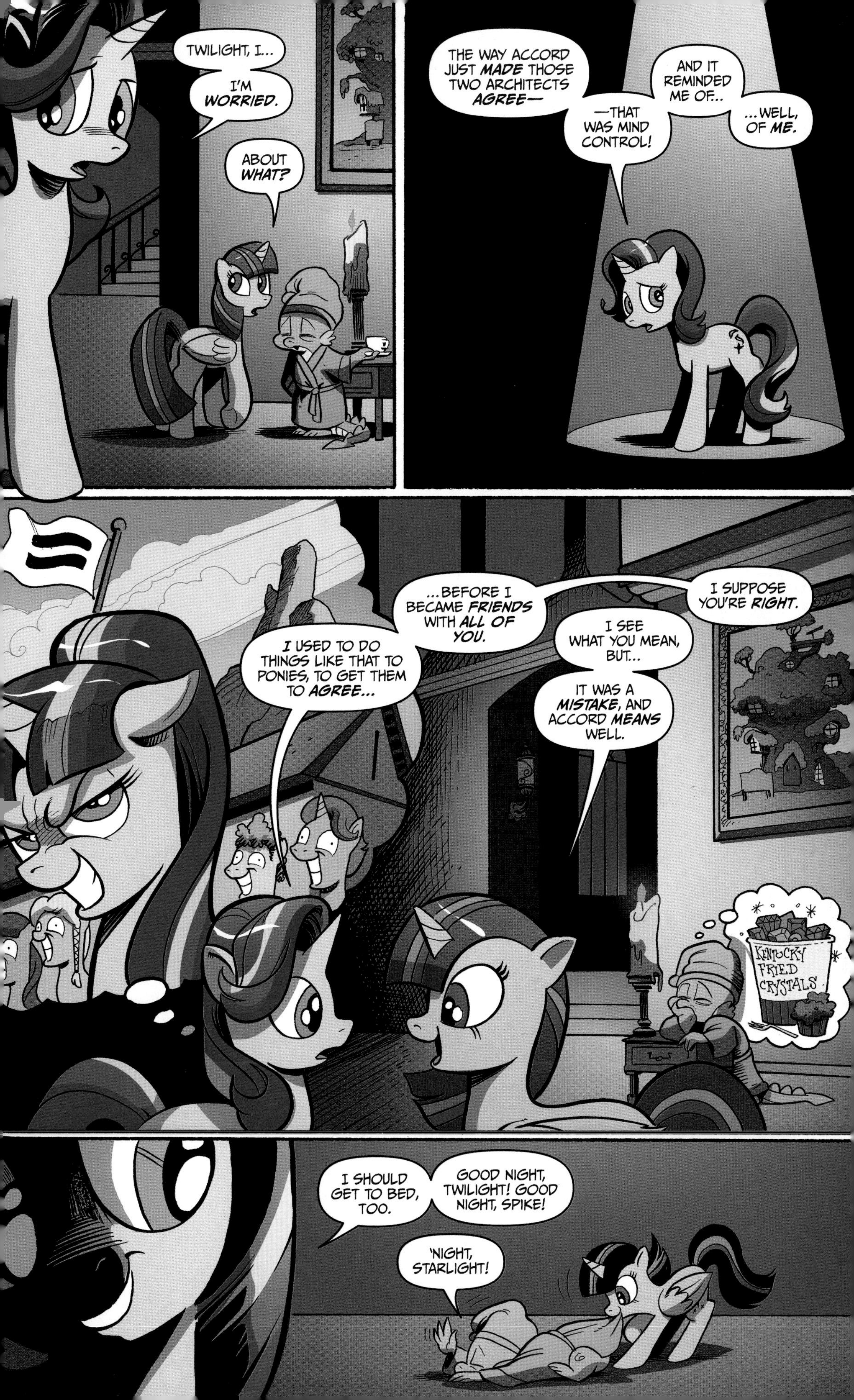
TWILIGHT, I...
I'M WORRIED.
ABOUT WHAT?
THE WAY ACCORD JUST MADE THOSE TWO ARCHITECTS AGREE—
—THAT WAS MIND CONTROL!
AND IT REMINDED ME OF...
...WELL, OF ME.
I USED TO DO THINGS LIKE THAT TO PONIES, TO GET THEM TO AGREE...
...BEFORE I BECAME FRIENDS WITH ALL OF YOU.
I SEE WHAT YOU MEAN, BUT...
IT WAS A MISTAKE, AND ACCORD MEANS WELL.
I SUPPOSE YOU'RE RIGHT.
KENTUCKY FRIED CRYSTALS
I SHOULD GET TO BED, TOO.
GOOD NIGHT, TWILIGHT! GOOD NIGHT, SPIKE!
'NIGHT, STARLIGHT!

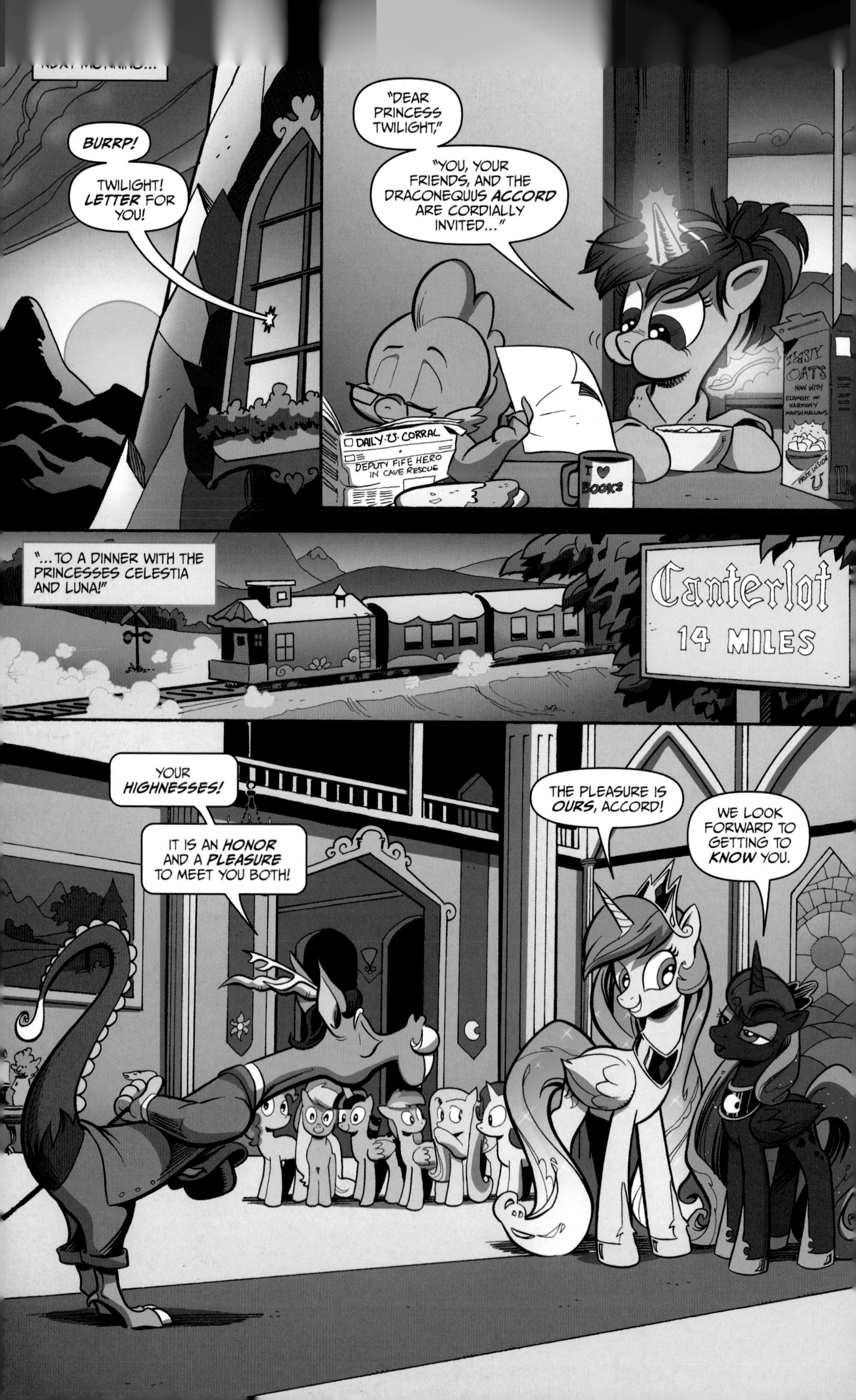
BURRP!
TWILIGHT! LETTER FOR YOU!
"DEAR PRINCESS TWILIGHT,"
"YOU, YOUR FRIENDS, AND THE DRACONEQUUS ACCORD ARE CORDIALLY INVITED..."
DAILY·U·CORRAL
DEPUTY FIFE HERO IN CAVE RESCUE
I ♥ BOOKS
TASTY OATS
NOW WITH ELEMENT OF HARMONY MARSHMALLOWS
PRIZE INSIDE
"...TO A DINNER WITH THE PRINCESSES CELESTIA AND LUNA!"
Canterlot
14 MILES
YOUR HIGHNESSES!
IT IS AN HONOR AND A PLEASURE TO MEET YOU BOTH!
THE PLEASURE IS OURS, ACCORD!
WE LOOK FORWARD TO GETTING TO KNOW YOU.

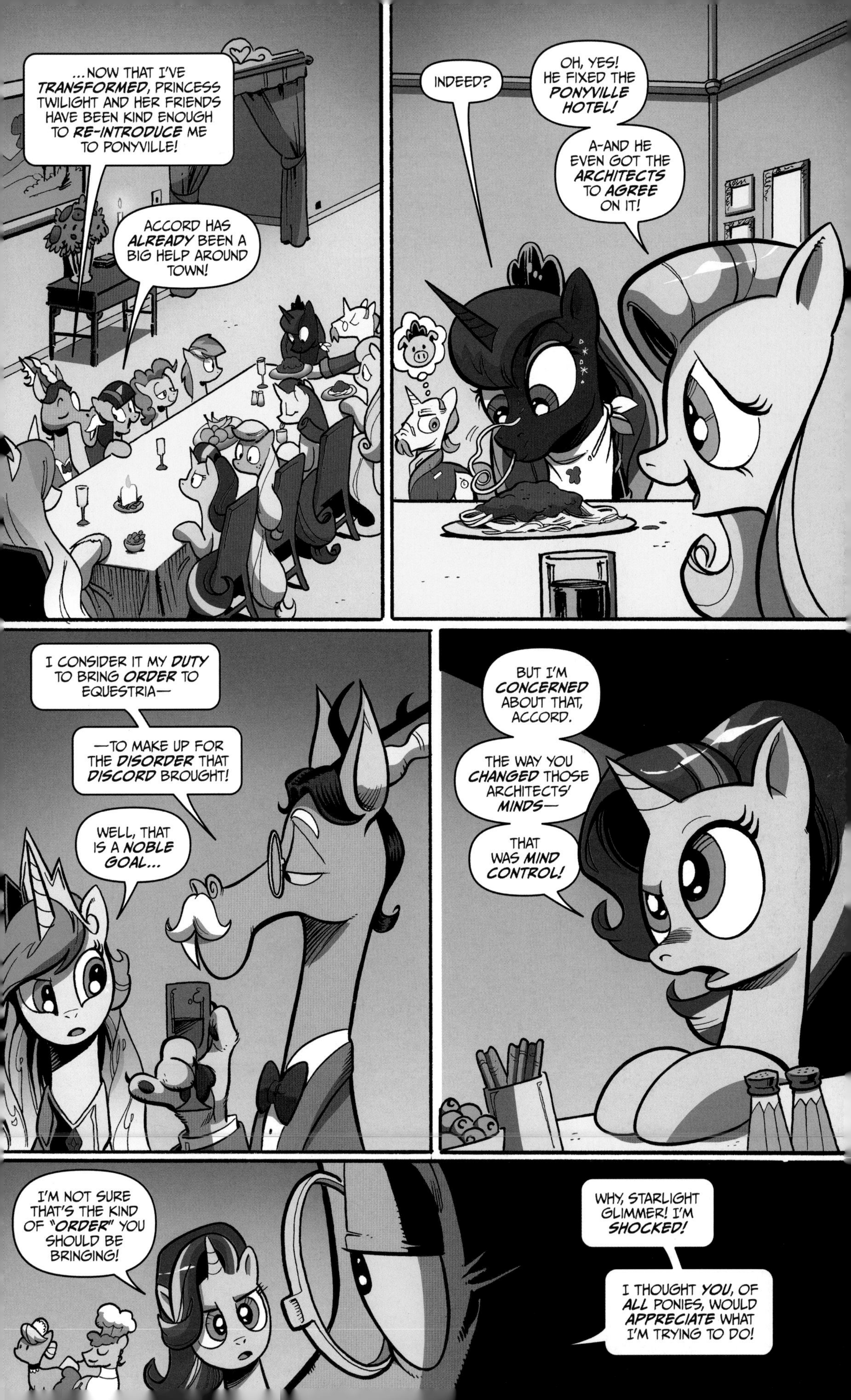
...NOW THAT I'VE TRANSFORMED, PRINCESS TWILIGHT AND HER FRIENDS HAVE BEEN KIND ENOUGH TO RE-INTRODUCE ME TO PONYVILLE!
ACCORD HAS ALREADY BEEN A BIG HELP AROUND TOWN!
INDEED?
OH, YES! HE FIXED THE PONYVILLE HOTEL!
A-AND HE EVEN GOT THE ARCHITECTS TO AGREE ON IT!
I CONSIDER IT MY DUTY TO BRING ORDER TO EQUESTRIA—
—TO MAKE UP FOR THE DISORDER THAT DISCORD BROUGHT!
WELL, THAT IS A NOBLE GOAL...
BUT I'M CONCERNED ABOUT THAT, ACCORD.
THE WAY YOU CHANGED THOSE ARCHITECTS' MINDS—
THAT WAS MIND CONTROL!
I'M NOT SURE THAT'S THE KIND OF "ORDER" YOU SHOULD BE BRINGING!
WHY, STARLIGHT GLIMMER! I'M SHOCKED!
I THOUGHT YOU, OF ALL PONIES, WOULD APPRECIATE WHAT I'M TRYING TO DO!

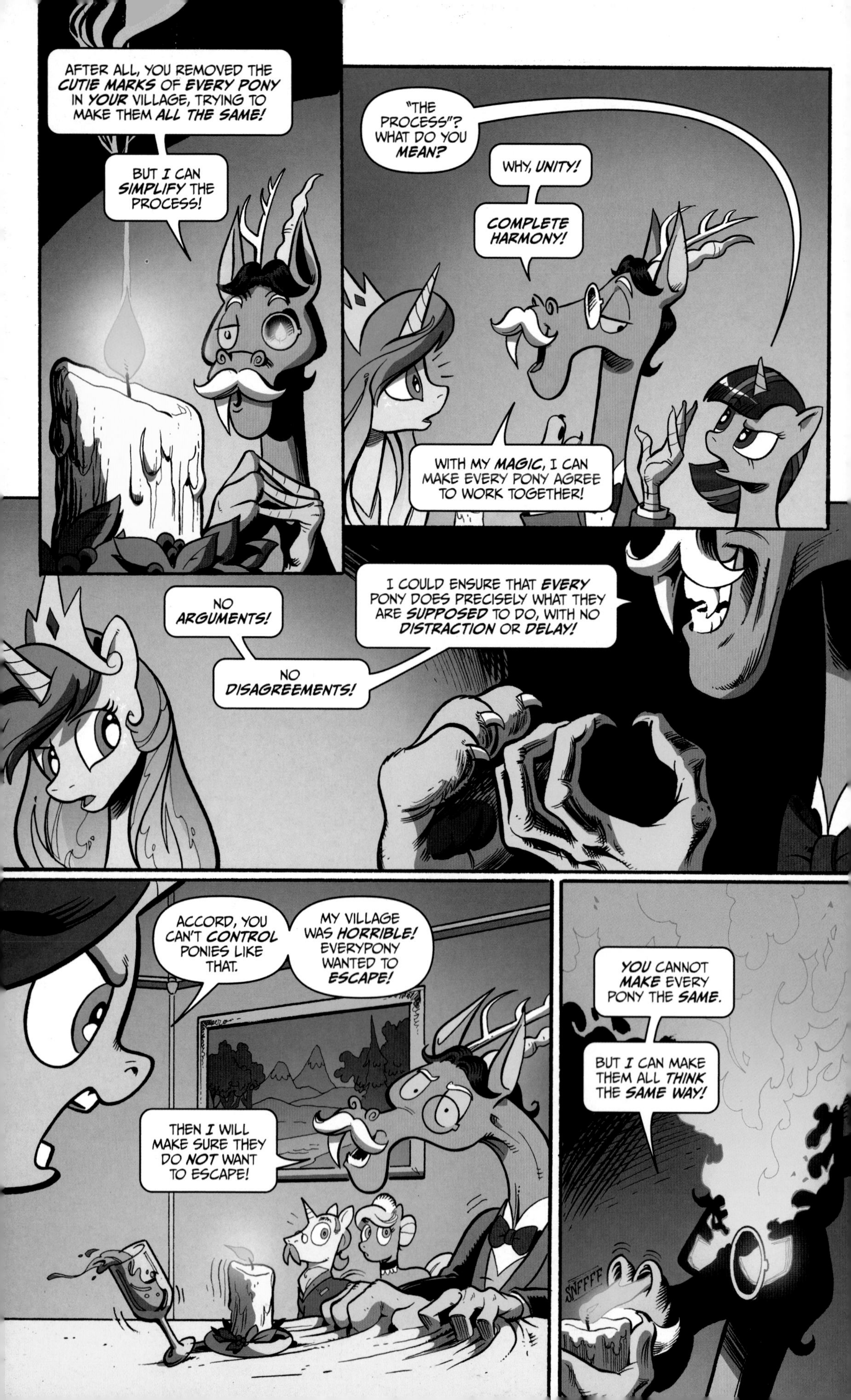

AFTER ALL, YOU REMOVED THE CUTIE MARKS OF EVERY PONY IN YOUR VILLAGE, TRYING TO MAKE THEM ALL THE SAME!
BUT I CAN SIMPLIFY THE PROCESS!
"THE PROCESS"? WHAT DO YOU MEAN?
WHY, UNITY!
COMPLETE HARMONY!
WITH MY MAGIC, I CAN MAKE EVERY PONY AGREE TO WORK TOGETHER!
I COULD ENSURE THAT EVERY PONY DOES PRECISELY WHAT THEY ARE SUPPOSED TO DO, WITH NO DISTRACTION OR DELAY!
NO ARGUMENTS!
NO DISAGREEMENTS!
ACCORD, YOU CAN'T CONTROL PONIES LIKE THAT.
MY VILLAGE WAS HORRIBLE! EVERYPONY WANTED TO ESCAPE!
THEN I WILL MAKE SURE THEY DO NOT WANT TO ESCAPE!
YOU CANNOT MAKE EVERY PONY THE SAME.
BUT I CAN MAKE THEM ALL THINK THE SAME WAY!
SNFFFF

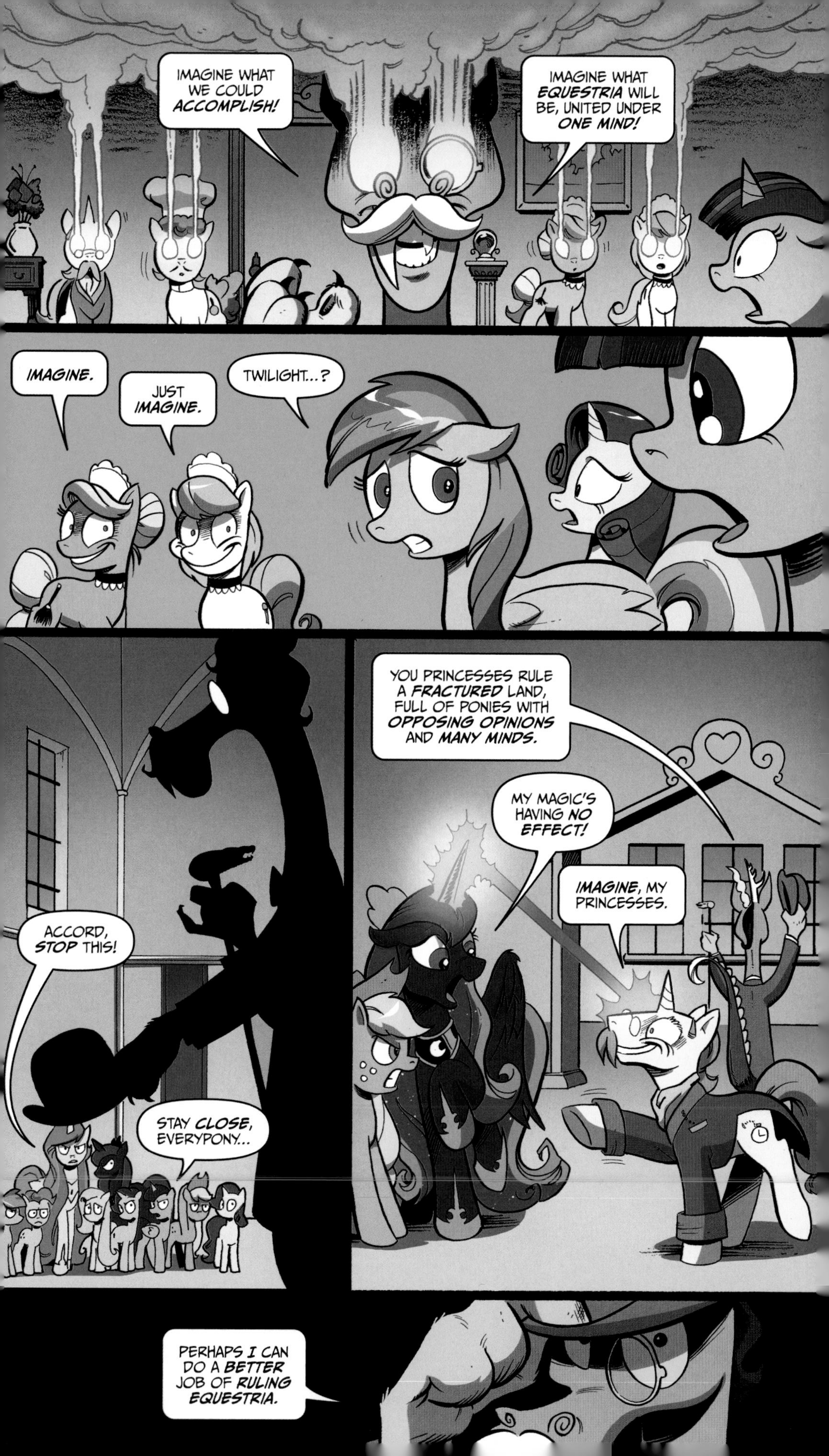
IMAGINE WHAT WE COULD ACCOMPLISH!
IMAGINE WHAT EQUESTRIA WILL BE, UNITED UNDER ONE MIND!
IMAGINE.
JUST IMAGINE.
TWILIGHT...?
ACCORD, STOP THIS!
STAY CLOSE, EVERYPONY...
YOU PRINCESSES RULE A FRACTURED LAND, FULL OF PONIES WITH OPPOSING OPINIONS AND MANY MINDS.
MY MAGIC'S HAVING NO EFFECT!
IMAGINE, MY PRINCESSES.
PERHAPS I CAN DO A BETTER JOB OF RULING EQUESTRIA.

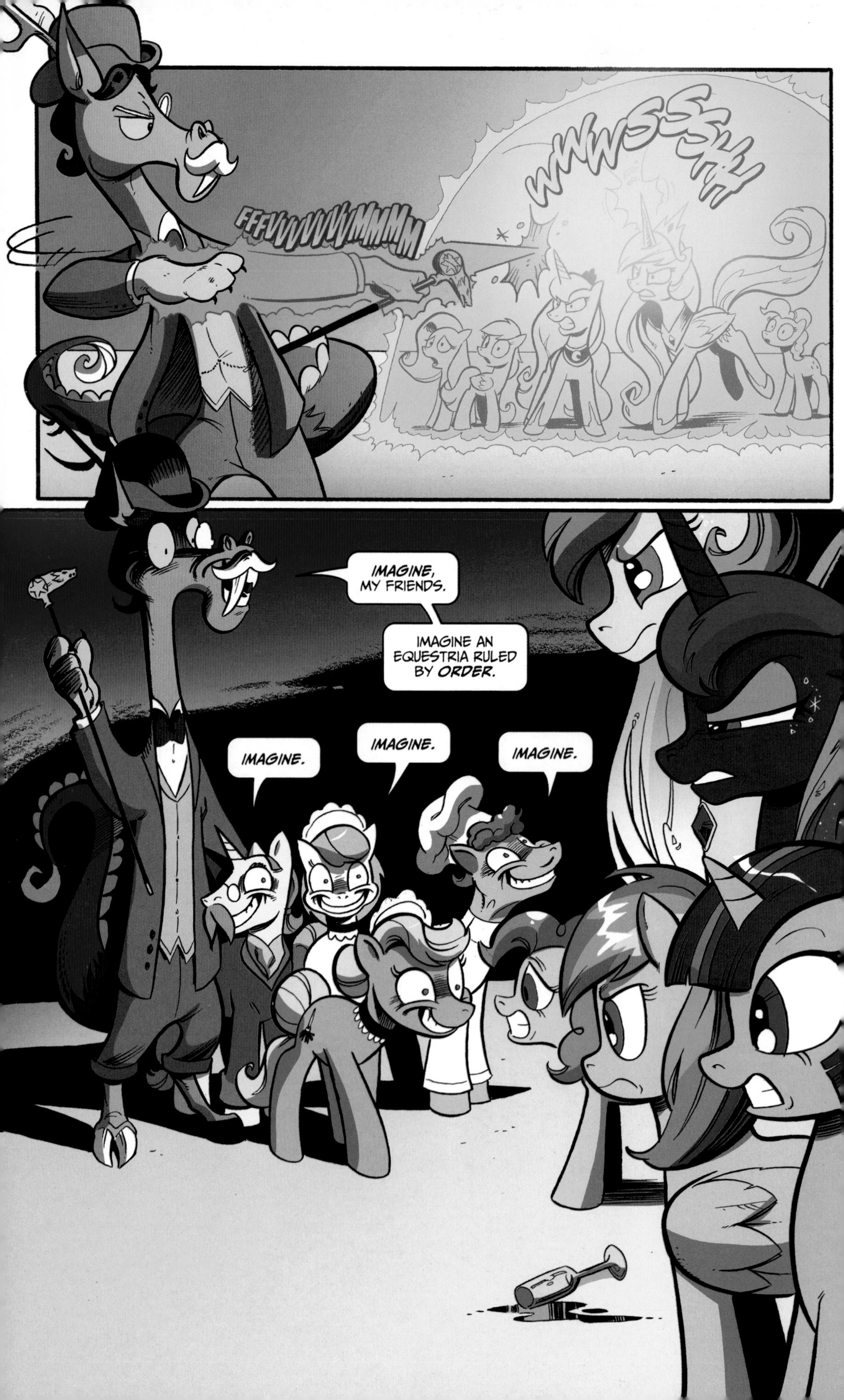
FFFVVVVVVVVMMMM
WWWSSSHH
IMAGINE, MY FRIENDS.
IMAGINE AN EQUESTRIA RULED BY ORDER.
IMAGINE.
IMAGINE.
IMAGINE.

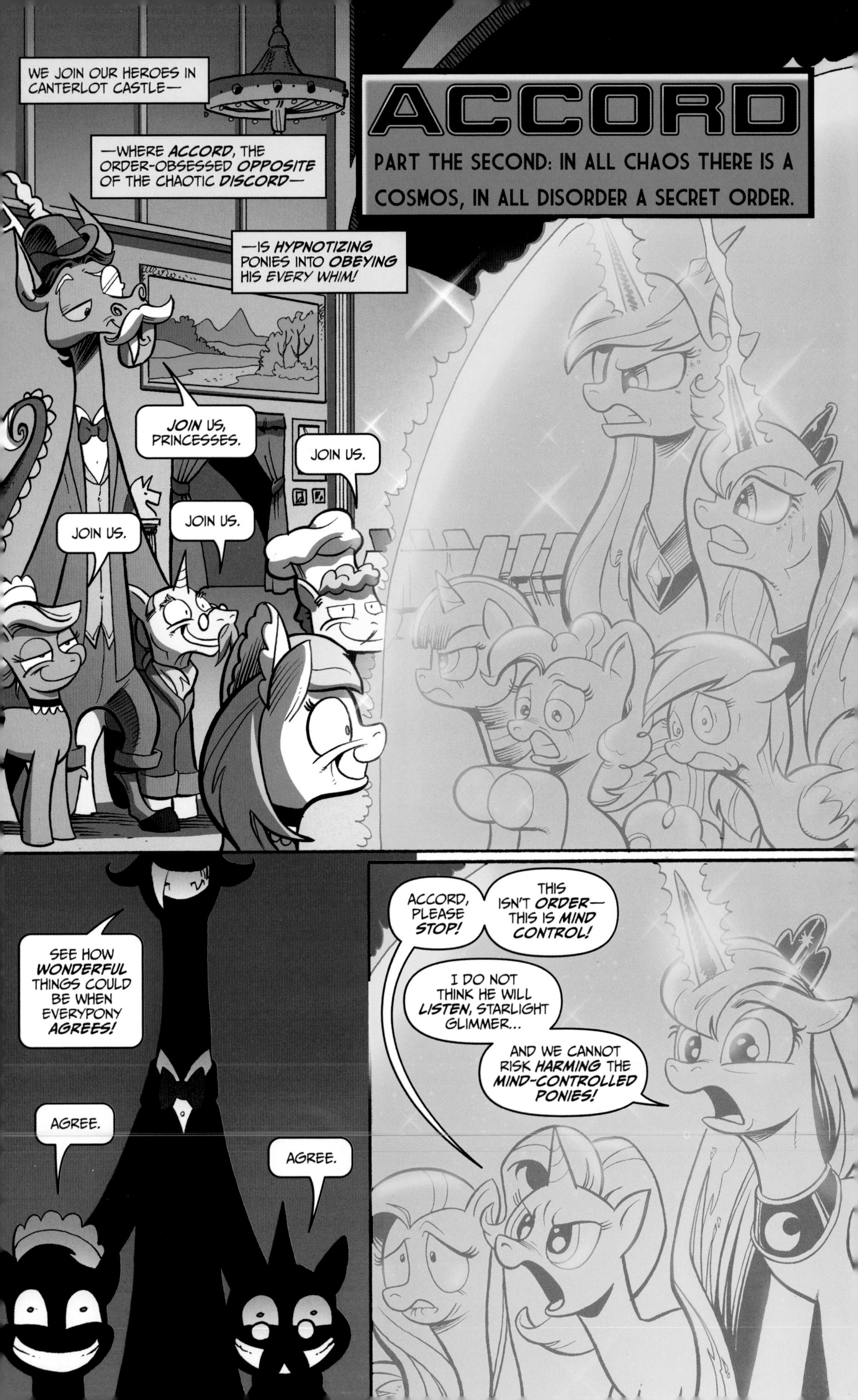
WE JOIN OUR HEROES IN CANTERLOT CASTLE—
ACCORD
PART THE SECOND: IN ALL CHAOS THERE IS A COSMOS, IN ALL DISORDER A SECRET ORDER.
—WHERE ACCORD, THE ORDER-OBSESSED OPPOSITE OF THE CHAOTIC DISCORD—
—IS HYPNOTIZING PONIES INTO OBEYING HIS EVERY WHIM!
JOIN US, PRINCESSES.
JOIN US.
JOIN US.
JOIN US.
SEE HOW WONDERFUL THINGS COULD BE WHEN EVERYPONY AGREES!
AGREE.
AGREE.
ACCORD, PLEASE STOP!
THIS ISN'T ORDER—THIS IS MIND CONTROL!
I DO NOT THINK HE WILL LISTEN, STARLIGHT GLIMMER...
AND WE CANNOT RISK HARMING THE MIND-CONTROLLED PONIES!

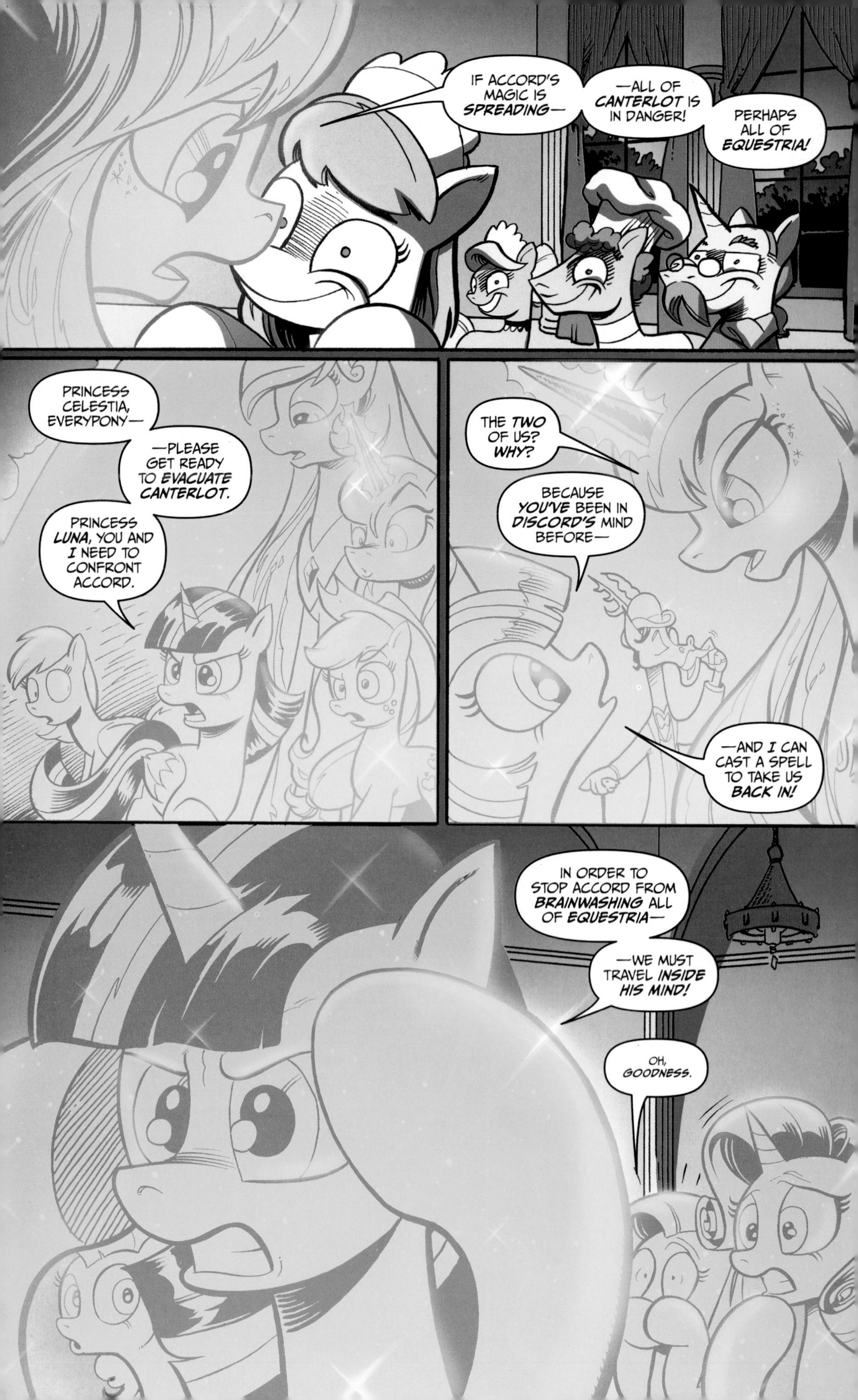
IF ACCORD'S MAGIC IS SPREADING—
—ALL OF CANTERLOT IS IN DANGER!
PERHAPS ALL OF EQUESTRIA!
PRINCESS CELESTIA, EVERYPONY—
—PLEASE GET READY TO EVACUATE CANTERLOT.
PRINCESS LUNA, YOU AND I NEED TO CONFRONT ACCORD.
THE TWO OF US? WHY?
BECAUSE YOU'VE BEEN IN DISCORD'S MIND BEFORE—
—AND I CAN CAST A SPELL TO TAKE US BACK IN!
IN ORDER TO STOP ACCORD FROM BRAINWASHING ALL OF EQUESTRIA—
—WE MUST TRAVEL INSIDE HIS MIND!
OH, GOODNESS.

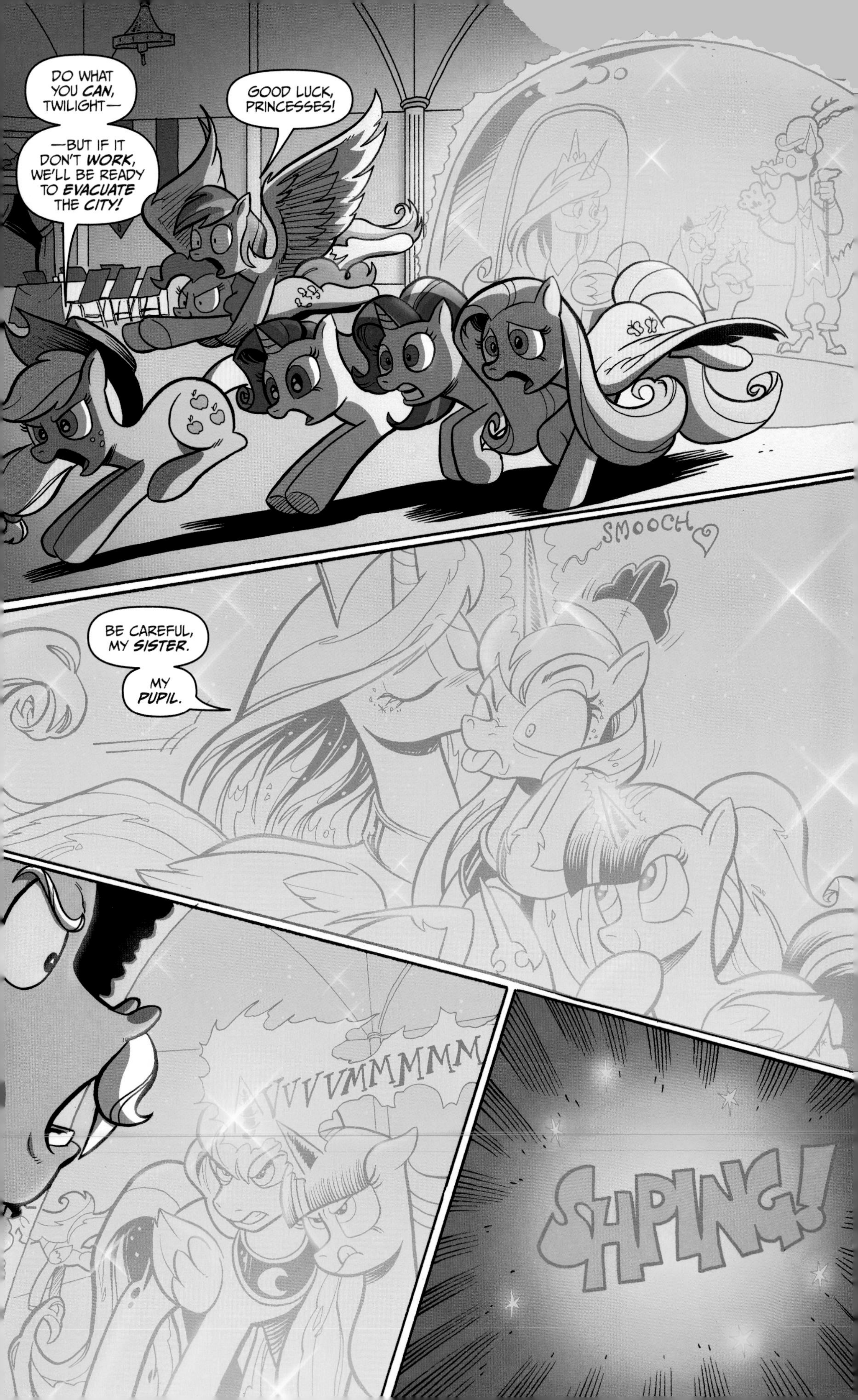
DO WHAT YOU CAN, TWILIGHT—
—BUT IF IT DON'T WORK, WE'LL BE READY TO EVACUATE THE CITY!
GOOD LUCK, PRINCESSES!
SMOOCH
BE CAREFUL, MY SISTER.
MY PUPIL.
VVVVMMMMMM
SHPING!

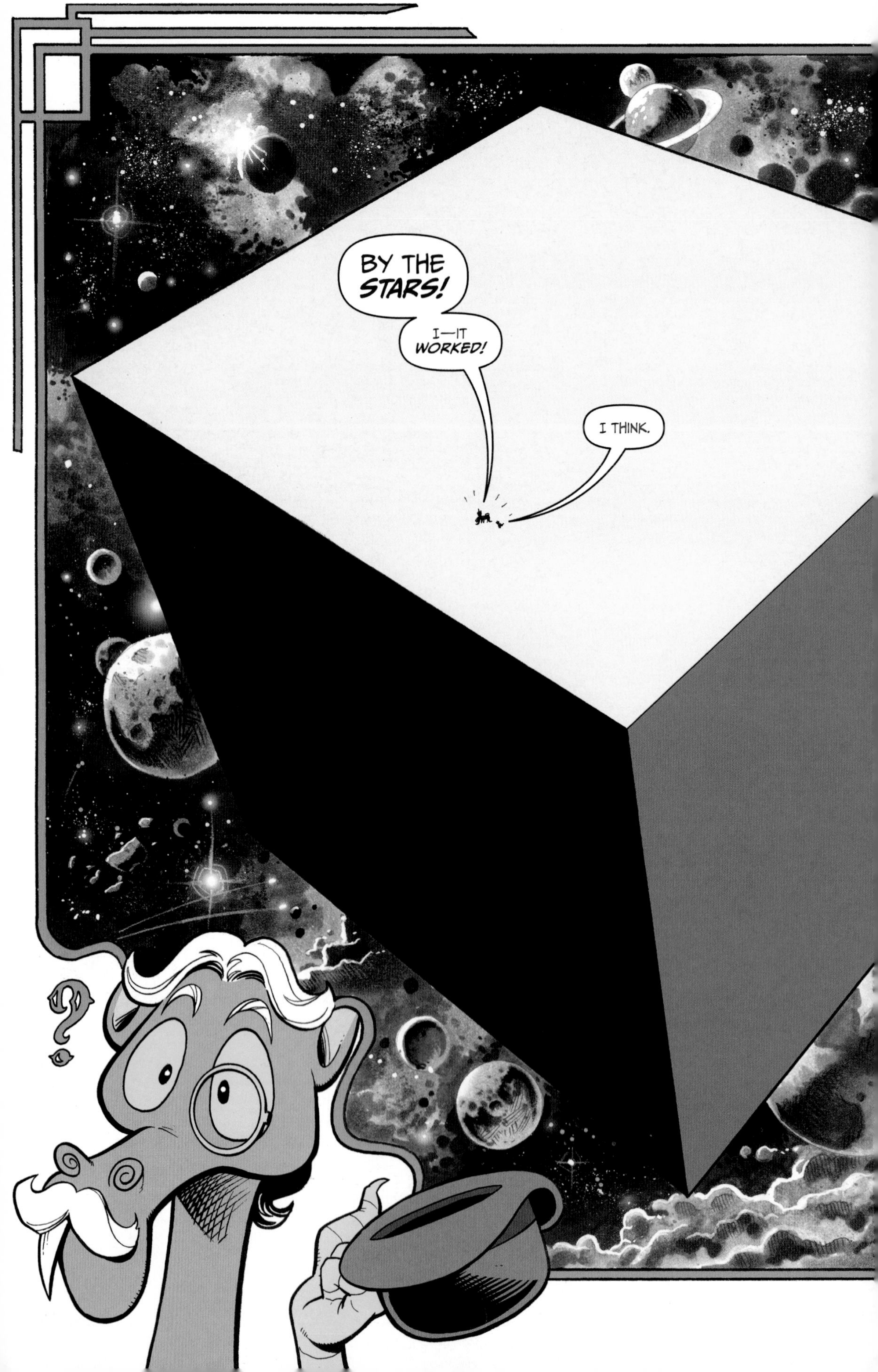
BY THE STARS!
I—IT WORKED!
I THINK.
?

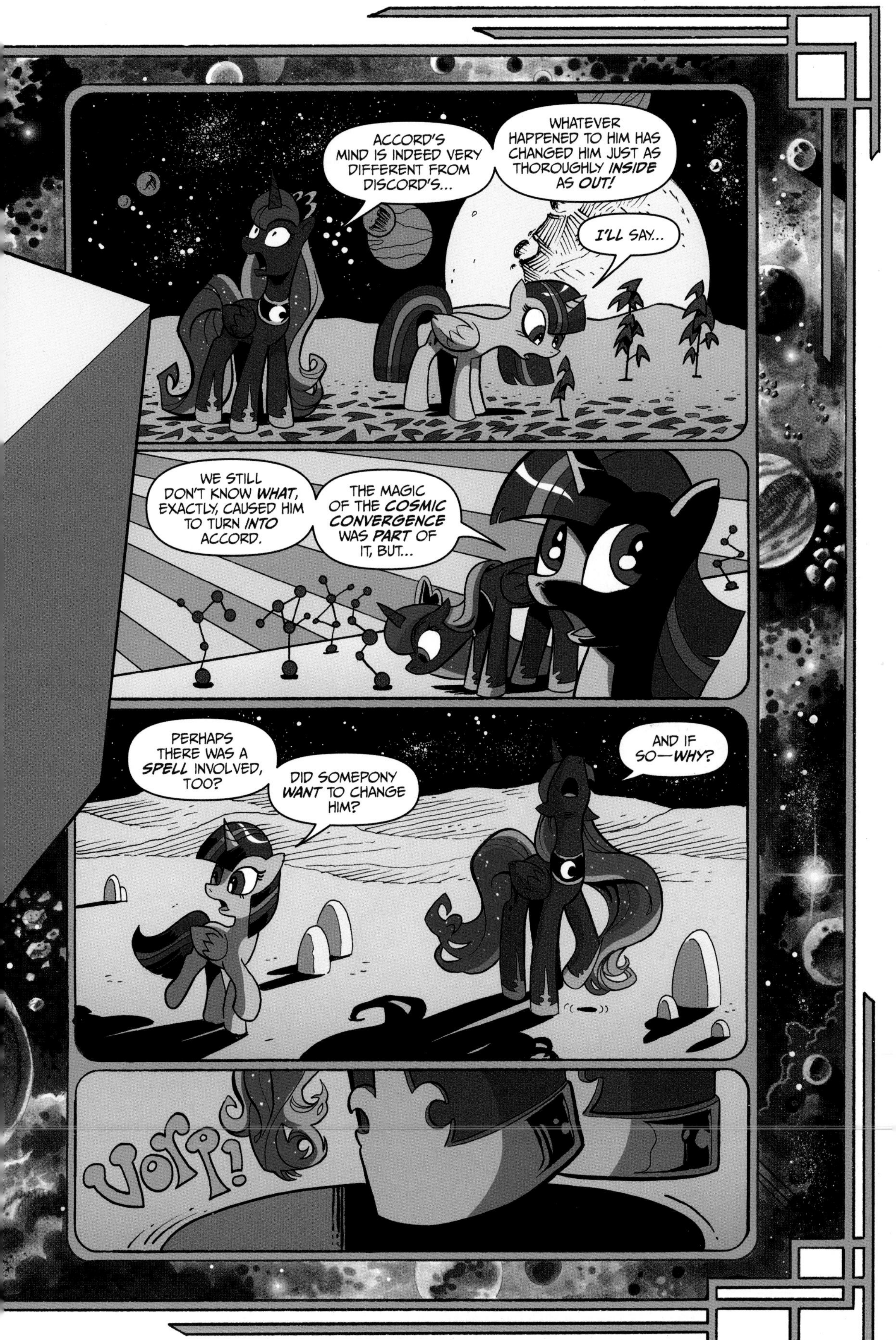
ACCORD'S MIND IS INDEED VERY DIFFERENT FROM DISCORD'S...
WHATEVER HAPPENED TO HIM HAS CHANGED HIM JUST AS THOROUGHLY *INSIDE* AS *OUT!*
I'LL SAY...
WE STILL DON'T KNOW *WHAT*, EXACTLY, CAUSED HIM TO TURN *INTO* ACCORD.
THE MAGIC OF THE *COSMIC CONVERGENCE* WAS *PART* OF IT, BUT...
PERHAPS THERE WAS A *SPELL* INVOLVED, TOO?
DID SOMEPONY *WANT* TO CHANGE HIM?
AND IF SO—*WHY?*
VORP!

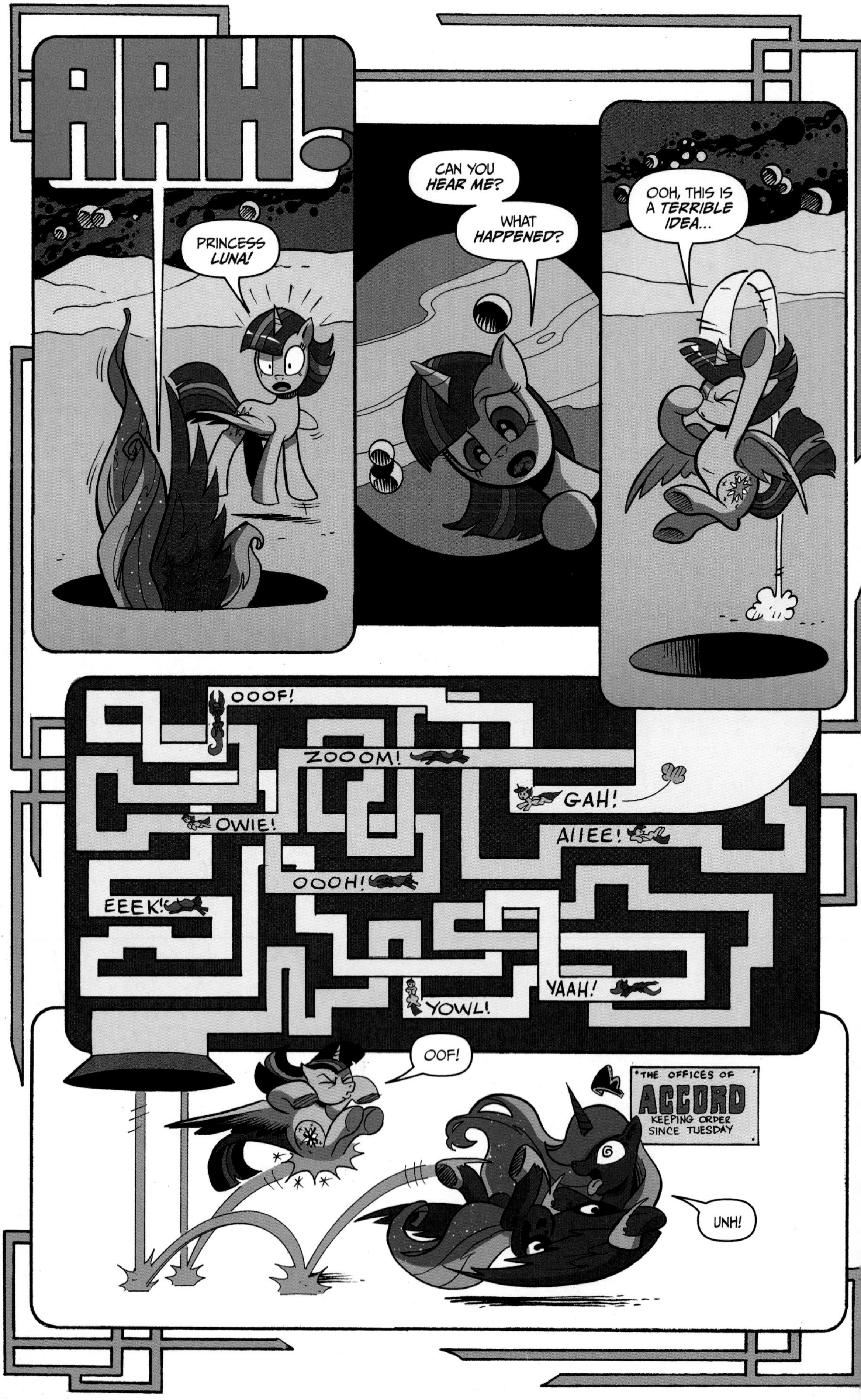
AAH!
PRINCESS LUNA!
CAN YOU HEAR ME?
WHAT HAPPENED?
OOH, THIS IS A TERRIBLE IDEA...
OOOF!
ZOOOM!
GAH!
OWIE!
AIIEE!
OOOH!
EEEK!
YAAH!
YOWL!
OOF!
THE OFFICES OF ACCORD KEEPING ORDER SINCE TUESDAY
UNH!

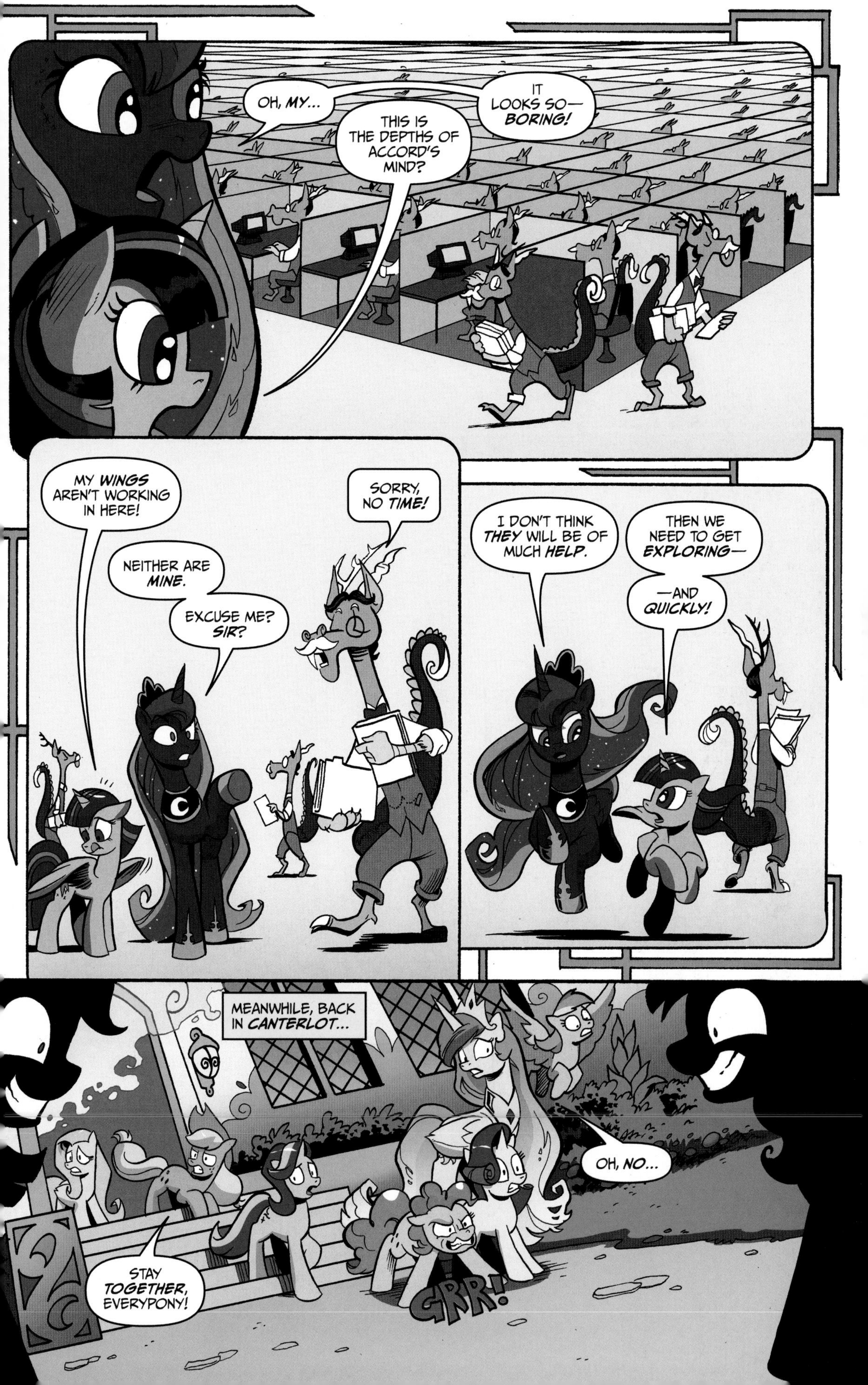
OH, MY...
IT LOOKS SO— BORING!
THIS IS THE DEPTHS OF ACCORD'S MIND?
MY WINGS AREN'T WORKING IN HERE!
NEITHER ARE MINE.
EXCUSE ME? SIR?
SORRY, NO TIME!
I DON'T THINK THEY WILL BE OF MUCH HELP.
THEN WE NEED TO GET EXPLORING—
—AND QUICKLY!
MEANWHILE, BACK IN CANTERLOT...
OH, NO...
STAY TOGETHER, EVERYPONY!
GRR!

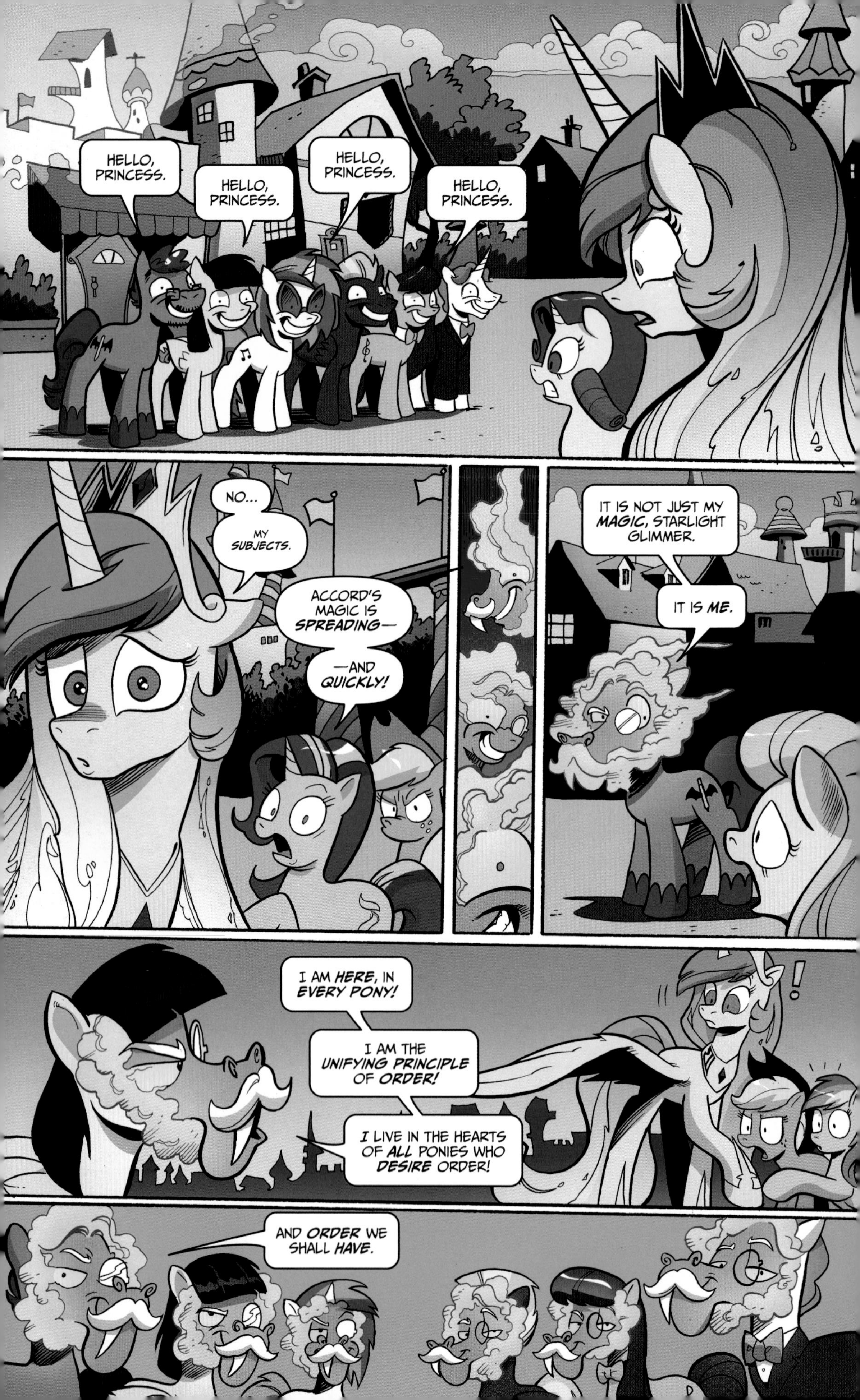
HELLO, PRINCESS.
HELLO, PRINCESS.
HELLO, PRINCESS.
HELLO, PRINCESS.
NO...
MY SUBJECTS.
ACCORD'S MAGIC IS SPREADING—
—AND QUICKLY!
IT IS NOT JUST MY MAGIC, STARLIGHT GLIMMER.
IT IS ME.
I AM HERE, IN EVERY PONY!
I AM THE UNIFYING PRINCIPLE OF ORDER!
I LIVE IN THE HEARTS OF ALL PONIES WHO DESIRE ORDER!
AND ORDER WE SHALL HAVE.

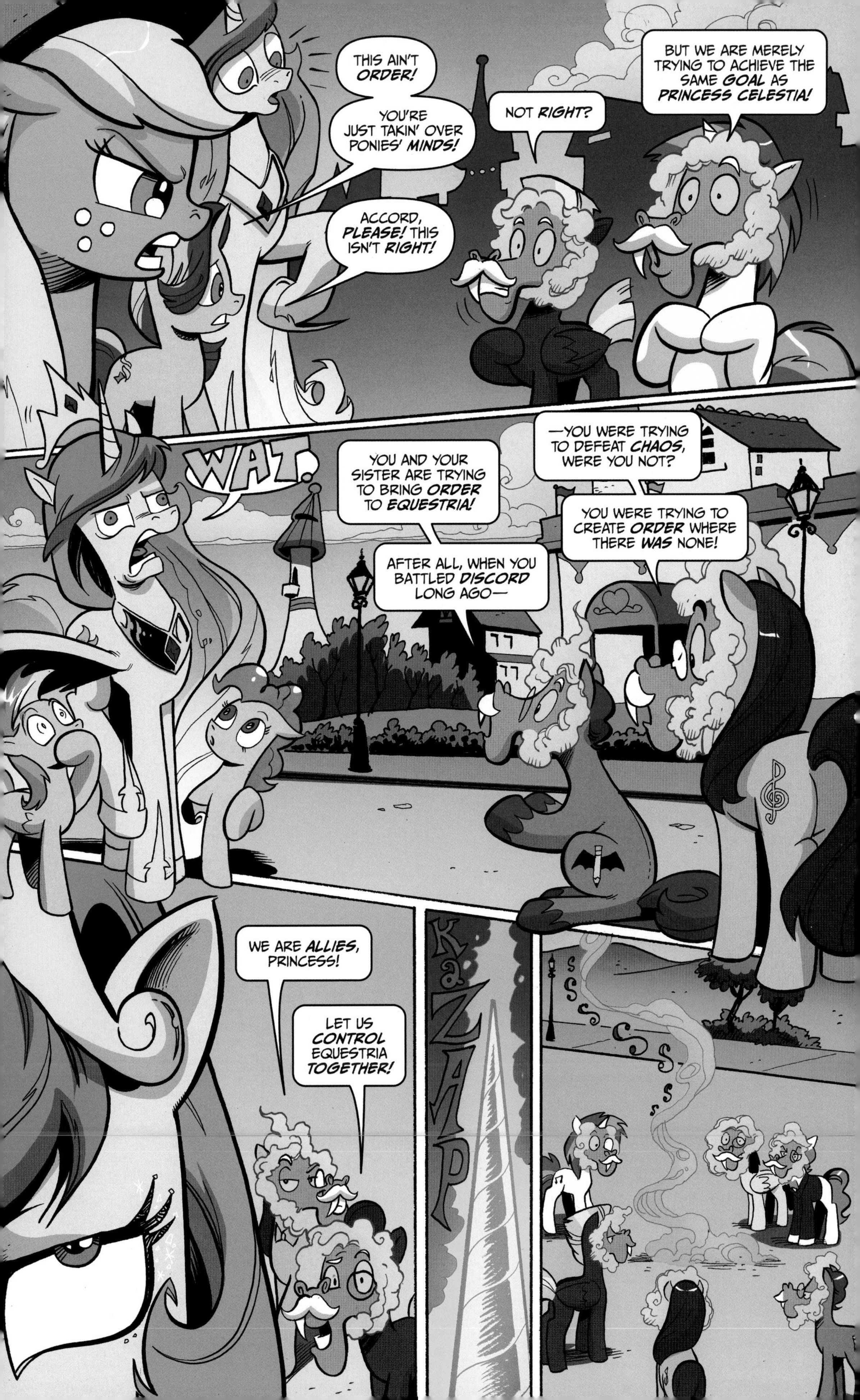

THIS AIN'T ORDER!
YOU'RE JUST TAKIN' OVER PONIES' MINDS!
ACCORD, PLEASE! THIS ISN'T RIGHT!
NOT RIGHT?
BUT WE ARE MERELY TRYING TO ACHIEVE THE SAME GOAL AS PRINCESS CELESTIA!
WAT.
YOU AND YOUR SISTER ARE TRYING TO BRING ORDER TO EQUESTRIA!
AFTER ALL, WHEN YOU BATTLED DISCORD LONG AGO—
—YOU WERE TRYING TO DEFEAT CHAOS, WERE YOU NOT?
YOU WERE TRYING TO CREATE ORDER WHERE THERE WAS NONE!
WE ARE ALLIES, PRINCESS!
LET US CONTROL EQUESTRIA TOGETHER!
KAZAP
SSSSSSS

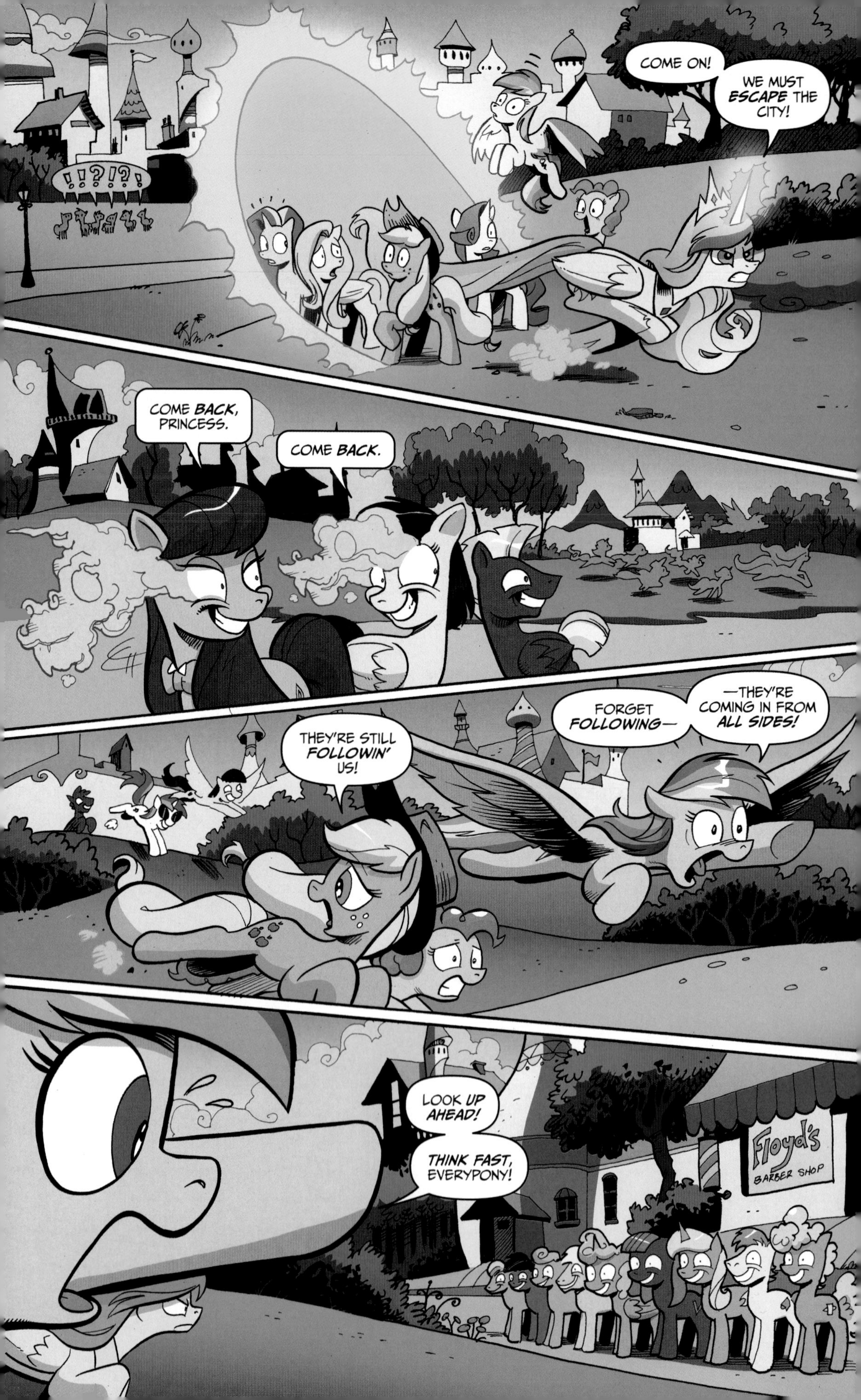

!!?!?!
COME ON!
WE MUST ESCAPE THE CITY!
COME BACK, PRINCESS.
COME BACK.
THEY'RE STILL FOLLOWIN' US!
FORGET FOLLOWING—
—THEY'RE COMING IN FROM ALL SIDES!
LOOK UP AHEAD!
THINK FAST, EVERYPONY!
Floyd's BARBER SHOP

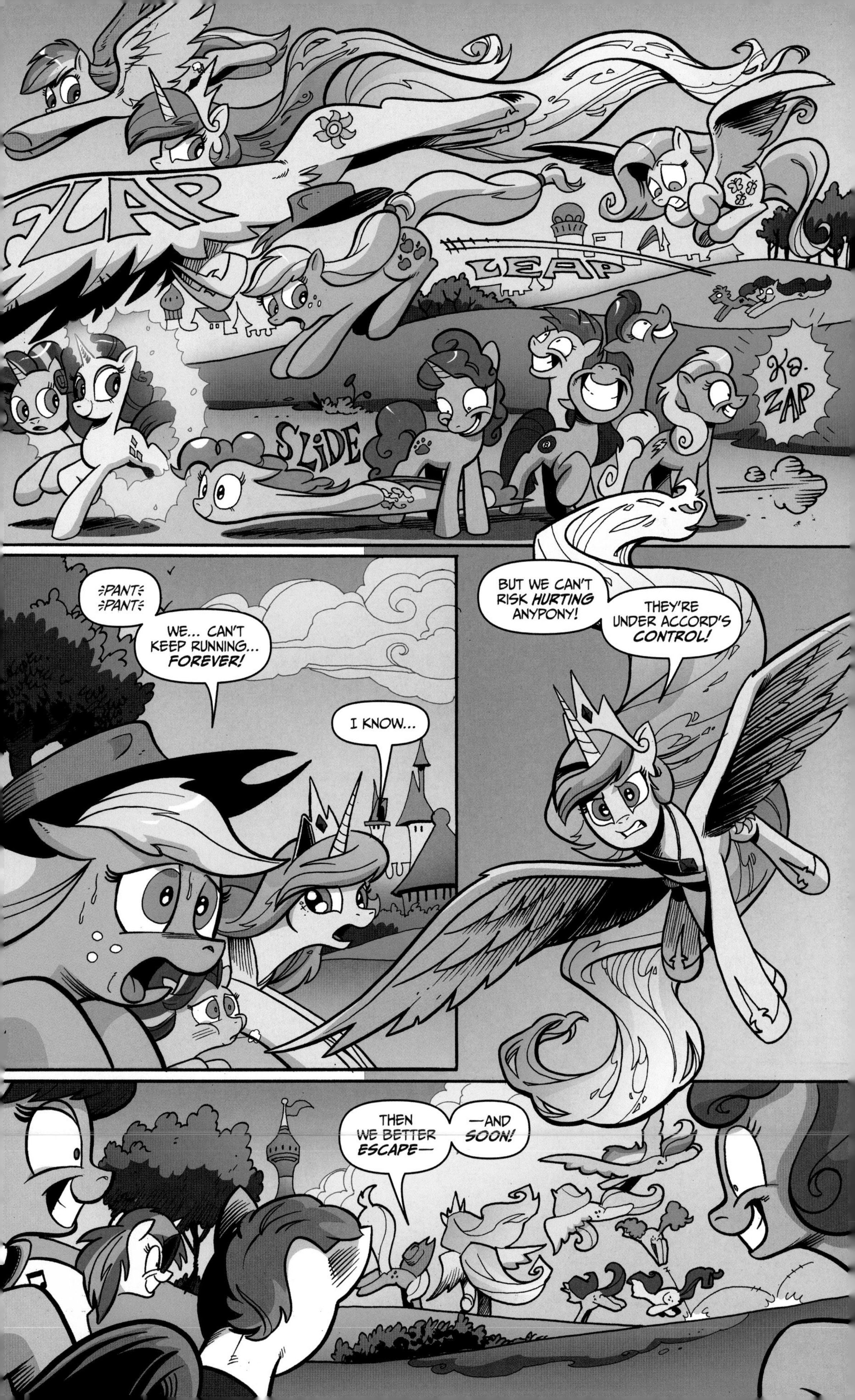
ZAP
LEAP
SLIDE
KA-ZAP
PANT PANT
WE... CAN'T KEEP RUNNING... FOREVER!
I KNOW...
BUT WE CAN'T RISK HURTING ANYPONY!
THEY'RE UNDER ACCORD'S CONTROL!
THEN WE BETTER ESCAPE—
—AND SOON!

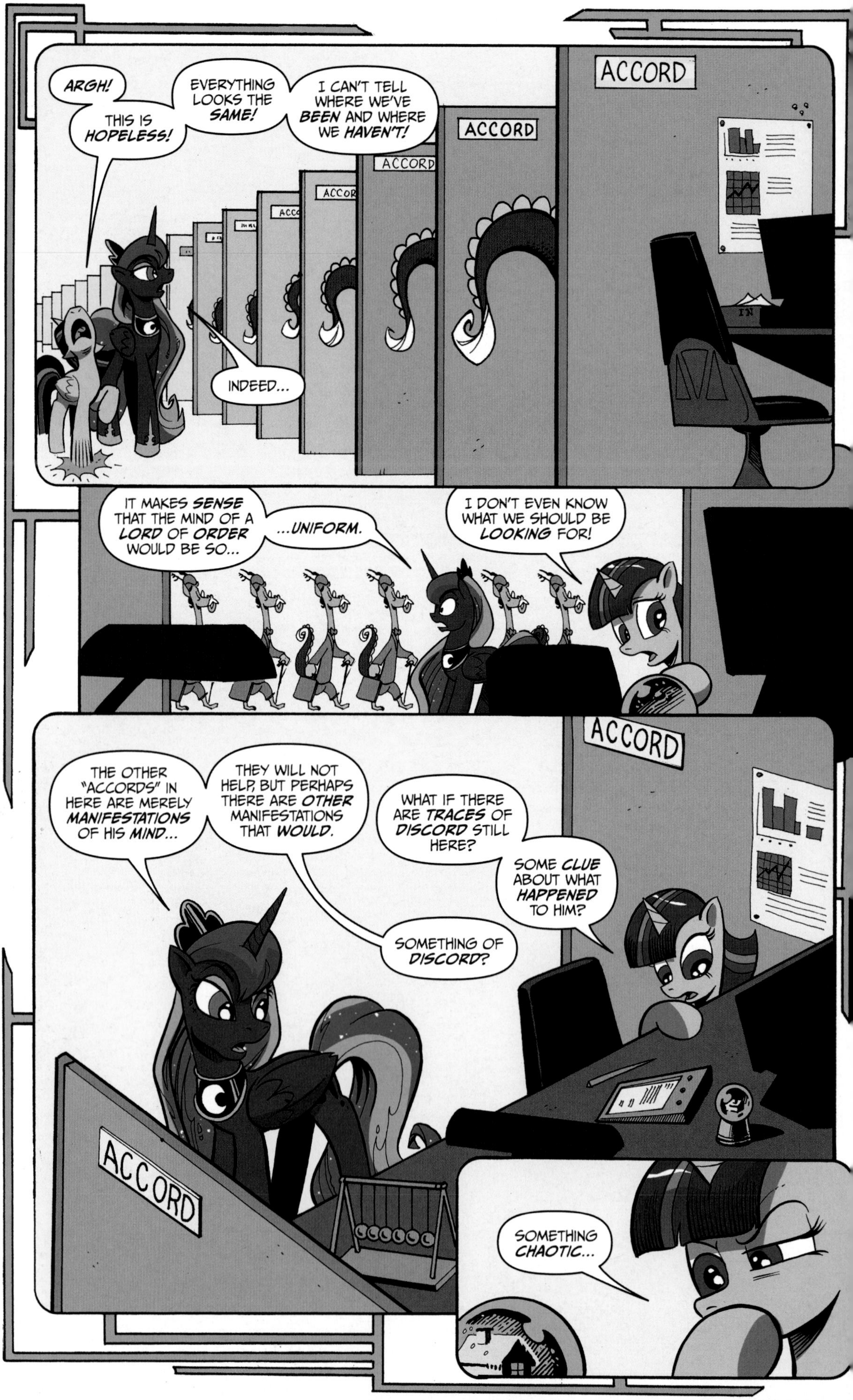
ARGH!
THIS IS HOPELESS!
EVERYTHING LOOKS THE SAME!
I CAN'T TELL WHERE WE'VE BEEN AND WHERE WE HAVEN'T!
ACCORD
INDEED...
IT MAKES SENSE THAT THE MIND OF A LORD OF ORDER WOULD BE SO...
...UNIFORM.
I DON'T EVEN KNOW WHAT WE SHOULD BE LOOKING FOR!
THE OTHER "ACCORDS" IN HERE ARE MERELY MANIFESTATIONS OF HIS MIND...
THEY WILL NOT HELP, BUT PERHAPS THERE ARE OTHER MANIFESTATIONS THAT WOULD.
WHAT IF THERE ARE TRACES OF DISCORD STILL HERE?
SOME CLUE ABOUT WHAT HAPPENED TO HIM?
SOMETHING OF DISCORD?
ACCORD
SOMETHING CHAOTIC...

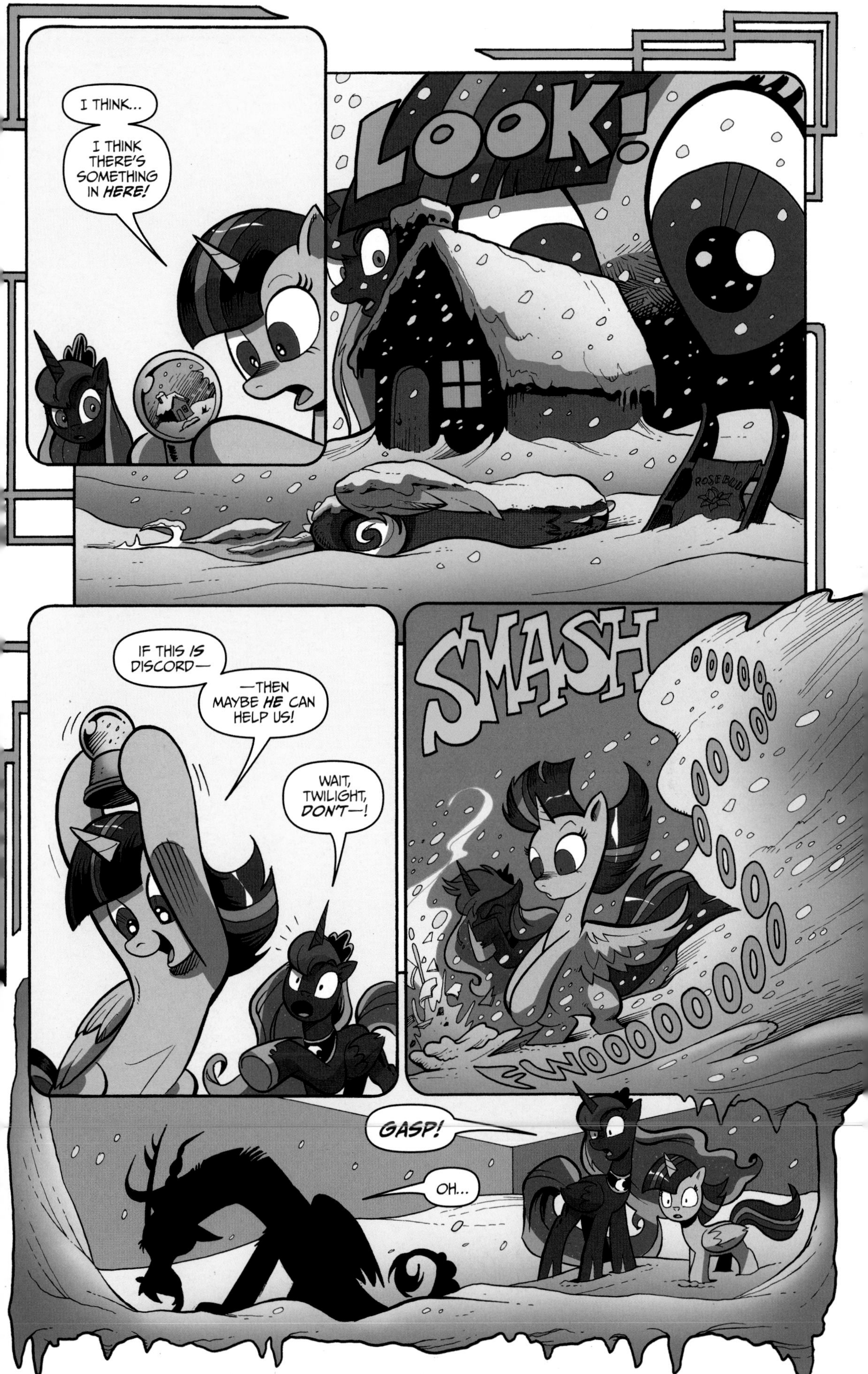
I THINK...
I THINK THERE'S SOMETHING IN *HERE!*
LOOK!
ROSEBUD
IF THIS *IS* DISCORD—
—THEN MAYBE *HE* CAN HELP US!
WAIT, TWILIGHT, *DON'T*—!
SMASH
WOOOOOOOOOOOOOOOOOOOOO
GASP!
OH...

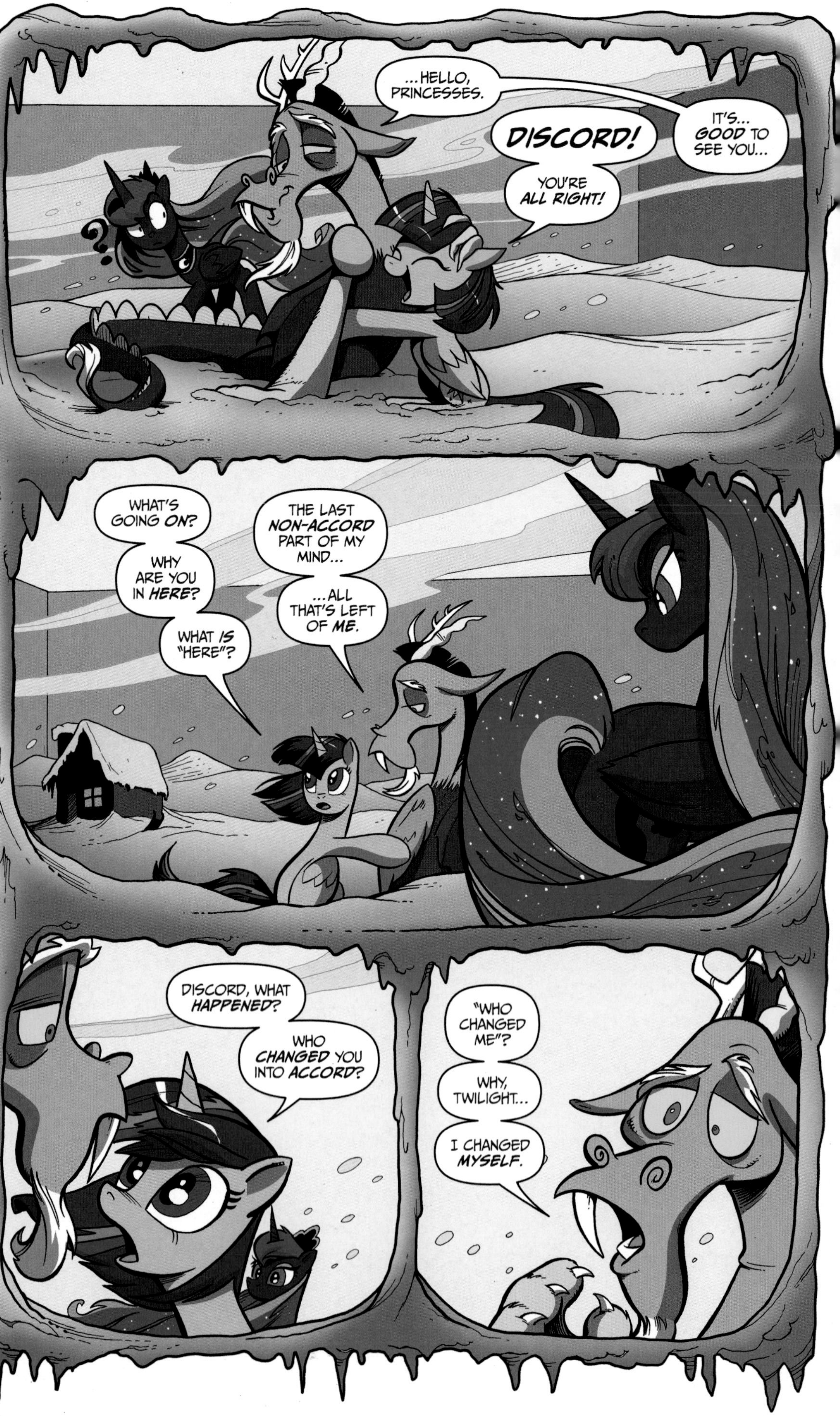

...HELLO, PRINCESSES.
DISCORD!
YOU'RE ALL RIGHT!
IT'S... GOOD TO SEE YOU...
WHAT'S GOING ON?
WHY ARE YOU IN HERE?
WHAT IS "HERE"?
THE LAST NON-ACCORD PART OF MY MIND...
...ALL THAT'S LEFT OF ME.
DISCORD, WHAT HAPPENED?
WHO CHANGED YOU INTO ACCORD?
"WHO CHANGED ME"?
WHY, TWILIGHT...
I CHANGED MYSELF.

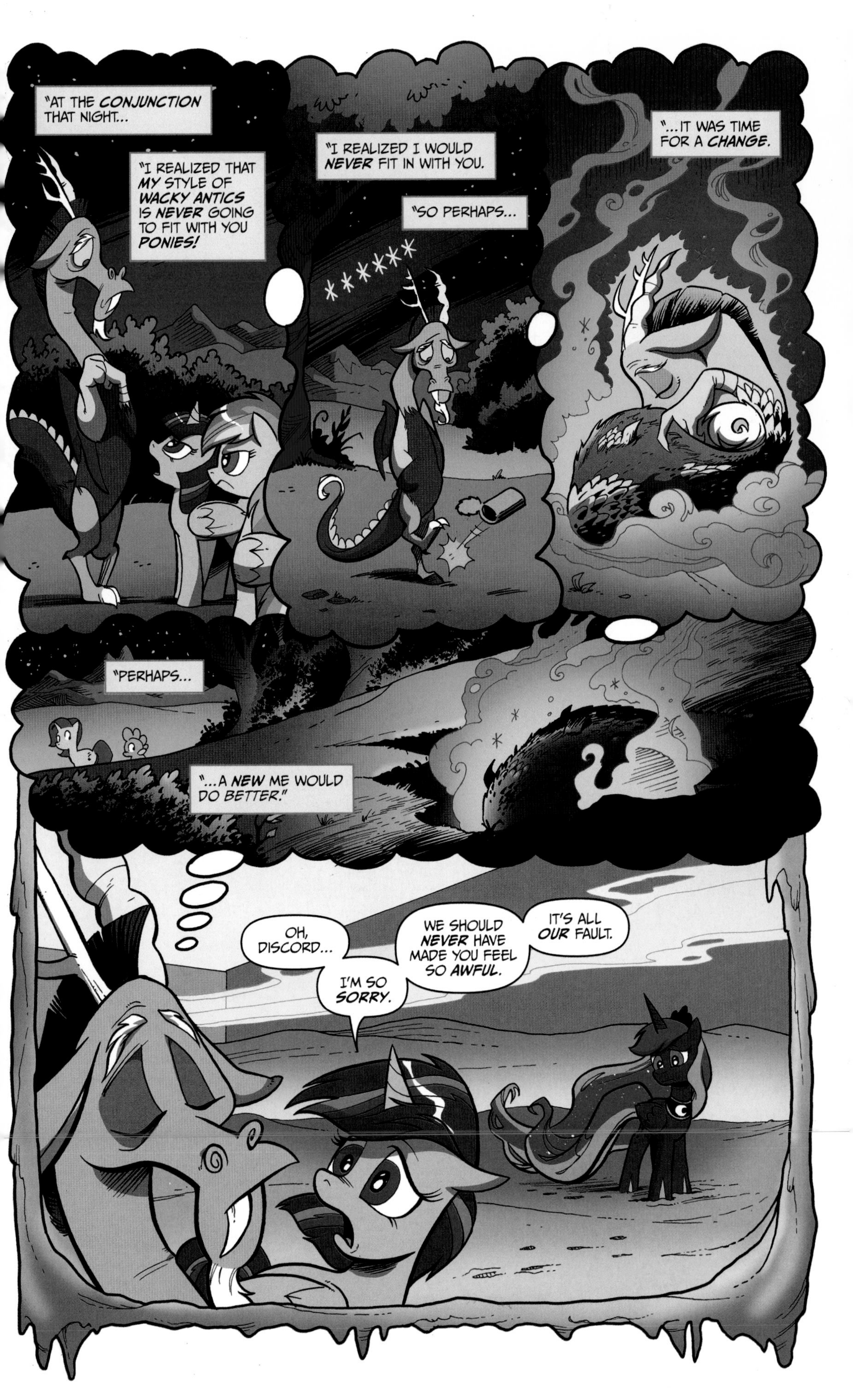
"AT THE CONJUNCTION THAT NIGHT...
"I REALIZED THAT MY STYLE OF WACKY ANTICS IS NEVER GOING TO FIT WITH YOU PONIES!
"I REALIZED I WOULD NEVER FIT IN WITH YOU.
"SO PERHAPS...
"...IT WAS TIME FOR A CHANGE.
"PERHAPS...
"...A NEW ME WOULD DO BETTER."
OH, DISCORD...
I'M SO SORRY.
WE SHOULD NEVER HAVE MADE YOU FEEL SO AWFUL.
IT'S ALL OUR FAULT.

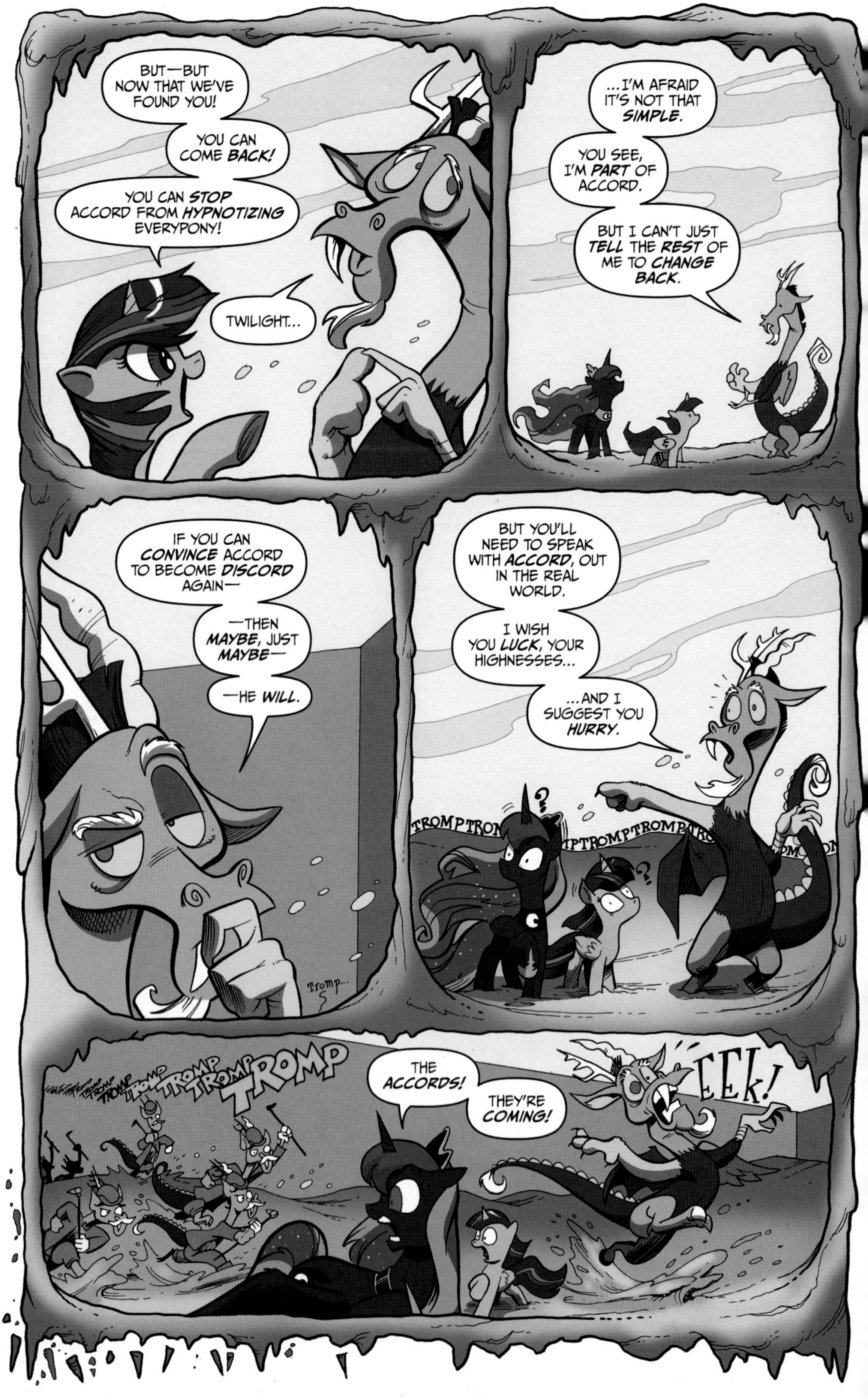

BUT—BUT NOW THAT WE'VE FOUND YOU!
YOU CAN COME BACK!
YOU CAN STOP ACCORD FROM HYPNOTIZING EVERYPONY!
TWILIGHT...
...I'M AFRAID IT'S NOT THAT SIMPLE.
YOU SEE, I'M PART OF ACCORD.
BUT I CAN'T JUST TELL THE REST OF ME TO CHANGE BACK.
IF YOU CAN CONVINCE ACCORD TO BECOME DISCORD AGAIN—
—THEN MAYBE, JUST MAYBE—
—HE WILL.
Tromp...
BUT YOU'LL NEED TO SPEAK WITH ACCORD, OUT IN THE REAL WORLD.
I WISH YOU LUCK, YOUR HIGHNESSES...
...AND I SUGGEST YOU HURRY.
TROMPTROMPTROMPTROMPTROMP
TROMP TROMP TROMP TROMP TROMP
THE ACCORDS!
THEY'RE COMING!
EEK!

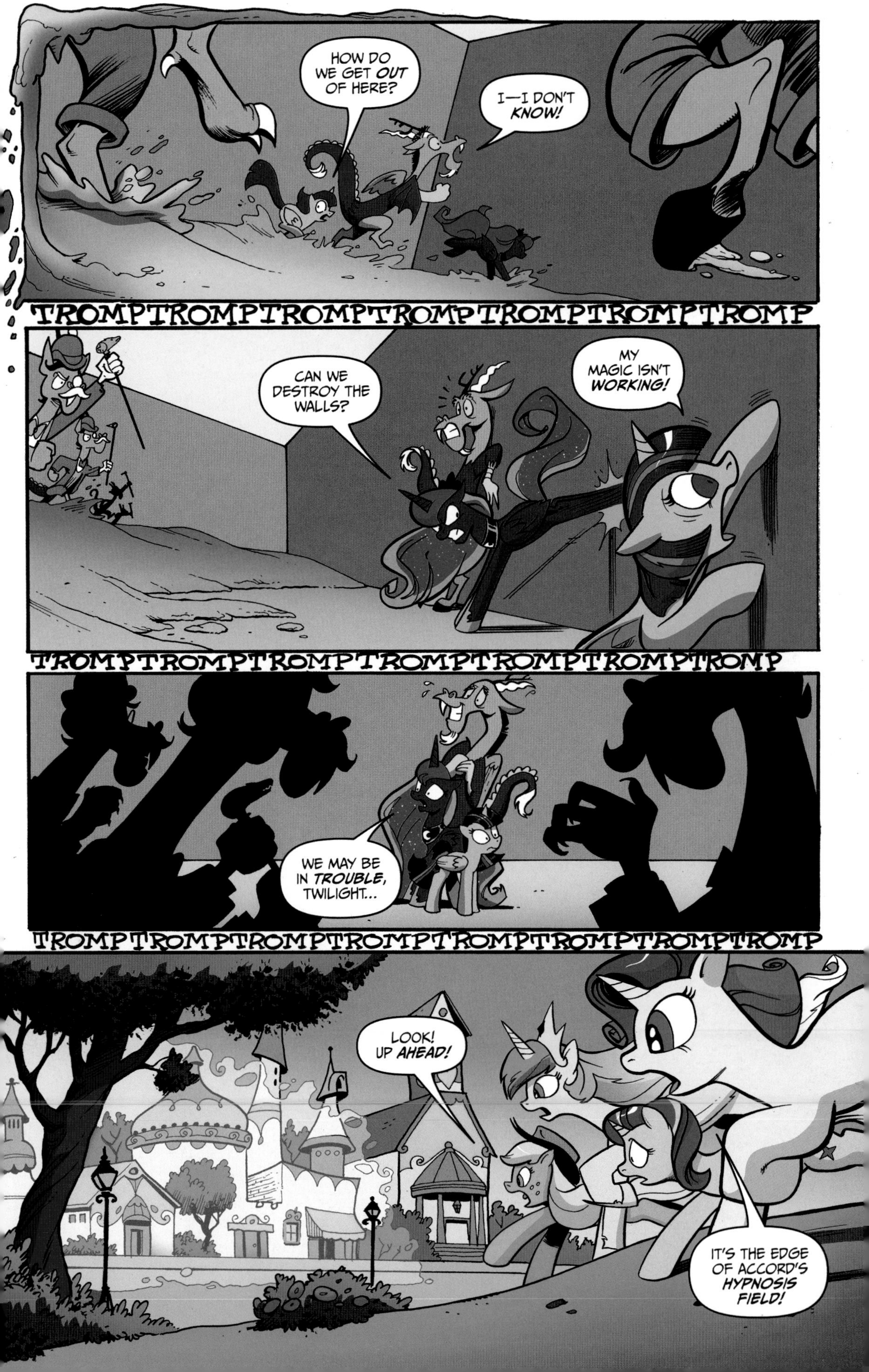
HOW DO WE GET OUT OF HERE?
I—I DON'T KNOW!
TROMPTROMPTROMPTROMPTROMPTROMPTROMP
CAN WE DESTROY THE WALLS?
MY MAGIC ISN'T WORKING!
TROMPTROMPTROMPTROMPTROMPTROMP
WE MAY BE IN TROUBLE, TWILIGHT...
TROMPTROMPTROMPTROMPTROMPTROMPTROMPTROMP
LOOK! UP AHEAD!
IT'S THE EDGE OF ACCORD'S HYPNOSIS FIELD!

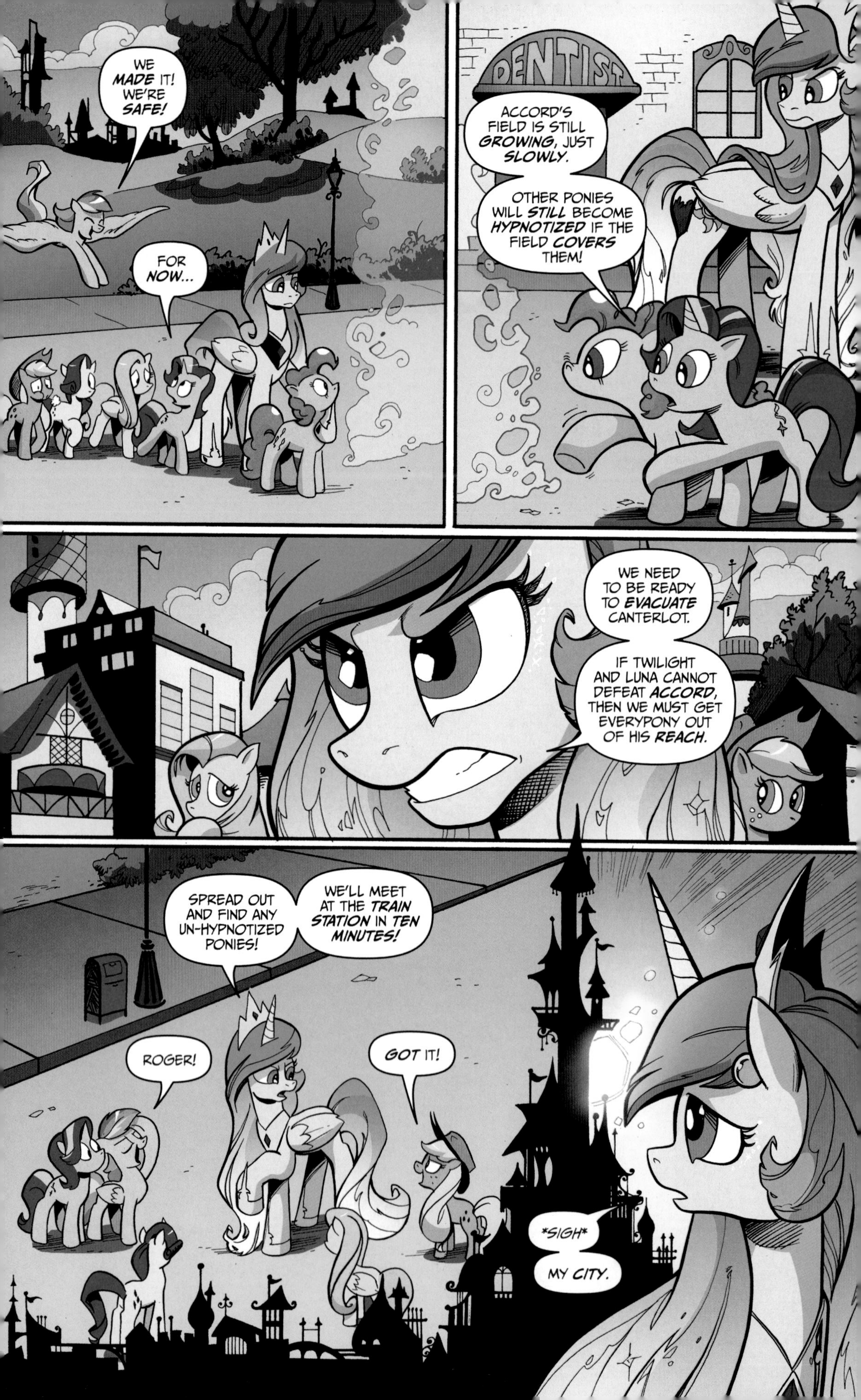
WE MADE IT! WE'RE SAFE!
FOR NOW...
ACCORD'S FIELD IS STILL GROWING, JUST SLOWLY.
OTHER PONIES WILL STILL BECOME HYPNOTIZED IF THE FIELD COVERS THEM!
DENTIST
WE NEED TO BE READY TO EVACUATE CANTERLOT.
IF TWILIGHT AND LUNA CANNOT DEFEAT ACCORD, THEN WE MUST GET EVERYPONY OUT OF HIS REACH.
SPREAD OUT AND FIND ANY UN-HYPNOTIZED PONIES!
WE'LL MEET AT THE TRAIN STATION IN TEN MINUTES!
ROGER!
GOT IT!
SIGH
MY CITY.

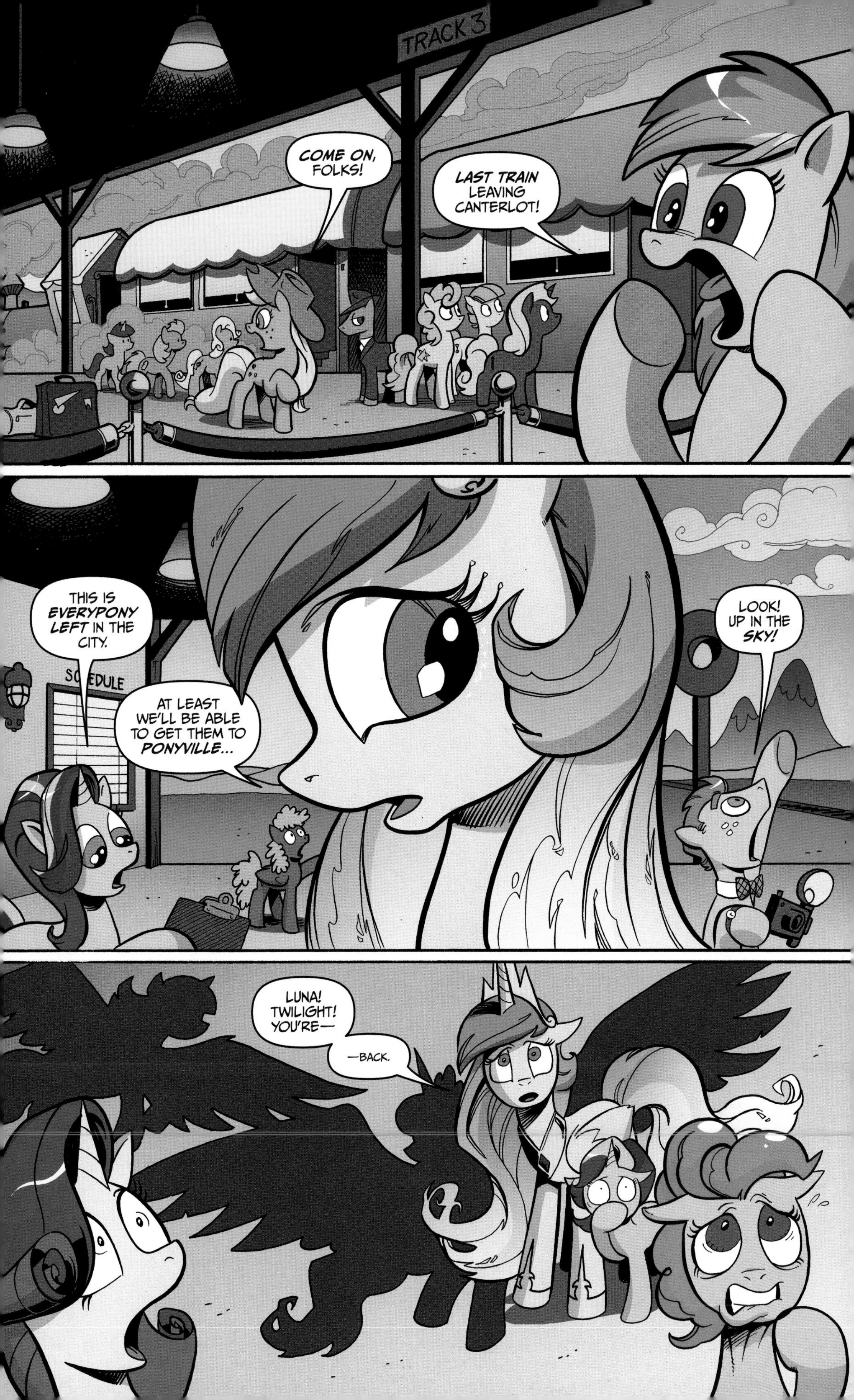
TRACK 3
COME ON, FOLKS!
LAST TRAIN LEAVING CANTERLOT!
THIS IS EVERYPONY LEFT IN THE CITY.
SCHEDULE
AT LEAST WE'LL BE ABLE TO GET THEM TO PONYVILLE...
LOOK! UP IN THE SKY!
LUNA! TWILIGHT! YOU'RE—
—BACK.

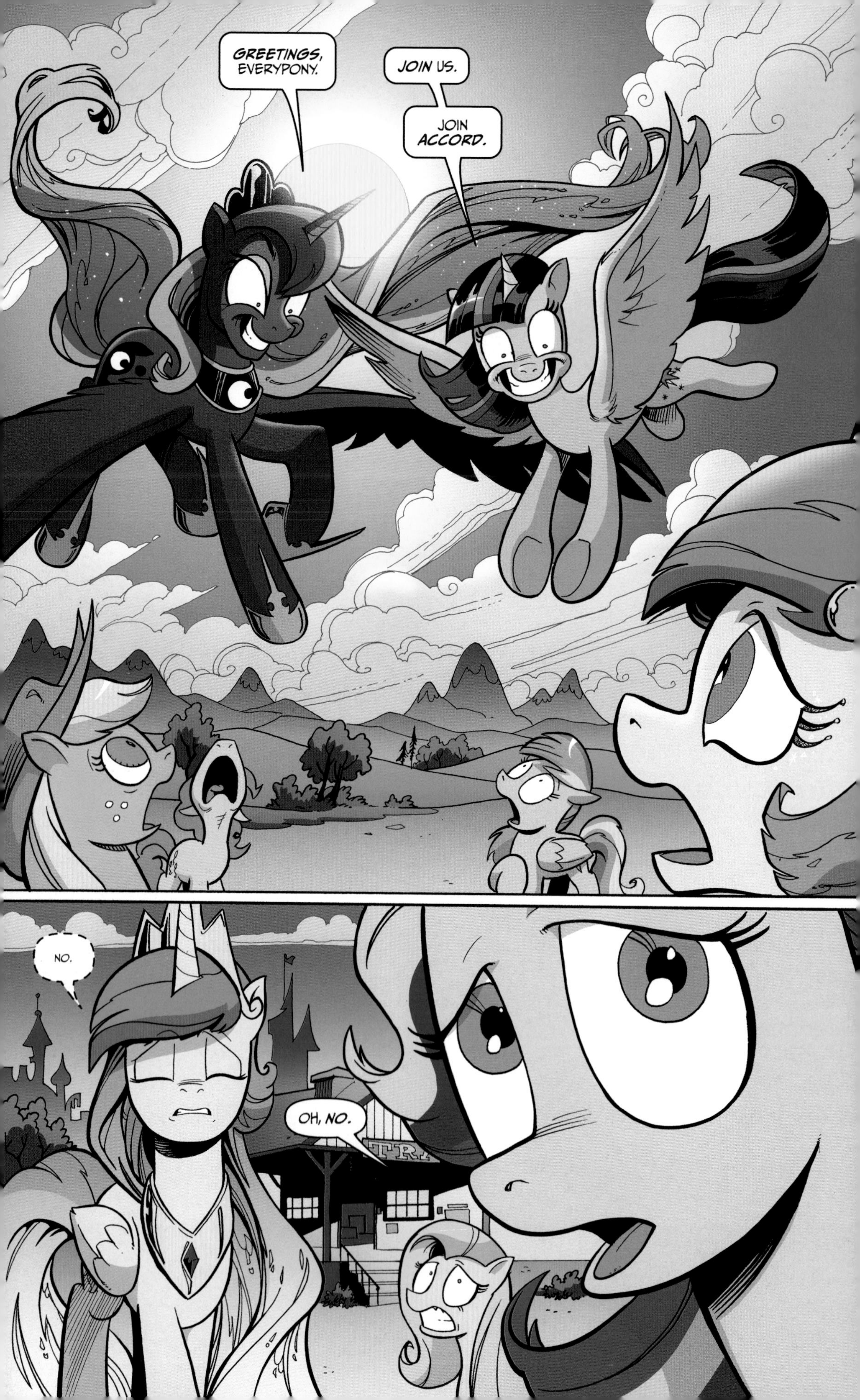
GREETINGS, EVERYPONY.
JOIN US.
JOIN ACCORD.
NO.
OH, NO.

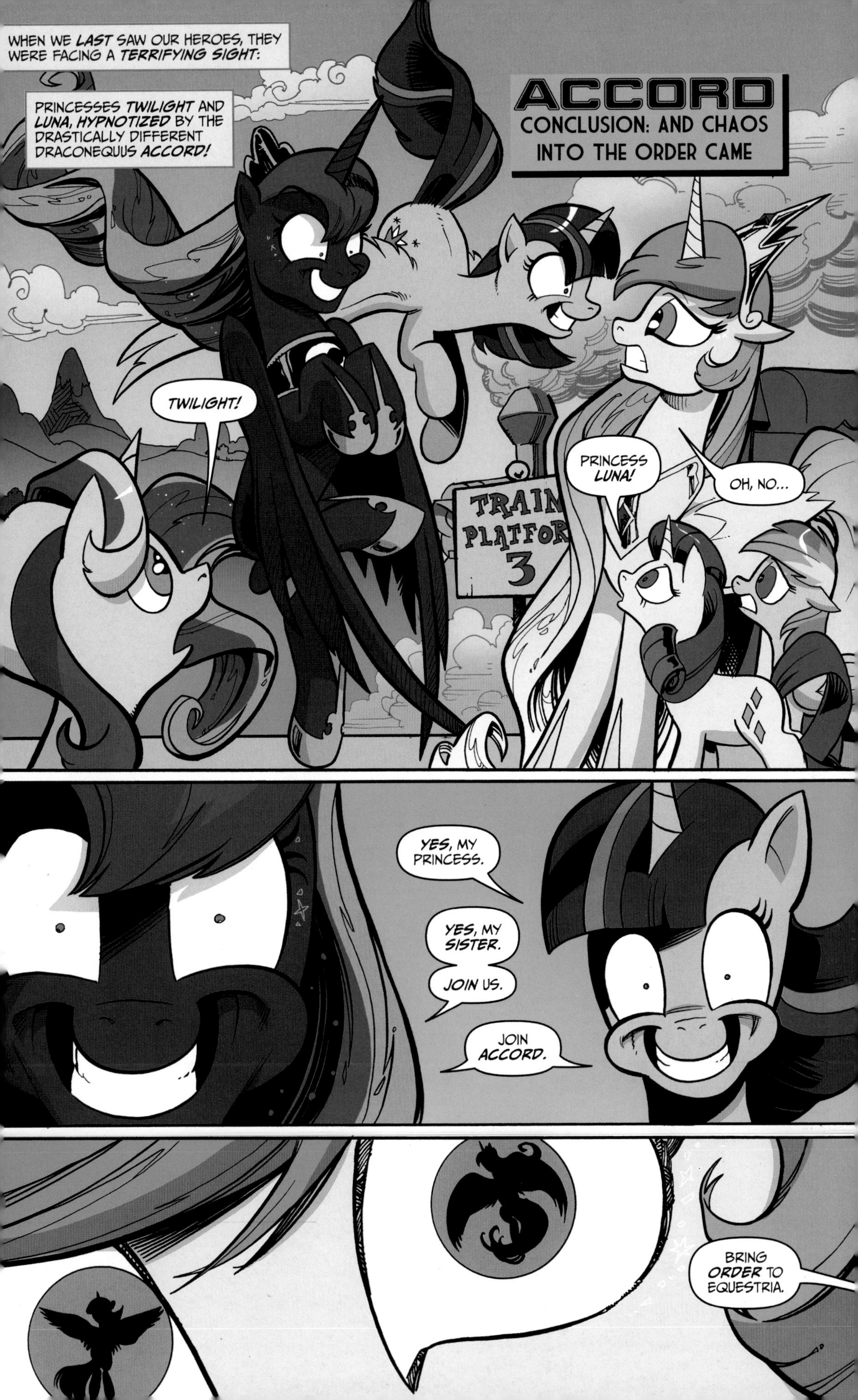
WHEN WE LAST SAW OUR HEROES, THEY WERE FACING A TERRIFYING SIGHT:
PRINCESSES TWILIGHT AND LUNA, HYPNOTIZED BY THE DRASTICALLY DIFFERENT DRACONEQUUS ACCORD!
ACCORD
CONCLUSION: AND CHAOS INTO THE ORDER CAME
TWILIGHT!
TRAIN PLATFOR 3
PRINCESS LUNA!
OH, NO...
YES, MY PRINCESS.
YES, MY SISTER.
JOIN US.
JOIN ACCORD.
BRING ORDER TO EQUESTRIA.

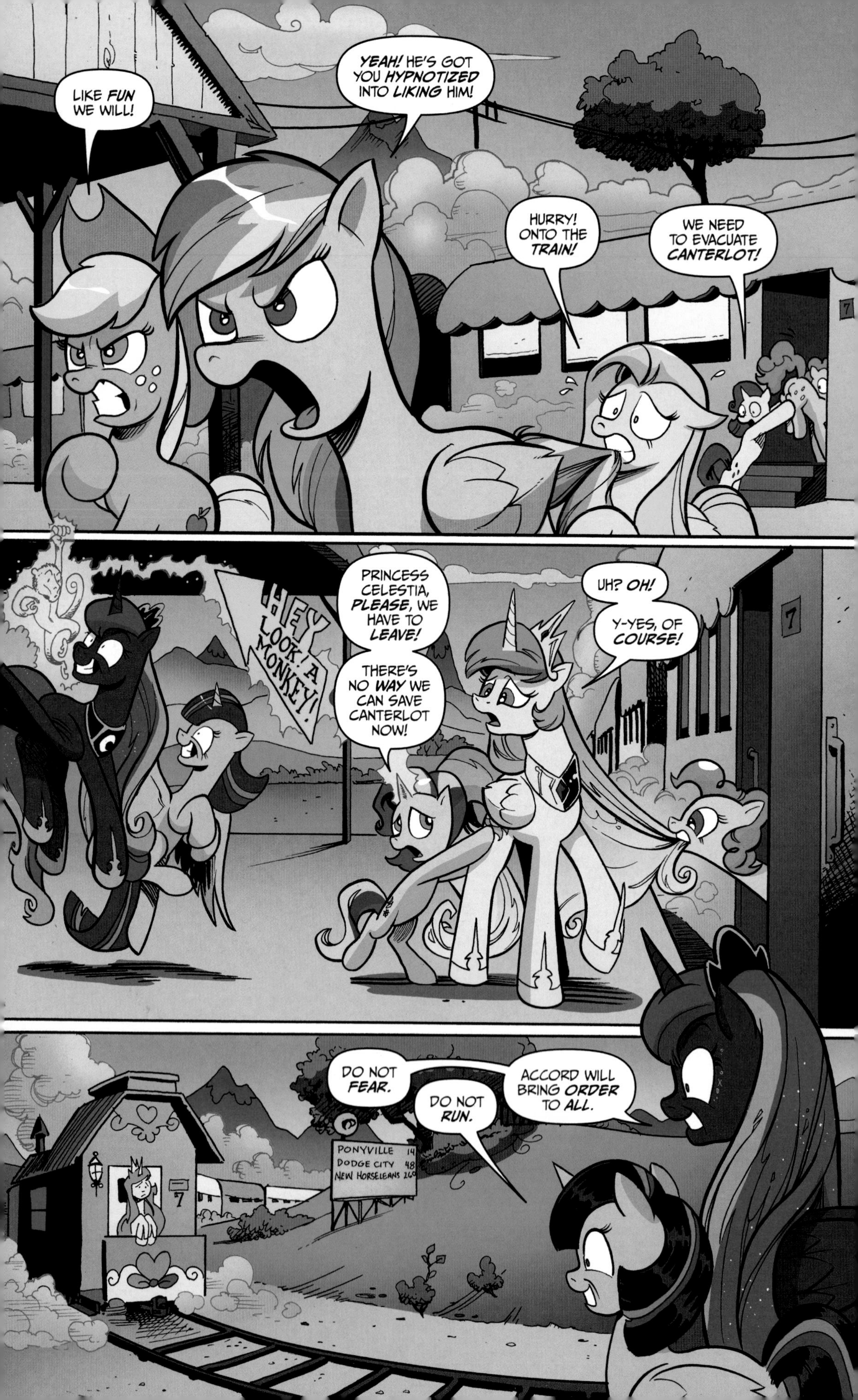

LIKE *FUN* WE WILL!
YEAH! HE'S GOT YOU *HYPNOTIZED* INTO *LIKING* HIM!
HURRY! ONTO THE *TRAIN!*
WE NEED TO EVACUATE *CANTERLOT!*
HEY LOOK! A MONKEY!
PRINCESS CELESTIA, *PLEASE*, WE HAVE TO *LEAVE!*
THERE'S NO *WAY* WE CAN SAVE CANTERLOT NOW!
UH? *OH!*
Y-YES, OF *COURSE!*
DO NOT *FEAR.*
DO NOT *RUN.*
ACCORD WILL BRING *ORDER* TO *ALL*.
PONYVILLE 14
DODGE CITY 48
NEW HORSELEANS 260

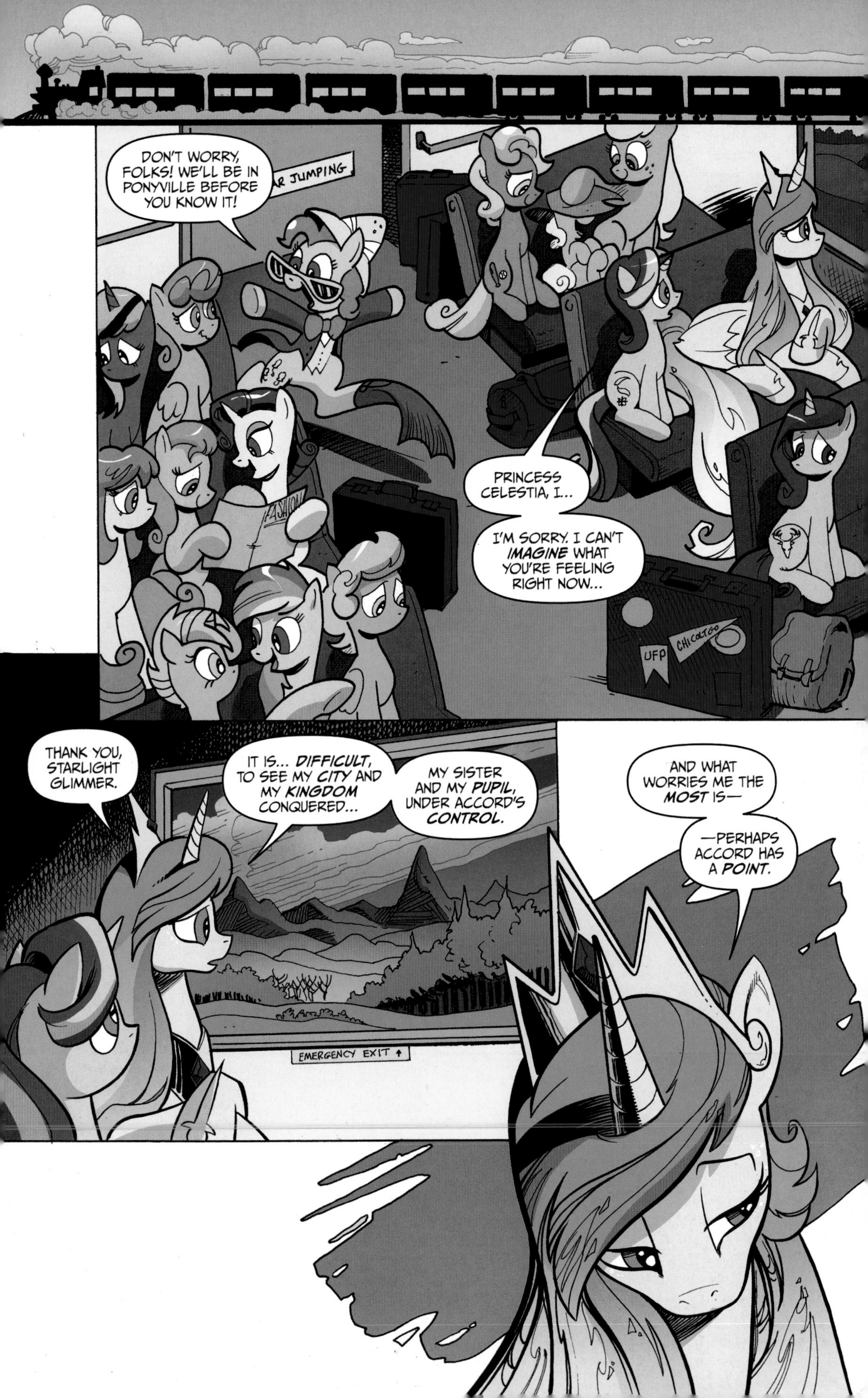
DON'T WORRY, FOLKS! WE'LL BE IN PONYVILLE BEFORE YOU KNOW IT!
AR JUMPING
FASHION
PRINCESS CELESTIA, I...
I'M SORRY. I CAN'T *IMAGINE* WHAT YOU'RE FEELING RIGHT NOW...
UFP
CHICOLTGO
THANK YOU, STARLIGHT GLIMMER.
IT IS... *DIFFICULT*, TO SEE MY *CITY* AND MY *KINGDOM* CONQUERED...
MY SISTER AND MY *PUPIL*, UNDER ACCORD'S *CONTROL*.
EMERGENCY EXIT
AND WHAT WORRIES ME THE *MOST* IS—
—PERHAPS ACCORD HAS A *POINT*.

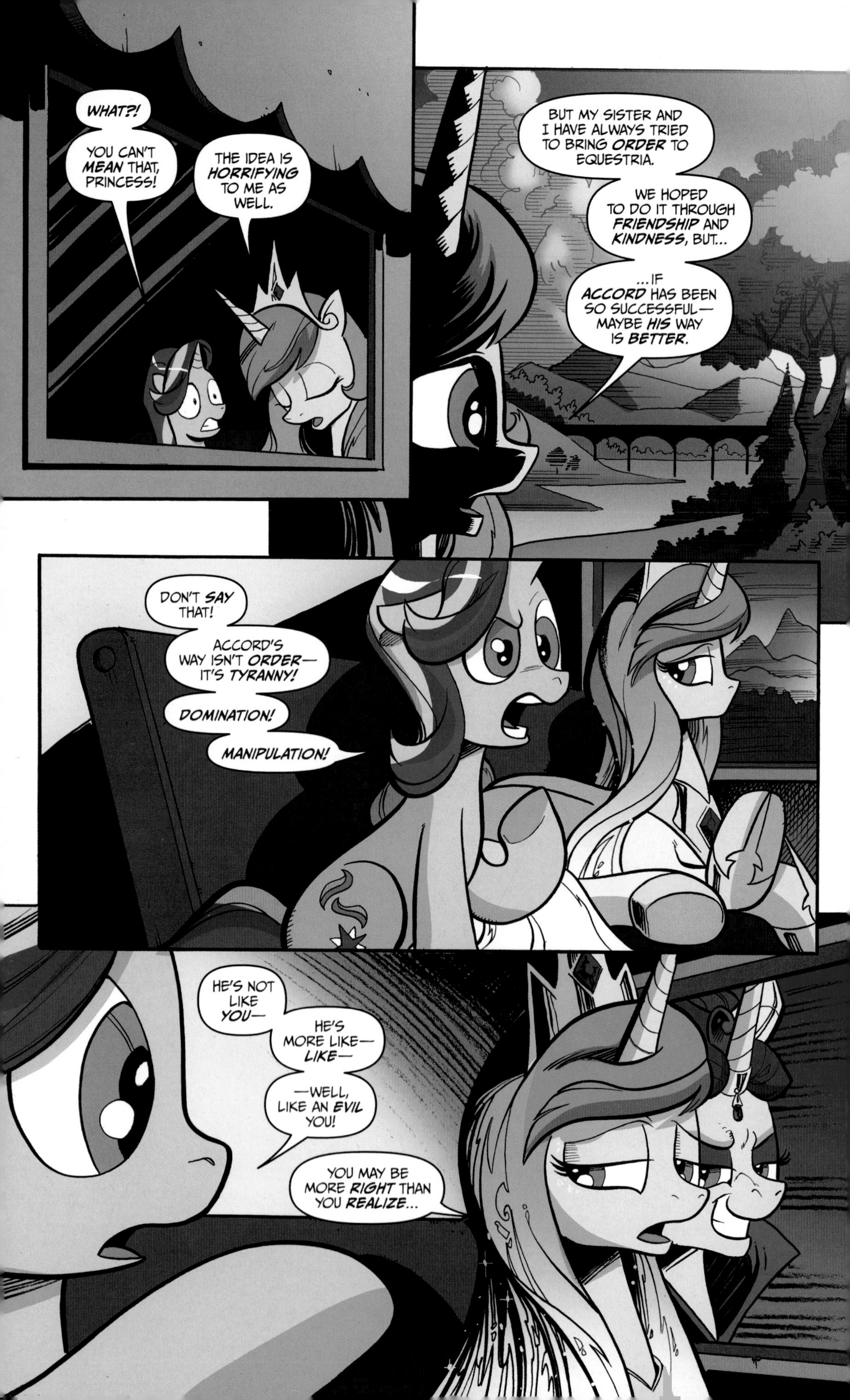
WHAT?!
YOU CAN'T MEAN THAT, PRINCESS!
THE IDEA IS HORRIFYING TO ME AS WELL.
BUT MY SISTER AND I HAVE ALWAYS TRIED TO BRING ORDER TO EQUESTRIA.
WE HOPED TO DO IT THROUGH FRIENDSHIP AND KINDNESS, BUT...
...IF ACCORD HAS BEEN SO SUCCESSFUL— MAYBE HIS WAY IS BETTER.
DON'T SAY THAT!
ACCORD'S WAY ISN'T ORDER— IT'S TYRANNY!
DOMINATION!
MANIPULATION!
HE'S NOT LIKE YOU—
HE'S MORE LIKE— LIKE—
—WELL, LIKE AN EVIL YOU!
YOU MAY BE MORE RIGHT THAN YOU REALIZE...

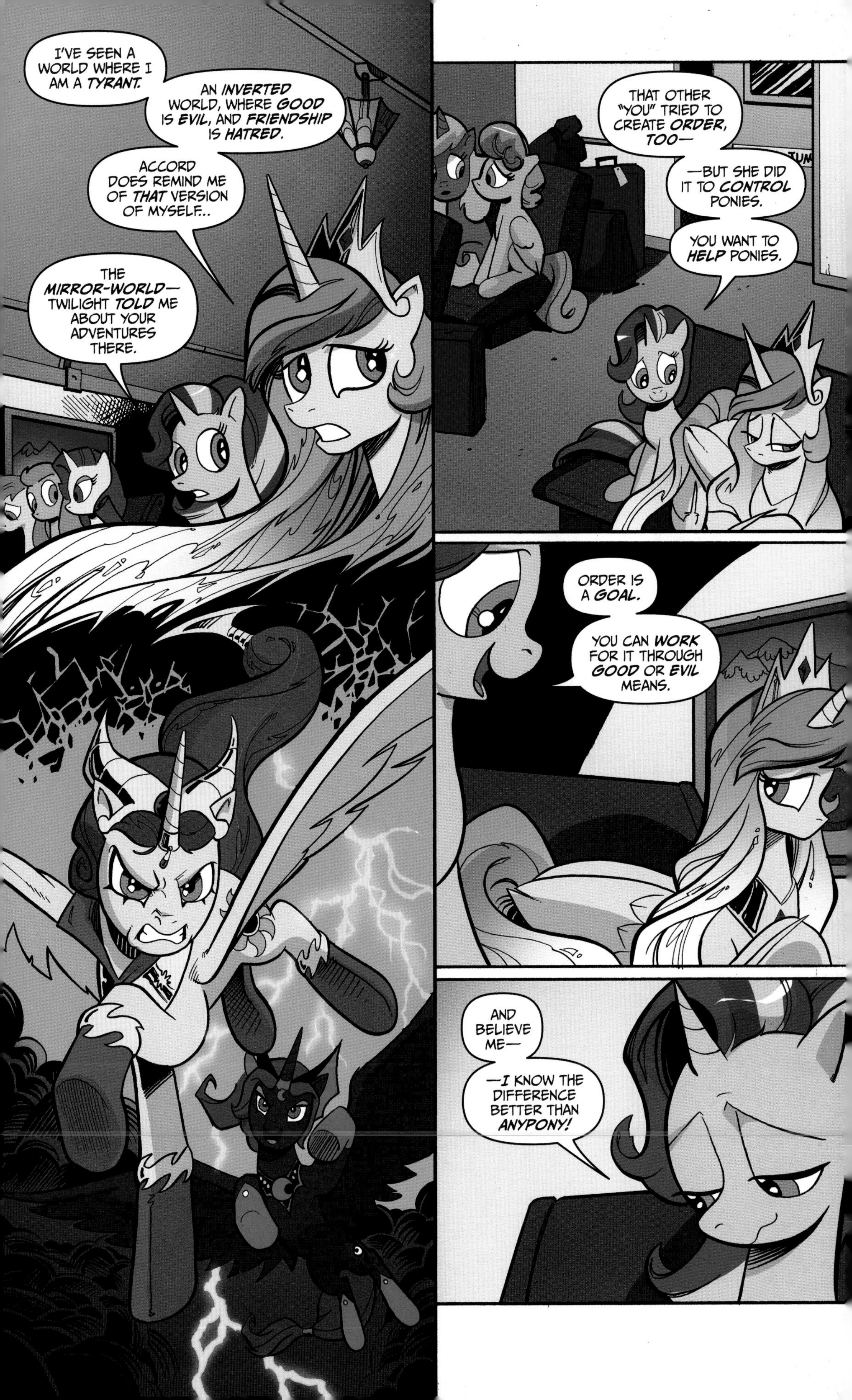
I'VE SEEN A WORLD WHERE I AM A *TYRANT.*
AN *INVERTED* WORLD, WHERE *GOOD* IS *EVIL,* AND *FRIENDSHIP* IS *HATRED.*
ACCORD DOES REMIND ME OF *THAT* VERSION OF MYSELF...
THE *MIRROR-WORLD*— TWILIGHT *TOLD* ME ABOUT YOUR ADVENTURES THERE.
THAT OTHER "YOU" TRIED TO CREATE *ORDER, TOO*—
—BUT SHE DID IT TO *CONTROL* PONIES.
YOU WANT TO *HELP* PONIES.
ORDER IS A *GOAL.*
YOU CAN *WORK* FOR IT THROUGH *GOOD* OR *EVIL* MEANS.
AND BELIEVE ME—
—*I* KNOW THE DIFFERENCE BETTER THAN *ANYPONY!*

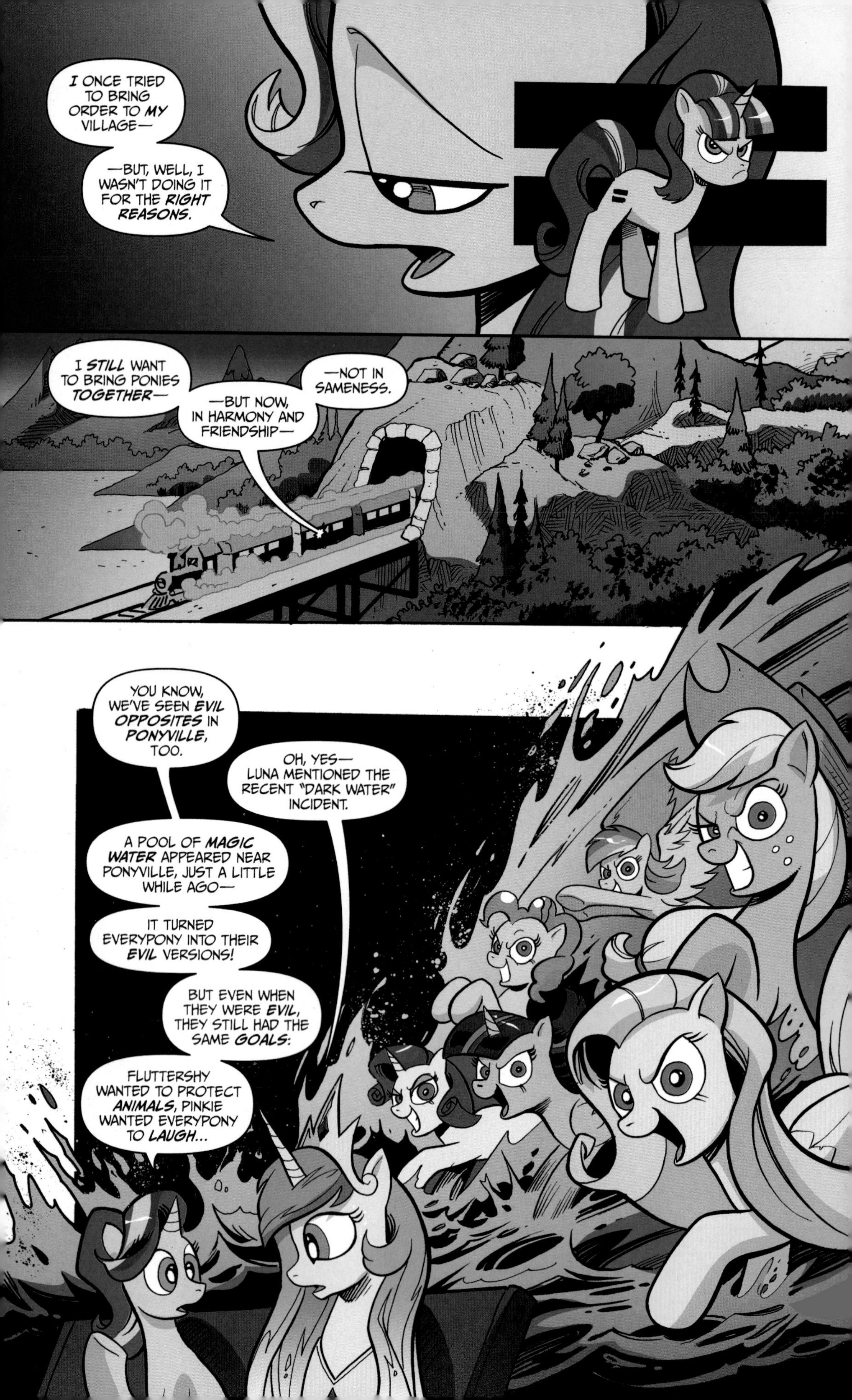
I ONCE TRIED TO BRING ORDER TO MY VILLAGE—
—BUT, WELL, I WASN'T DOING IT FOR THE RIGHT REASONS.
I STILL WANT TO BRING PONIES TOGETHER—
—BUT NOW, IN HARMONY AND FRIENDSHIP—
—NOT IN SAMENESS.
YOU KNOW, WE'VE SEEN EVIL OPPOSITES IN PONYVILLE, TOO.
OH, YES— LUNA MENTIONED THE RECENT "DARK WATER" INCIDENT.
A POOL OF MAGIC WATER APPEARED NEAR PONYVILLE, JUST A LITTLE WHILE AGO—
IT TURNED EVERYPONY INTO THEIR EVIL VERSIONS!
BUT EVEN WHEN THEY WERE EVIL, THEY STILL HAD THE SAME GOALS:
FLUTTERSHY WANTED TO PROTECT ANIMALS, PINKIE WANTED EVERYPONY TO LAUGH...

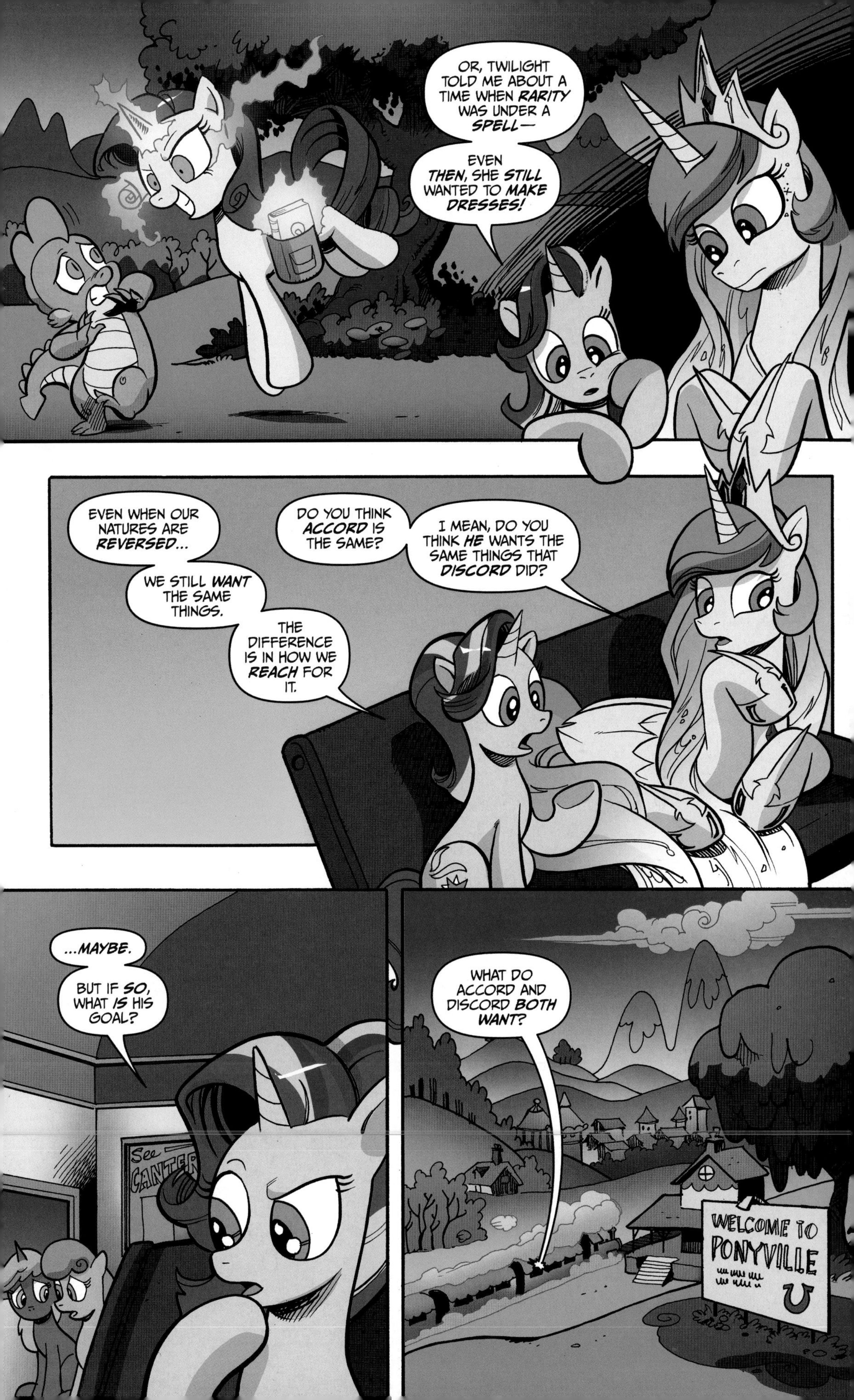
OR, TWILIGHT TOLD ME ABOUT A TIME WHEN RARITY WAS UNDER A SPELL—
EVEN THEN, SHE STILL WANTED TO MAKE DRESSES!
EVEN WHEN OUR NATURES ARE REVERSED...
WE STILL WANT THE SAME THINGS.
THE DIFFERENCE IS IN HOW WE REACH FOR IT.
DO YOU THINK ACCORD IS THE SAME?
I MEAN, DO YOU THINK HE WANTS THE SAME THINGS THAT DISCORD DID?
...MAYBE.
BUT IF SO, WHAT IS HIS GOAL?
See CANTER
WHAT DO ACCORD AND DISCORD BOTH WANT?
WELCOME TO PONYVILLE

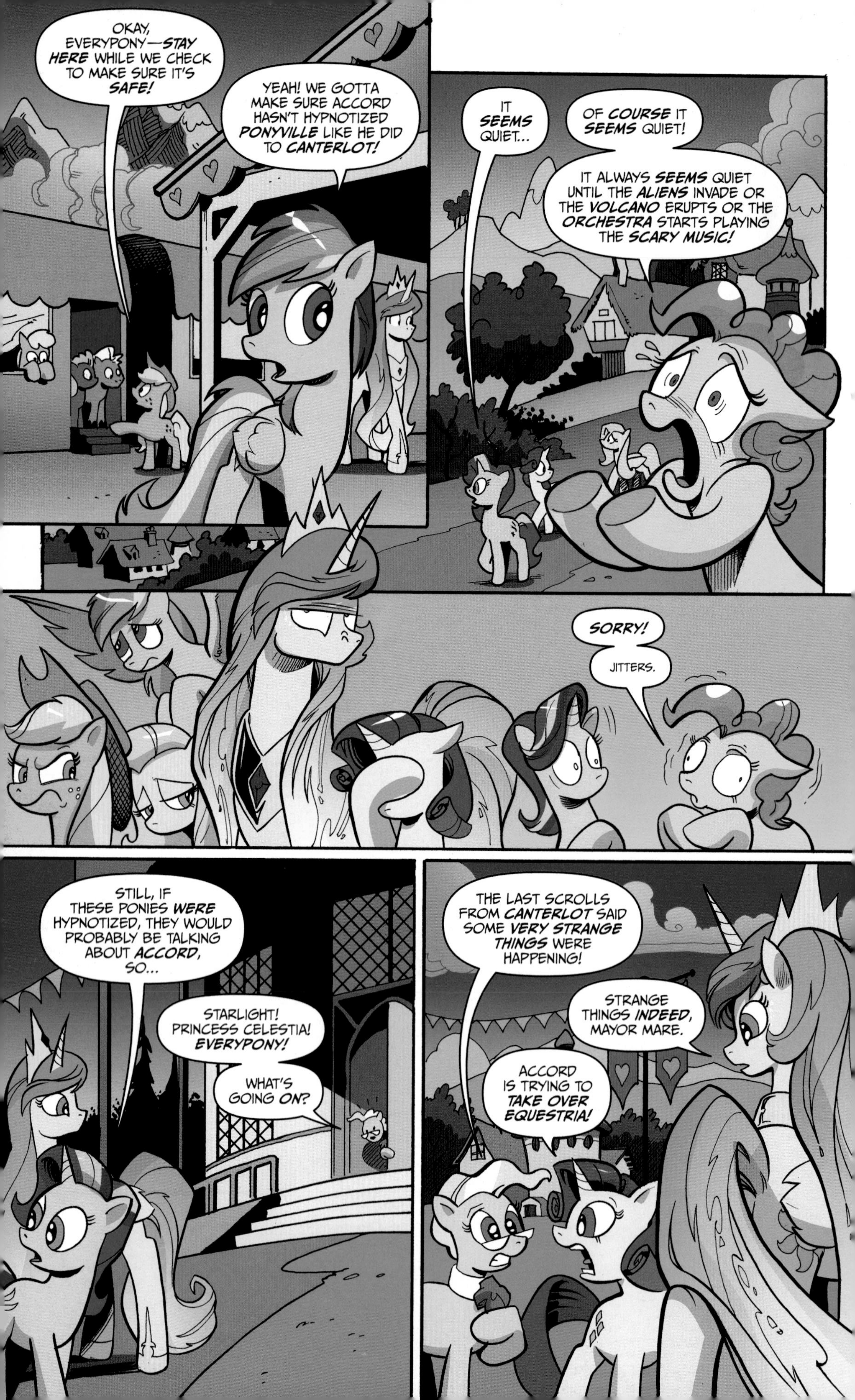
OKAY, EVERYPONY—STAY HERE WHILE WE CHECK TO MAKE SURE IT'S SAFE!
YEAH! WE GOTTA MAKE SURE ACCORD HASN'T HYPNOTIZED PONYVILLE LIKE HE DID TO CANTERLOT!
IT SEEMS QUIET...
OF COURSE IT SEEMS QUIET!
IT ALWAYS SEEMS QUIET UNTIL THE ALIENS INVADE OR THE VOLCANO ERUPTS OR THE ORCHESTRA STARTS PLAYING THE SCARY MUSIC!
SORRY!
JITTERS.
STILL, IF THESE PONIES WERE HYPNOTIZED, THEY WOULD PROBABLY BE TALKING ABOUT ACCORD, SO...
STARLIGHT! PRINCESS CELESTIA! EVERYPONY!
WHAT'S GOING ON?
THE LAST SCROLLS FROM CANTERLOT SAID SOME VERY STRANGE THINGS WERE HAPPENING!
STRANGE THINGS INDEED, MAYOR MARE.
ACCORD IS TRYING TO TAKE OVER EQUESTRIA!

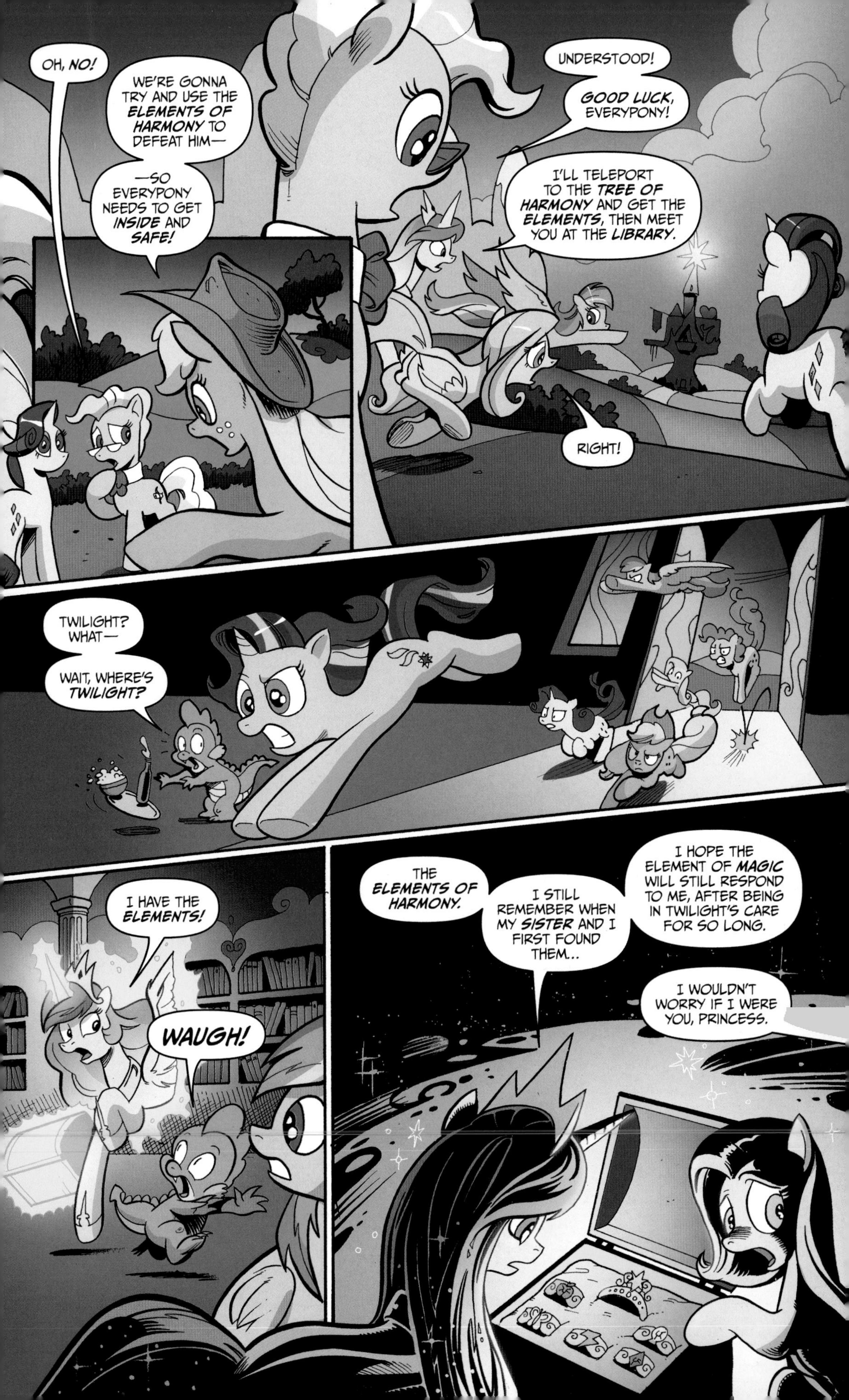
OH, NO!
WE'RE GONNA TRY AND USE THE ELEMENTS OF HARMONY TO DEFEAT HIM—
—SO EVERYPONY NEEDS TO GET INSIDE AND SAFE!
UNDERSTOOD!
GOOD LUCK, EVERYPONY!
I'LL TELEPORT TO THE TREE OF HARMONY AND GET THE ELEMENTS, THEN MEET YOU AT THE LIBRARY.
RIGHT!
TWILIGHT? WHAT—
WAIT, WHERE'S TWILIGHT?
I HAVE THE ELEMENTS!
WAUGH!
THE ELEMENTS OF HARMONY.
I STILL REMEMBER WHEN MY SISTER AND I FIRST FOUND THEM...
I HOPE THE ELEMENT OF MAGIC WILL STILL RESPOND TO ME, AFTER BEING IN TWILIGHT'S CARE FOR SO LONG.
I WOULDN'T WORRY IF I WERE YOU, PRINCESS.

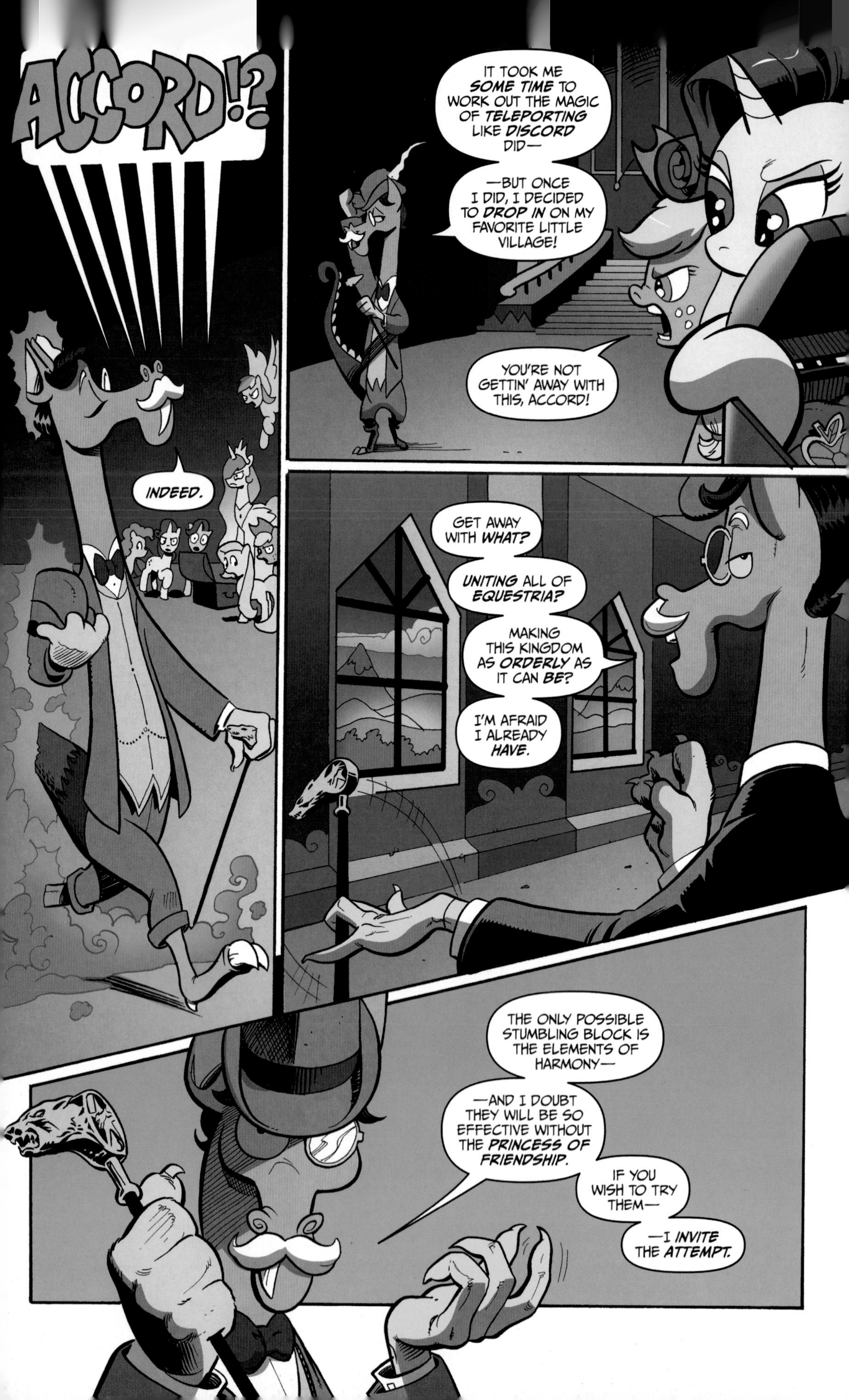
ACCORD!?
INDEED.
IT TOOK ME SOME TIME TO WORK OUT THE MAGIC OF TELEPORTING LIKE DISCORD DID—
—BUT ONCE I DID, I DECIDED TO DROP IN ON MY FAVORITE LITTLE VILLAGE!
YOU'RE NOT GETTIN' AWAY WITH THIS, ACCORD!
GET AWAY WITH WHAT?
UNITING ALL OF EQUESTRIA?
MAKING THIS KINGDOM AS ORDERLY AS IT CAN BE?
I'M AFRAID I ALREADY HAVE.
THE ONLY POSSIBLE STUMBLING BLOCK IS THE ELEMENTS OF HARMONY—
—AND I DOUBT THEY WILL BE SO EFFECTIVE WITHOUT THE PRINCESS OF FRIENDSHIP.
IF YOU WISH TO TRY THEM—
—I INVITE THE ATTEMPT.

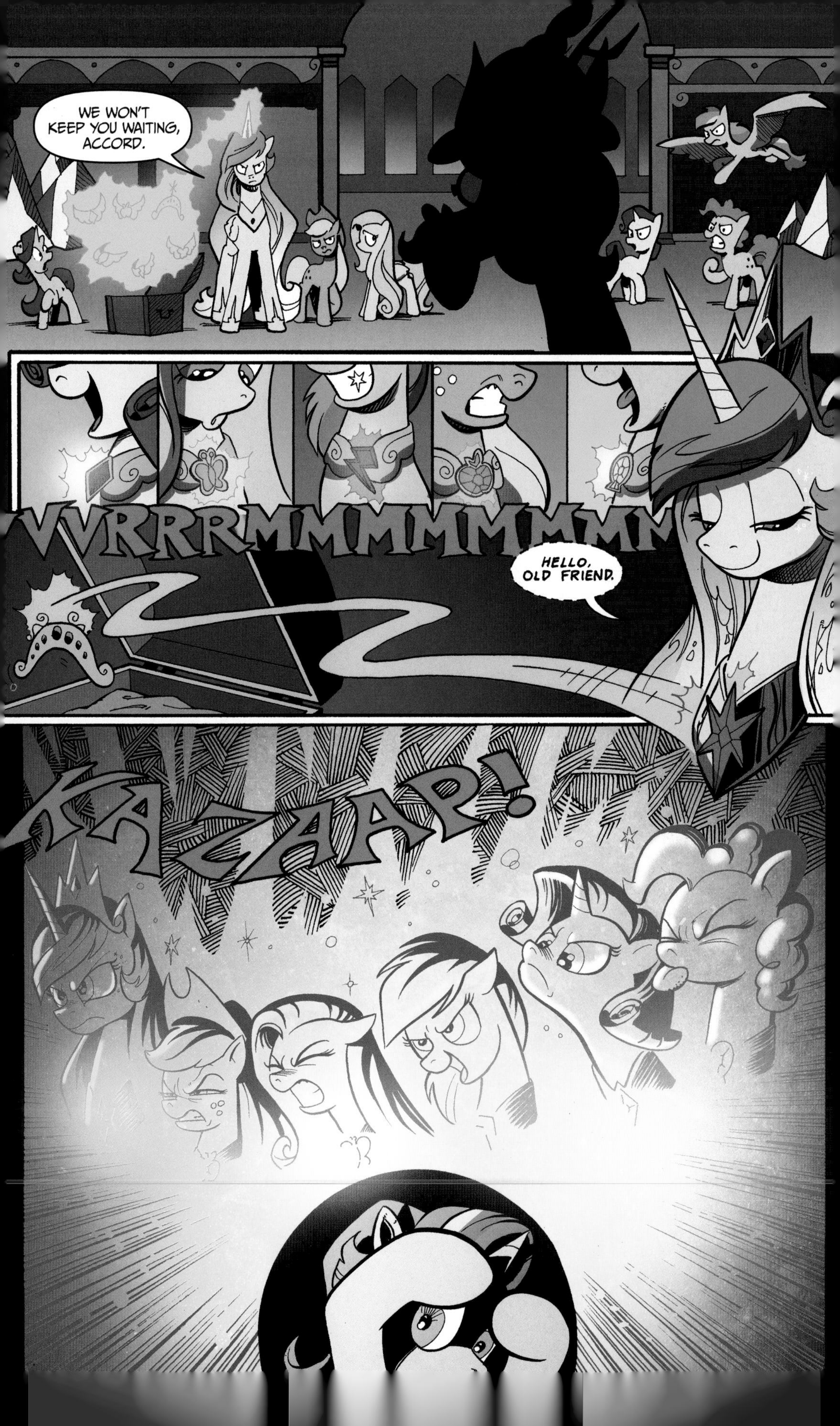

WE WON'T KEEP YOU WAITING, ACCORD.
VVRRRMMMMMMMMM
HELLO, OLD FRIEND.
KAZAAP!

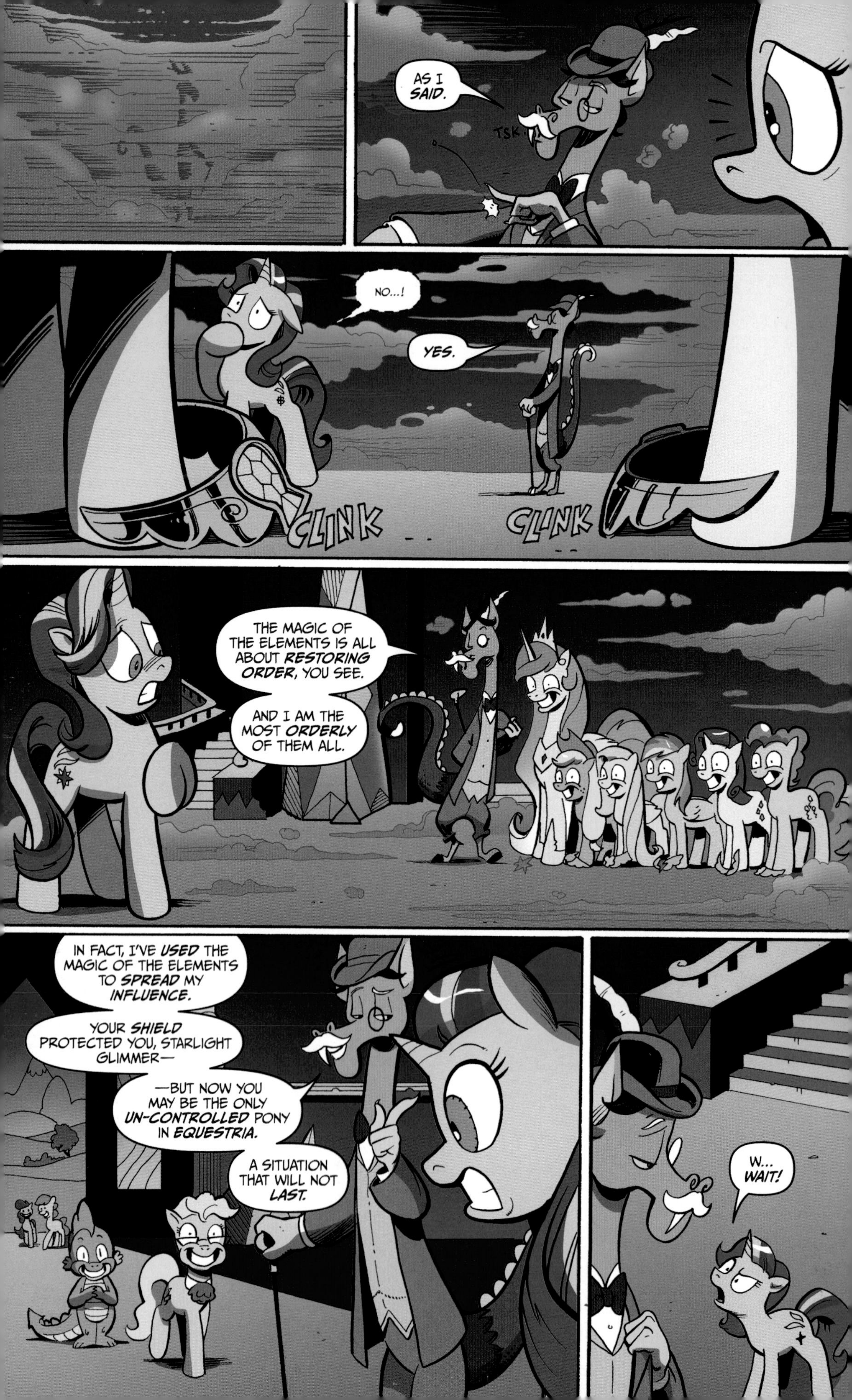
AS I SAID.
TSK.
NO...!
YES.
CLINK
CLINK
THE MAGIC OF THE ELEMENTS IS ALL ABOUT RESTORING ORDER, YOU SEE.
AND I AM THE MOST ORDERLY OF THEM ALL.
IN FACT, I'VE USED THE MAGIC OF THE ELEMENTS TO SPREAD MY INFLUENCE.
YOUR SHIELD PROTECTED YOU, STARLIGHT GLIMMER—
—BUT NOW YOU MAY BE THE ONLY UN-CONTROLLED PONY IN EQUESTRIA.
A SITUATION THAT WILL NOT LAST.
W... WAIT!

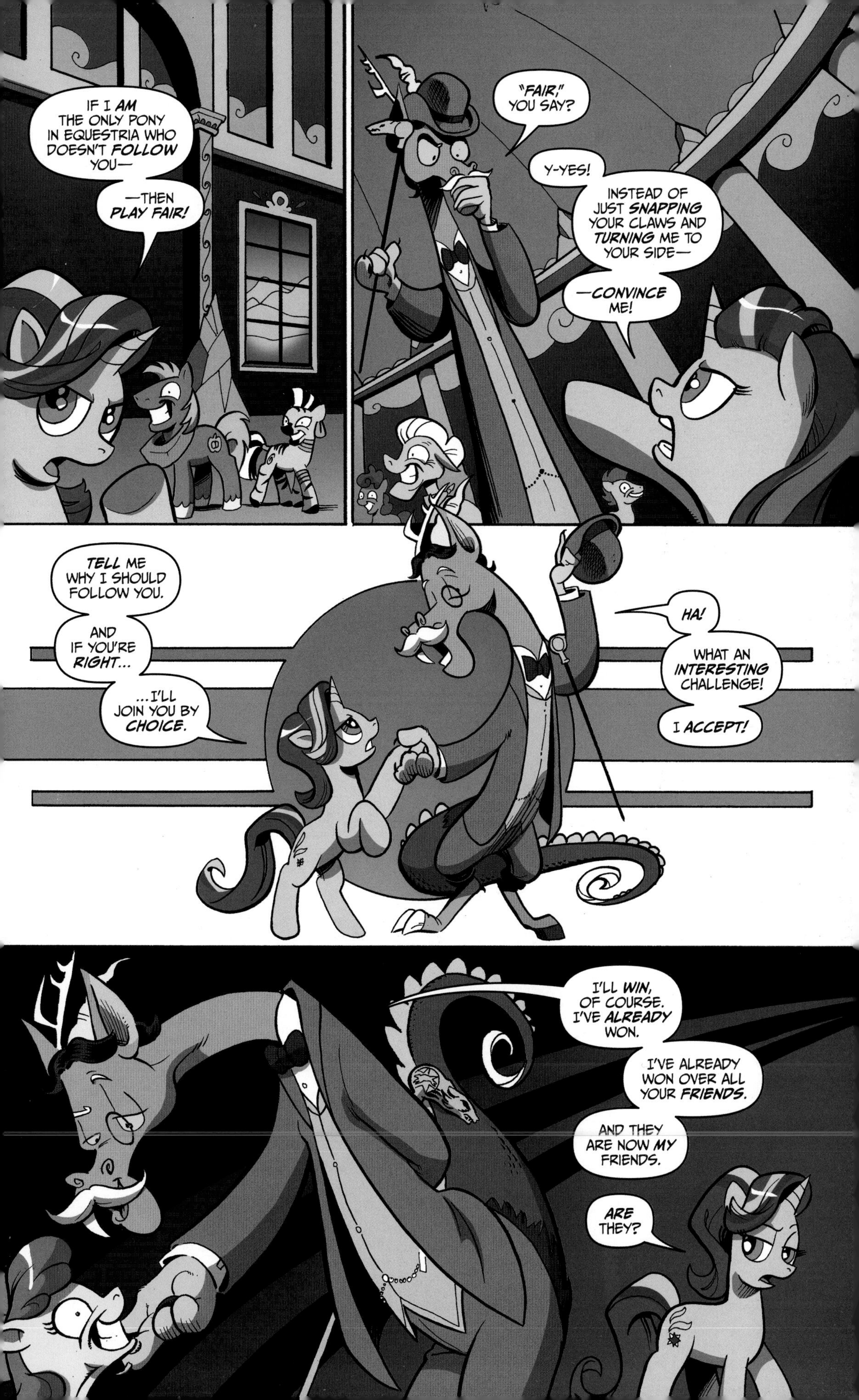
IF I *AM* THE ONLY PONY IN EQUESTRIA WHO DOESN'T *FOLLOW* YOU—
—THEN *PLAY FAIR!*
"FAIR," YOU SAY?
Y-YES!
INSTEAD OF JUST *SNAPPING* YOUR CLAWS AND *TURNING* ME TO YOUR SIDE—
—*CONVINCE* ME!
TELL ME WHY I SHOULD FOLLOW YOU.
AND IF YOU'RE *RIGHT*...
...I'LL JOIN YOU BY *CHOICE*.
HA!
WHAT AN *INTERESTING* CHALLENGE!
I *ACCEPT!*
I'LL *WIN*, OF COURSE. I'VE *ALREADY* WON.
I'VE ALREADY WON OVER ALL YOUR *FRIENDS*.
AND THEY ARE NOW *MY* FRIENDS.
ARE THEY?

WHY, OF **COURSE!**

JUST LOOK AT EVERYPONY THAT HAS JOINED ME!

THEY *THINK* LIKE ME, THEY *ACT* LIKE ME.

JOIN ME.

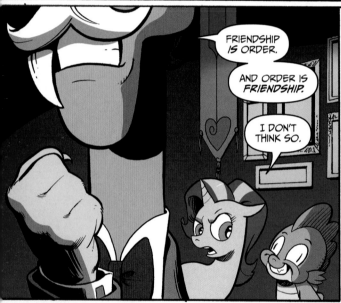

FRIENDSHIP *IS* ORDER.

AND ORDER IS *FRIENDSHIP.*

I DON'T THINK SO.

MY OLD VILLAGE WAS BASED ON *ORDER.*

BUT WE WEREN'T *FRIENDS.*

FRIENDSHIP ISN'T SOMETHING THAT KEEPS YOU *LOCKED* INTO *ONE WAY* OF *THINKING.*

FRIENDSHIP ISN'T ABOUT BEING *THE SAME!*

AFTER ALL, *DISCORD* WASN'T THE SAME AS *ANYPONY—*

—AND EVEN *HE* WANTED *FRIENDS!*

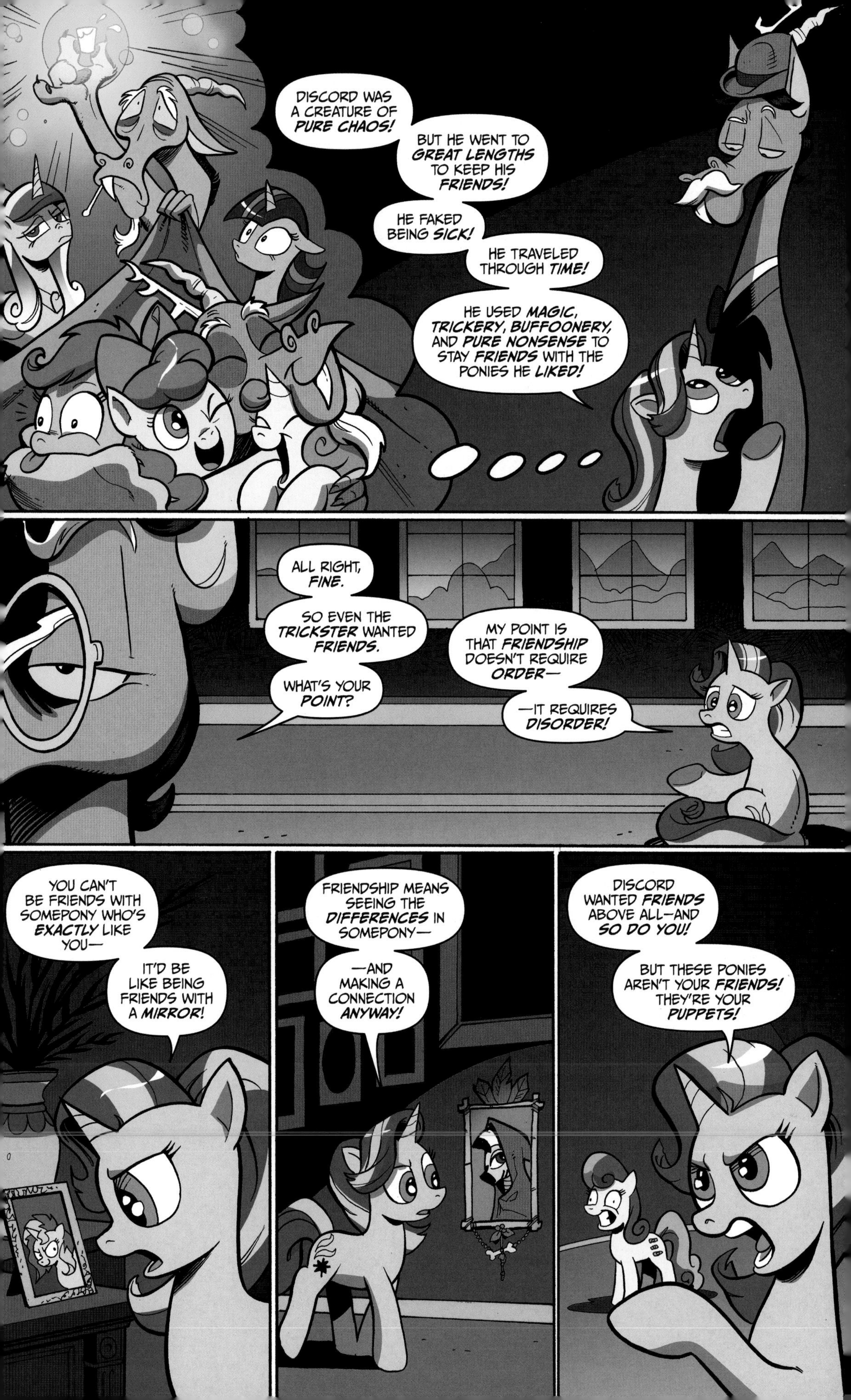

DISCORD WAS A CREATURE OF PURE CHAOS!
BUT HE WENT TO GREAT LENGTHS TO KEEP HIS FRIENDS!
HE FAKED BEING SICK!
HE TRAVELED THROUGH TIME!
HE USED MAGIC, TRICKERY, BUFFOONERY, AND PURE NONSENSE TO STAY FRIENDS WITH THE PONIES HE LIKED!
ALL RIGHT, FINE.
SO EVEN THE TRICKSTER WANTED FRIENDS.
WHAT'S YOUR POINT?
MY POINT IS THAT FRIENDSHIP DOESN'T REQUIRE ORDER—
—IT REQUIRES DISORDER!
YOU CAN'T BE FRIENDS WITH SOMEPONY WHO'S EXACTLY LIKE YOU—
IT'D BE LIKE BEING FRIENDS WITH A MIRROR!
FRIENDSHIP MEANS SEEING THE DIFFERENCES IN SOMEPONY—
—AND MAKING A CONNECTION ANYWAY!
DISCORD WANTED FRIENDS ABOVE ALL—AND SO DO YOU!
BUT THESE PONIES AREN'T YOUR FRIENDS! THEY'RE YOUR PUPPETS!

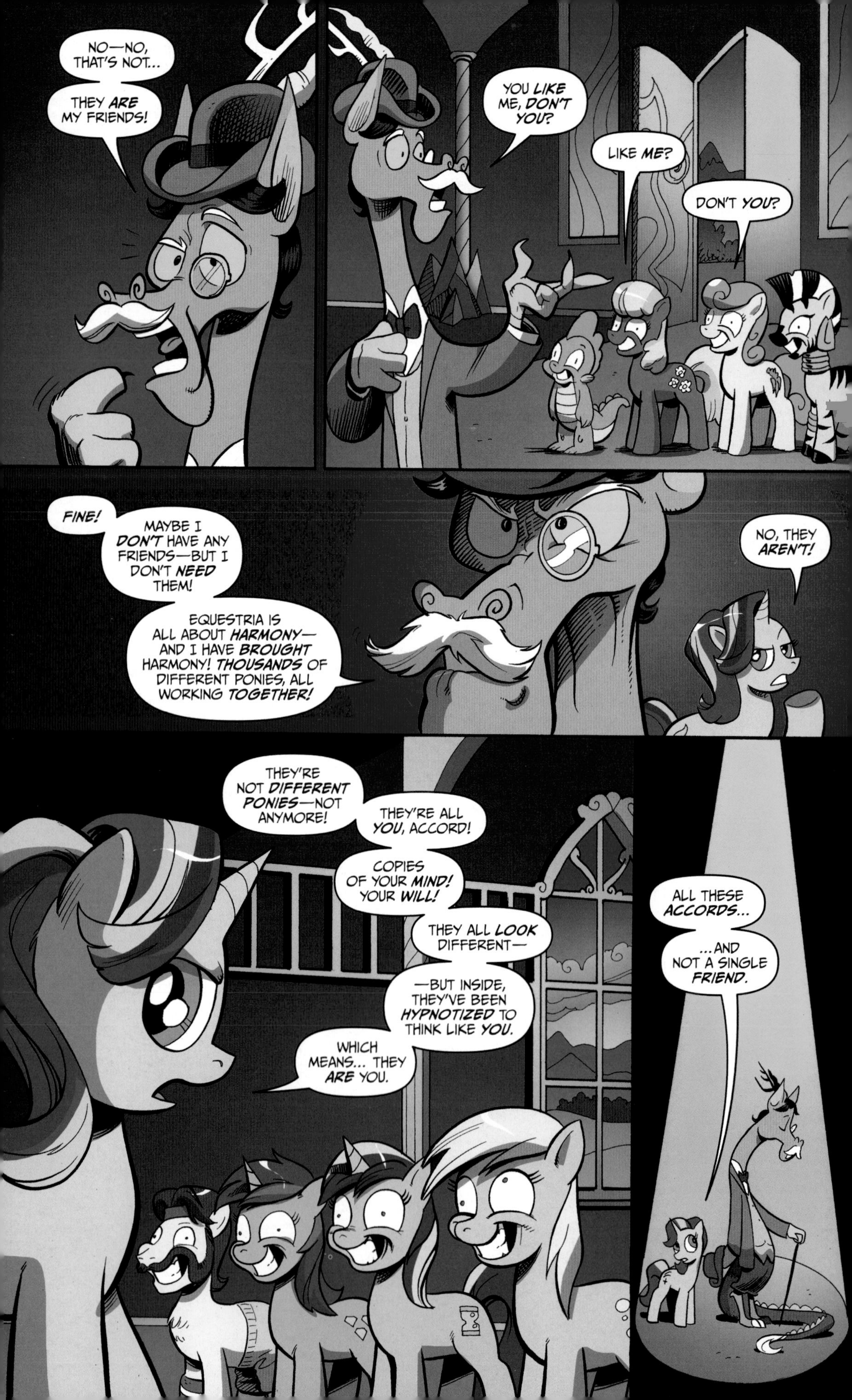
NO—NO, THAT'S NOT...
THEY *ARE* MY FRIENDS!
YOU *LIKE* ME, *DON'T YOU?*
LIKE *ME?*
DON'T *YOU?*
FINE!
MAYBE I *DON'T* HAVE ANY FRIENDS—BUT I DON'T *NEED* THEM!
EQUESTRIA IS ALL ABOUT *HARMONY*—AND I HAVE *BROUGHT* HARMONY! *THOUSANDS* OF DIFFERENT PONIES, ALL WORKING *TOGETHER!*
NO, THEY *AREN'T!*
THEY'RE NOT *DIFFERENT PONIES*—NOT ANYMORE!
THEY'RE ALL *YOU*, ACCORD!
COPIES OF YOUR *MIND!* YOUR *WILL!*
THEY ALL *LOOK* DIFFERENT—
—BUT INSIDE, THEY'VE BEEN *HYPNOTIZED* TO THINK LIKE *YOU.*
WHICH MEANS... THEY *ARE* YOU.
ALL THESE *ACCORDS*...
...AND NOT A SINGLE *FRIEND.*

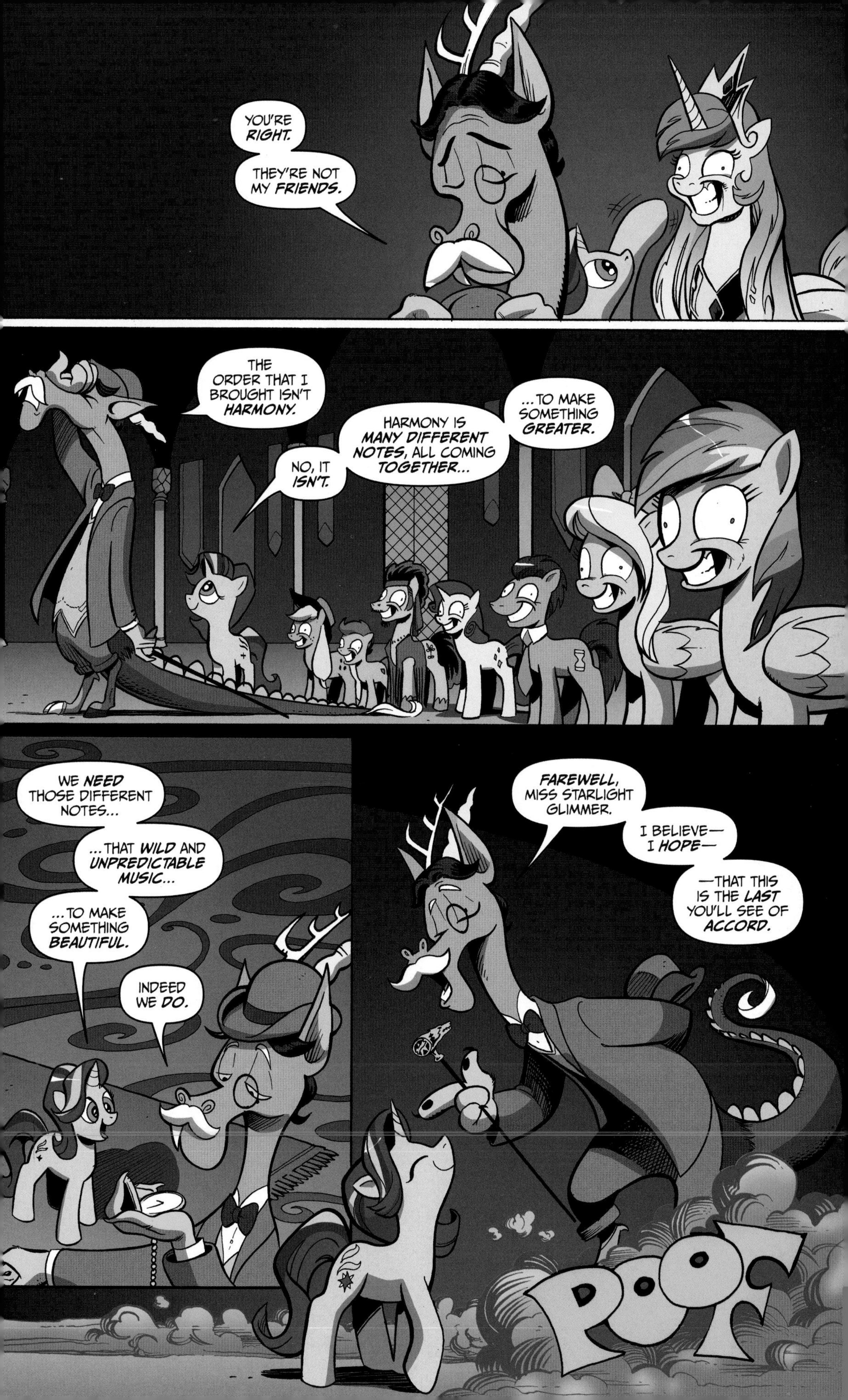
YOU'RE RIGHT.
THEY'RE NOT MY FRIENDS.
THE ORDER THAT I BROUGHT ISN'T HARMONY.
NO, IT ISN'T.
HARMONY IS MANY DIFFERENT NOTES, ALL COMING TOGETHER...
...TO MAKE SOMETHING GREATER.
WE NEED THOSE DIFFERENT NOTES...
...THAT WILD AND UNPREDICTABLE MUSIC...
...TO MAKE SOMETHING BEAUTIFUL.
INDEED WE DO.
FAREWELL, MISS STARLIGHT GLIMMER.
I BELIEVE— I HOPE—
—THAT THIS IS THE LAST YOU'LL SEE OF ACCORD.
POOF

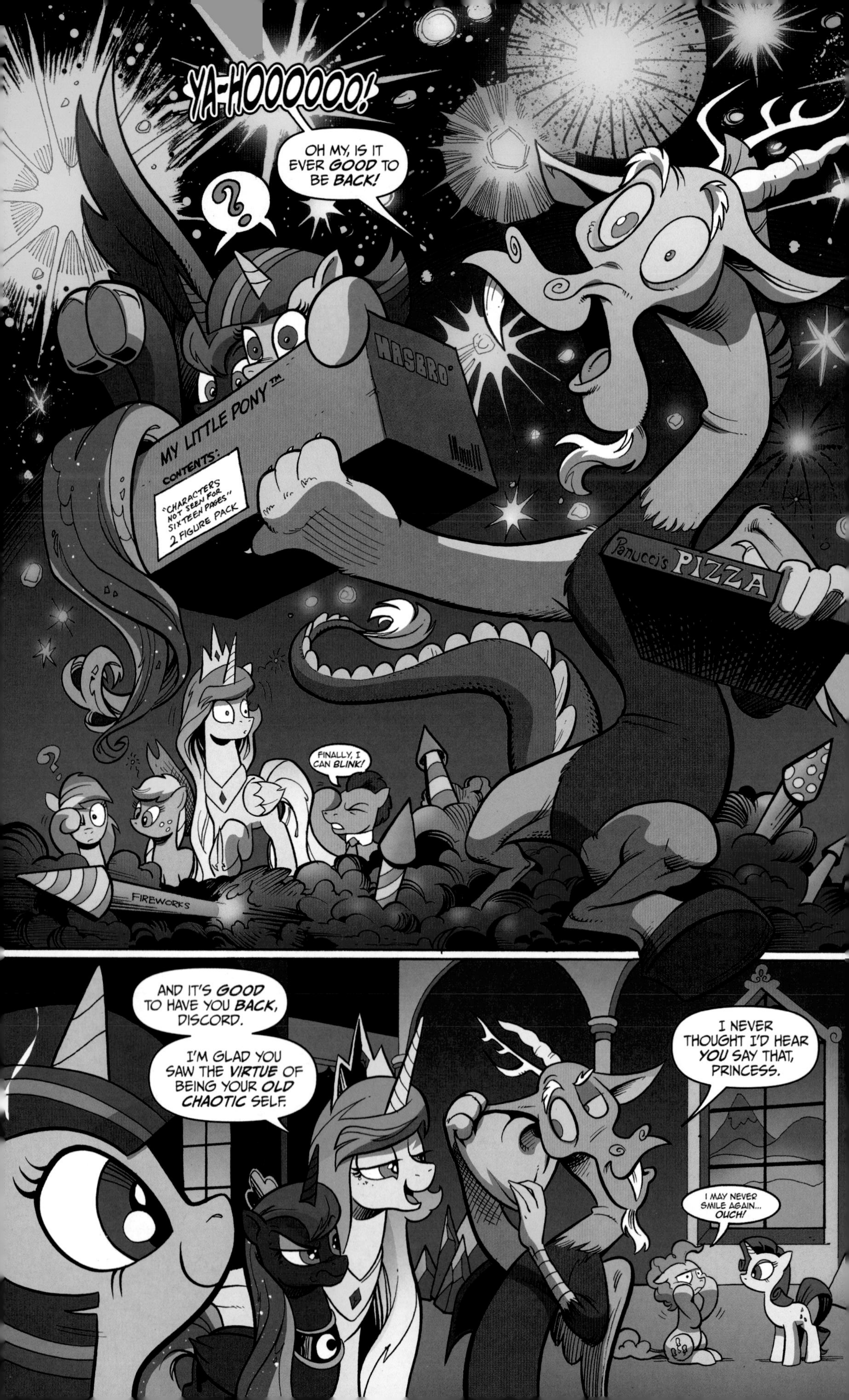
YA-HOOOOOO!
OH MY, IS IT EVER GOOD TO BE BACK!
?
HASBRO
MY LITTLE PONY™
CONTENTS:
"CHARACTERS NOT SEEN FOR SIXTEEN PAGES" 2 FIGURE PACK
Panucci's PIZZA
FINALLY, I CAN BLINK!
FIREWORKS
AND IT'S GOOD TO HAVE YOU BACK, DISCORD.
I'M GLAD YOU SAW THE VIRTUE OF BEING YOUR OLD CHAOTIC SELF.
I NEVER THOUGHT I'D HEAR YOU SAY THAT, PRINCESS.
I MAY NEVER SMILE AGAIN... OUCH!

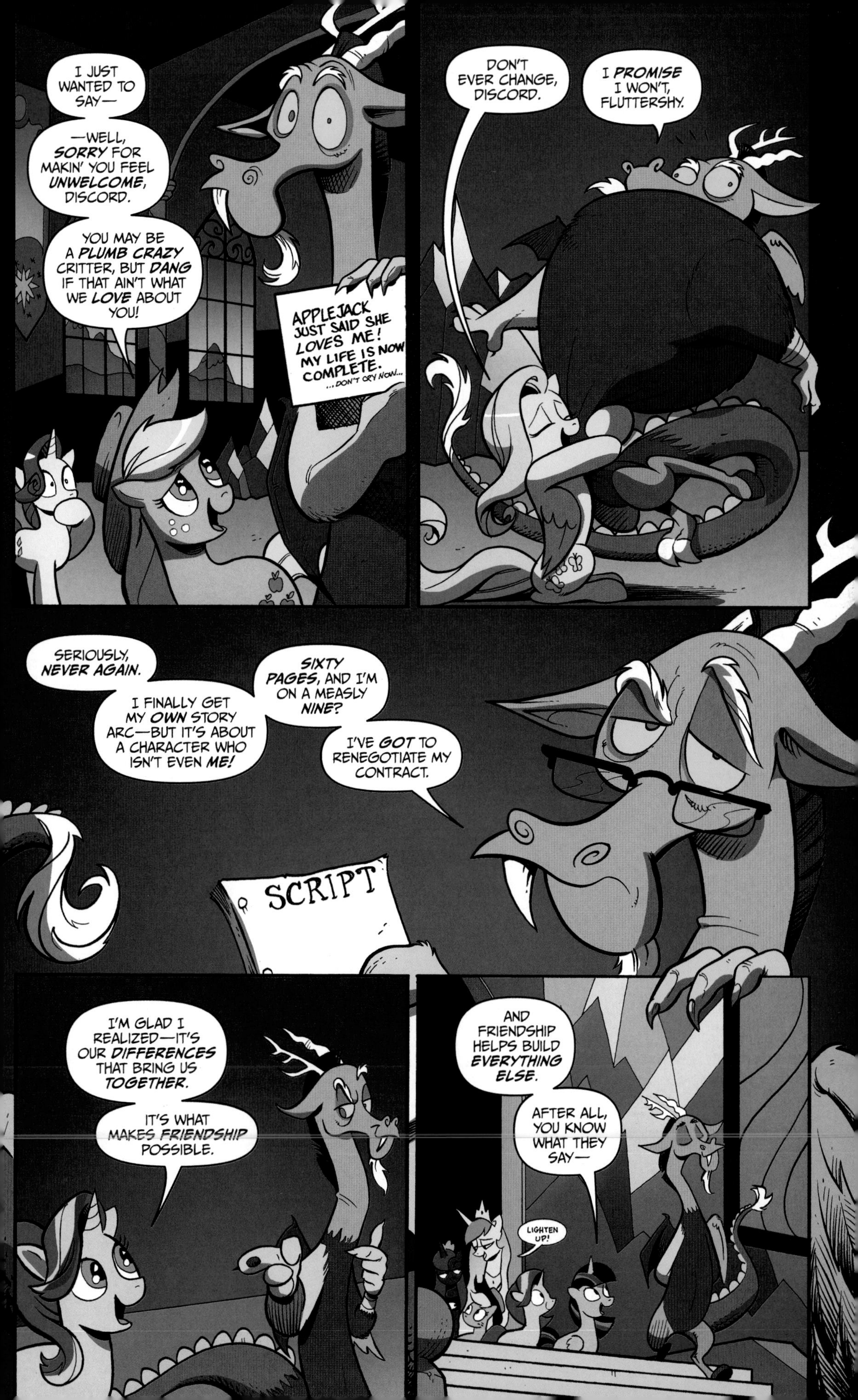
I JUST WANTED TO SAY—
—WELL, SORRY FOR MAKIN' YOU FEEL UNWELCOME, DISCORD.
YOU MAY BE A PLUMB CRAZY CRITTER, BUT DANG IF THAT AIN'T WHAT WE LOVE ABOUT YOU!
APPLEJACK JUST SAID SHE LOVES ME! MY LIFE IS NOW COMPLETE.
...DON'T CRY NOW...
DON'T EVER CHANGE, DISCORD.
I PROMISE I WON'T, FLUTTERSHY.
SERIOUSLY, NEVER AGAIN.
I FINALLY GET MY OWN STORY ARC—BUT IT'S ABOUT A CHARACTER WHO ISN'T EVEN ME!
SIXTY PAGES, AND I'M ON A MEASLY NINE?
I'VE GOT TO RENEGOTIATE MY CONTRACT.
SCRIPT
I'M GLAD I REALIZED—IT'S OUR DIFFERENCES THAT BRING US TOGETHER.
IT'S WHAT MAKES FRIENDSHIP POSSIBLE.
AND FRIENDSHIP HELPS BUILD EVERYTHING ELSE.
AFTER ALL, YOU KNOW WHAT THEY SAY—
LIGHTEN UP!

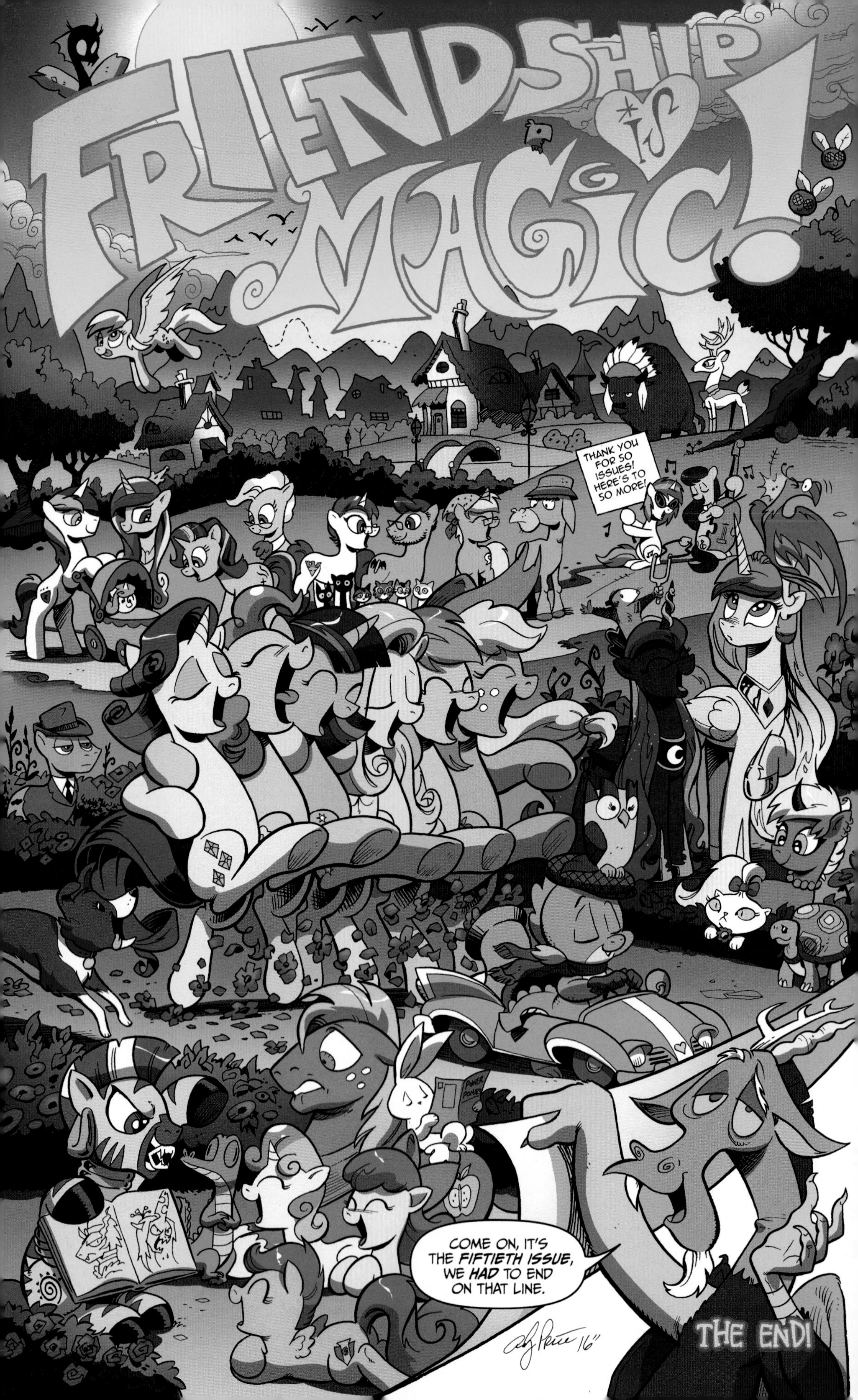
FRIENDSHIP IS MAGIC!
THANK YOU FOR 50 ISSUES! HERE'S TO 50 MORE!
POWER PONIES
COME ON, IT'S THE *FIFTIETH ISSUE*, WE *HAD* TO END ON THAT LINE.
THE END!

My Little Pony

Friendship is Magic

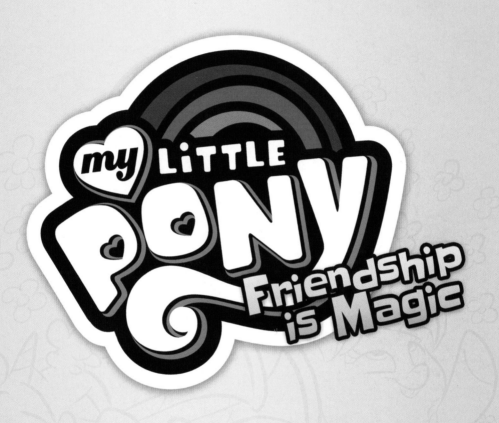

art by Sara Richard

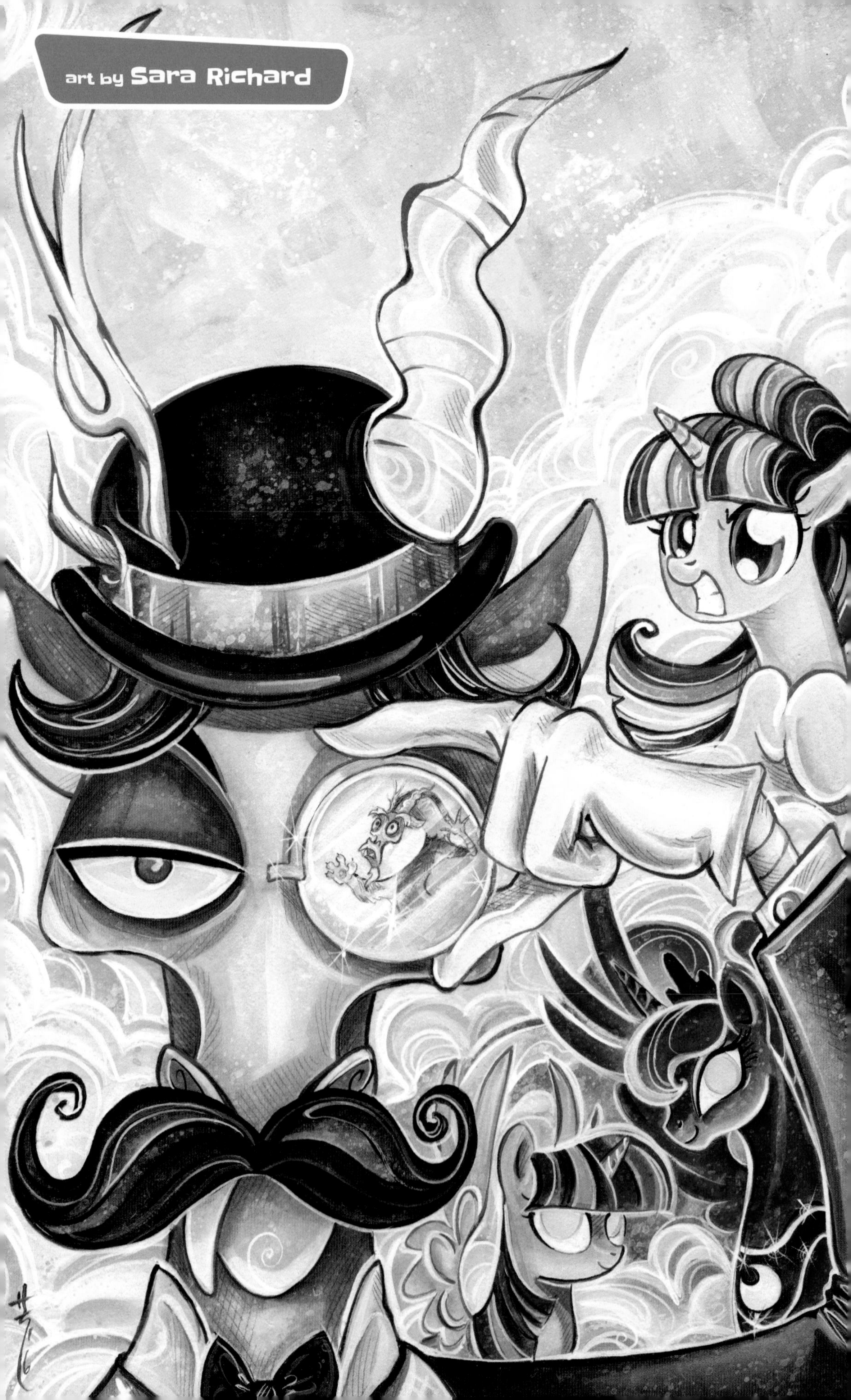

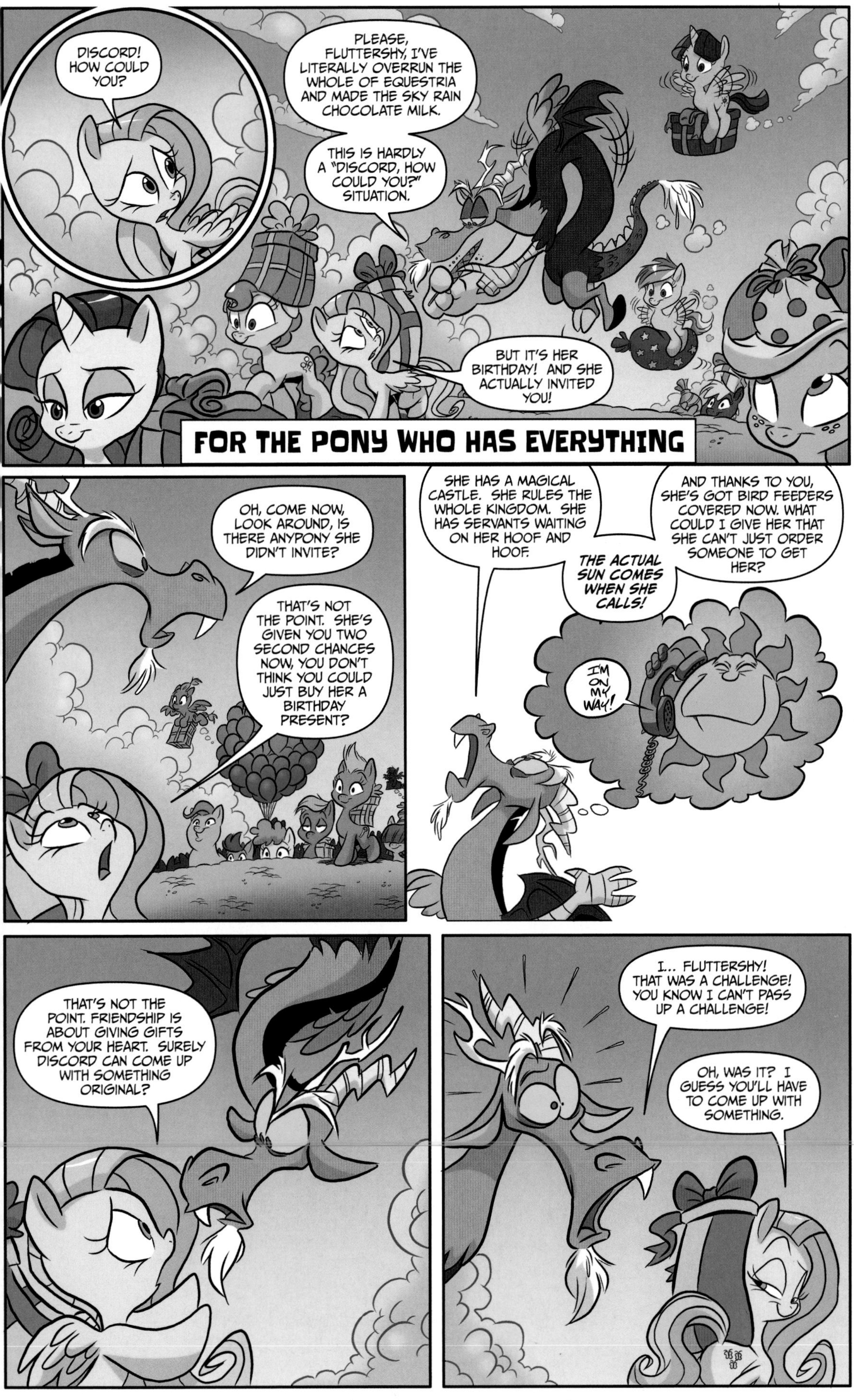

DISCORD! HOW COULD YOU?
PLEASE, FLUTTERSHY, I'VE LITERALLY OVERRUN THE WHOLE OF EQUESTRIA AND MADE THE SKY RAIN CHOCOLATE MILK.
THIS IS HARDLY A "DISCORD, HOW COULD YOU?" SITUATION.
BUT IT'S HER BIRTHDAY! AND SHE ACTUALLY INVITED YOU!
FOR THE PONY WHO HAS EVERYTHING
OH, COME NOW, LOOK AROUND, IS THERE ANYPONY SHE DIDN'T INVITE?
THAT'S NOT THE POINT. SHE'S GIVEN YOU TWO SECOND CHANCES NOW, YOU DON'T THINK YOU COULD JUST BUY HER A BIRTHDAY PRESENT?
SHE HAS A MAGICAL CASTLE. SHE RULES THE WHOLE KINGDOM. SHE HAS SERVANTS WAITING ON HER HOOF AND HOOF.
THE ACTUAL SUN COMES WHEN SHE CALLS!
AND THANKS TO YOU, SHE'S GOT BIRD FEEDERS COVERED NOW. WHAT COULD I GIVE HER THAT SHE CAN'T JUST ORDER SOMEONE TO GET HER?
I'M ON MY WAY!
THAT'S NOT THE POINT. FRIENDSHIP IS ABOUT GIVING GIFTS FROM YOUR HEART. SURELY DISCORD CAN COME UP WITH SOMETHING ORIGINAL?
I... FLUTTERSHY! THAT WAS A CHALLENGE! YOU KNOW I CAN'T PASS UP A CHALLENGE!
OH, WAS IT? I GUESS YOU'LL HAVE TO COME UP WITH SOMETHING.

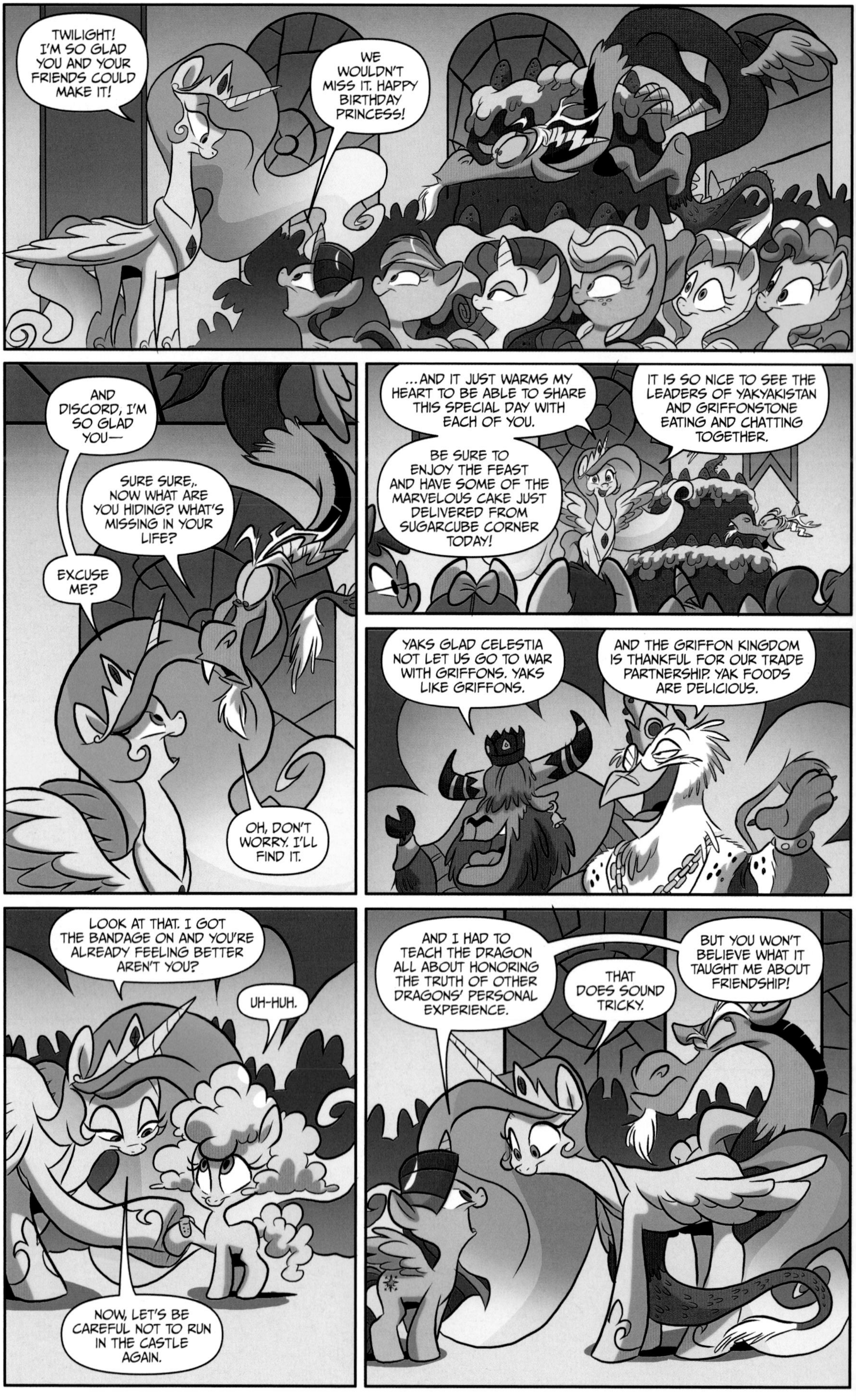
TWILIGHT! I'M SO GLAD YOU AND YOUR FRIENDS COULD MAKE IT!
WE WOULDN'T MISS IT. HAPPY BIRTHDAY PRINCESS!
AND DISCORD, I'M SO GLAD YOU—
SURE SURE,. NOW WHAT ARE YOU HIDING? WHAT'S MISSING IN YOUR LIFE?
EXCUSE ME?
OH, DON'T WORRY. I'LL FIND IT.
...AND IT JUST WARMS MY HEART TO BE ABLE TO SHARE THIS SPECIAL DAY WITH EACH OF YOU.
IT IS SO NICE TO SEE THE LEADERS OF YAKYAKISTAN AND GRIFFONSTONE EATING AND CHATTING TOGETHER.
BE SURE TO ENJOY THE FEAST AND HAVE SOME OF THE MARVELOUS CAKE JUST DELIVERED FROM SUGARCUBE CORNER TODAY!
YAKS GLAD CELESTIA NOT LET US GO TO WAR WITH GRIFFONS. YAKS LIKE GRIFFONS.
AND THE GRIFFON KINGDOM IS THANKFUL FOR OUR TRADE PARTNERSHIP. YAK FOODS ARE DELICIOUS.
LOOK AT THAT. I GOT THE BANDAGE ON AND YOU'RE ALREADY FEELING BETTER AREN'T YOU?
UH-HUH.
NOW, LET'S BE CAREFUL NOT TO RUN IN THE CASTLE AGAIN.
AND I HAD TO TEACH THE DRAGON ALL ABOUT HONORING THE TRUTH OF OTHER DRAGONS' PERSONAL EXPERIENCE.
THAT DOES SOUND TRICKY.
BUT YOU WON'T BELIEVE WHAT IT TAUGHT ME ABOUT FRIENDSHIP!

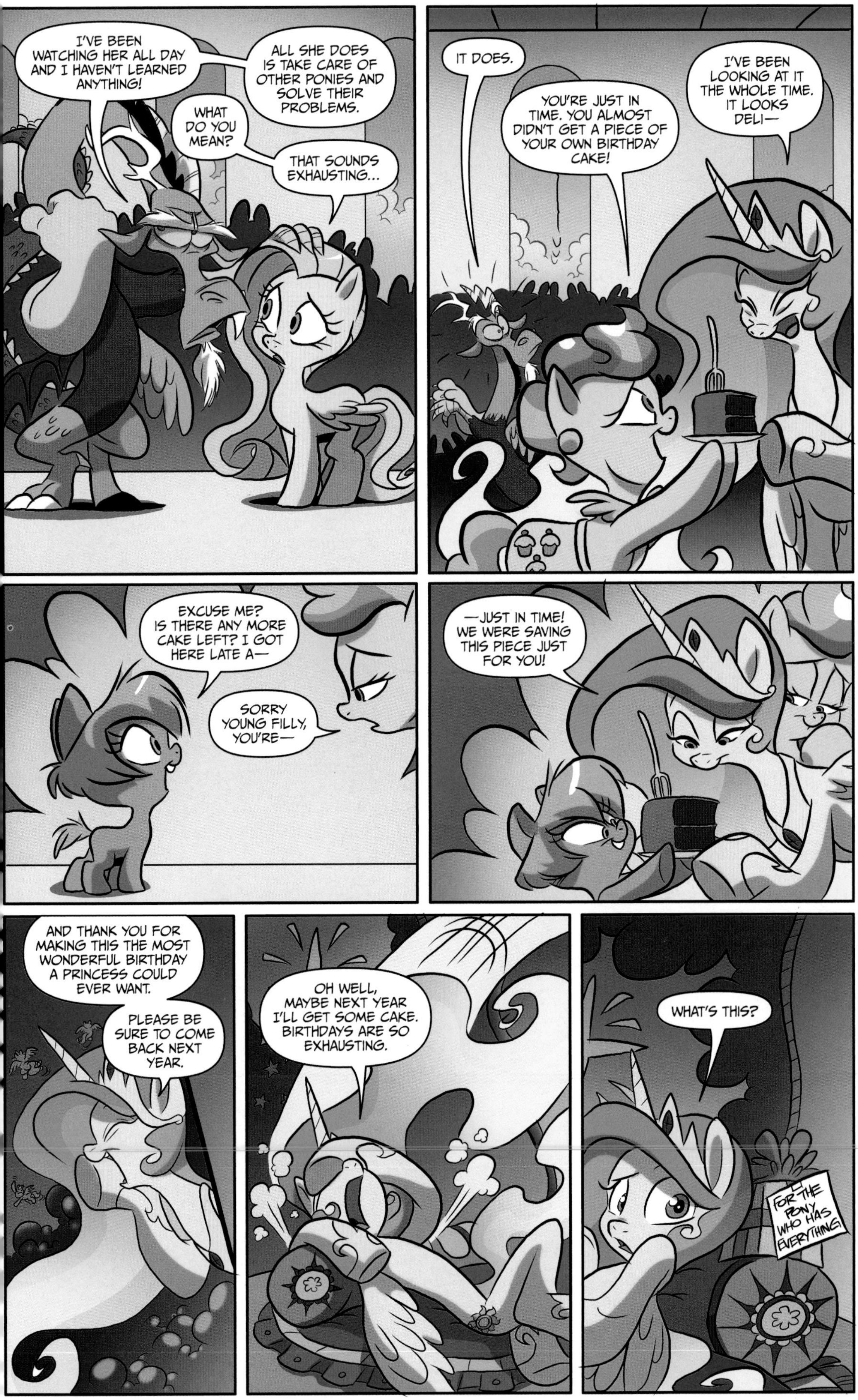

I'VE BEEN WATCHING HER ALL DAY AND I HAVEN'T LEARNED ANYTHING!
ALL SHE DOES IS TAKE CARE OF OTHER PONIES AND SOLVE THEIR PROBLEMS.
WHAT DO YOU MEAN?
THAT SOUNDS EXHAUSTING...
IT DOES.
YOU'RE JUST IN TIME. YOU ALMOST DIDN'T GET A PIECE OF YOUR OWN BIRTHDAY CAKE!
I'VE BEEN LOOKING AT IT THE WHOLE TIME. IT LOOKS DELI—
EXCUSE ME? IS THERE ANY MORE CAKE LEFT? I GOT HERE LATE A—
SORRY YOUNG FILLY, YOU'RE—
—JUST IN TIME! WE WERE SAVING THIS PIECE JUST FOR YOU!
AND THANK YOU FOR MAKING THIS THE MOST WONDERFUL BIRTHDAY A PRINCESS COULD EVER WANT.
PLEASE BE SURE TO COME BACK NEXT YEAR.
OH WELL, MAYBE NEXT YEAR I'LL GET SOME CAKE. BIRTHDAYS ARE SO EXHAUSTING.
WHAT'S THIS?
FOR THE PONY WHO HAS EVERYTHING

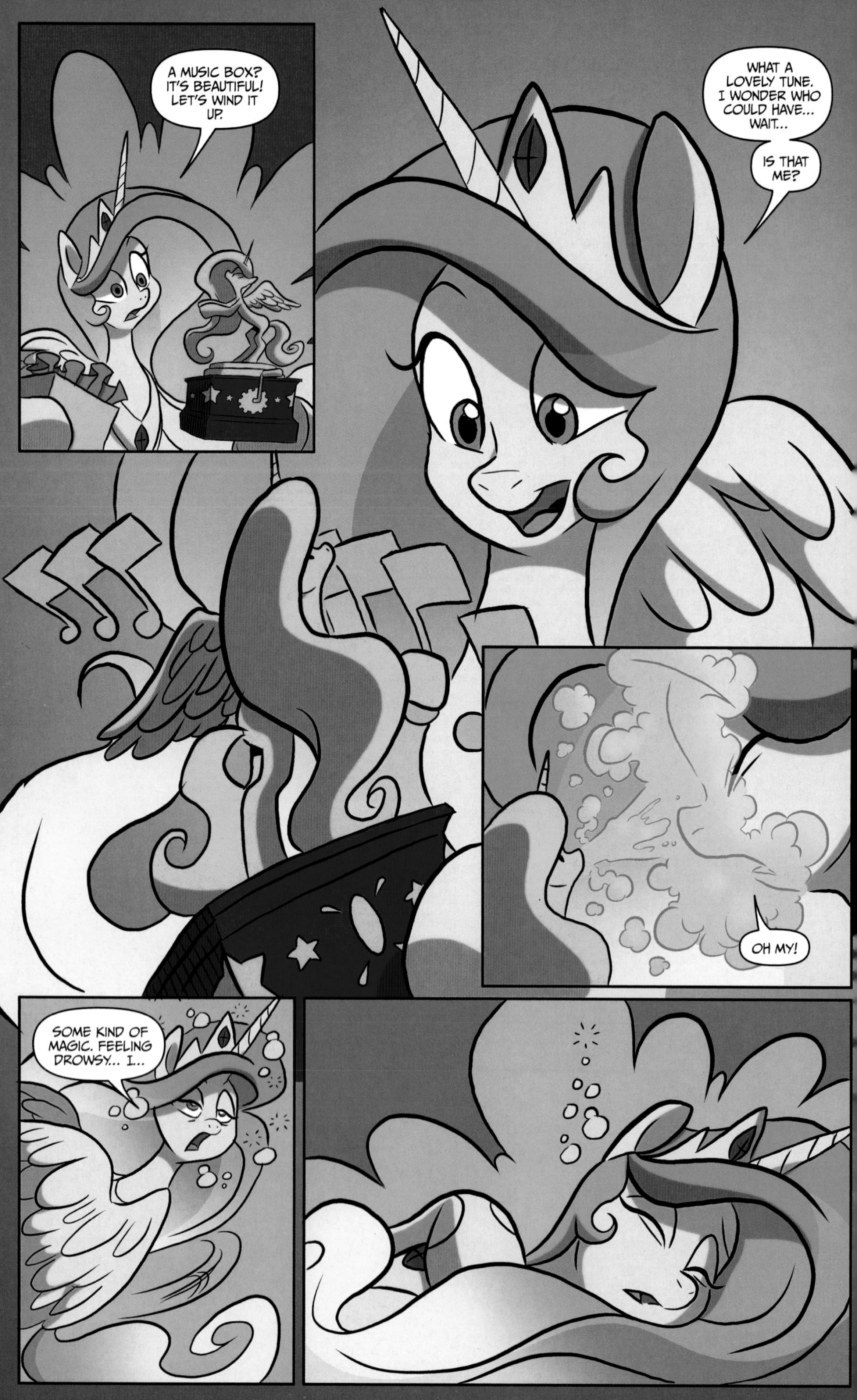
A MUSIC BOX? IT'S BEAUTIFUL! LET'S WIND IT UP.
WHAT A LOVELY TUNE. I WONDER WHO COULD HAVE... WAIT...
IS THAT ME?
OH MY!
SOME KIND OF MAGIC. FEELING DROWSY... I...

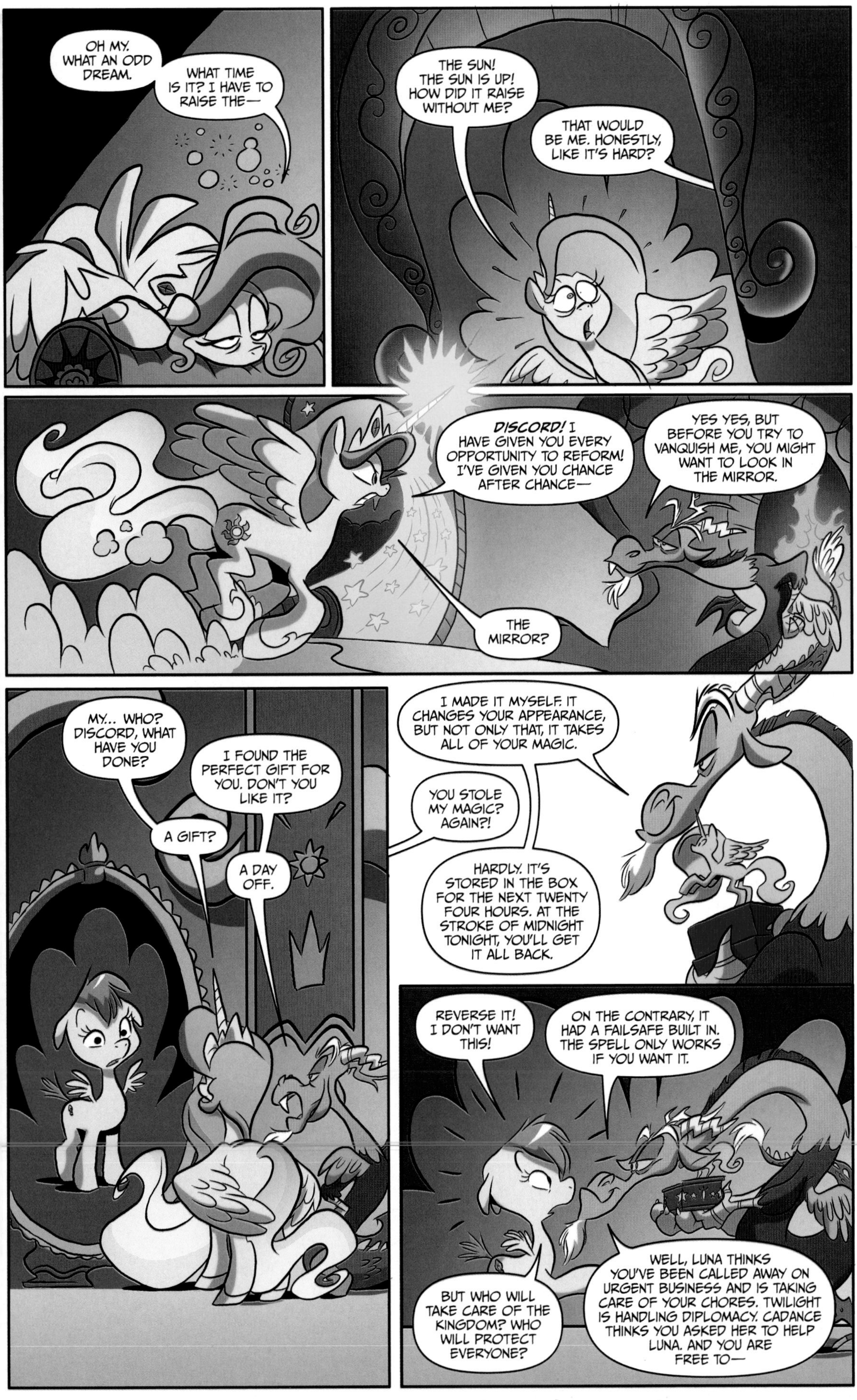
OH MY. WHAT AN ODD DREAM.
WHAT TIME IS IT? I HAVE TO RAISE THE—
THE SUN! THE SUN IS UP! HOW DID IT RAISE WITHOUT ME?
THAT WOULD BE ME. HONESTLY, LIKE IT'S HARD?
DISCORD! I HAVE GIVEN YOU EVERY OPPORTUNITY TO REFORM! I'VE GIVEN YOU CHANCE AFTER CHANCE—
YES YES, BUT BEFORE YOU TRY TO VANQUISH ME, YOU MIGHT WANT TO LOOK IN THE MIRROR.
THE MIRROR?
MY... WHO? DISCORD, WHAT HAVE YOU DONE?
I FOUND THE PERFECT GIFT FOR YOU. DON'T YOU LIKE IT?
A GIFT?
A DAY OFF.
I MADE IT MYSELF. IT CHANGES YOUR APPEARANCE, BUT NOT ONLY THAT, IT TAKES ALL OF YOUR MAGIC.
YOU STOLE MY MAGIC? AGAIN?!
HARDLY. IT'S STORED IN THE BOX FOR THE NEXT TWENTY FOUR HOURS. AT THE STROKE OF MIDNIGHT TONIGHT, YOU'LL GET IT ALL BACK.
REVERSE IT! I DON'T WANT THIS!
ON THE CONTRARY, IT HAD A FAILSAFE BUILT IN. THE SPELL ONLY WORKS IF YOU WANT IT.
BUT WHO WILL TAKE CARE OF THE KINGDOM? WHO WILL PROTECT EVERYONE?
WELL, LUNA THINKS YOU'VE BEEN CALLED AWAY ON URGENT BUSINESS AND IS TAKING CARE OF YOUR CHORES. TWILIGHT IS HANDLING DIPLOMACY. CADANCE THINKS YOU ASKED HER TO HELP LUNA. AND YOU ARE FREE TO—

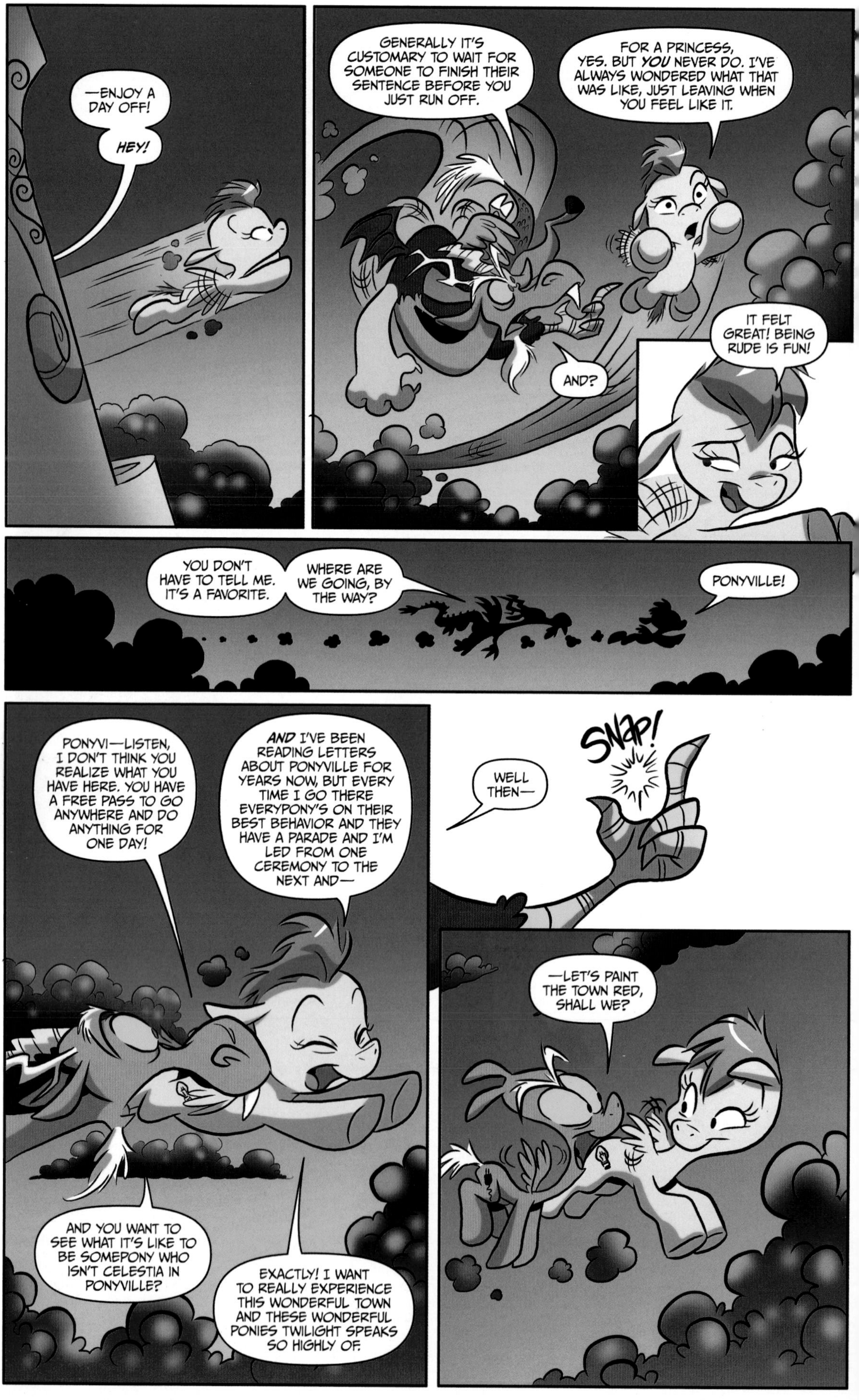
—ENJOY A DAY OFF!
HEY!
GENERALLY IT'S CUSTOMARY TO WAIT FOR SOMEONE TO FINISH THEIR SENTENCE BEFORE YOU JUST RUN OFF.
FOR A PRINCESS, YES. BUT YOU NEVER DO. I'VE ALWAYS WONDERED WHAT THAT WAS LIKE, JUST LEAVING WHEN YOU FEEL LIKE IT.
AND?
IT FELT GREAT! BEING RUDE IS FUN!
WHERE ARE WE GOING, BY THE WAY?
PONYVILLE!
YOU DON'T HAVE TO TELL ME. IT'S A FAVORITE.
PONYVI—LISTEN, I DON'T THINK YOU REALIZE WHAT YOU HAVE HERE. YOU HAVE A FREE PASS TO GO ANYWHERE AND DO ANYTHING FOR ONE DAY!
AND I'VE BEEN READING LETTERS ABOUT PONYVILLE FOR YEARS NOW, BUT EVERY TIME I GO THERE EVERYPONY'S ON THEIR BEST BEHAVIOR AND THEY HAVE A PARADE AND I'M LED FROM ONE CEREMONY TO THE NEXT AND—
AND YOU WANT TO SEE WHAT IT'S LIKE TO BE SOMEPONY WHO ISN'T CELESTIA IN PONYVILLE?
EXACTLY! I WANT TO REALLY EXPERIENCE THIS WONDERFUL TOWN AND THESE WONDERFUL PONIES TWILIGHT SPEAKS SO HIGHLY OF.
WELL THEN—
SNAP!
—LET'S PAINT THE TOWN RED, SHALL WE?

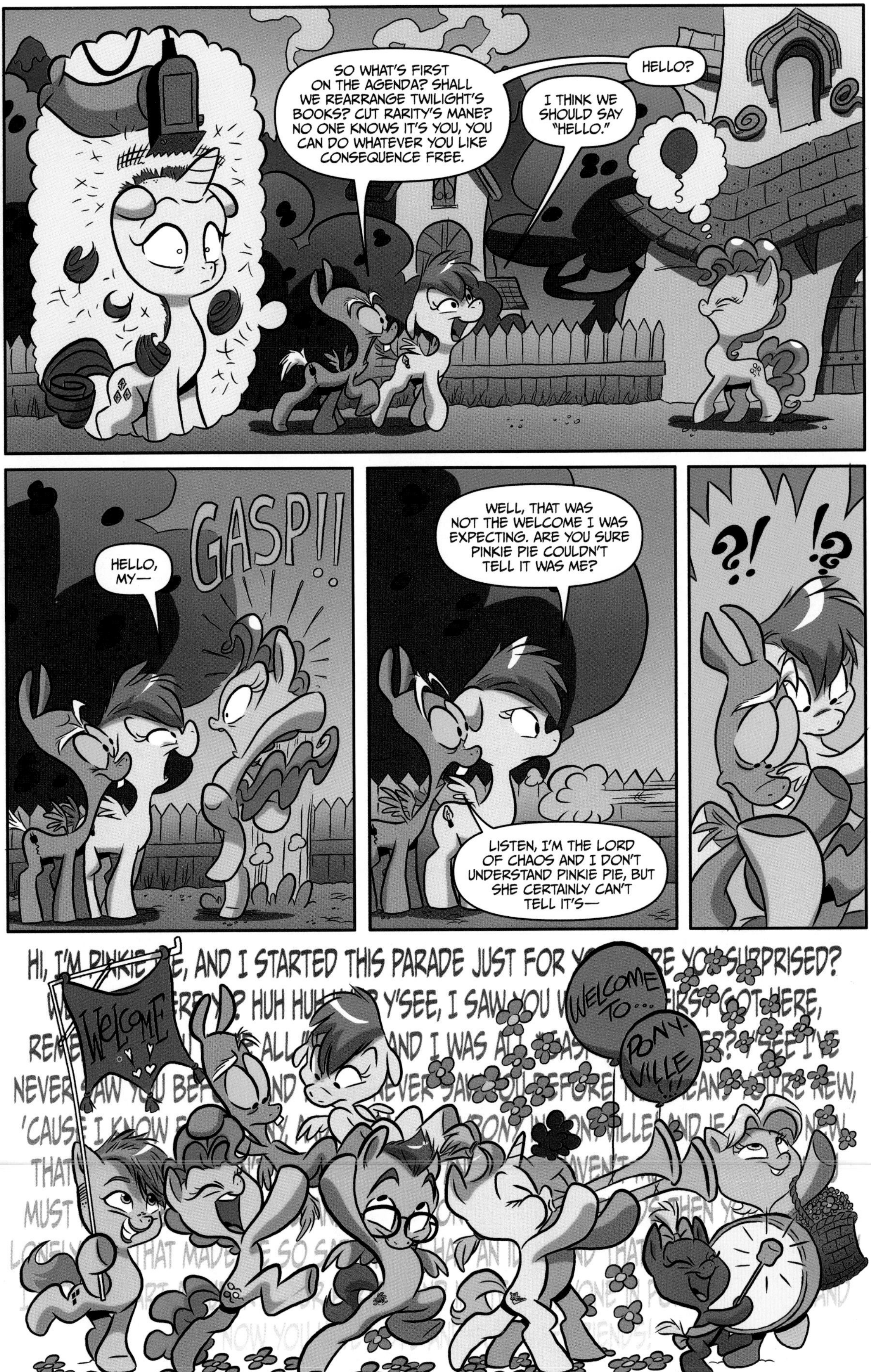
SO WHAT'S FIRST ON THE AGENDA? SHALL WE REARRANGE TWILIGHT'S BOOKS? CUT RARITY'S MANE? NO ONE KNOWS IT'S YOU, YOU CAN DO WHATEVER YOU LIKE CONSEQUENCE FREE.
I THINK WE SHOULD SAY "HELLO."
HELLO?
HELLO, MY—
GASP!!
WELL, THAT WAS NOT THE WELCOME I WAS EXPECTING. ARE YOU SURE PINKIE PIE COULDN'T TELL IT WAS ME?
LISTEN, I'M THE LORD OF CHAOS AND I DON'T UNDERSTAND PINKIE PIE, BUT SHE CERTAINLY CAN'T TELL IT'S—
?!
!?
HI, I'M
, AND I STARTED THIS PARADE JUST FOR
SURPRISED?
HUH HUH
Y'SEE, I SAW YOU
GOT HERE,
AND I WAS
NEVER
'CAUSE I KNOW
THAT
MUST
THAT MADE
NOW YOU
WELCOME
WELCOME TO...
PONY-VILLE!!!

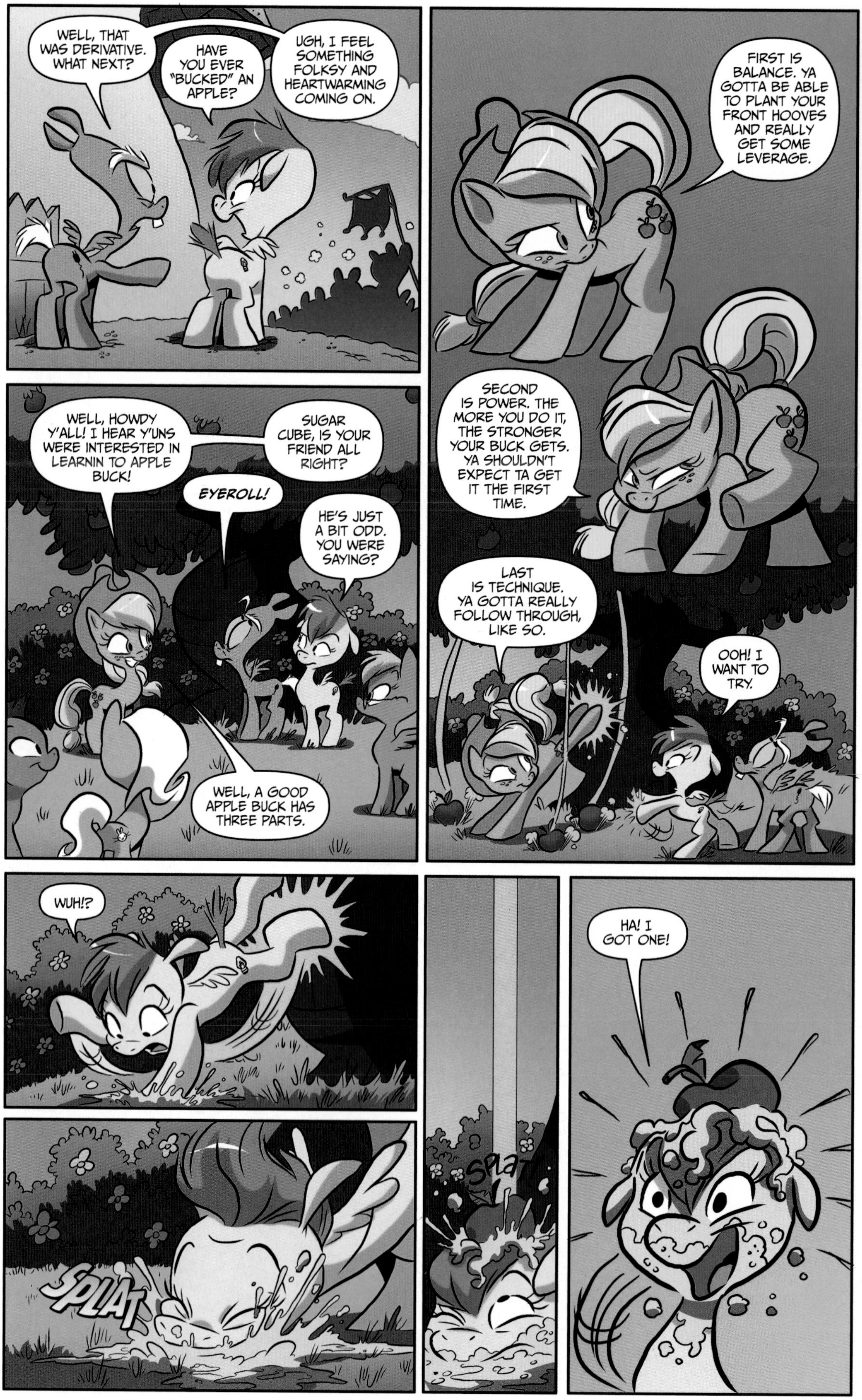

WELL, THAT WAS DERIVATIVE. WHAT NEXT?
HAVE YOU EVER "BUCKED" AN APPLE?
UGH, I FEEL SOMETHING FOLKSY AND HEARTWARMING COMING ON.
FIRST IS BALANCE. YA GOTTA BE ABLE TO PLANT YOUR FRONT HOOVES AND REALLY GET SOME LEVERAGE.
WELL, HOWDY Y'ALL! I HEAR Y'UNS WERE INTERESTED IN LEARNIN TO APPLE BUCK!
SUGAR CUBE, IS YOUR FRIEND ALL RIGHT?
EYEROLL!
HE'S JUST A BIT ODD. YOU WERE SAYING?
WELL, A GOOD APPLE BUCK HAS THREE PARTS.
SECOND IS POWER. THE MORE YOU DO IT, THE STRONGER YOUR BUCK GETS. YA SHOULDN'T EXPECT TA GET IT THE FIRST TIME.
LAST IS TECHNIQUE. YA GOTTA REALLY FOLLOW THROUGH, LIKE SO.
OOH! I WANT TO TRY.
WUH!?
SPLAT
SPLAT
HA! I GOT ONE!

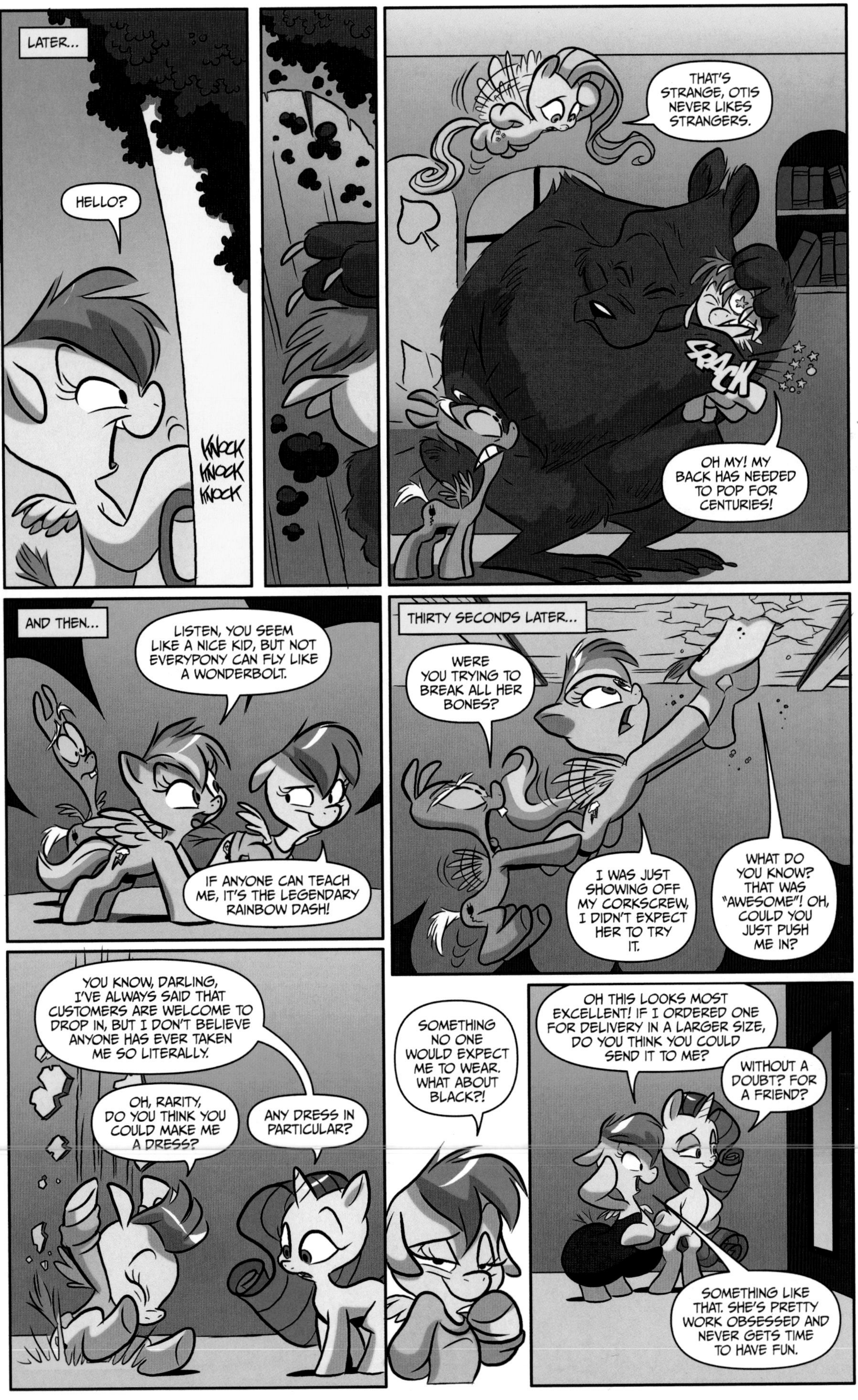
LATER...
HELLO?
KNOCK KNOCK KNOCK
THAT'S STRANGE, OTIS NEVER LIKES STRANGERS.
CRACK
OH MY! MY BACK HAS NEEDED TO POP FOR CENTURIES!
AND THEN...
LISTEN, YOU SEEM LIKE A NICE KID, BUT NOT EVERYPONY CAN FLY LIKE A WONDERBOLT.
IF ANYONE CAN TEACH ME, IT'S THE LEGENDARY RAINBOW DASH!
THIRTY SECONDS LATER...
WERE YOU TRYING TO BREAK ALL HER BONES?
I WAS JUST SHOWING OFF MY CORKSCREW, I DIDN'T EXPECT HER TO TRY IT.
WHAT DO YOU KNOW? THAT WAS "AWESOME"! OH, COULD YOU JUST PUSH ME IN?
YOU KNOW, DARLING, I'VE ALWAYS SAID THAT CUSTOMERS ARE WELCOME TO DROP IN, BUT I DON'T BELIEVE ANYONE HAS EVER TAKEN ME SO LITERALLY.
OH, RARITY, DO YOU THINK YOU COULD MAKE ME A DRESS?
ANY DRESS IN PARTICULAR?
SOMETHING NO ONE WOULD EXPECT ME TO WEAR. WHAT ABOUT BLACK?!
OH THIS LOOKS MOST EXCELLENT! IF I ORDERED ONE FOR DELIVERY IN A LARGER SIZE, DO YOU THINK YOU COULD SEND IT TO ME?
WITHOUT A DOUBT? FOR A FRIEND?
SOMETHING LIKE THAT. SHE'S PRETTY WORK OBSESSED AND NEVER GETS TIME TO HAVE FUN.

YOU LEAVE AN IMMORTAL PRINCESS ALONE WITH A FASHION DESIGNER FOR FIVE MINUTES AND THE NEXT THING YOU KNOW—

—SHE'S RUN OFF TO THE SWEET SHOP.

YOU'RE HERE! COME HELP ME! I ORDERED ONE OF EVERYTHING AND I DON'T THINK I CAN FINISH IT ALL.

YOU KNOW, WHEN YOU FIRST TOLD ME WHAT YOU DID TO THE MUSIC BOX, I THOUGHT ABOUT TURNING YOU BACK TO STONE.

AND NOW?

I THINK YOU ARE SURPRISINGLY INSIGHTFUL. I NEVER WOULD HAVE ADMITTED THAT I NEEDED A DAY OFF.

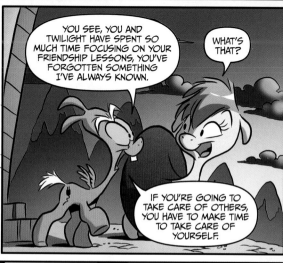

YOU SEE, YOU AND TWILIGHT HAVE SPENT SO MUCH TIME FOCUSING ON YOUR FRIENDSHIP LESSONS, YOU'VE FORGOTTEN SOMETHING I'VE ALWAYS KNOWN.

WHAT'S THAT?

IF YOU'RE GOING TO TAKE CARE OF OTHERS, YOU HAVE TO MAKE TIME TO TAKE CARE OF YOURSELF.

I DON'T THINK I CAN FLY BACK WITH ALL THE CAKE I ATE.

WHY NOT THE TRAIN, PRINCESS?

OOOH! THE TRAIN! I'VE ALWAYS THOUGHT TRAINS WERE ROMANTIC.

A SENTIMENT ONLY SHARED BY PONIES WHO DON'T RIDE TRAINS REGULARLY.

HAHAHAHAHAHA!

HEY, DISCORD. THANK YOU FOR THIS. YOU'RE A GOOD FRIEND.

DON'T GET SAPPY ON ME NOW. LET'S JUST HOPE YOUR SISTER DIDN'T BURN THE PLACE DOWN.

BUT IF YOU EVER DO SOMETHING LIKE THIS WITHOUT ASKING AGAIN, YOU'LL BE SPENDING THE NEXT CENTURY AS MY BIRD FEEDER.

FAIR ENOUGH. AND BY THE BY, THAT'S NOT SO MUCH THE SUN AS A GIANT BALLOON FILLED WITH ANGRY LAVA MONSTERS. SO...YOU MAY NEED TO DEAL WITH THAT.

OH, DISCORD.

WELL, I KNEW YOU WOULDN'T COME IF THERE WAS WORK TO BE DONE.

THE END!

my LITTLE PONY
Friendship is Magic

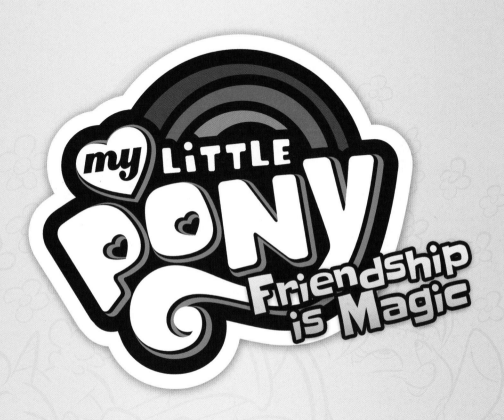

art by Tony Fleecs

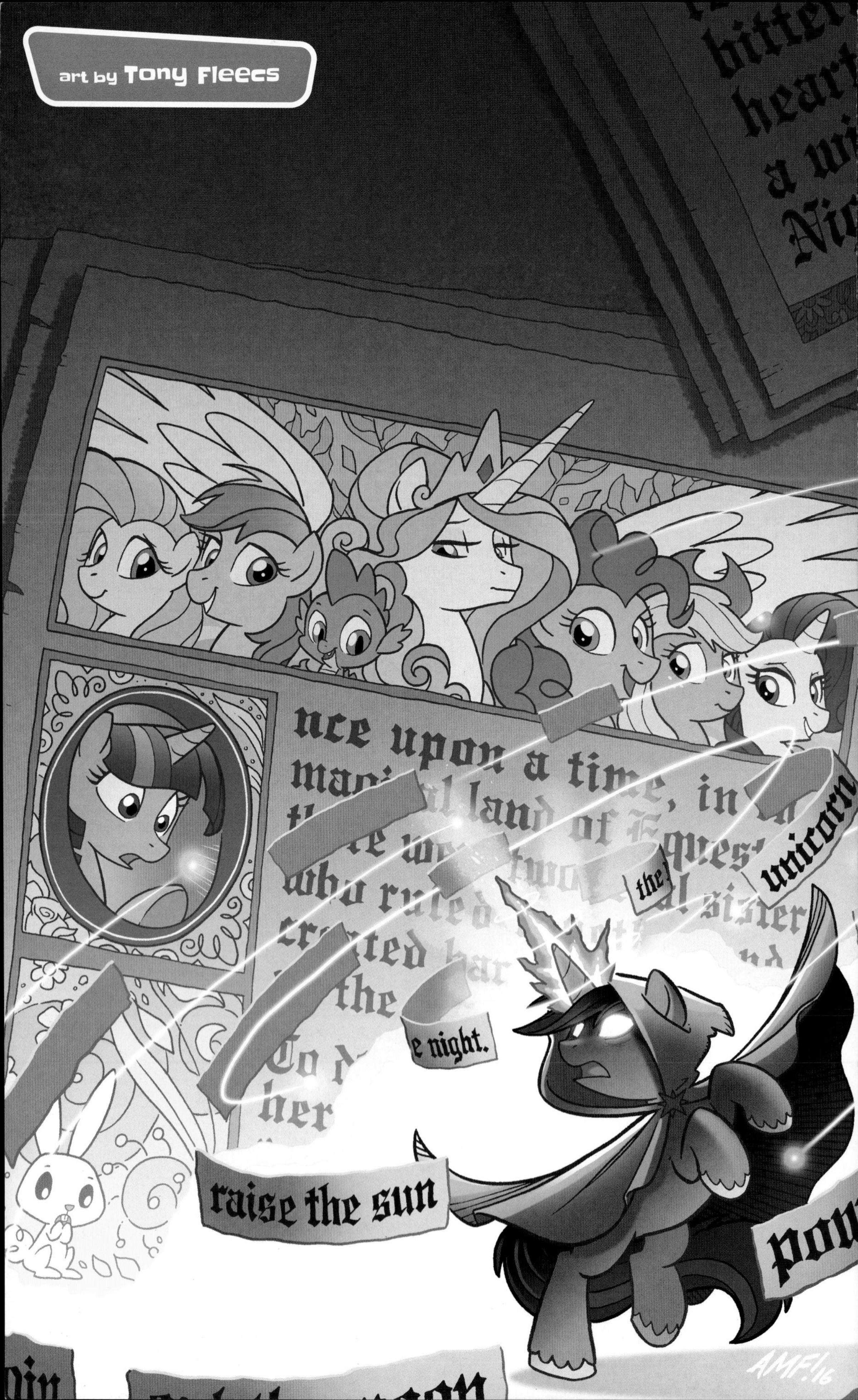
unicorn
the
e night.
raise the sun
A.M.F. '16

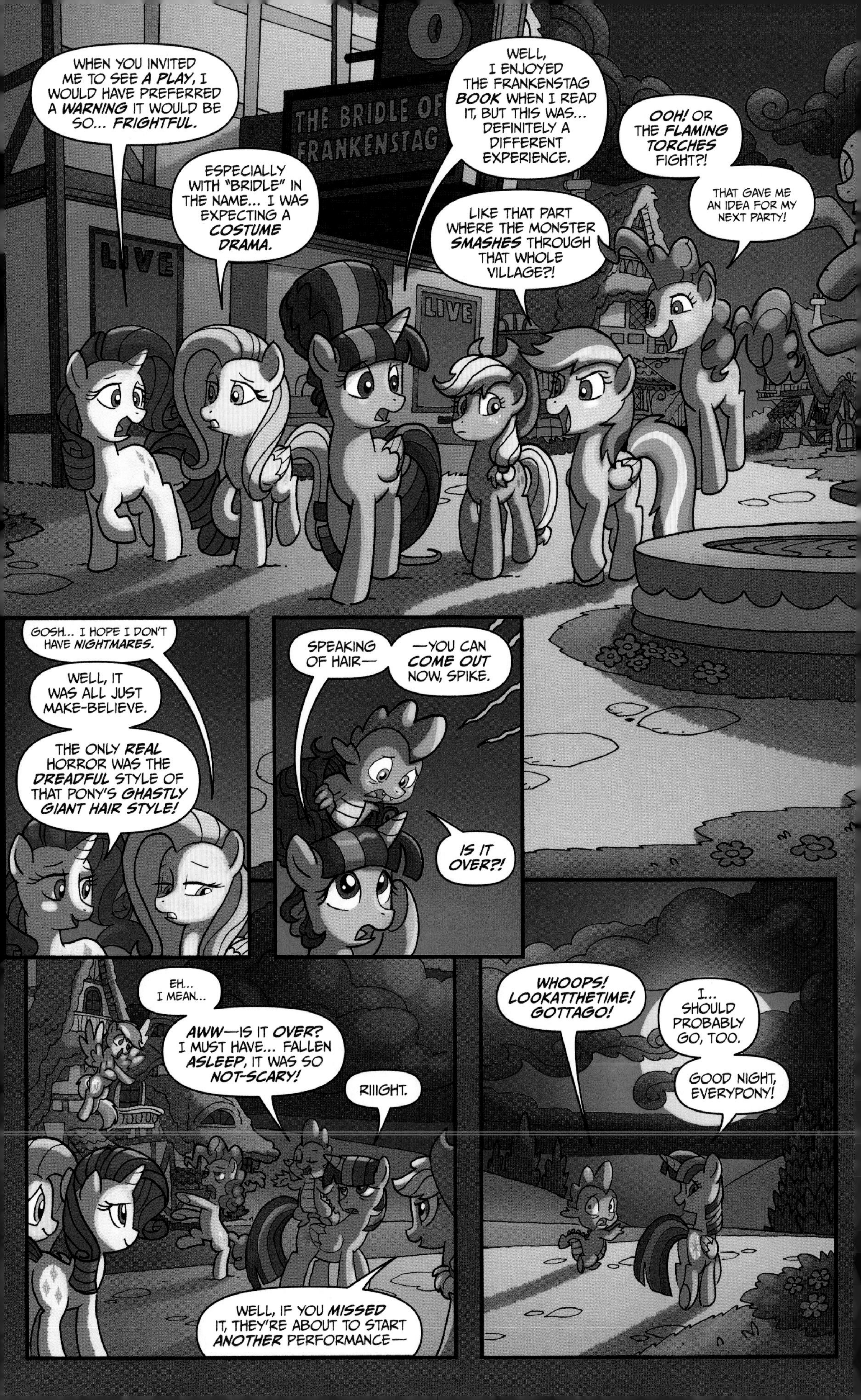

THE BRIDLE OF FRANKENSTAG
LIVE
LIVE
WHEN YOU INVITED ME TO SEE A PLAY, I WOULD HAVE PREFERRED A WARNING IT WOULD BE SO... FRIGHTFUL.
ESPECIALLY WITH "BRIDLE" IN THE NAME... I WAS EXPECTING A COSTUME DRAMA.
WELL, I ENJOYED THE FRANKENSTAG BOOK WHEN I READ IT, BUT THIS WAS... DEFINITELY A DIFFERENT EXPERIENCE.
LIKE THAT PART WHERE THE MONSTER SMASHES THROUGH THAT WHOLE VILLAGE?!
OOH! OR THE FLAMING TORCHES FIGHT?!
THAT GAVE ME AN IDEA FOR MY NEXT PARTY!
GOSH... I HOPE I DON'T HAVE NIGHTMARES.
WELL, IT WAS ALL JUST MAKE-BELIEVE.
THE ONLY REAL HORROR WAS THE DREADFUL STYLE OF THAT PONY'S GHASTLY GIANT HAIR STYLE!
SPEAKING OF HAIR—
—YOU CAN COME OUT NOW, SPIKE.
IS IT OVER?!
EH... I MEAN...
AWW—IS IT OVER? I MUST HAVE... FALLEN ASLEEP, IT WAS SO NOT-SCARY!
RIIIGHT.
WELL, IF YOU MISSED IT, THEY'RE ABOUT TO START ANOTHER PERFORMANCE—
WHOOPS! LOOKATTHETIME! GOTTAGO!
I... SHOULD PROBABLY GO, TOO.
GOOD NIGHT, EVERYPONY!

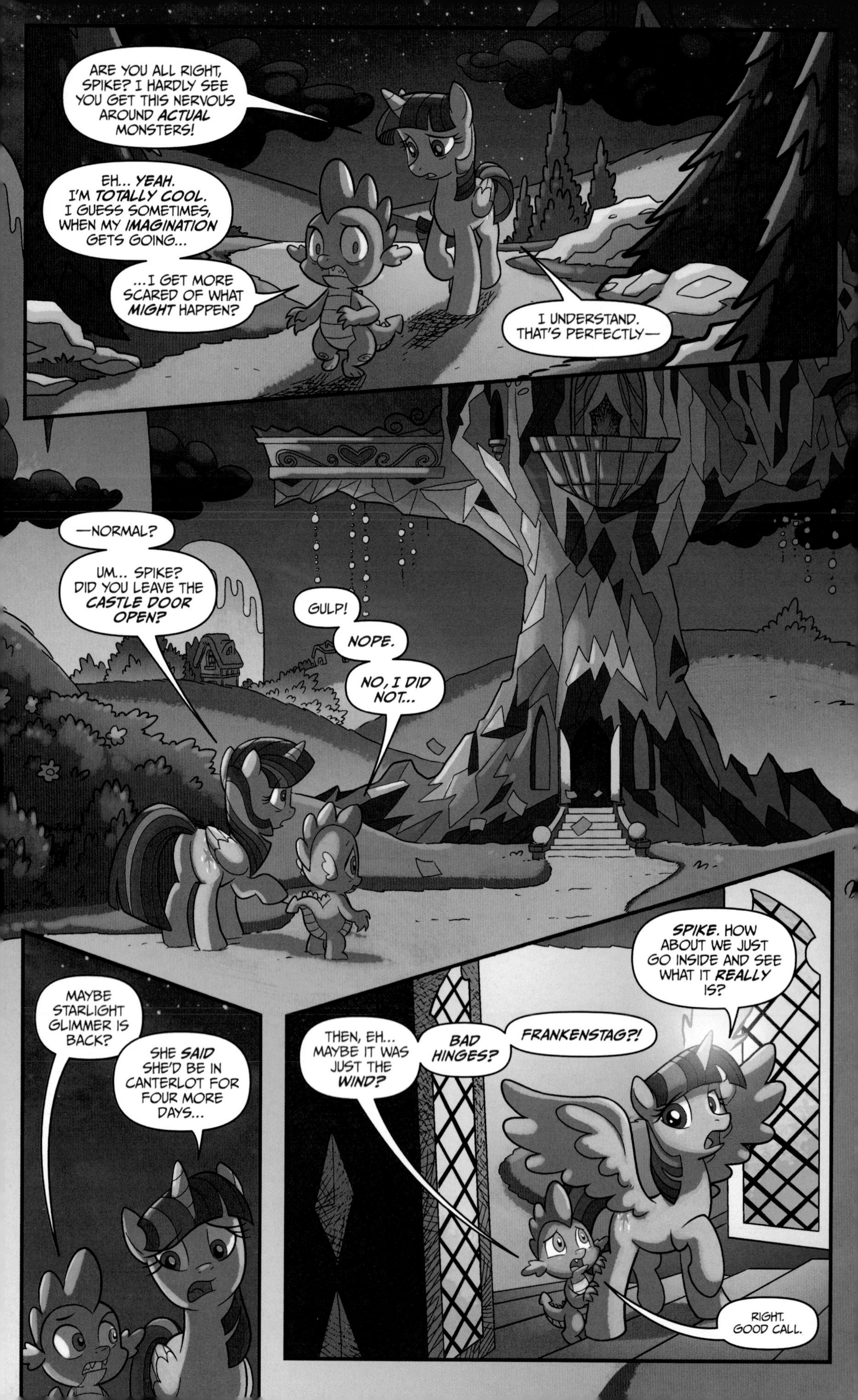
ARE YOU ALL RIGHT, SPIKE? I HARDLY SEE YOU GET THIS NERVOUS AROUND ACTUAL MONSTERS!
EH... YEAH. I'M TOTALLY COOL. I GUESS SOMETIMES, WHEN MY IMAGINATION GETS GOING...
...I GET MORE SCARED OF WHAT MIGHT HAPPEN?
I UNDERSTAND. THAT'S PERFECTLY—
—NORMAL?
UM... SPIKE? DID YOU LEAVE THE CASTLE DOOR OPEN?
GULP!
NOPE.
NO, I DID NOT...
MAYBE STARLIGHT GLIMMER IS BACK?
SHE SAID SHE'D BE IN CANTERLOT FOR FOUR MORE DAYS...
THEN, EH... MAYBE IT WAS JUST THE WIND?
BAD HINGES?
FRANKENSTAG?!
SPIKE. HOW ABOUT WE JUST GO INSIDE AND SEE WHAT IT REALLY IS?
RIGHT. GOOD CALL.

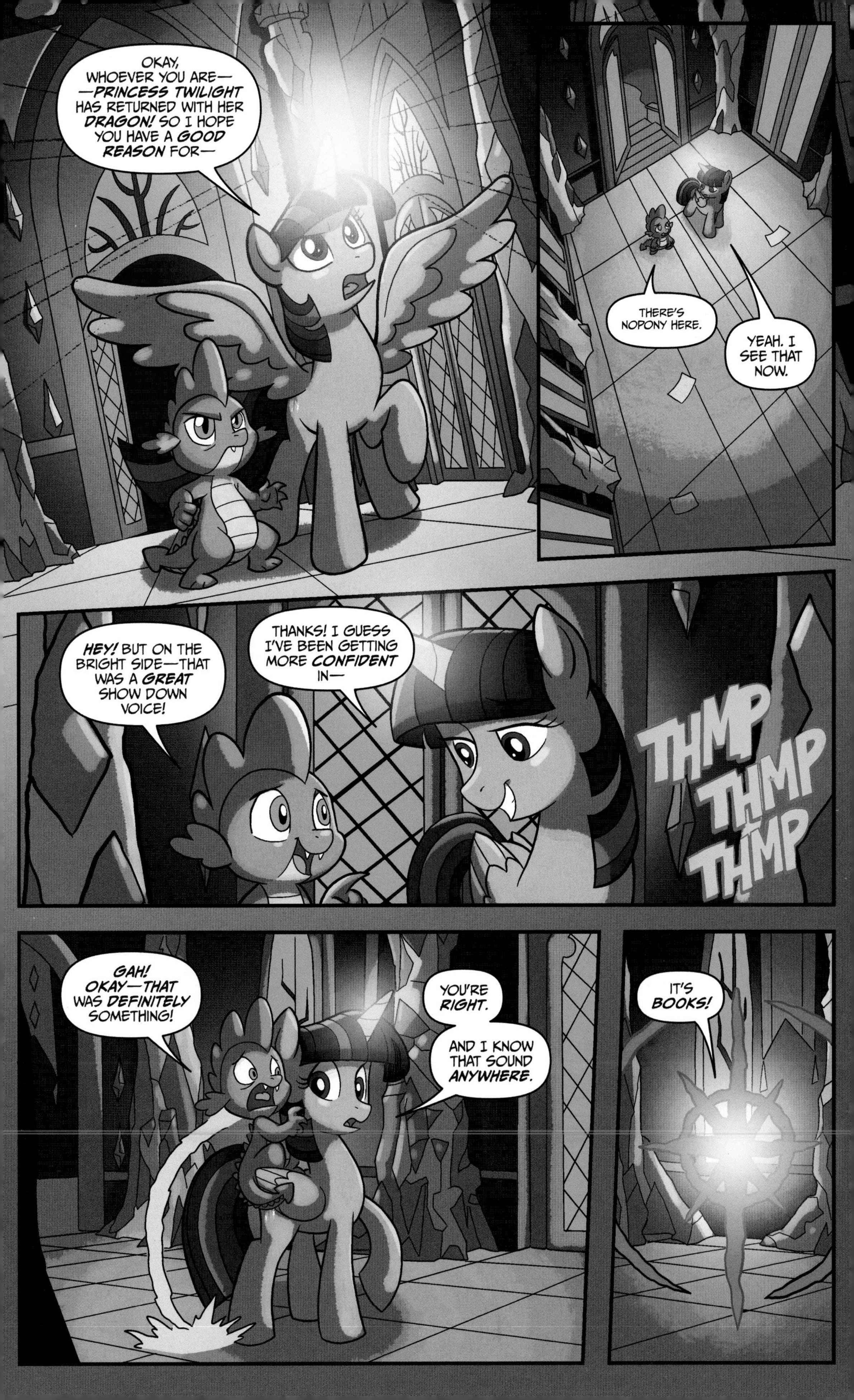

OKAY, WHOEVER YOU ARE— —PRINCESS TWILIGHT HAS RETURNED WITH HER DRAGON! SO I HOPE YOU HAVE A GOOD REASON FOR—
THERE'S NOPONY HERE.
YEAH. I SEE THAT NOW.
HEY! BUT ON THE BRIGHT SIDE—THAT WAS A GREAT SHOW DOWN VOICE!
THANKS! I GUESS I'VE BEEN GETTING MORE CONFIDENT IN—
THMP THMP THMP
GAH! OKAY—THAT WAS DEFINITELY SOMETHING!
YOU'RE RIGHT.
AND I KNOW THAT SOUND ANYWHERE.
IT'S BOOKS!

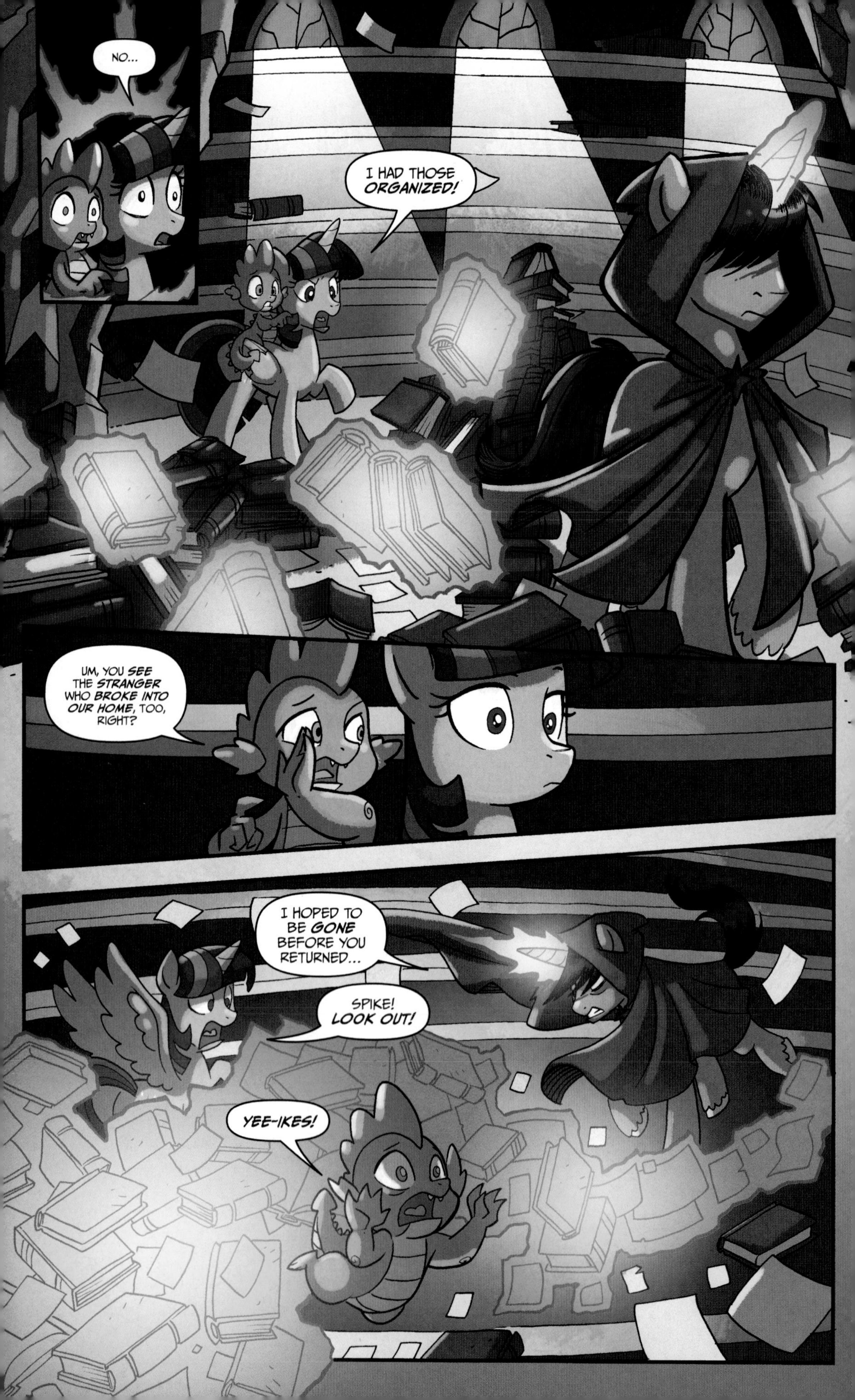
NO...
I HAD THOSE *ORGANIZED!*
UM, YOU **SEE** THE **STRANGER** WHO **BROKE INTO OUR HOME**, TOO, RIGHT?
I HOPED TO BE **GONE** BEFORE YOU RETURNED...
SPIKE! **LOOK OUT!**
YEE-IKES!

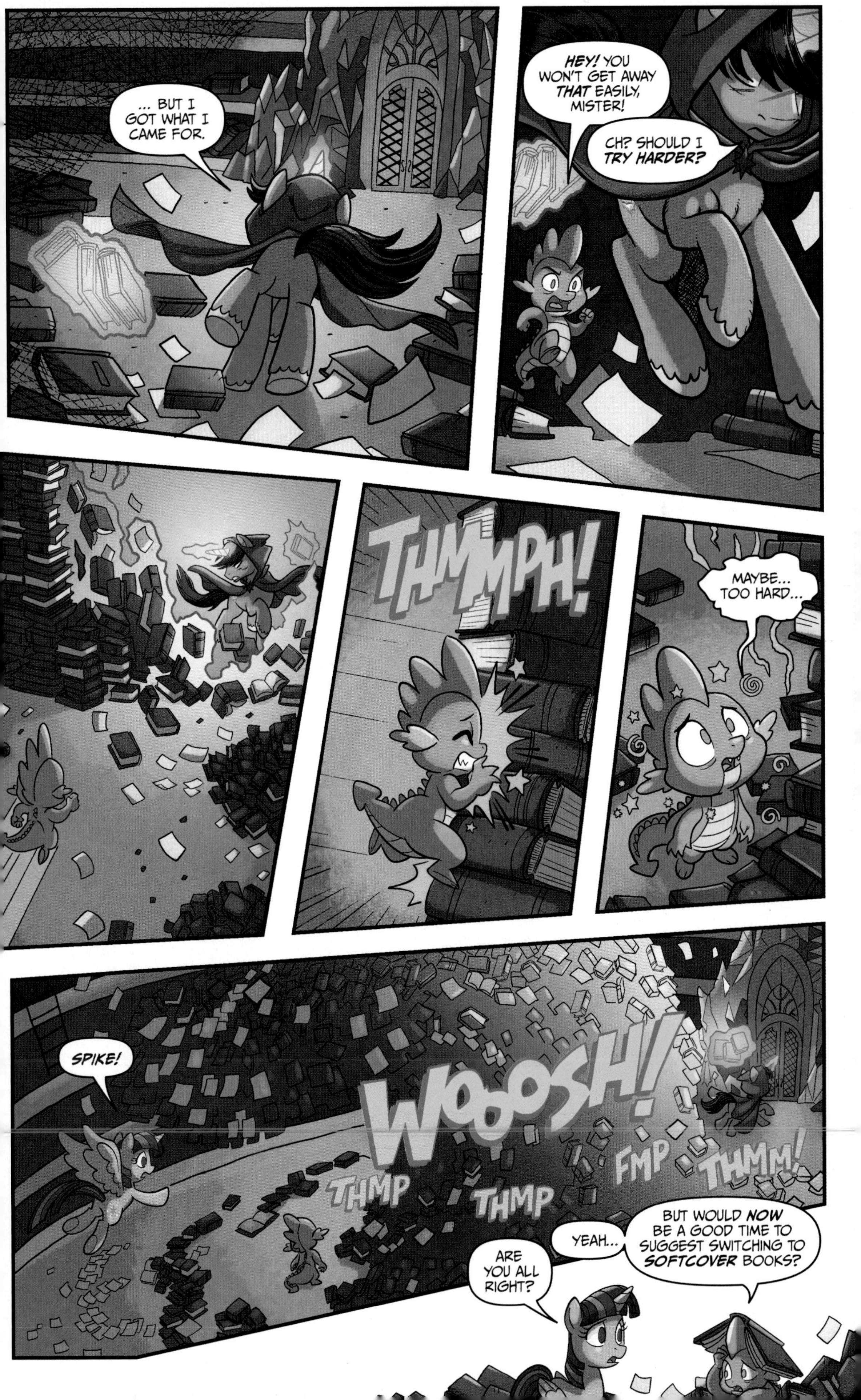
... BUT I GOT WHAT I CAME FOR.
HEY! YOU WON'T GET AWAY THAT EASILY, MISTER!
OH? SHOULD I TRY HARDER?
THMMPH!
MAYBE... TOO HARD...
SPIKE!
WOOOSH!
THMP
THMP
FMP
THMM!
ARE YOU ALL RIGHT?
YEAH...
BUT WOULD NOW BE A GOOD TIME TO SUGGEST SWITCHING TO SOFTCOVER BOOKS?

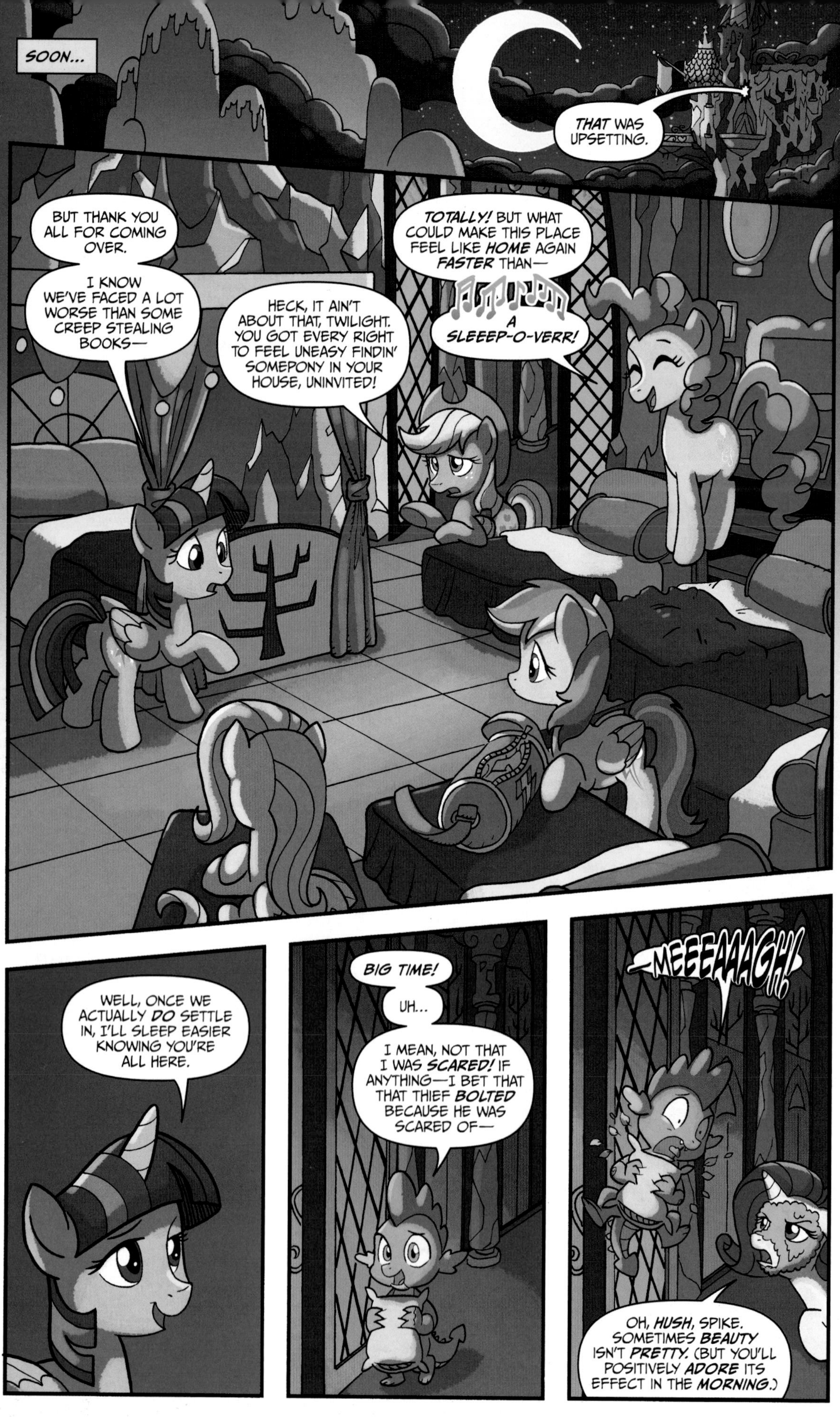
SOON...
THAT WAS UPSETTING.
BUT THANK YOU ALL FOR COMING OVER.
I KNOW WE'VE FACED A LOT WORSE THAN SOME CREEP STEALING BOOKS—
HECK, IT AIN'T ABOUT THAT, TWILIGHT. YOU GOT EVERY RIGHT TO FEEL UNEASY FINDIN' SOMEPONY IN YOUR HOUSE, UNINVITED!
TOTALLY! BUT WHAT COULD MAKE THIS PLACE FEEL LIKE HOME AGAIN FASTER THAN—
A SLEEEP-O-VERR!
WELL, ONCE WE ACTUALLY DO SETTLE IN, I'LL SLEEP EASIER KNOWING YOU'RE ALL HERE.
BIG TIME!
UH...
I MEAN, NOT THAT I WAS SCARED! IF ANYTHING—I BET THAT THAT THIEF BOLTED BECAUSE HE WAS SCARED OF—
—MEEEAAAGH!
OH, HUSH, SPIKE. SOMETIMES BEAUTY ISN'T PRETTY. (BUT YOU'LL POSITIVELY ADORE ITS EFFECT IN THE MORNING.)

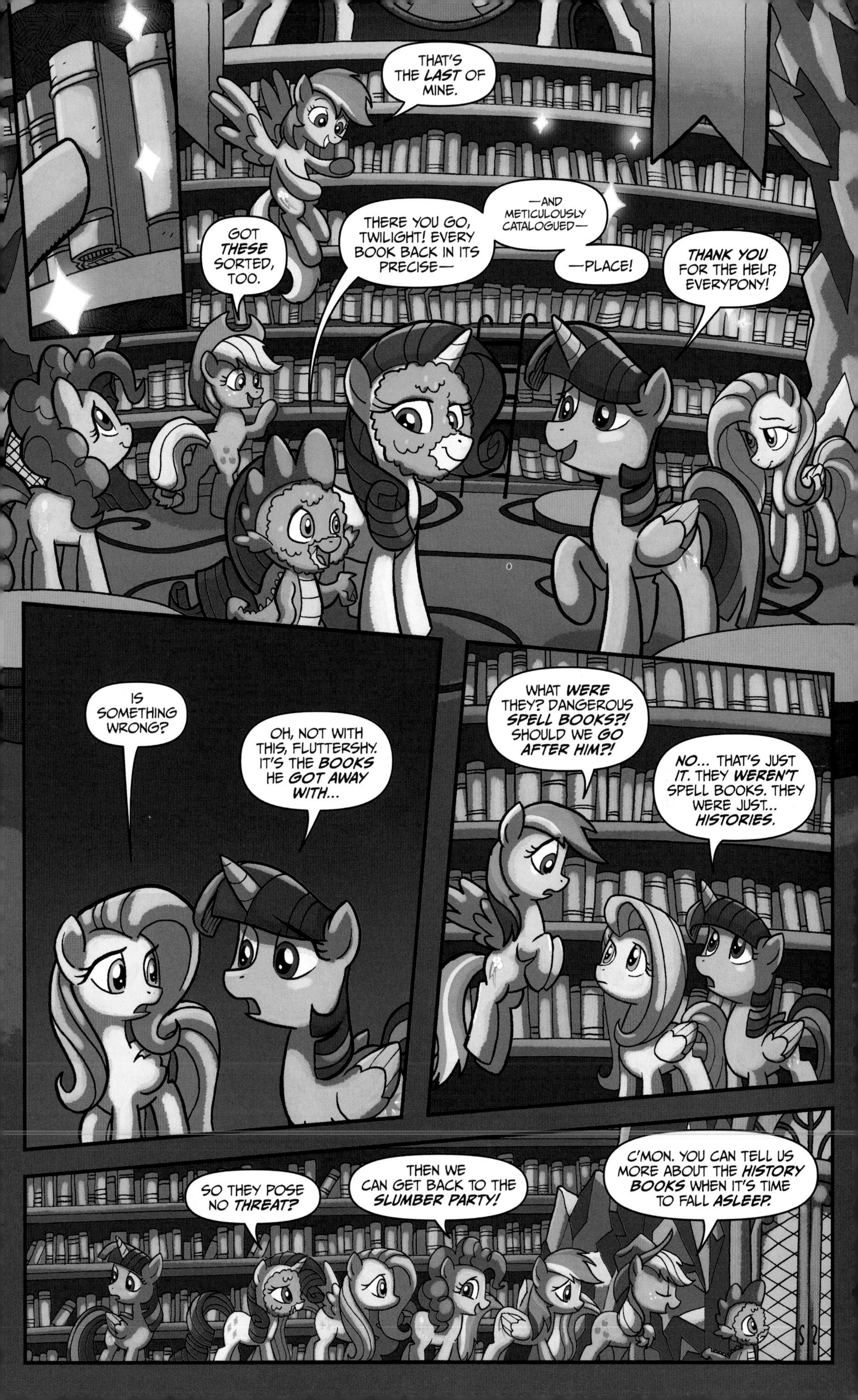
THAT'S THE LAST OF MINE.
GOT THESE SORTED, TOO.
THERE YOU GO, TWILIGHT! EVERY BOOK BACK IN ITS PRECISE—
—AND METICULOUSLY CATALOGUED—
—PLACE!
THANK YOU FOR THE HELP, EVERYPONY!
IS SOMETHING WRONG?
OH, NOT WITH THIS, FLUTTERSHY. IT'S THE BOOKS HE GOT AWAY WITH...
WHAT WERE THEY? DANGEROUS SPELL BOOKS?! SHOULD WE GO AFTER HIM?!
NO... THAT'S JUST IT. THEY WEREN'T SPELL BOOKS. THEY WERE JUST... HISTORIES.
SO THEY POSE NO THREAT?
THEN WE CAN GET BACK TO THE SLUMBER PARTY!
C'MON. YOU CAN TELL US MORE ABOUT THE HISTORY BOOKS WHEN IT'S TIME TO FALL ASLEEP.

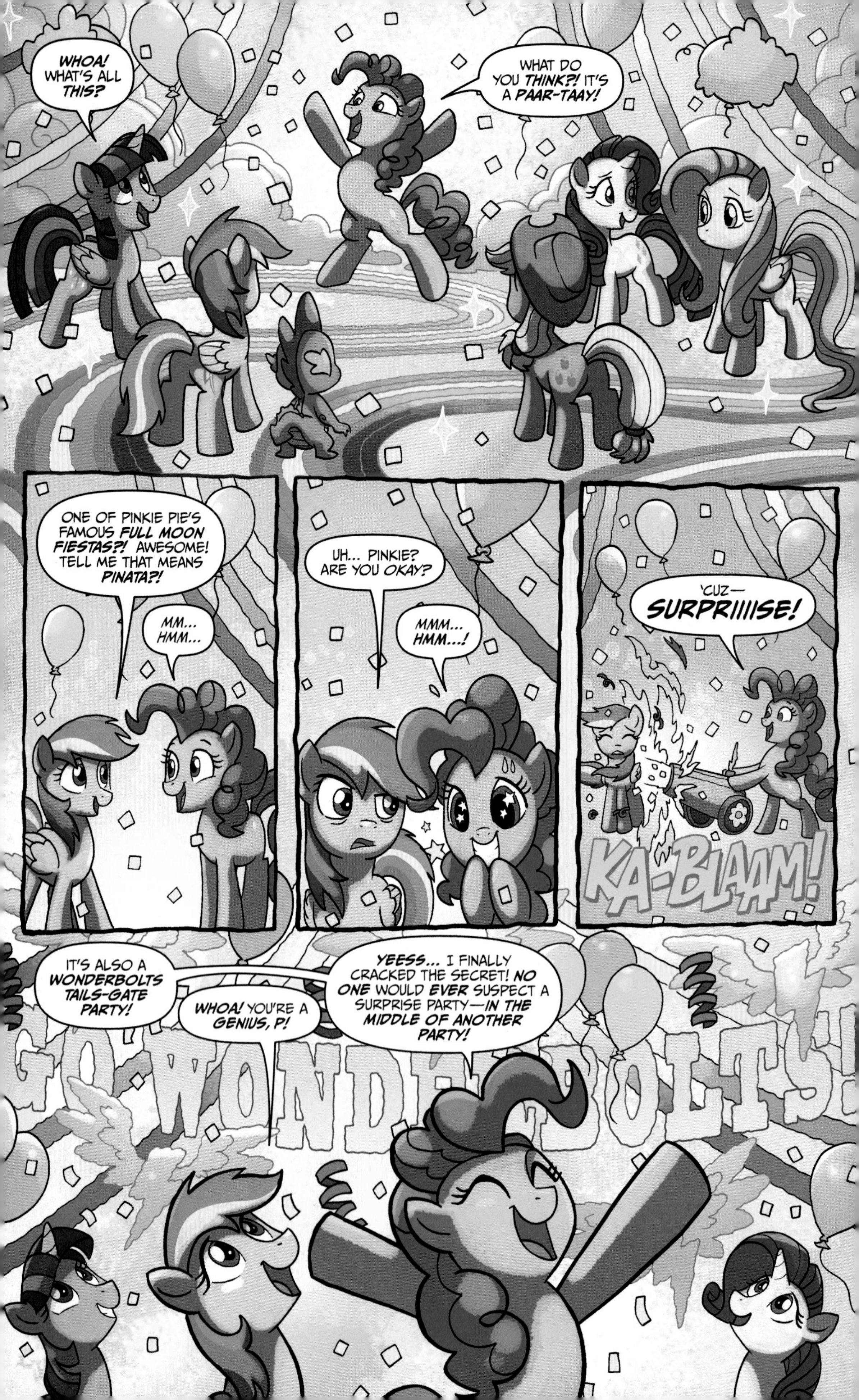
WHOA! WHAT'S ALL THIS?
WHAT DO YOU THINK?! IT'S A PAAR-TAAY!
ONE OF PINKIE PIE'S FAMOUS FULL MOON FIESTAS?! AWESOME! TELL ME THAT MEANS PINATA?!
MM... HMM...
UH... PINKIE? ARE YOU OKAY?
MMM... HMM...!
'CUZ— SURPRIIIISE!
KA-BLAAM!
IT'S ALSO A WONDERBOLTS TAILS-GATE PARTY!
WHOA! YOU'RE A GENIUS, P!
YEESS... I FINALLY CRACKED THE SECRET! NO ONE WOULD EVER SUSPECT A SURPRISE PARTY—IN THE MIDDLE OF ANOTHER PARTY!

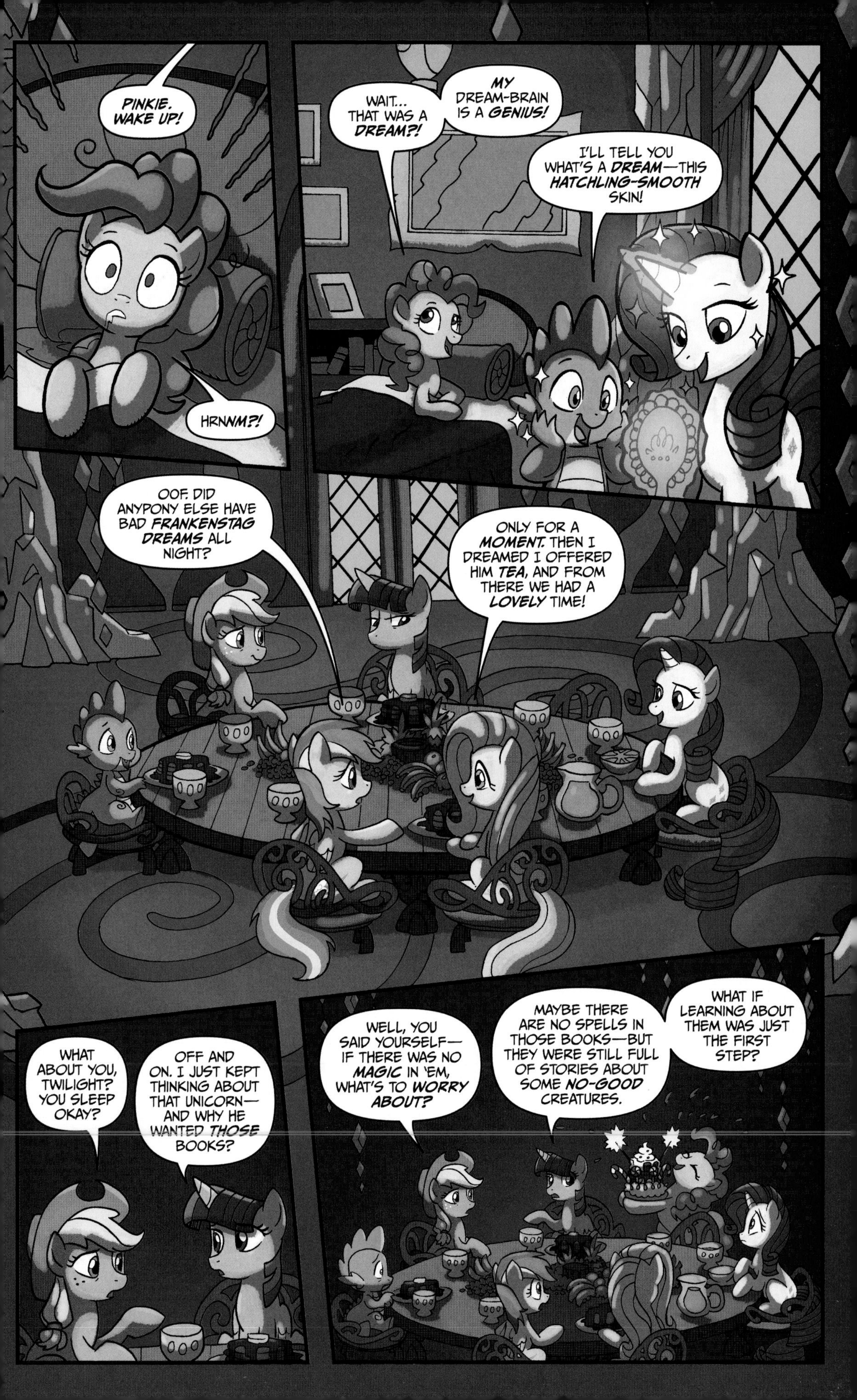
PINKIE. WAKE UP!
HRNNM?!
WAIT... THAT WAS A DREAM?!
MY DREAM-BRAIN IS A GENIUS!
I'LL TELL YOU WHAT'S A DREAM—THIS HATCHLING-SMOOTH SKIN!
OOF. DID ANYPONY ELSE HAVE BAD FRANKENSTAG DREAMS ALL NIGHT?
ONLY FOR A MOMENT. THEN I DREAMED I OFFERED HIM TEA, AND FROM THERE WE HAD A LOVELY TIME!
WHAT ABOUT YOU, TWILIGHT? YOU SLEEP OKAY?
OFF AND ON. I JUST KEPT THINKING ABOUT THAT UNICORN—AND WHY HE WANTED THOSE BOOKS?
WELL, YOU SAID YOURSELF—IF THERE WAS NO MAGIC IN 'EM, WHAT'S TO WORRY ABOUT?
MAYBE THERE ARE NO SPELLS IN THOSE BOOKS—BUT THEY WERE STILL FULL OF STORIES ABOUT SOME NO-GOOD CREATURES.
WHAT IF LEARNING ABOUT THEM WAS JUST THE FIRST STEP?

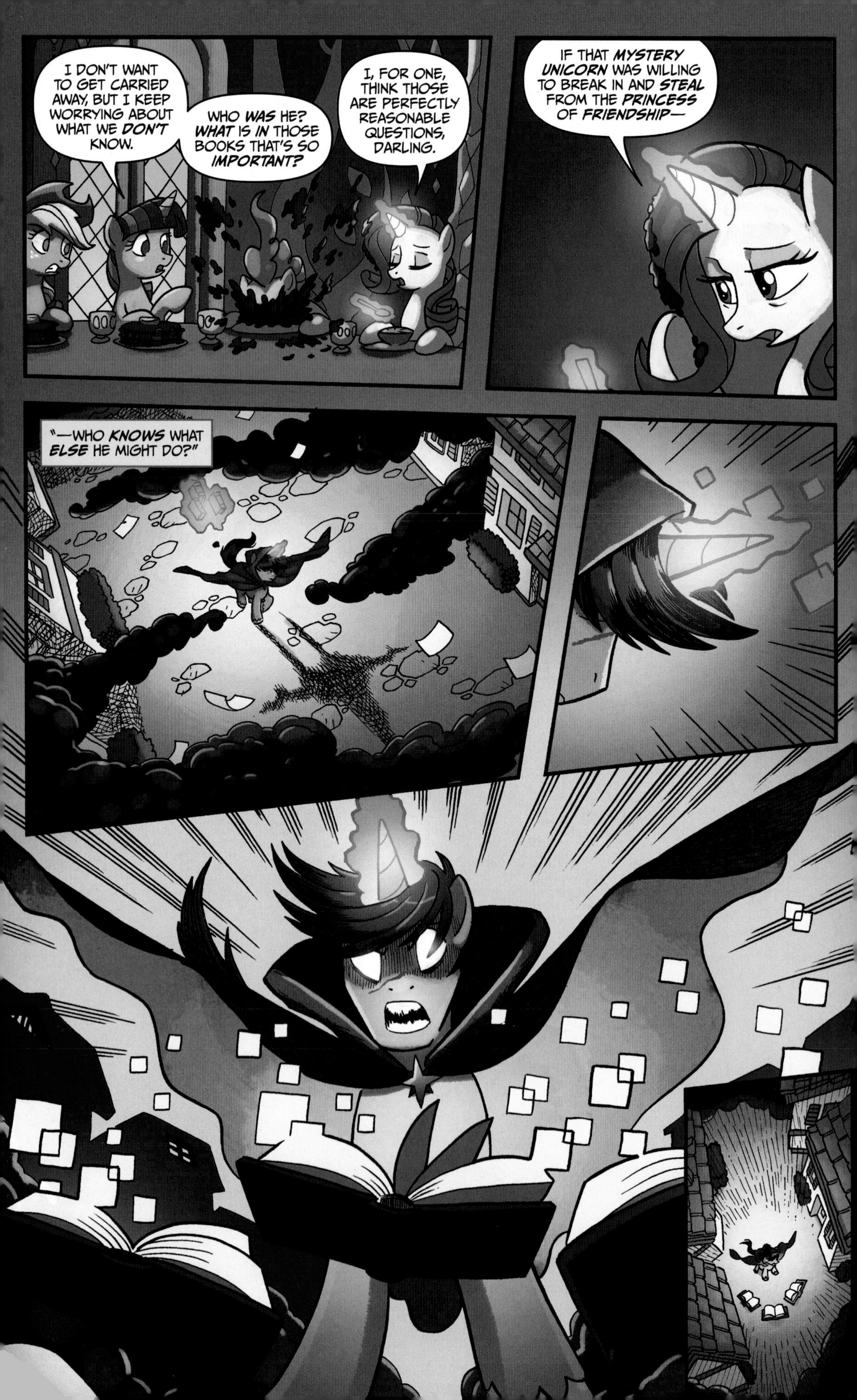
I DON'T WANT TO GET CARRIED AWAY, BUT I KEEP WORRYING ABOUT WHAT WE DON'T KNOW.
WHO WAS HE? WHAT IS IN THOSE BOOKS THAT'S SO IMPORTANT?
I, FOR ONE, THINK THOSE ARE PERFECTLY REASONABLE QUESTIONS, DARLING.
IF THAT MYSTERY UNICORN WAS WILLING TO BREAK IN AND STEAL FROM THE PRINCESS OF FRIENDSHIP—
"—WHO KNOWS WHAT ELSE HE MIGHT DO?"

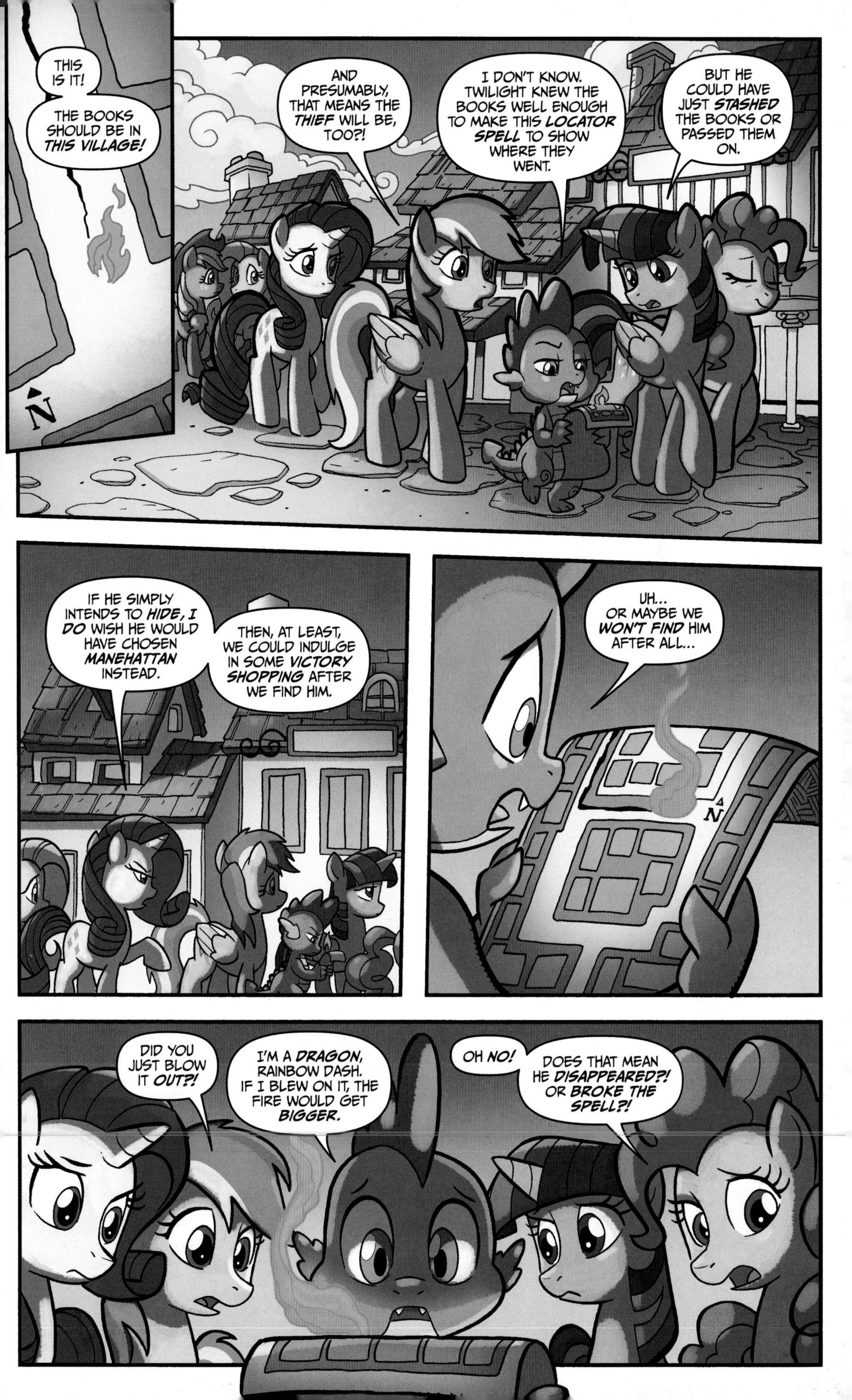
THIS IS IT!
THE BOOKS SHOULD BE IN THIS VILLAGE!
AND PRESUMABLY, THAT MEANS THE THIEF WILL BE, TOO?!
I DON'T KNOW. TWILIGHT KNEW THE BOOKS WELL ENOUGH TO MAKE THIS LOCATOR SPELL TO SHOW WHERE THEY WENT.
BUT HE COULD HAVE JUST STASHED THE BOOKS OR PASSED THEM ON.
IF HE SIMPLY INTENDS TO HIDE, I DO WISH HE WOULD HAVE CHOSEN MANEHATTAN INSTEAD.
THEN, AT LEAST, WE COULD INDULGE IN SOME VICTORY SHOPPING AFTER WE FIND HIM.
UH... OR MAYBE WE WON'T FIND HIM AFTER ALL...
DID YOU JUST BLOW IT OUT?!
I'M A DRAGON, RAINBOW DASH. IF I BLEW ON IT, THE FIRE WOULD GET BIGGER.
OH NO!
DOES THAT MEAN HE DISAPPEARED?! OR BROKE THE SPELL?!

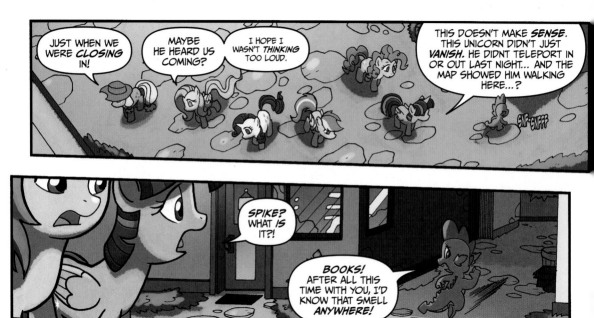

JUST WHEN WE WERE *CLOSING IN!*

MAYBE HE HEARD US COMING?

I HOPE I WASN'T *THINKING* TOO LOUD.

THIS DOESN'T MAKE *SENSE.* THIS UNICORN DIDN'T JUST *VANISH.* HE DIDN'T TELEPORT IN OR OUT LAST NIGHT... AND THE MAP SHOWED HIM WALKING HERE...?

SNF-SNFFF

SPIKE? WHAT *IS* IT?!

BOOKS! AFTER ALL THIS TIME WITH YOU, I'D KNOW THAT SMELL *ANYWHERE!*

HA! WELL, WE *DO* HAVE A *SPELL*—BUT NO *MYSTERY COLT!* AT LEAST WE FOUND YOUR—

—BOOKS? UH... TWILIGHT? DID THEY *USED* TO BE *BLANK?!*

NO. THE SPELL MUST HAVE *ERASED* THEM!

BUT *THAT* MEANS THE *THIEF* IS PROBABLY STILL *CLOSE!*

I SAY WE *SPLIT UP* AND CHECK THE MOST LIKELY SPOTS BEFORE HE GETS AWAY!

GOOD IDEA. LET'S GO IN PAIRS SINCE HE SEEMS TO BE A *SLIPPERY* SON OF A—

I CALL THE CANDY STORE!

WHY WOULD A *MAGICAL* THIEF BE IN A *CANDY STORE?*

SORRY! CAN'T STOP TO THINK! GOTTA FIND A THIEF!

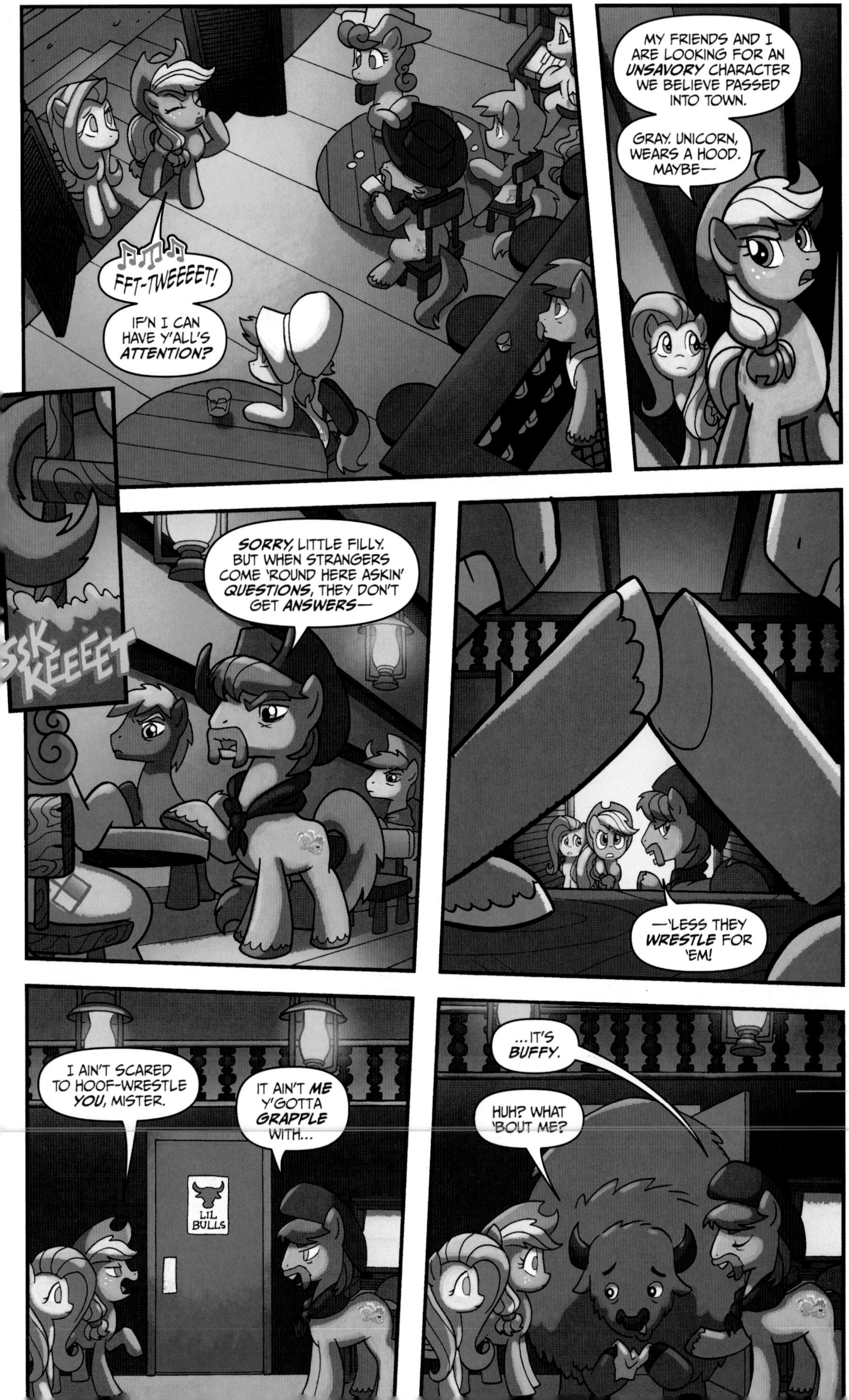
FFT-TWEEEET!
IF'N I CAN HAVE Y'ALL'S ATTENTION?
MY FRIENDS AND I ARE LOOKING FOR AN UNSAVORY CHARACTER WE BELIEVE PASSED INTO TOWN.
GRAY. UNICORN, WEARS A HOOD. MAYBE—
SSK KEEEEET
SORRY, LITTLE FILLY. BUT WHEN STRANGERS COME 'ROUND HERE ASKIN' QUESTIONS, THEY DON'T GET ANSWERS—
—'LESS THEY WRESTLE FOR 'EM!
I AIN'T SCARED TO HOOF-WRESTLE YOU, MISTER.
IT AIN'T ME Y'GOTTA GRAPPLE WITH...
LIL BULLS
...IT'S BUFFY.
HUH? WHAT 'BOUT ME?

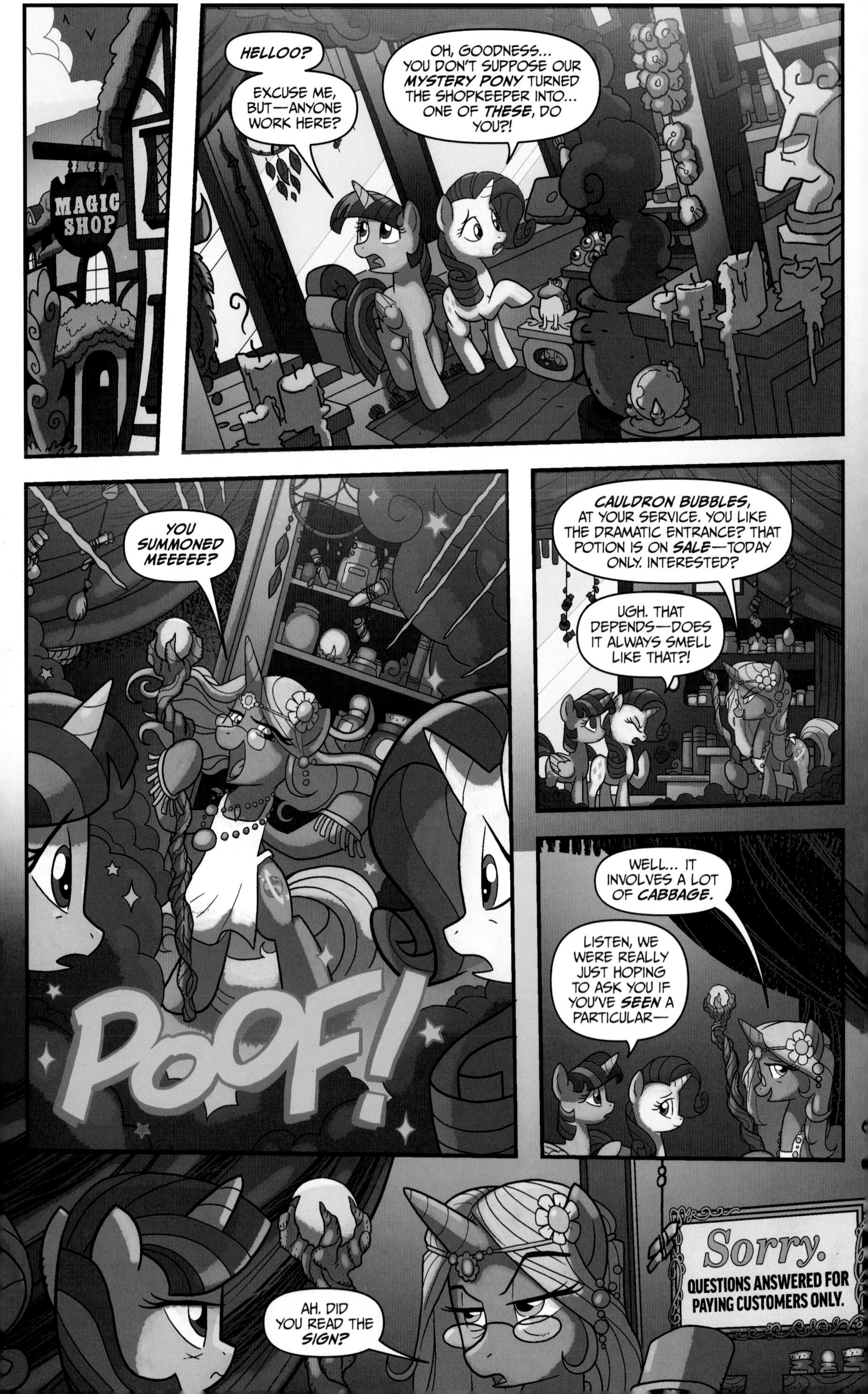
MAGIC SHOP
HELLOO?
EXCUSE ME, BUT—ANYONE WORK HERE?
OH, GOODNESS... YOU DON'T SUPPOSE OUR MYSTERY PONY TURNED THE SHOPKEEPER INTO... ONE OF THESE, DO YOU?!
YOU SUMMONED MEEEEE?
POOF!
CAULDRON BUBBLES, AT YOUR SERVICE. YOU LIKE THE DRAMATIC ENTRANCE? THAT POTION IS ON SALE—TODAY ONLY. INTERESTED?
UGH. THAT DEPENDS—DOES IT ALWAYS SMELL LIKE THAT?!
WELL... IT INVOLVES A LOT OF CABBAGE.
LISTEN, WE WERE REALLY JUST HOPING TO ASK YOU IF YOU'VE SEEN A PARTICULAR—
AH. DID YOU READ THE SIGN?
Sorry.
QUESTIONS ANSWERED FOR PAYING CUSTOMERS ONLY.

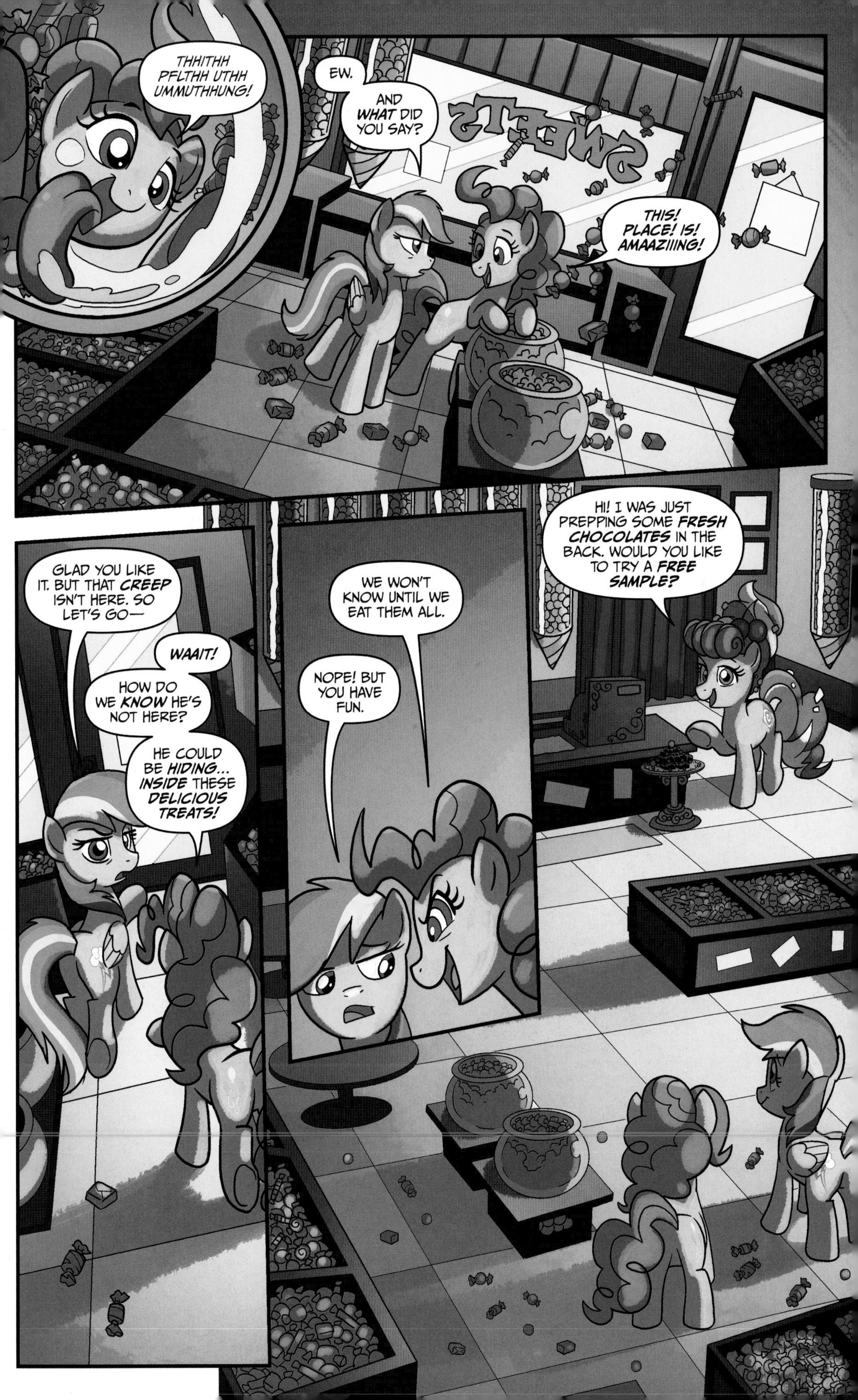
THHITHH PFLTHH UTHH UMMUTHHUNG!
EW.
AND WHAT DID YOU SAY?
SWEETS
THIS! PLACE! IS! AMAAZIIING!
GLAD YOU LIKE IT. BUT THAT CREEP ISN'T HERE. SO LET'S GO—
WAAIT!
HOW DO WE KNOW HE'S NOT HERE?
HE COULD BE HIDING... INSIDE THESE DELICIOUS TREATS!
WE WON'T KNOW UNTIL WE EAT THEM ALL.
NOPE! BUT YOU HAVE FUN.
HI! I WAS JUST PREPPING SOME FRESH CHOCOLATES IN THE BACK. WOULD YOU LIKE TO TRY A FREE SAMPLE?

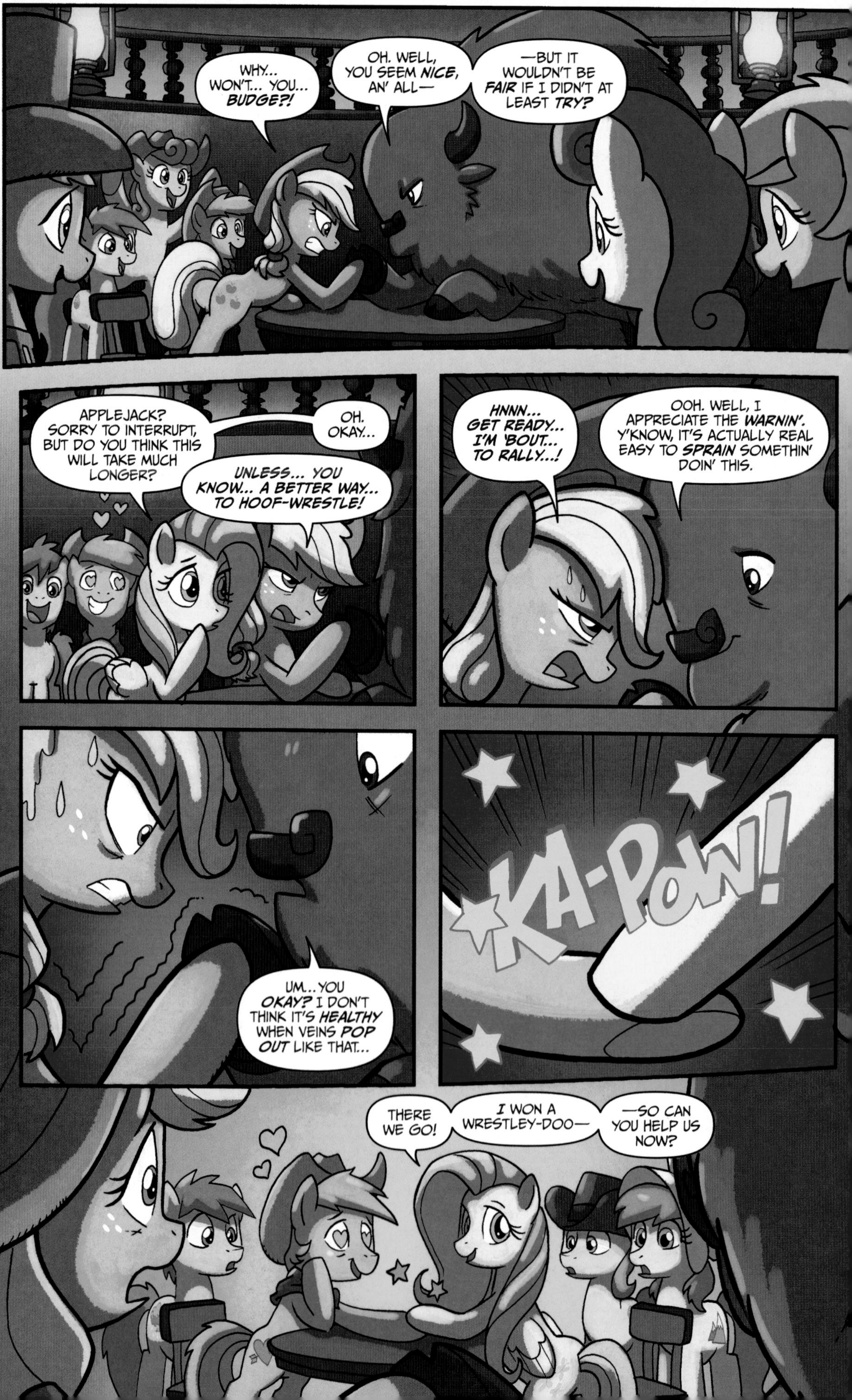
WHY... WON'T... YOU... BUDGE?!
OH. WELL, YOU SEEM NICE, AN' ALL—
—BUT IT WOULDN'T BE FAIR IF I DIDN'T AT LEAST TRY?
APPLEJACK? SORRY TO INTERRUPT, BUT DO YOU THINK THIS WILL TAKE MUCH LONGER?
OH. OKAY...
UNLESS... YOU KNOW... A BETTER WAY... TO HOOF-WRESTLE!
HNNN... GET READY... I'M 'BOUT... TO RALLY...!
OOH. WELL, I APPRECIATE THE WARNIN'. Y'KNOW, IT'S ACTUALLY REAL EASY TO SPRAIN SOMETHIN' DOIN' THIS.
UM...YOU OKAY? I DON'T THINK IT'S HEALTHY WHEN VEINS POP OUT LIKE THAT...
KA-POW!
THERE WE GO!
I WON A WRESTLEY-DOO—
—SO CAN YOU HELP US NOW?

AH! THERE, NOW I *DEFINITELY* REMEMBER A UNICORN OF THAT DESCRIPTION COMING IN HERE JUST EARLIER!

HE WANTED TO USE MY BACK ROOM TO CAST A VERY *STRANGE* SPELL AWAY FROM PRYING EYES...

WHAT SPELL?!

KA-SHING!

HMM... IT'S AT THE *TIP* OF MY *TONGUE*...

I'LL BUY A NEW *QUILL* AND INK, TOO.

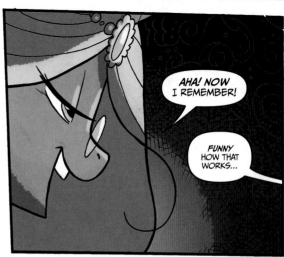

AHA! NOW I REMEMBER!

FUNNY HOW THAT WORKS...

YES! YES! KAY?! THAT UNICORN JUST CAME TO TOWN ASKING QUESTIONS!

SAID HIS NAME WAS SHADOW LOCK! NOW WILL YOU *GET* HER OUT OF HERE?!

SAID HIS *SPELL* CAN *ERASE* THE CONTENTS OF A BOOK, OR OTHER *WRITING*—

— AND MAKE ANYPONY WHO'D READ IT *FORGET* WHAT THEY'D LEARNED!

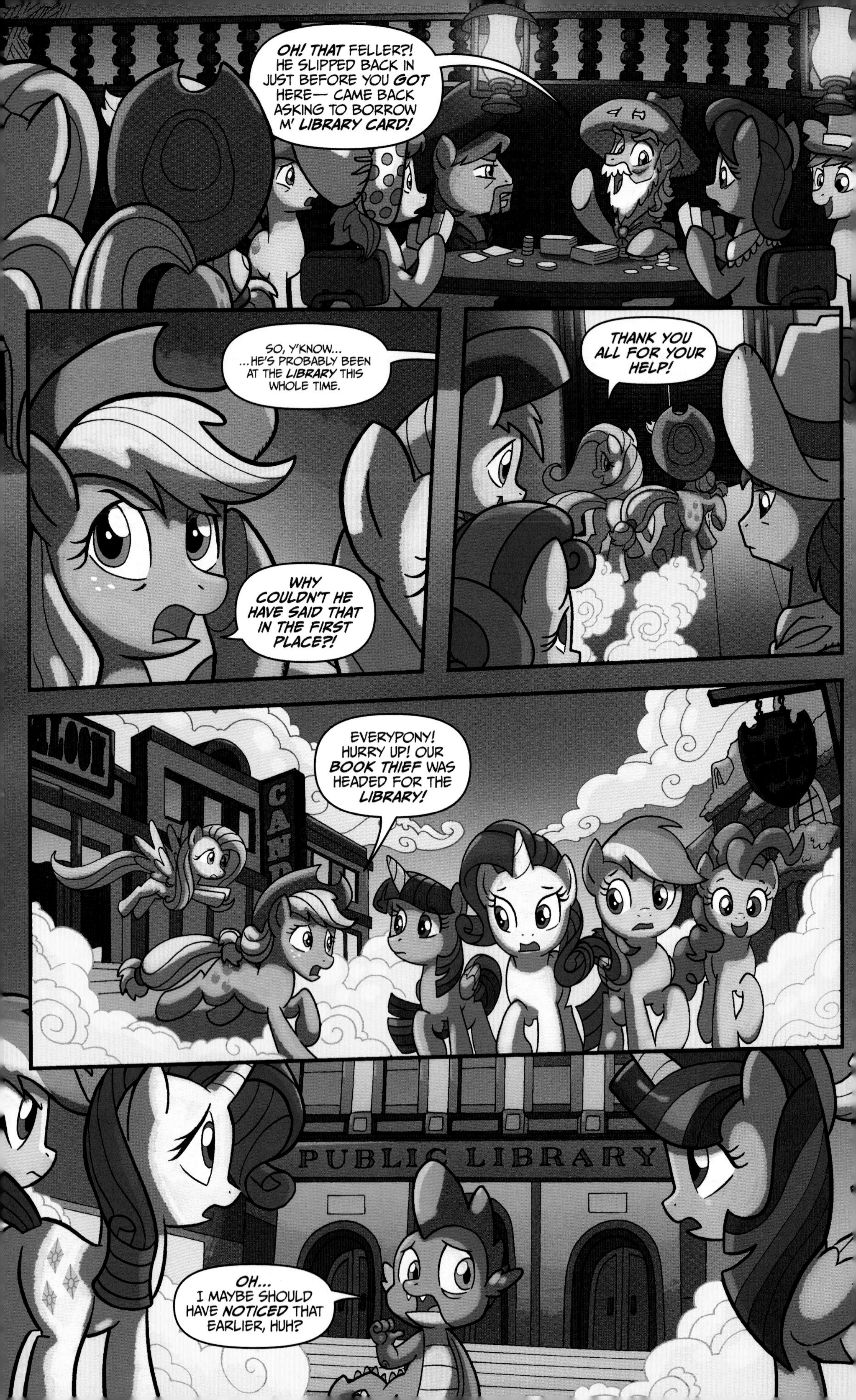
OH! THAT FELLER?! HE SLIPPED BACK IN JUST BEFORE YOU GOT HERE— CAME BACK ASKING TO BORROW M' LIBRARY CARD!
SO, Y'KNOW... ...HE'S PROBABLY BEEN AT THE LIBRARY THIS WHOLE TIME.
WHY COULDN'T HE HAVE SAID THAT IN THE FIRST PLACE?!
THANK YOU ALL FOR YOUR HELP!
EVERYPONY! HURRY UP! OUR BOOK THIEF WAS HEADED FOR THE LIBRARY!
PUBLIC LIBRARY
OH... I MAYBE SHOULD HAVE NOTICED THAT EARLIER, HUH?

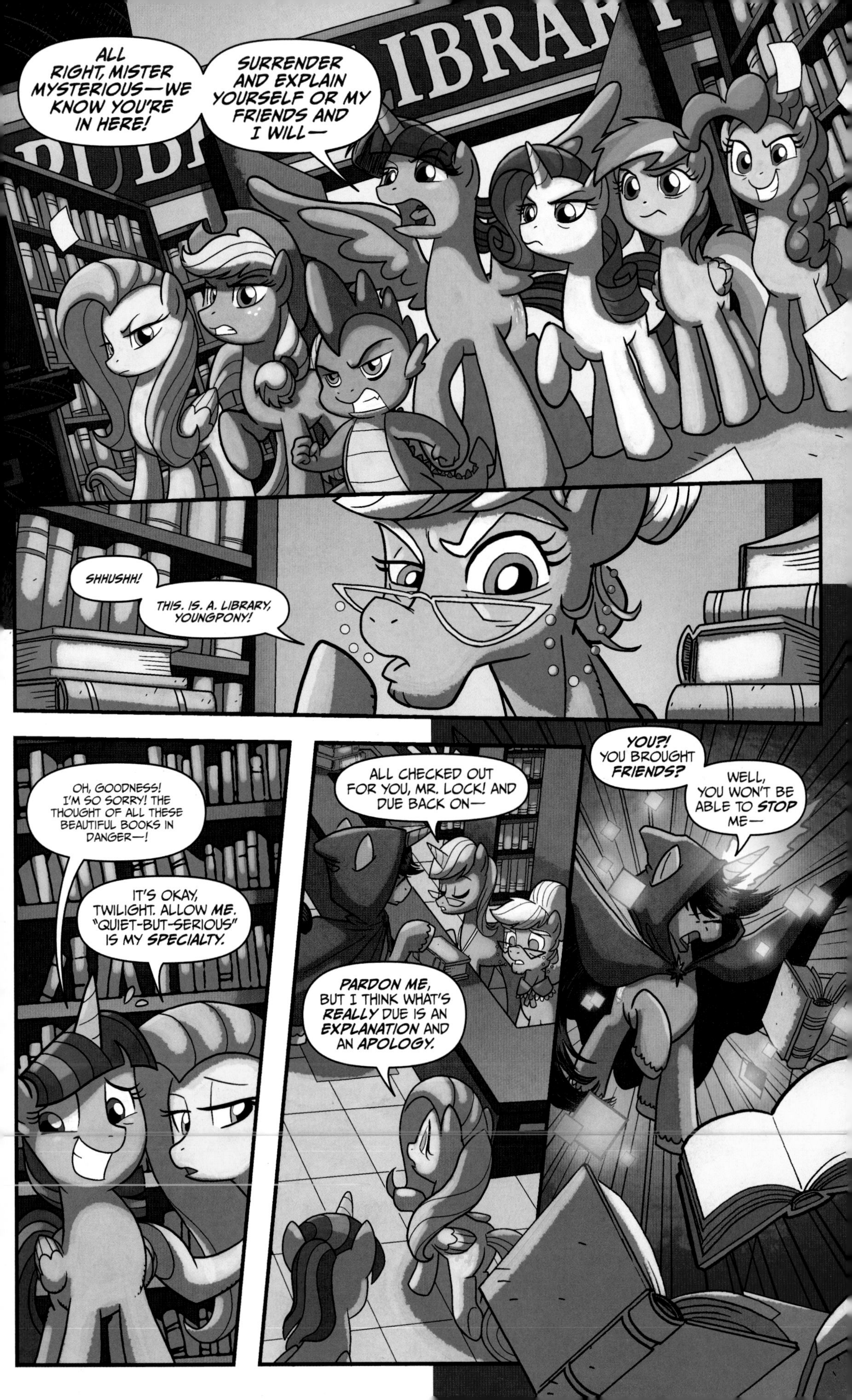
LIBRARY
ALL RIGHT, MISTER MYSTERIOUS—WE KNOW YOU'RE IN HERE!
SURRENDER AND EXPLAIN YOURSELF OR MY FRIENDS AND I WILL—
SHHUSHH!
THIS. IS. A. LIBRARY, YOUNGPONY!
OH, GOODNESS! I'M SO SORRY! THE THOUGHT OF ALL THESE BEAUTIFUL BOOKS IN DANGER—!
IT'S OKAY, TWILIGHT. ALLOW ME. "QUIET-BUT-SERIOUS" IS MY SPECIALTY.
ALL CHECKED OUT FOR YOU, MR. LOCK! AND DUE BACK ON—
PARDON ME, BUT I THINK WHAT'S REALLY DUE IS AN EXPLANATION AND AN APOLOGY.
YOU?! YOU BROUGHT FRIENDS?
WELL, YOU WON'T BE ABLE TO STOP ME—

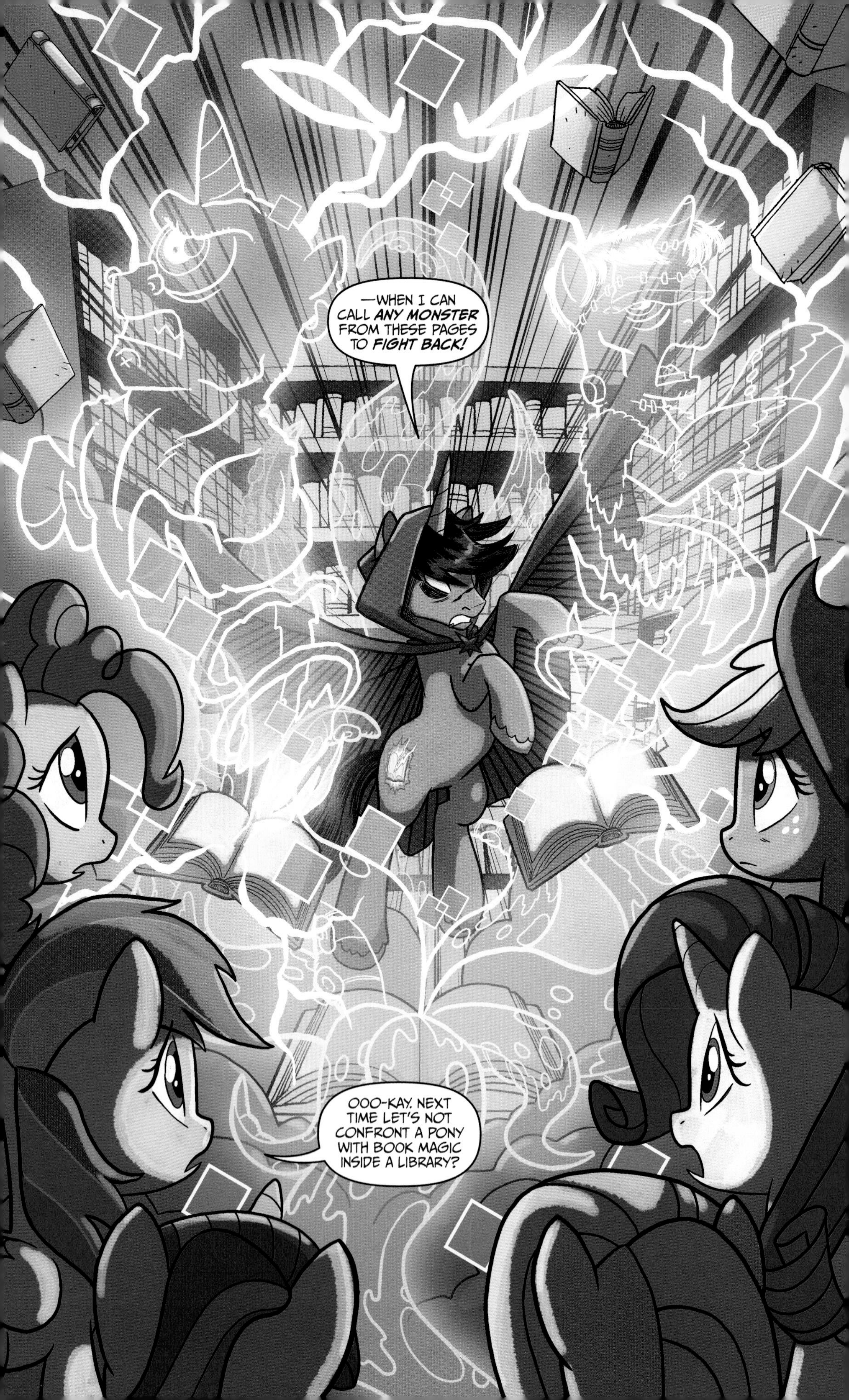
—WHEN I CAN CALL ANY MONSTER FROM THESE PAGES TO FIGHT BACK!
OOO-KAY. NEXT TIME LET'S NOT CONFRONT A PONY WITH BOOK MAGIC INSIDE A LIBRARY?

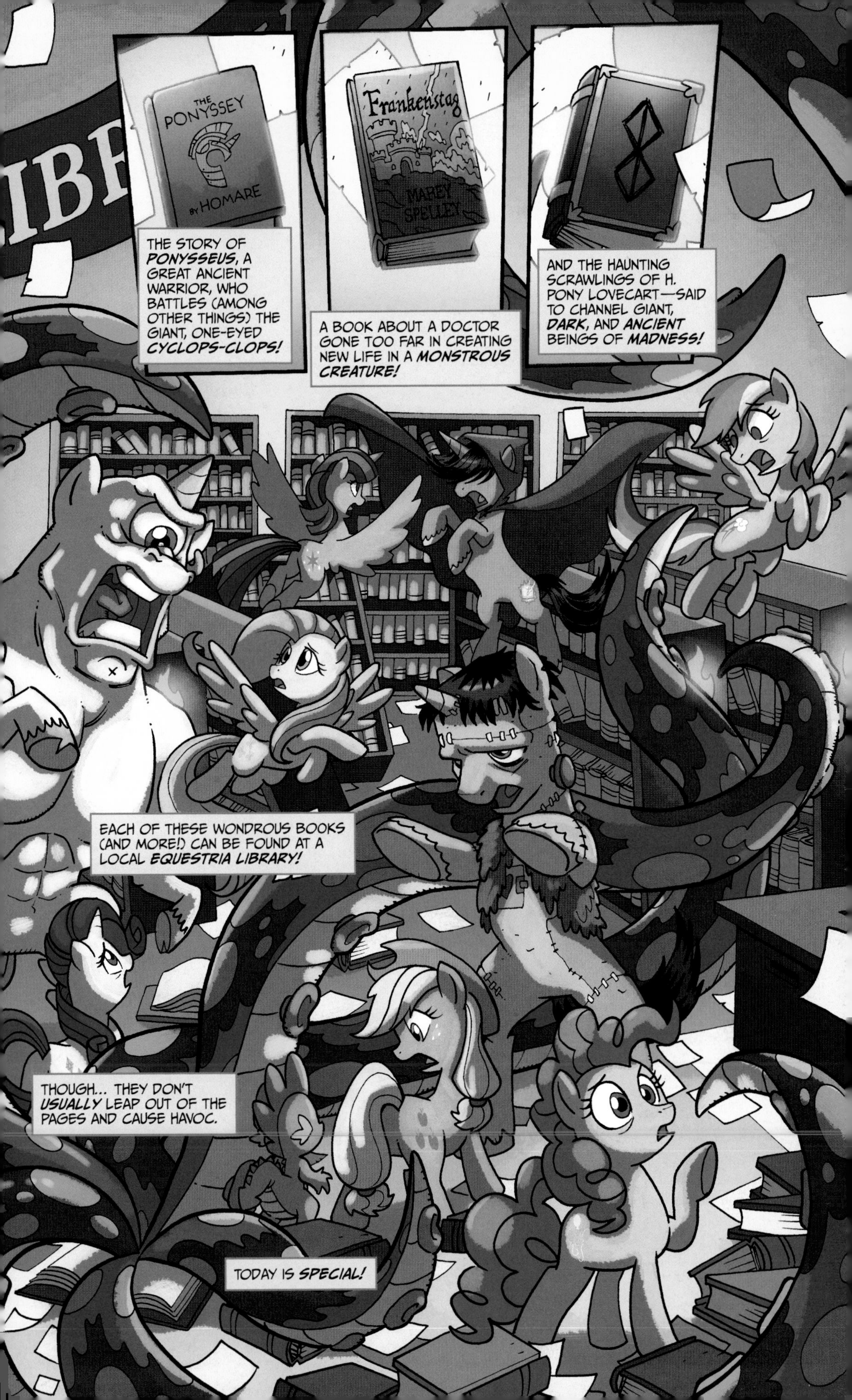
IBR
THE PONYSSEY
BY HOMARE
Frankenstag
MAREY SPELLEY
THE STORY OF PONYSSEUS, A GREAT ANCIENT WARRIOR, WHO BATTLES (AMONG OTHER THINGS) THE GIANT, ONE-EYED CYCLOPS-CLOPS!
A BOOK ABOUT A DOCTOR GONE TOO FAR IN CREATING NEW LIFE IN A MONSTROUS CREATURE!
AND THE HAUNTING SCRAWLINGS OF H. PONY LOVECART—SAID TO CHANNEL GIANT, DARK, AND ANCIENT BEINGS OF MADNESS!
EACH OF THESE WONDROUS BOOKS (AND MORE!) CAN BE FOUND AT A LOCAL EQUESTRIA LIBRARY!
THOUGH... THEY DON'T USUALLY LEAP OUT OF THE PAGES AND CAUSE HAVOC.
TODAY IS SPECIAL!

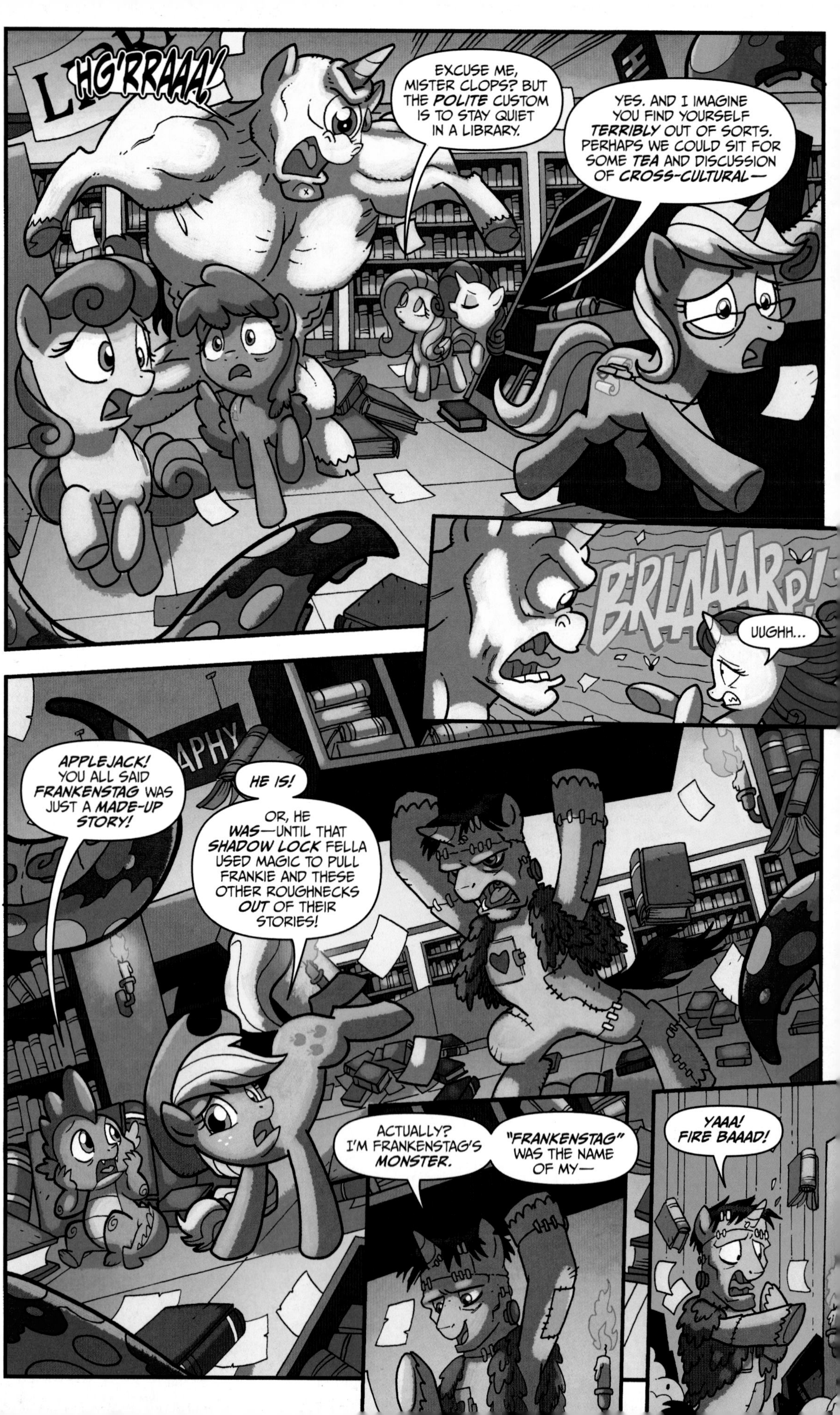

HG'RRAAA!
EXCUSE ME, MISTER CLOPS? BUT THE POLITE CUSTOM IS TO STAY QUIET IN A LIBRARY.
YES. AND I IMAGINE YOU FIND YOURSELF TERRIBLY OUT OF SORTS. PERHAPS WE COULD SIT FOR SOME TEA AND DISCUSSION OF CROSS-CULTURAL—
BRLAAARP!
UUGHH...
APHY
APPLEJACK! YOU ALL SAID FRANKENSTAG WAS JUST A MADE-UP STORY!
HE IS!
OR, HE WAS—UNTIL THAT SHADOW LOCK FELLA USED MAGIC TO PULL FRANKIE AND THESE OTHER ROUGHNECKS OUT OF THEIR STORIES!
ACTUALLY? I'M FRANKENSTAG'S MONSTER.
"FRANKENSTAG" WAS THE NAME OF MY—
YAAA! FIRE BAAAD!

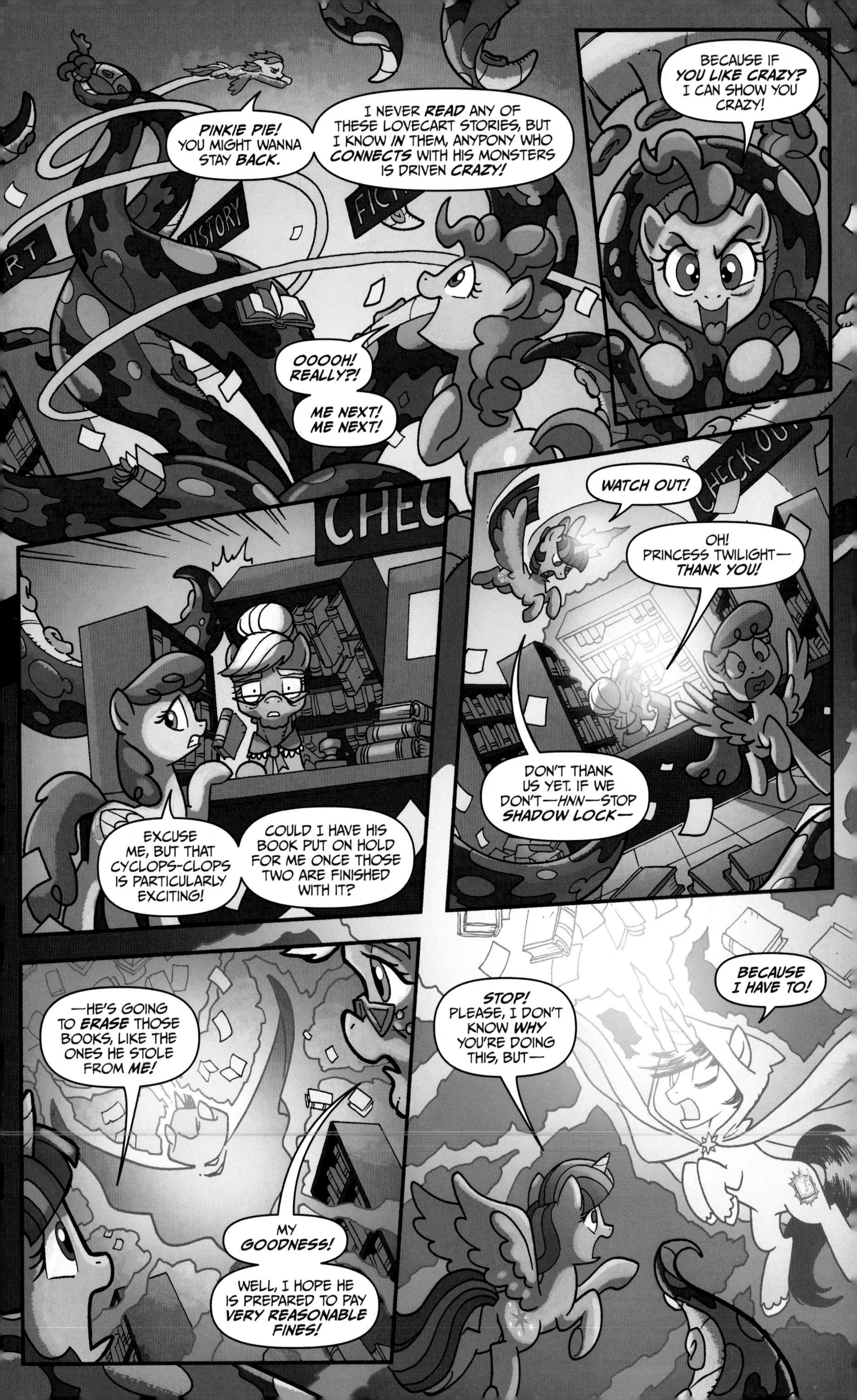

PINKIE PIE! YOU MIGHT WANNA STAY BACK.
I NEVER READ ANY OF THESE LOVECART STORIES, BUT I KNOW IN THEM, ANYPONY WHO CONNECTS WITH HIS MONSTERS IS DRIVEN CRAZY!
ART
HISTORY
OOOOH! REALLY?!
ME NEXT! ME NEXT!
BECAUSE IF YOU LIKE CRAZY? I CAN SHOW YOU CRAZY!
CHEC
EXCUSE ME, BUT THAT CYCLOPS-CLOPS IS PARTICULARLY EXCITING!
COULD I HAVE HIS BOOK PUT ON HOLD FOR ME ONCE THOSE TWO ARE FINISHED WITH IT?
CHECK OUT
WATCH OUT!
OH! PRINCESS TWILIGHT— THANK YOU!
DON'T THANK US YET. IF WE DON'T—HNN—STOP SHADOW LOCK—
—HE'S GOING TO ERASE THOSE BOOKS, LIKE THE ONES HE STOLE FROM ME!
MY GOODNESS!
WELL, I HOPE HE IS PREPARED TO PAY VERY REASONABLE FINES!
STOP! PLEASE, I DON'T KNOW WHY YOU'RE DOING THIS, BUT—
BECAUSE I HAVE TO!

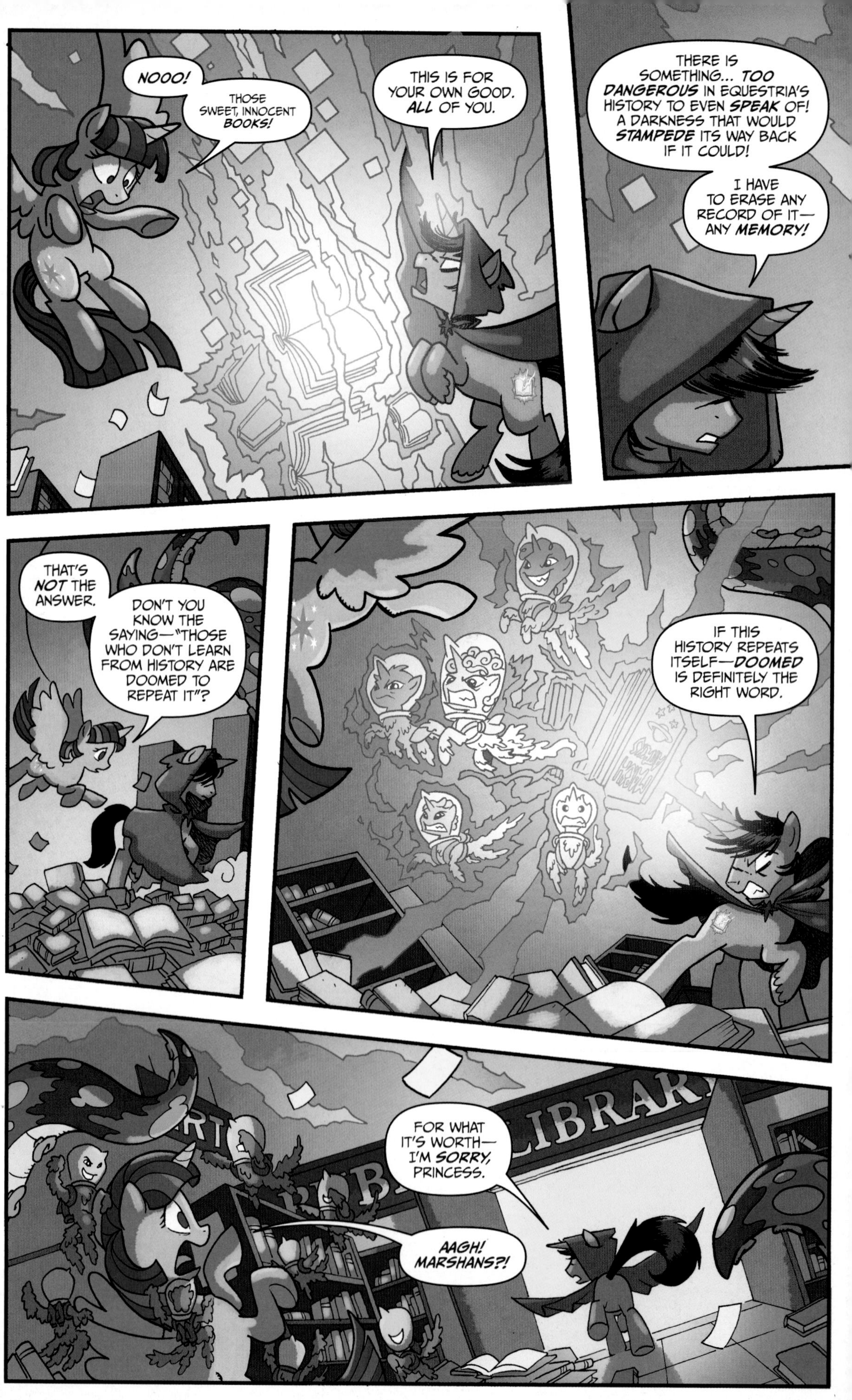
NOOO!
THOSE SWEET, INNOCENT BOOKS!
THIS IS FOR YOUR OWN GOOD. ALL OF YOU.
THERE IS SOMETHING... TOO DANGEROUS IN EQUESTRIA'S HISTORY TO EVEN SPEAK OF! A DARKNESS THAT WOULD STAMPEDE ITS WAY BACK IF IT COULD!
I HAVE TO ERASE ANY RECORD OF IT— ANY MEMORY!
THAT'S NOT THE ANSWER.
DON'T YOU KNOW THE SAYING—"THOSE WHO DON'T LEARN FROM HISTORY ARE DOOMED TO REPEAT IT"?
IF THIS HISTORY REPEATS ITSELF—DOOMED IS DEFINITELY THE RIGHT WORD.
FOR WHAT IT'S WORTH— I'M SORRY, PRINCESS.
AAGH! MARSHANS?!

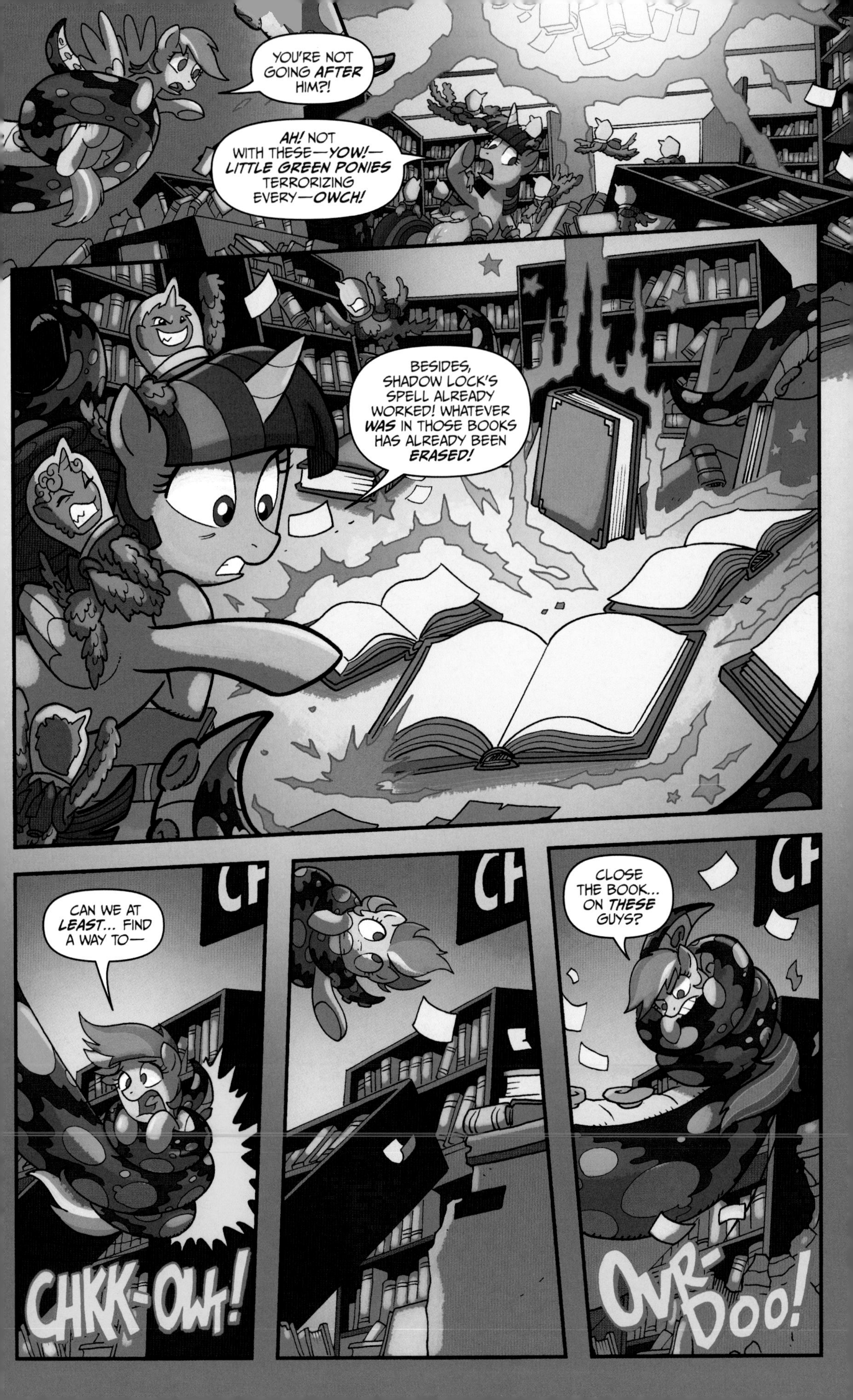

YOU'RE NOT GOING AFTER HIM?!
AH! NOT WITH THESE—YOW!—LITTLE GREEN PONIES TERRORIZING EVERY—OWCH!
BESIDES, SHADOW LOCK'S SPELL ALREADY WORKED! WHATEVER WAS IN THOSE BOOKS HAS ALREADY BEEN ERASED!
CAN WE AT LEAST... FIND A WAY TO—
CHKK-OWK!
CLOSE THE BOOK... ON THESE GUYS?
OVR-DOO!

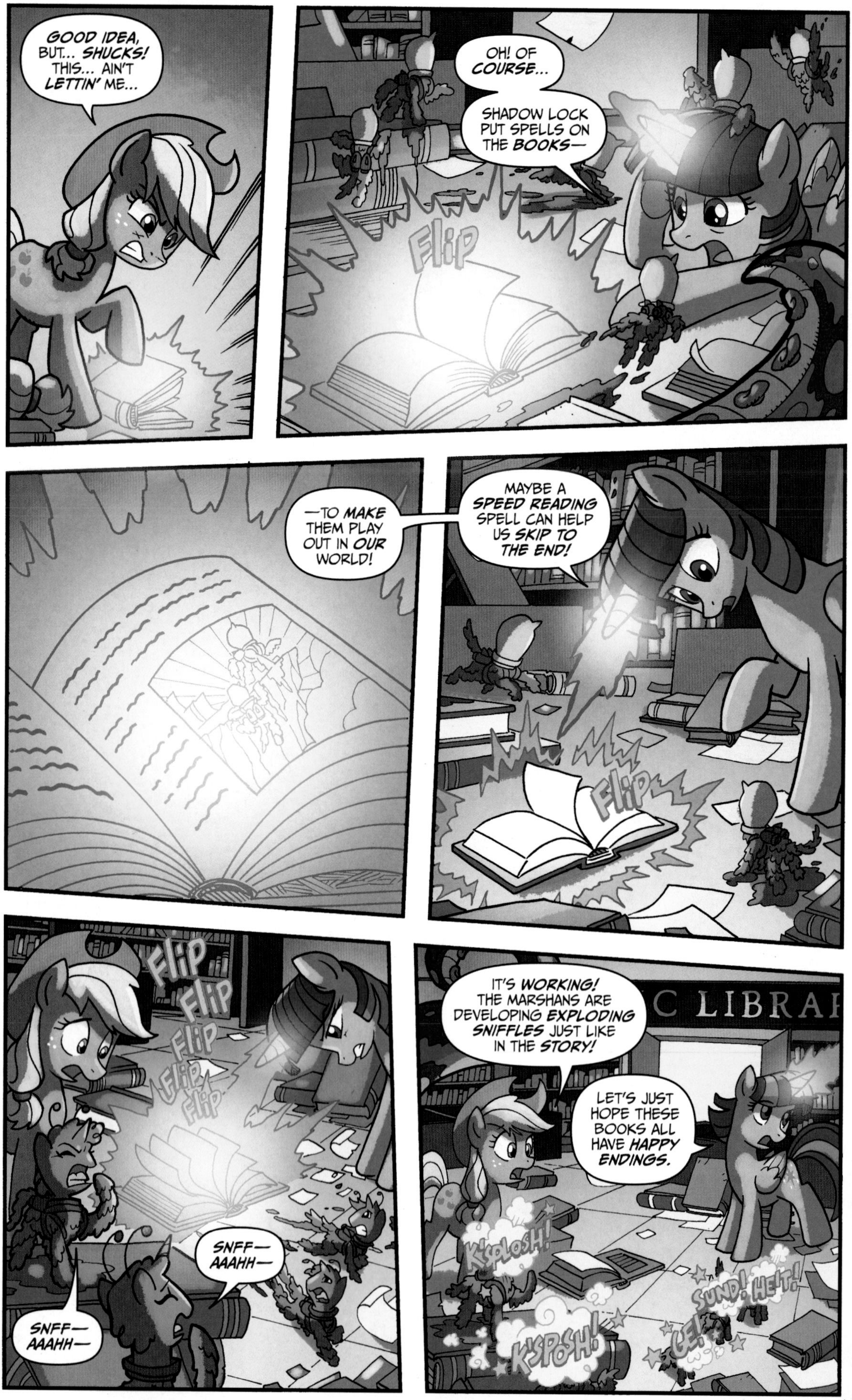
GOOD IDEA, BUT... SHUCKS! THIS... AIN'T LETTIN' ME...
OH! OF COURSE...
SHADOW LOCK PUT SPELLS ON THE BOOKS—
FLIP
—TO MAKE THEM PLAY OUT IN OUR WORLD!
MAYBE A SPEED READING SPELL CAN HELP US SKIP TO THE END!
FLIP
FLIP
FLIP
FLIP
FLIP
FLIP
SNFF— AAAHH—
SNFF— AAAHH—
IT'S WORKING! THE MARSHANS ARE DEVELOPING EXPLODING SNIFFLES JUST LIKE IN THE STORY!
C LIBRAR
LET'S JUST HOPE THESE BOOKS ALL HAVE HAPPY ENDINGS.
K'SPLOSH!
K'SPOSH!
GE!
SUND!
HEIT!

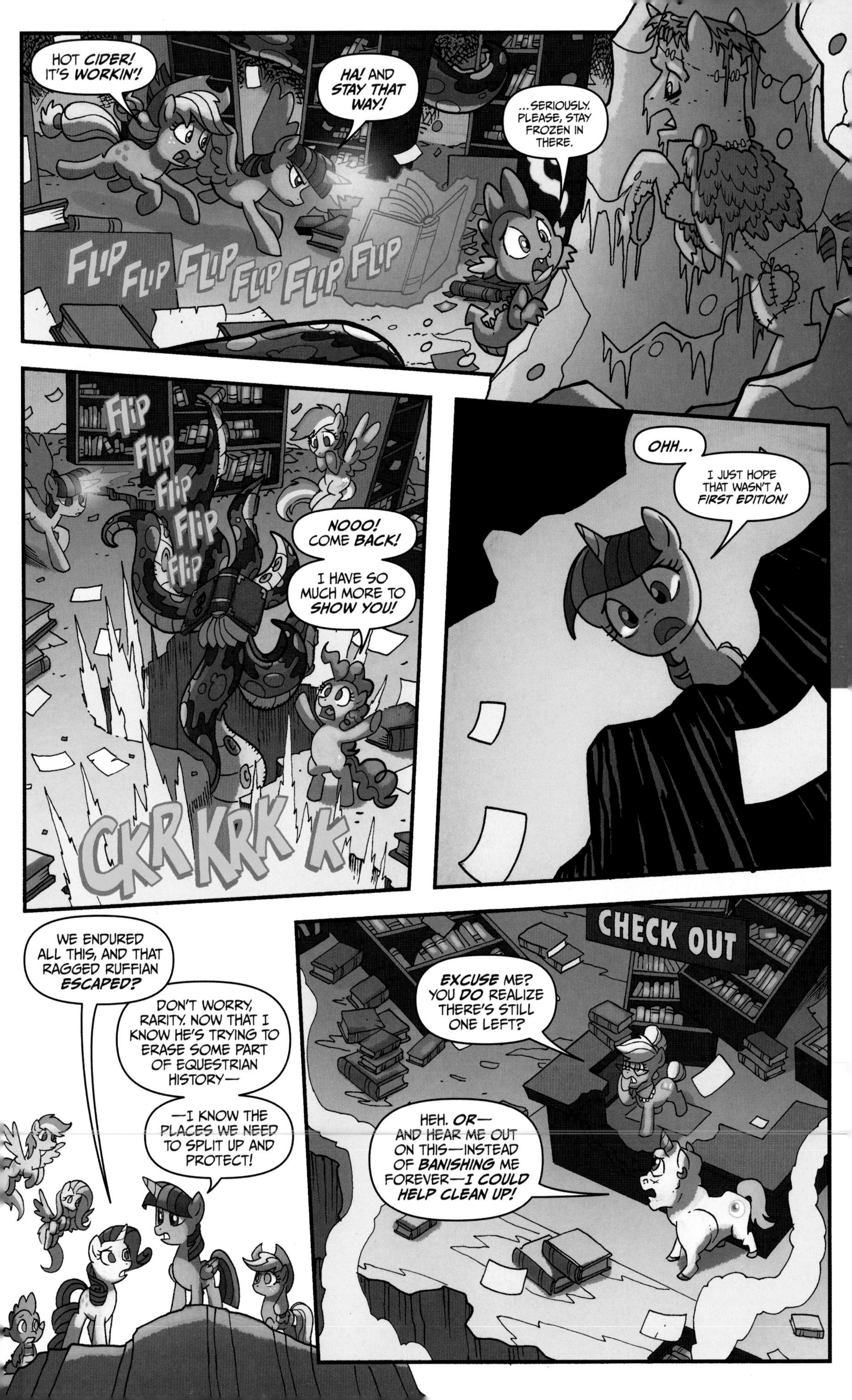
HOT CIDER! IT'S WORKIN'!
HA! AND STAY THAT WAY!
...SERIOUSLY. PLEASE, STAY FROZEN IN THERE.
FLIP FLIP FLIP FLIP FLIP FLIP
FLIP FLIP FLIP FLIP FLIP
NOOO! COME BACK!
I HAVE SO MUCH MORE TO SHOW YOU!
CKR KRK K
OHH...
I JUST HOPE THAT WASN'T A FIRST EDITION!
WE ENDURED ALL THIS, AND THAT RAGGED RUFFIAN ESCAPED?
DON'T WORRY, RARITY. NOW THAT I KNOW HE'S TRYING TO ERASE SOME PART OF EQUESTRIAN HISTORY—
—I KNOW THE PLACES WE NEED TO SPLIT UP AND PROTECT!
CHECK OUT
EXCUSE ME? YOU DO REALIZE THERE'S STILL ONE LEFT?
HEH. OR— AND HEAR ME OUT ON THIS—INSTEAD OF BANISHING ME FOREVER—I COULD HELP CLEAN UP!

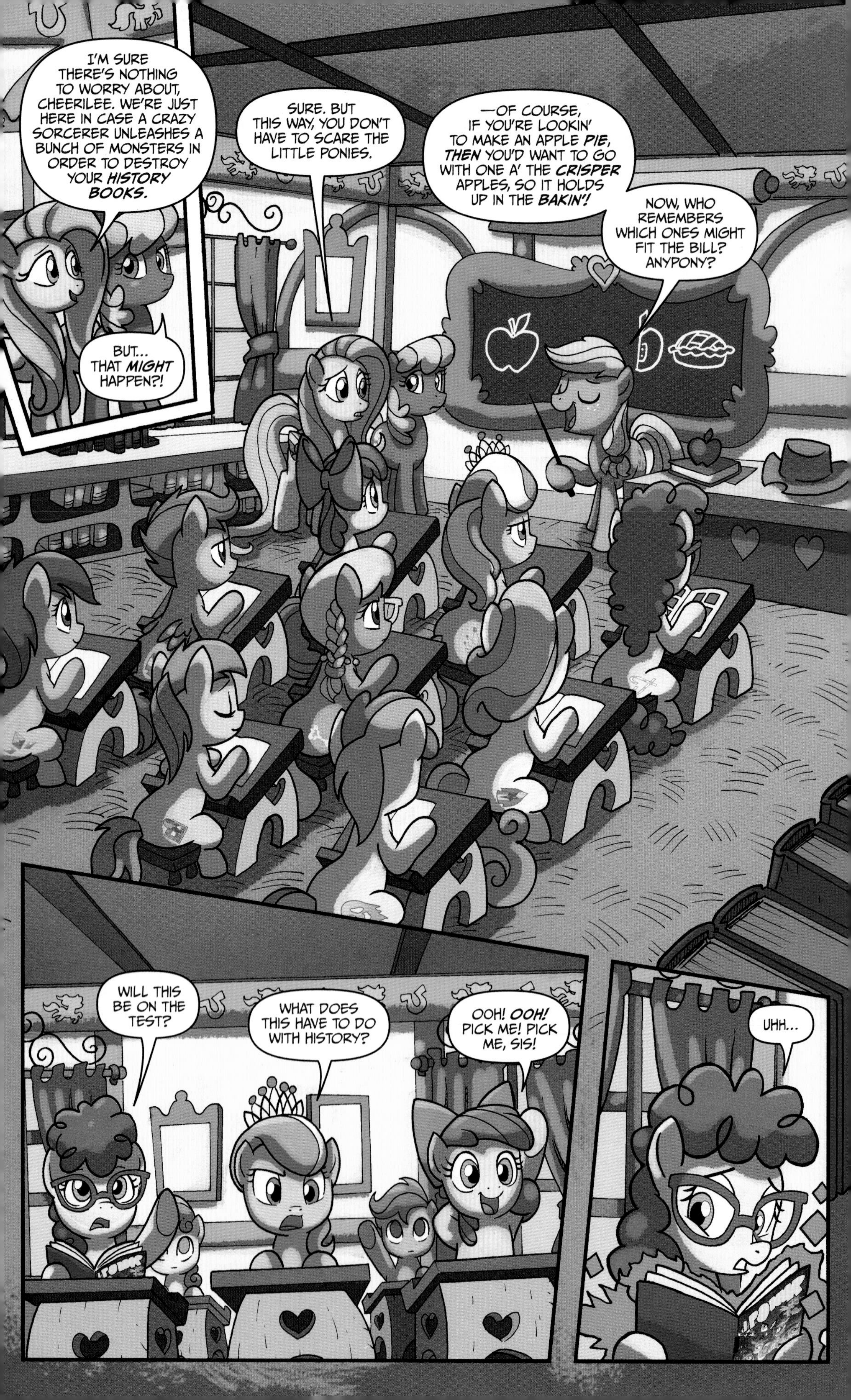
I'M SURE THERE'S NOTHING TO WORRY ABOUT, CHEERILEE. WE'RE JUST HERE IN CASE A CRAZY SORCERER UNLEASHES A BUNCH OF MONSTERS IN ORDER TO DESTROY YOUR *HISTORY BOOKS.*
BUT... THAT *MIGHT* HAPPEN?!
SURE. BUT THIS WAY, YOU DON'T HAVE TO SCARE THE LITTLE PONIES.
—OF COURSE, IF YOU'RE LOOKIN' TO MAKE AN APPLE *PIE, THEN* YOU'D WANT TO GO WITH ONE A' THE *CRISPER* APPLES, SO IT HOLDS UP IN THE *BAKIN'!*
NOW, WHO REMEMBERS WHICH ONES MIGHT FIT THE BILL? ANYPONY?
WILL THIS BE ON THE TEST?
WHAT DOES THIS HAVE TO DO WITH HISTORY?
OOH! *OOH!* PICK ME! PICK ME, SIS!
UHH...

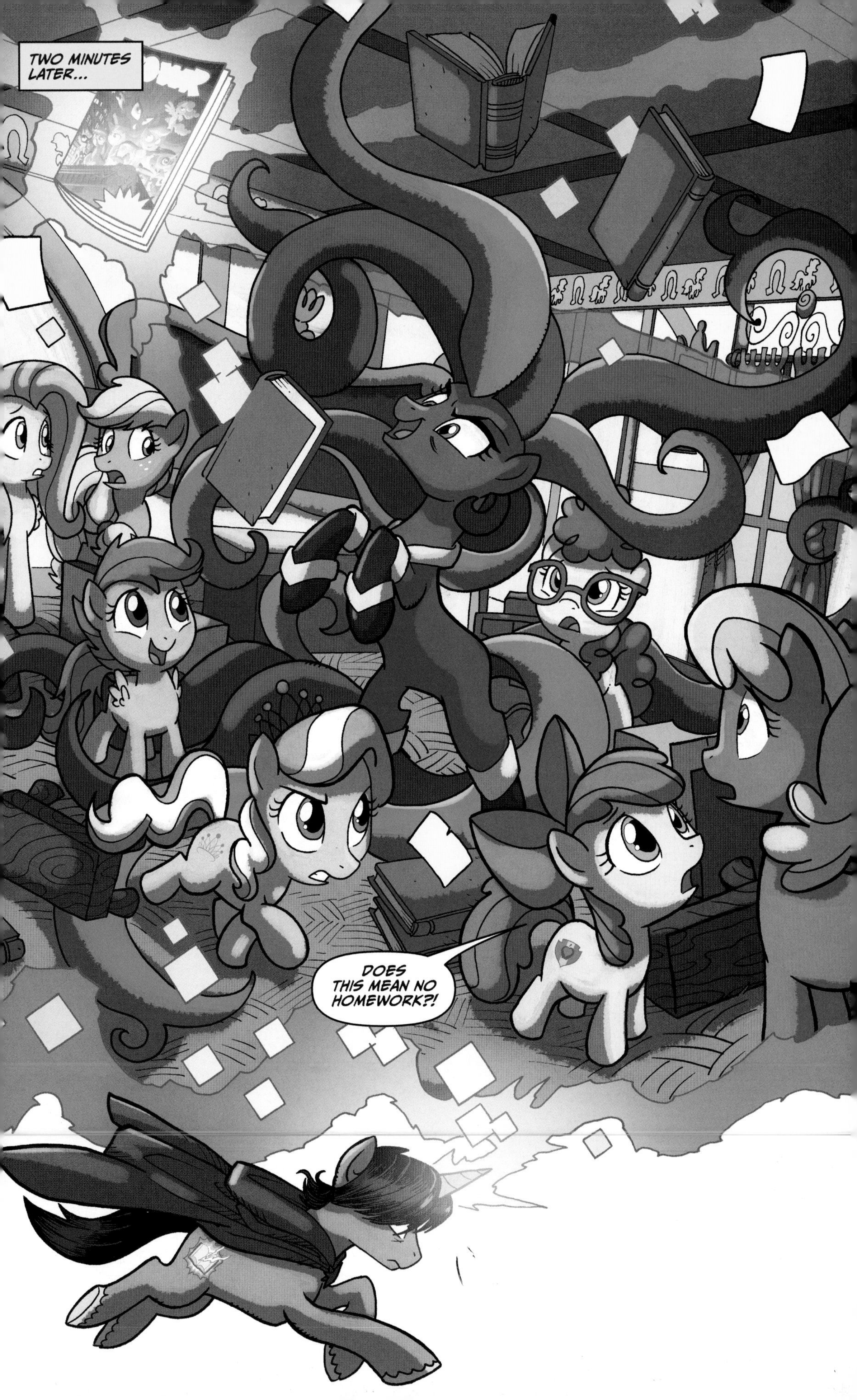
TWO MINUTES LATER...
DOES THIS MEAN NO HOMEWORK?!

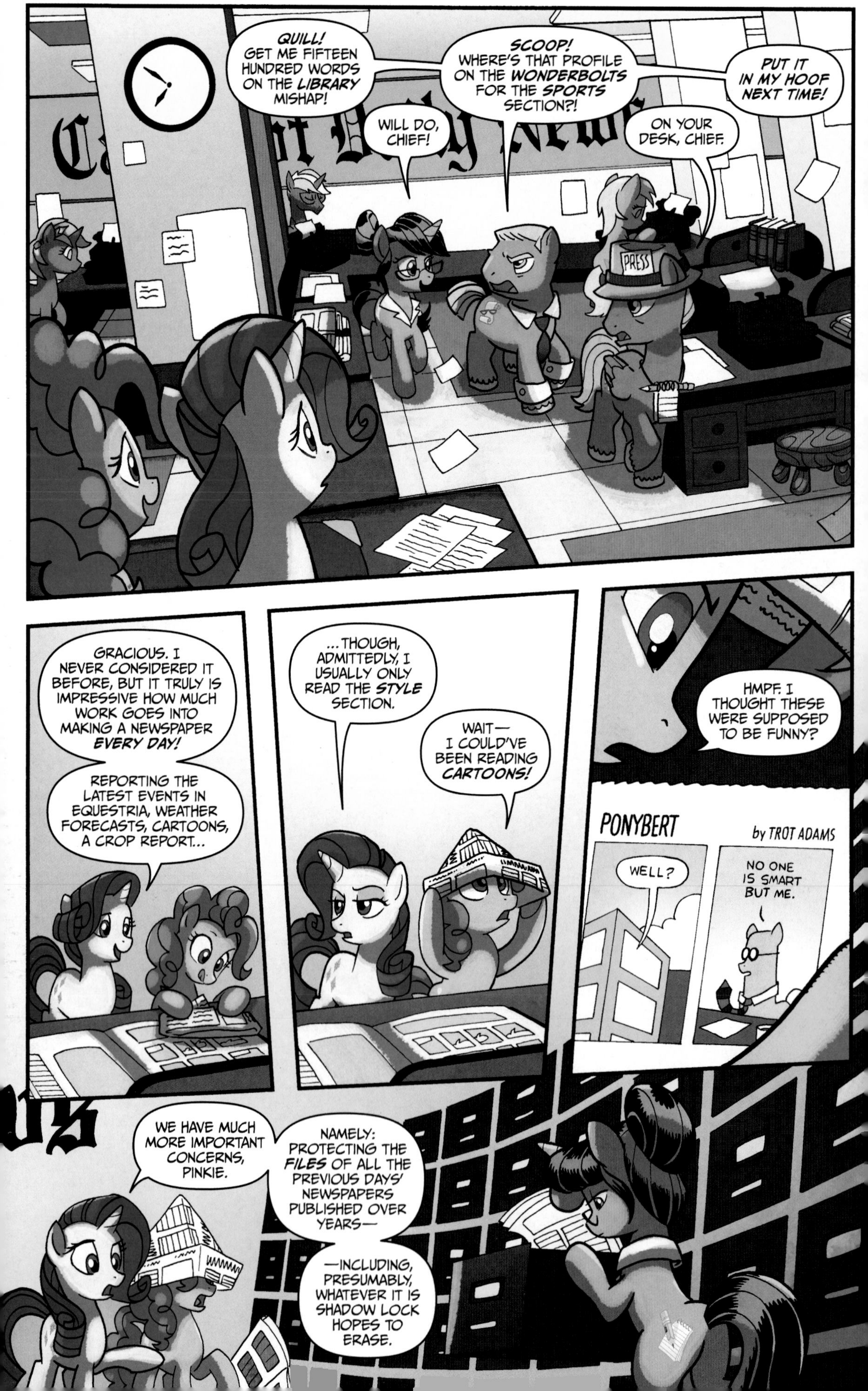
QUILL! GET ME FIFTEEN HUNDRED WORDS ON THE LIBRARY MISHAP!
WILL DO, CHIEF!
SCOOP! WHERE'S THAT PROFILE ON THE WONDERBOLTS FOR THE SPORTS SECTION?!
ON YOUR DESK, CHIEF.
PUT IT IN MY HOOF NEXT TIME!
PRESS
GRACIOUS. I NEVER CONSIDERED IT BEFORE, BUT IT TRULY IS IMPRESSIVE HOW MUCH WORK GOES INTO MAKING A NEWSPAPER EVERY DAY!
REPORTING THE LATEST EVENTS IN EQUESTRIA, WEATHER FORECASTS, CARTOONS, A CROP REPORT...
...THOUGH, ADMITTEDLY, I USUALLY ONLY READ THE STYLE SECTION.
WAIT— I COULD'VE BEEN READING CARTOONS!
HMPF. I THOUGHT THESE WERE SUPPOSED TO BE FUNNY?
PONYBERT
by TROT ADAMS
WELL?
NO ONE IS SMART BUT ME.
WE HAVE MUCH MORE IMPORTANT CONCERNS, PINKIE.
NAMELY: PROTECTING THE FILES OF ALL THE PREVIOUS DAYS' NEWSPAPERS PUBLISHED OVER YEARS—
—INCLUDING, PRESUMABLY, WHATEVER IT IS SHADOW LOCK HOPES TO ERASE.

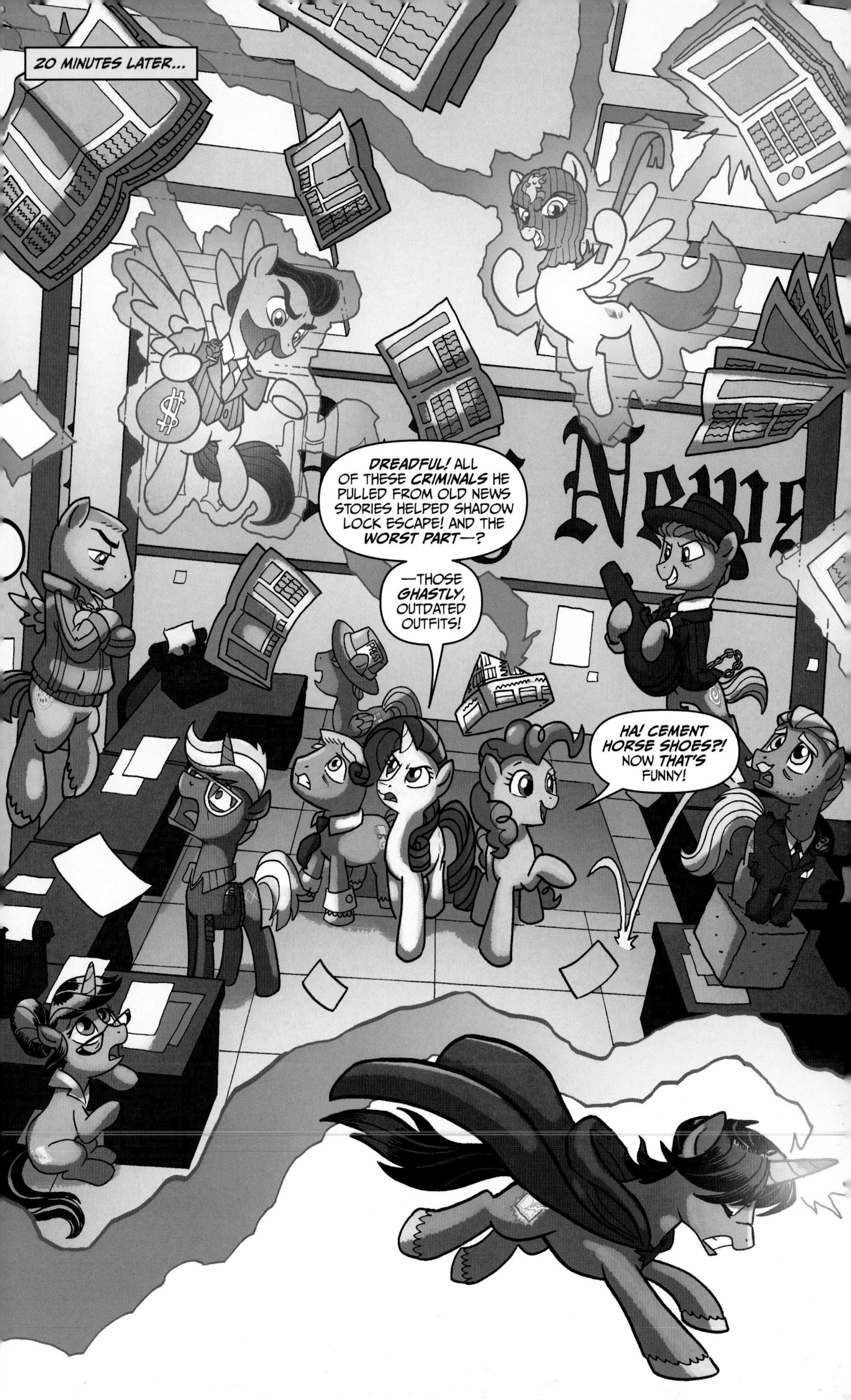
20 MINUTES LATER...
DREADFUL! ALL OF THESE CRIMINALS HE PULLED FROM OLD NEWS STORIES HELPED SHADOW LOCK ESCAPE! AND THE WORST PART—?
—THOSE GHASTLY, OUTDATED OUTFITS!
HA! CEMENT HORSE SHOES?! NOW THAT'S FUNNY!

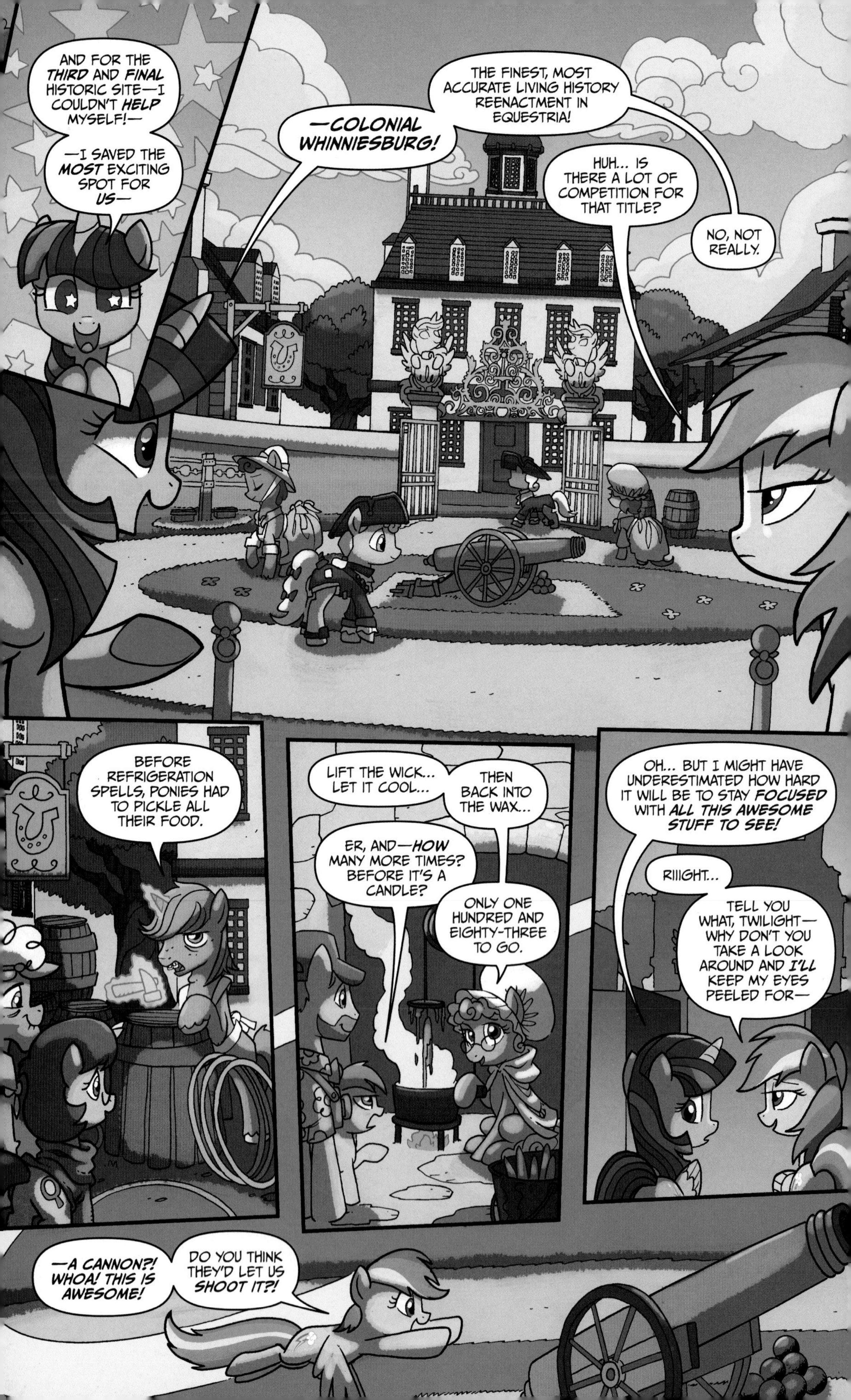

AND FOR THE THIRD AND FINAL HISTORIC SITE—I COULDN'T HELP MYSELF!—
—I SAVED THE MOST EXCITING SPOT FOR US—
—COLONIAL WHINNIESBURG!
THE FINEST, MOST ACCURATE LIVING HISTORY REENACTMENT IN EQUESTRIA!
HUH... IS THERE A LOT OF COMPETITION FOR THAT TITLE?
NO, NOT REALLY.
BEFORE REFRIGERATION SPELLS, PONIES HAD TO PICKLE ALL THEIR FOOD.
LIFT THE WICK... LET IT COOL...
THEN BACK INTO THE WAX...
ER, AND—HOW MANY MORE TIMES? BEFORE IT'S A CANDLE?
ONLY ONE HUNDRED AND EIGHTY-THREE TO GO.
OH... BUT I MIGHT HAVE UNDERESTIMATED HOW HARD IT WILL BE TO STAY FOCUSED WITH ALL THIS AWESOME STUFF TO SEE!
RIIIGHT...
TELL YOU WHAT, TWILIGHT— WHY DON'T YOU TAKE A LOOK AROUND AND I'LL KEEP MY EYES PEELED FOR—
—A CANNON?! WHOA! THIS IS AWESOME!
DO YOU THINK THEY'D LET US SHOOT IT?!

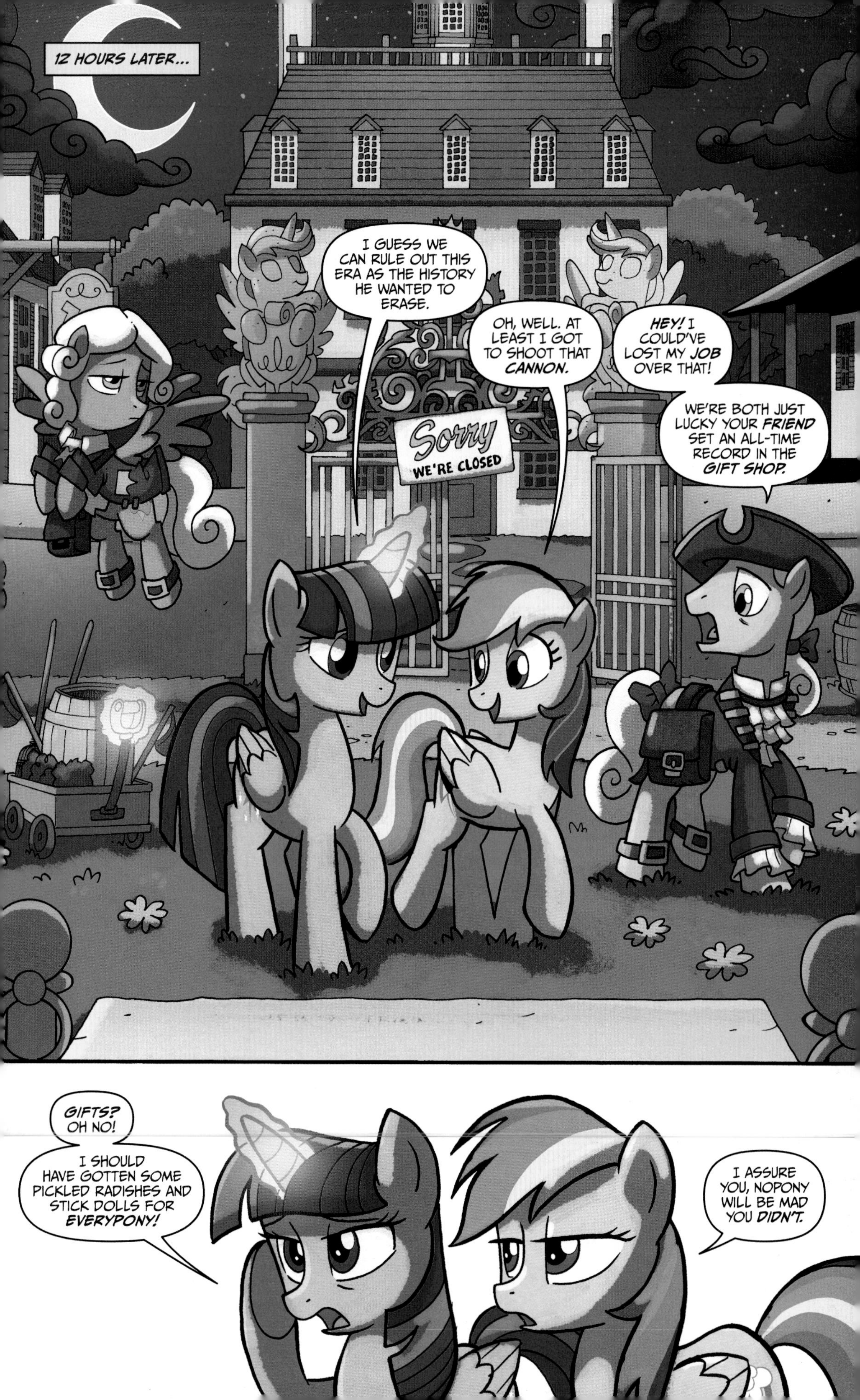
12 HOURS LATER...
I GUESS WE CAN RULE OUT THIS ERA AS THE HISTORY HE WANTED TO ERASE.
OH, WELL. AT LEAST I GOT TO SHOOT THAT CANNON.
HEY! I COULD'VE LOST MY JOB OVER THAT!
WE'RE BOTH JUST LUCKY YOUR FRIEND SET AN ALL-TIME RECORD IN THE GIFT SHOP.
Sorry WE'RE CLOSED
GIFTS? OH NO!
I SHOULD HAVE GOTTEN SOME PICKLED RADISHES AND STICK DOLLS FOR EVERYPONY!
I ASSURE YOU, NOPONY WILL BE MAD YOU DIDN'T.

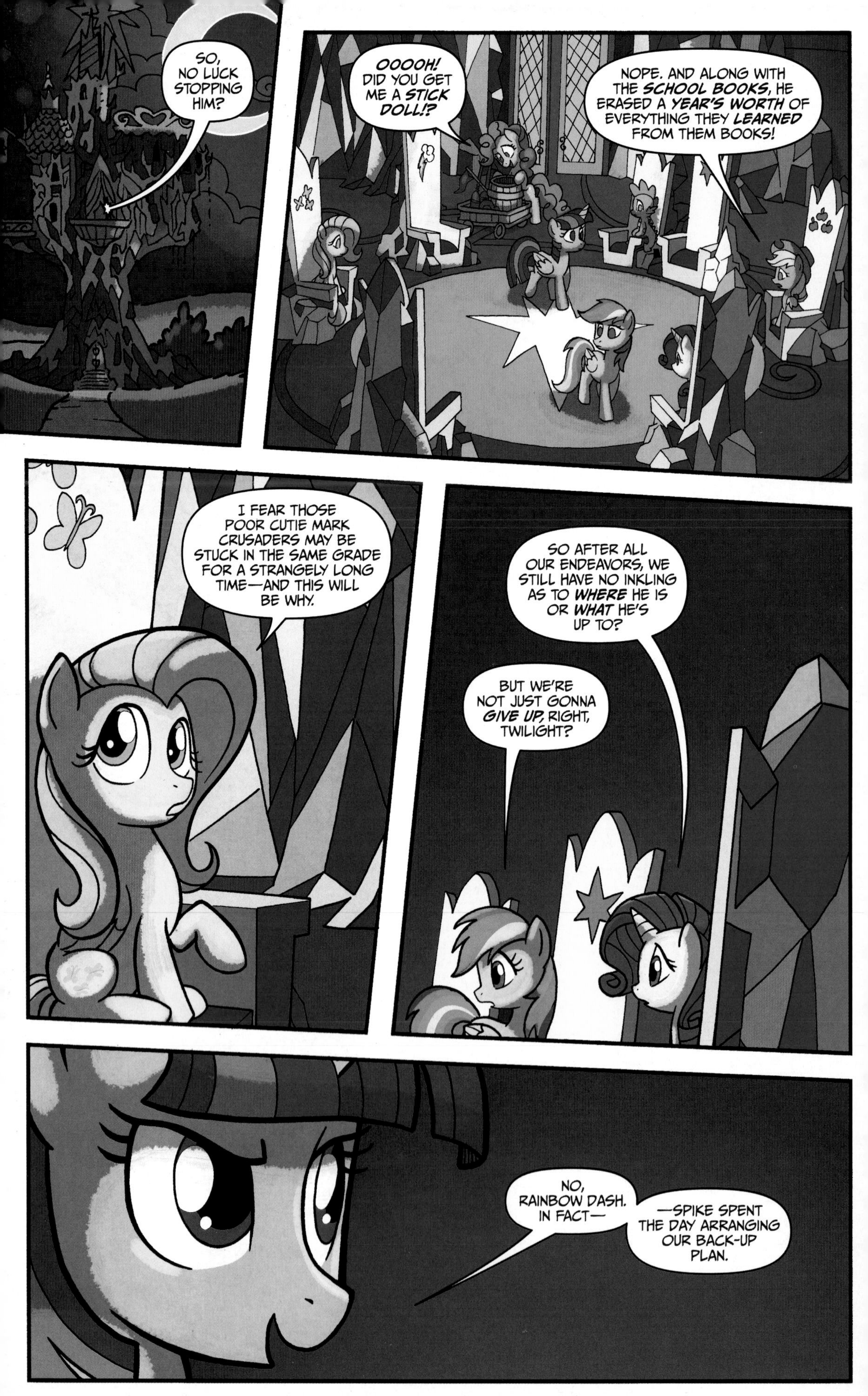
SO, NO LUCK STOPPING HIM?
OOOOH! DID YOU GET ME A STICK DOLL!?
NOPE. AND ALONG WITH THE SCHOOL BOOKS, HE ERASED A YEAR'S WORTH OF EVERYTHING THEY LEARNED FROM THEM BOOKS!
I FEAR THOSE POOR CUTIE MARK CRUSADERS MAY BE STUCK IN THE SAME GRADE FOR A STRANGELY LONG TIME—AND THIS WILL BE WHY.
SO AFTER ALL OUR ENDEAVORS, WE STILL HAVE NO INKLING AS TO WHERE HE IS OR WHAT HE'S UP TO?
BUT WE'RE NOT JUST GONNA GIVE UP, RIGHT, TWILIGHT?
NO, RAINBOW DASH. IN FACT—
—SPIKE SPENT THE DAY ARRANGING OUR BACK-UP PLAN.

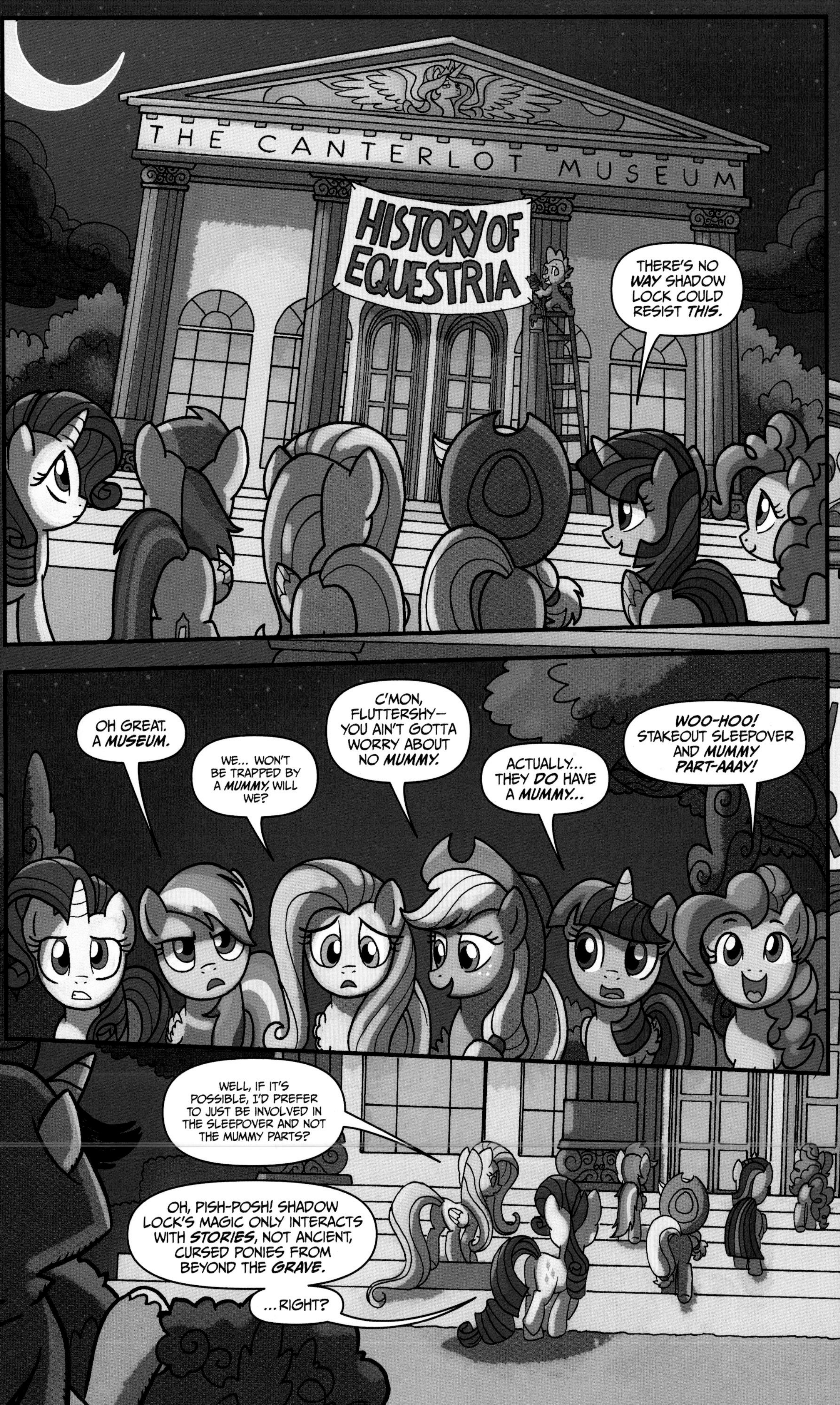
THE CANTERLOT MUSEUM
HISTORY OF EQUESTRIA
THERE'S NO WAY SHADOW LOCK COULD RESIST THIS.
OH GREAT. A MUSEUM.
WE... WON'T BE TRAPPED BY A MUMMY, WILL WE?
C'MON, FLUTTERSHY— YOU AIN'T GOTTA WORRY ABOUT NO MUMMY.
ACTUALLY... THEY DO HAVE A MUMMY...
WOO-HOO! STAKEOUT SLEEPOVER AND MUMMY PART-AAAY!
WELL, IF IT'S POSSIBLE, I'D PREFER TO JUST BE INVOLVED IN THE SLEEPOVER AND NOT THE MUMMY PARTS?
OH, PISH-POSH! SHADOW LOCK'S MAGIC ONLY INTERACTS WITH STORIES, NOT ANCIENT, CURSED PONIES FROM BEYOND THE GRAVE.
...RIGHT?

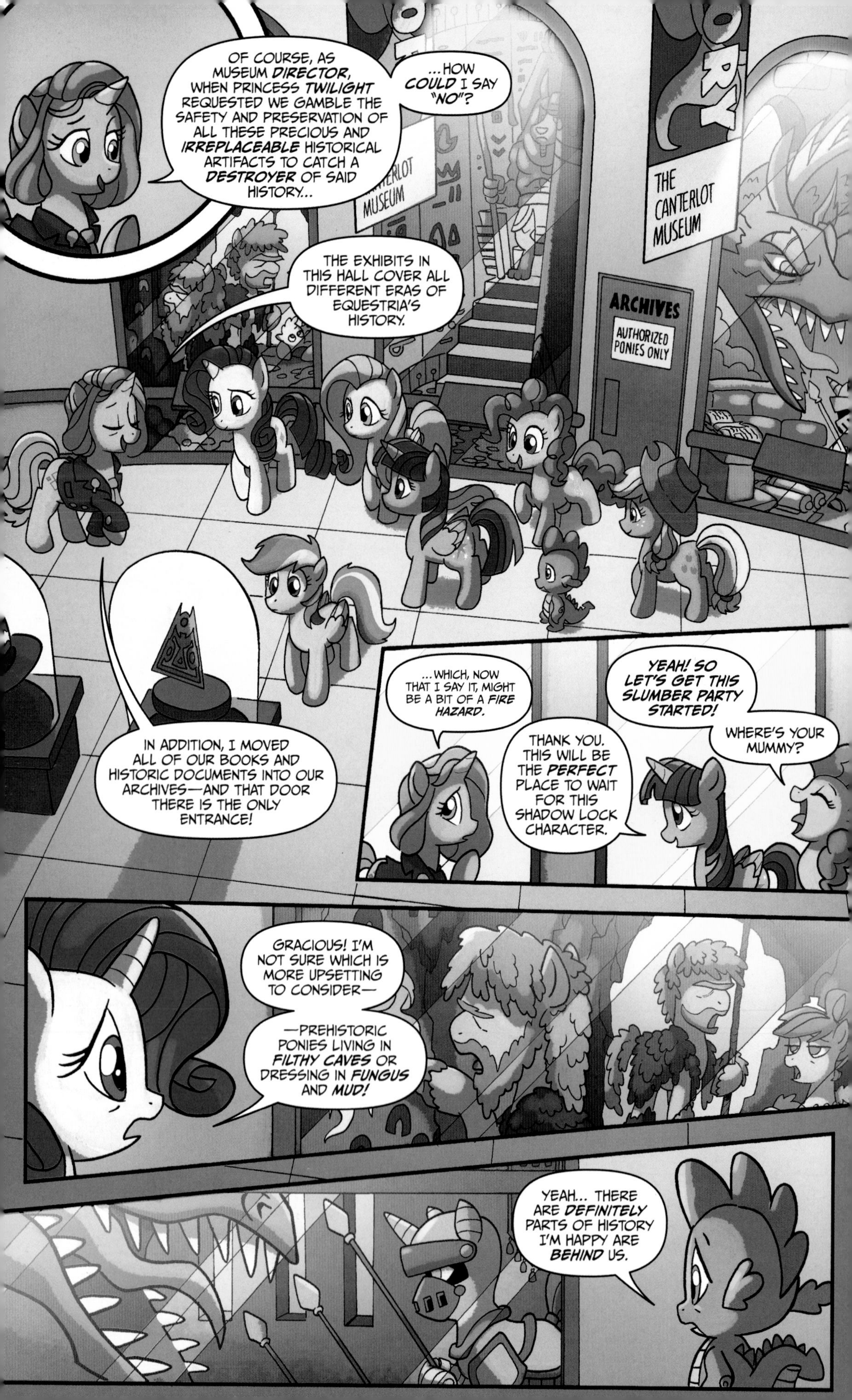
OF COURSE, AS MUSEUM DIRECTOR, WHEN PRINCESS TWILIGHT REQUESTED WE GAMBLE THE SAFETY AND PRESERVATION OF ALL THESE PRECIOUS AND IRREPLACEABLE HISTORICAL ARTIFACTS TO CATCH A DESTROYER OF SAID HISTORY...
...HOW COULD I SAY "NO"?
THE CANTERLOT MUSEUM
THE CANTERLOT MUSEUM
THE EXHIBITS IN THIS HALL COVER ALL DIFFERENT ERAS OF EQUESTRIA'S HISTORY.
ARCHIVES
AUTHORIZED PONIES ONLY
IN ADDITION, I MOVED ALL OF OUR BOOKS AND HISTORIC DOCUMENTS INTO OUR ARCHIVES—AND THAT DOOR THERE IS THE ONLY ENTRANCE!
...WHICH, NOW THAT I SAY IT, MIGHT BE A BIT OF A FIRE HAZARD.
THANK YOU. THIS WILL BE THE PERFECT PLACE TO WAIT FOR THIS SHADOW LOCK CHARACTER.
YEAH! SO LET'S GET THIS SLUMBER PARTY STARTED!
WHERE'S YOUR MUMMY?
GRACIOUS! I'M NOT SURE WHICH IS MORE UPSETTING TO CONSIDER—
—PREHISTORIC PONIES LIVING IN FILTHY CAVES OR DRESSING IN FUNGUS AND MUD!
YEAH... THERE ARE DEFINITELY PARTS OF HISTORY I'M HAPPY ARE BEHIND US.

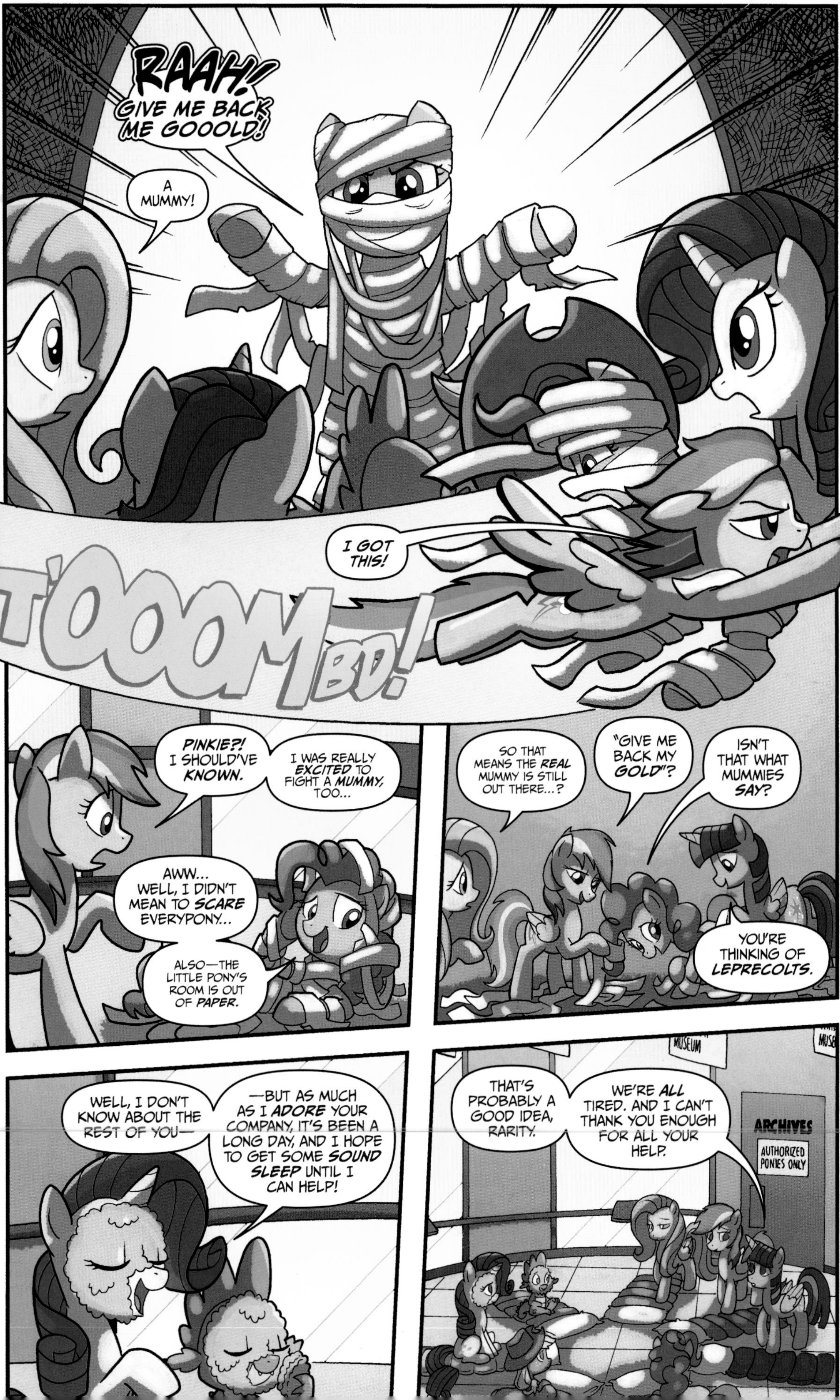
RAAH!! GIVE ME BACK ME GOOOLD!
A MUMMY!
I GOT THIS!
T'OOOMBD!
PINKIE?! I SHOULD'VE KNOWN.
I WAS REALLY EXCITED TO FIGHT A MUMMY, TOO...
AWW... WELL, I DIDN'T MEAN TO SCARE EVERYPONY...
ALSO—THE LITTLE PONY'S ROOM IS OUT OF PAPER.
SO THAT MEANS THE REAL MUMMY IS STILL OUT THERE...?
"GIVE ME BACK MY GOLD"?
ISN'T THAT WHAT MUMMIES SAY?
YOU'RE THINKING OF LEPRECOLTS.
WELL, I DON'T KNOW ABOUT THE REST OF YOU—
—BUT AS MUCH AS I ADORE YOUR COMPANY, IT'S BEEN A LONG DAY, AND I HOPE TO GET SOME SOUND SLEEP UNTIL I CAN HELP!
MUSEUM
THAT'S PROBABLY A GOOD IDEA, RARITY.
WE'RE ALL TIRED. AND I CAN'T THANK YOU ENOUGH FOR ALL YOUR HELP.
ARCHIVES
AUTHORIZED PONIES ONLY

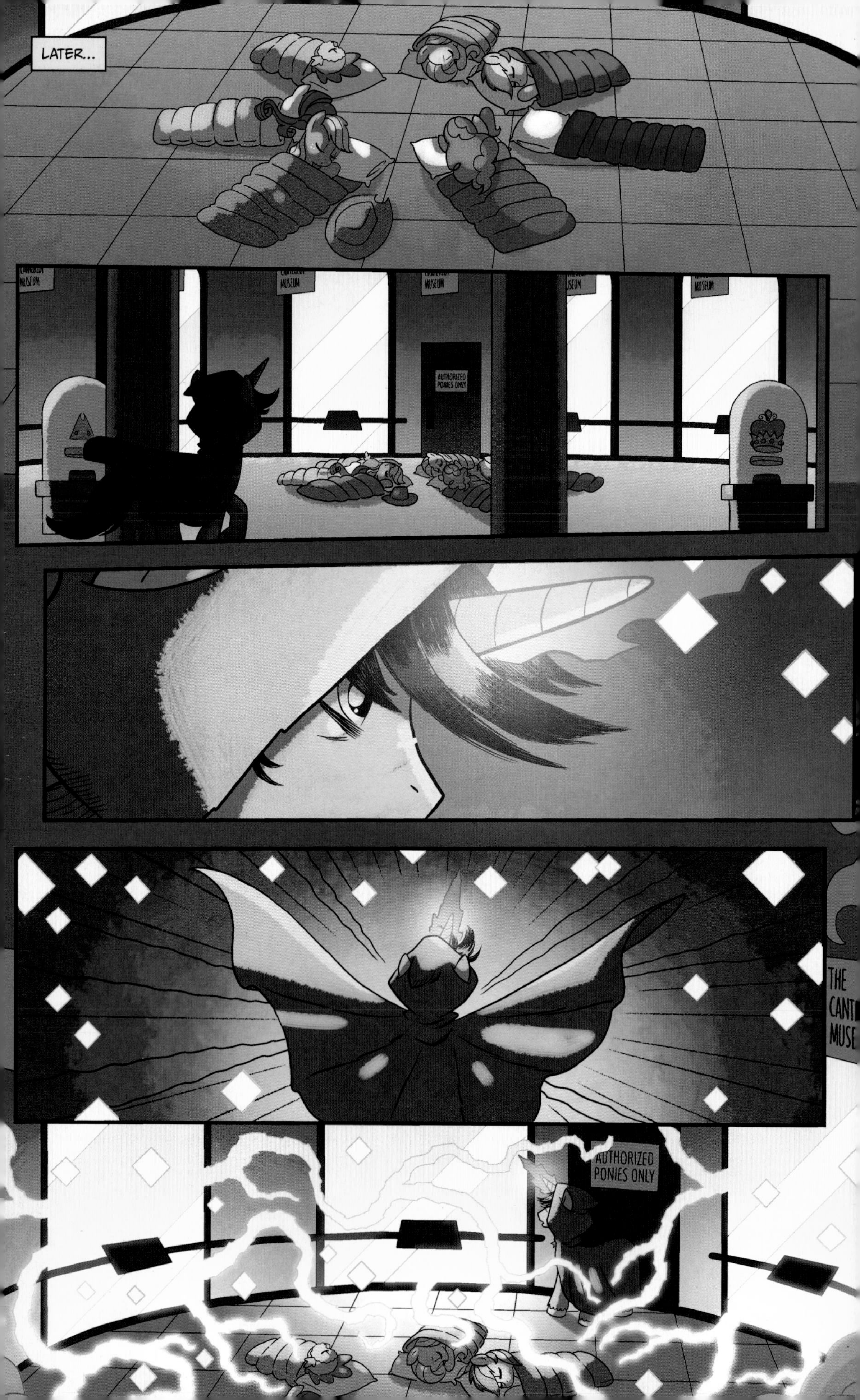
LATER...
CANTERLOT MUSEUM
CANTERLOT MUSEUM
CANTERLOT MUSEUM
CANTERLOT MUSEUM
CANTERLOT MUSEUM
AUTHORIZED PONIES ONLY
AUTHORIZED PONIES ONLY

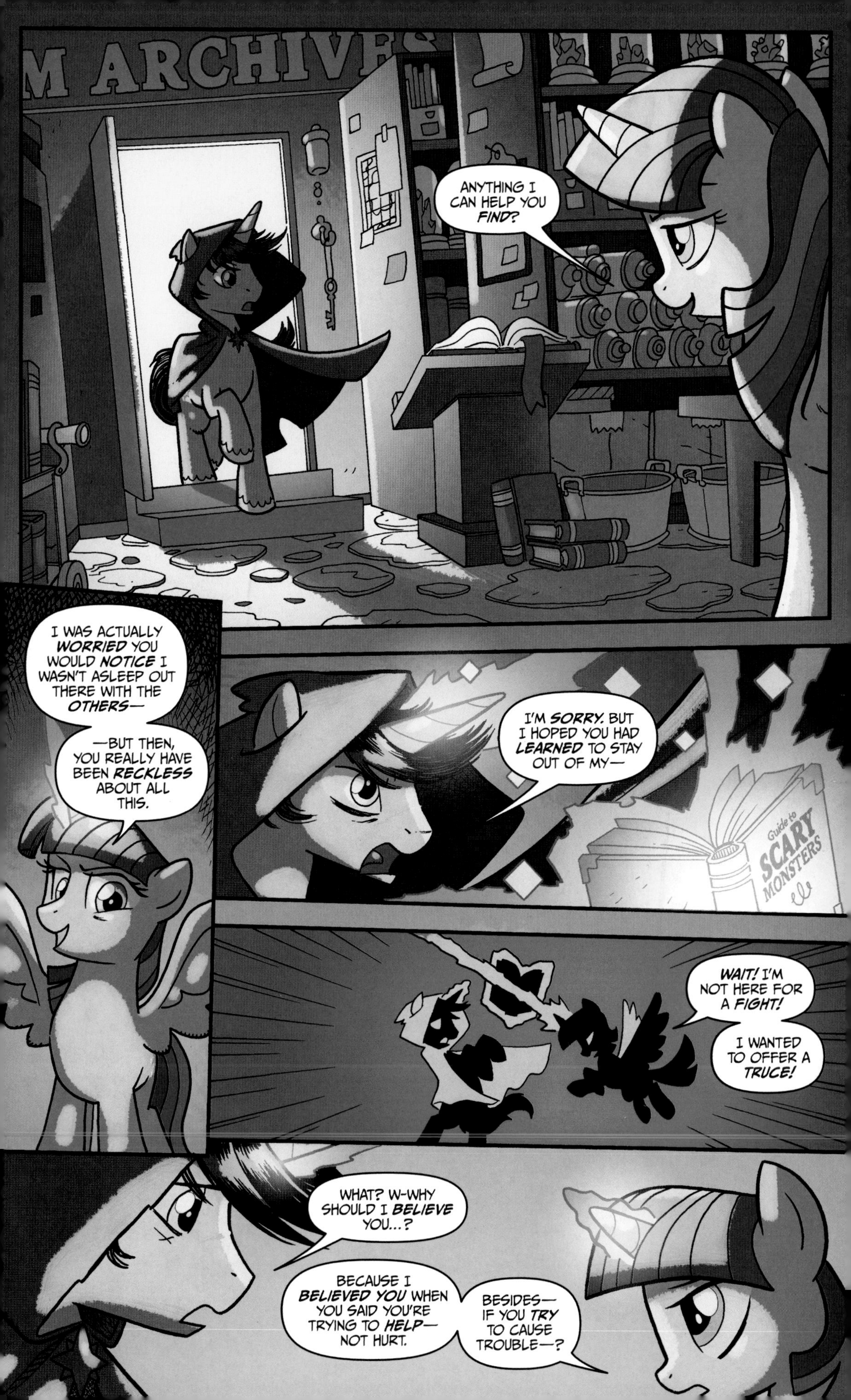
M ARCHIVES
ANYTHING I CAN HELP YOU FIND?
I WAS ACTUALLY WORRIED YOU WOULD NOTICE I WASN'T ASLEEP OUT THERE WITH THE OTHERS—
—BUT THEN, YOU REALLY HAVE BEEN RECKLESS ABOUT ALL THIS.
I'M SORRY. BUT I HOPED YOU HAD LEARNED TO STAY OUT OF MY—
Guide to SCARY MONSTERS
WAIT! I'M NOT HERE FOR A FIGHT!
I WANTED TO OFFER A TRUCE!
WHAT? W-WHY SHOULD I BELIEVE YOU...?
BECAUSE I BELIEVED YOU WHEN YOU SAID YOU'RE TRYING TO HELP— NOT HURT.
BESIDES— IF YOU TRY TO CAUSE TROUBLE—?

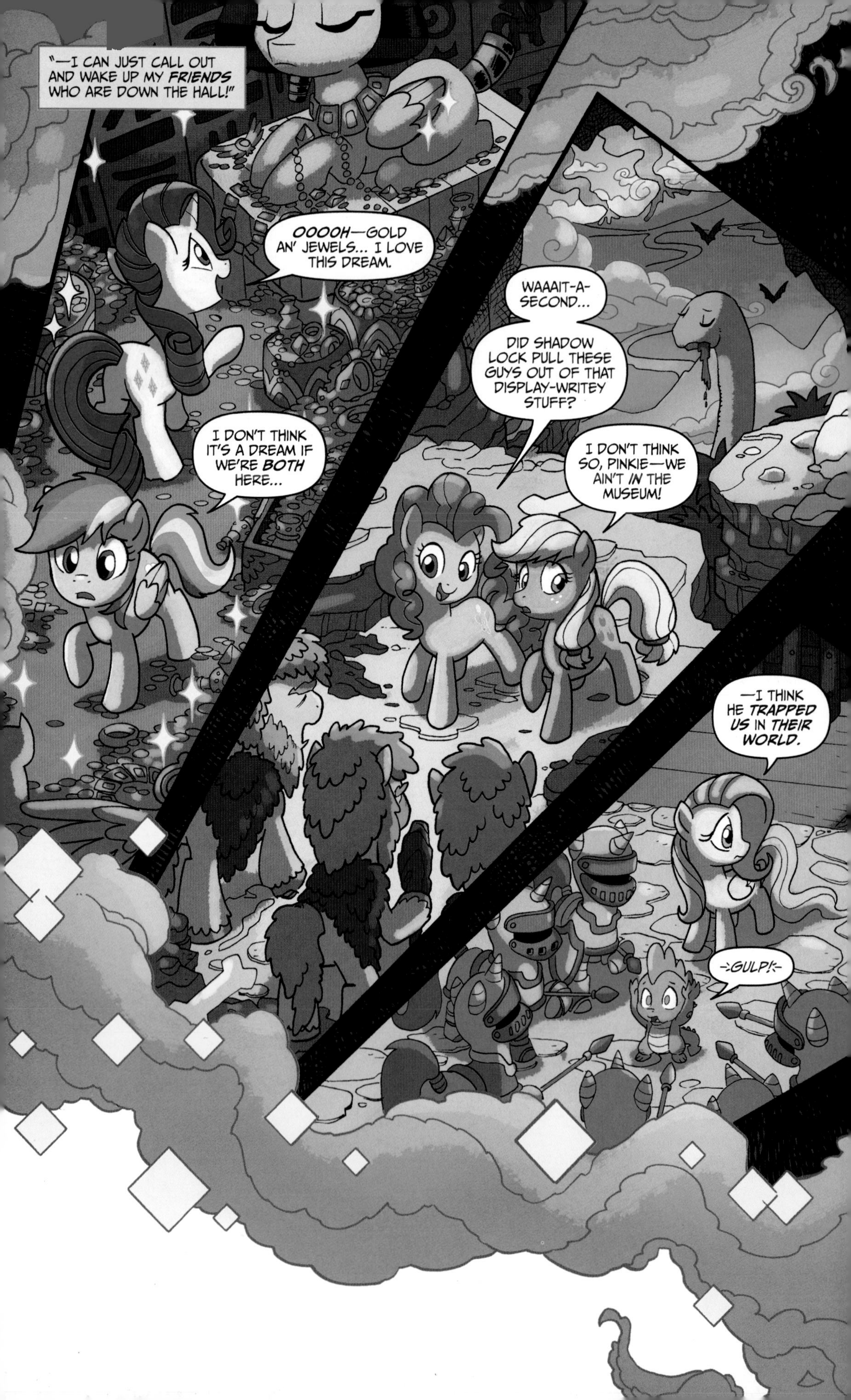
"—I CAN JUST CALL OUT AND WAKE UP MY FRIENDS WHO ARE DOWN THE HALL!"
OOOOH—GOLD AN' JEWELS... I LOVE THIS DREAM.
I DON'T THINK IT'S A DREAM IF WE'RE BOTH HERE...
WAAAIT-A-SECOND...
DID SHADOW LOCK PULL THESE GUYS OUT OF THAT DISPLAY-WRITEY STUFF?
I DON'T THINK SO, PINKIE—WE AIN'T IN THE MUSEUM!
—I THINK HE TRAPPED US IN THEIR WORLD.
-GULP!-

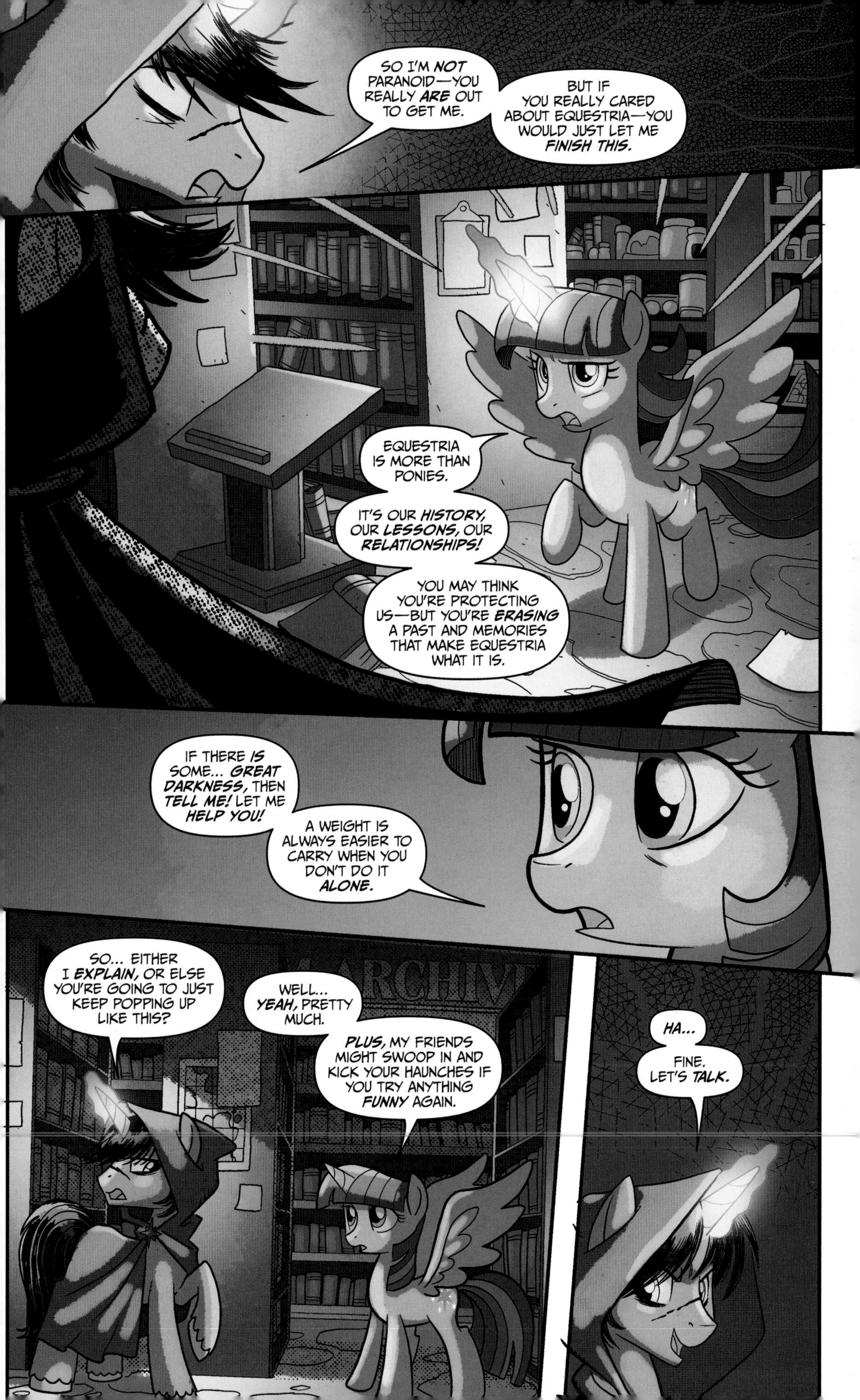
SO I'M NOT PARANOID—YOU REALLY ARE OUT TO GET ME.
BUT IF YOU REALLY CARED ABOUT EQUESTRIA—YOU WOULD JUST LET ME FINISH THIS.
EQUESTRIA IS MORE THAN PONIES.
IT'S OUR HISTORY, OUR LESSONS, OUR RELATIONSHIPS!
YOU MAY THINK YOU'RE PROTECTING US—BUT YOU'RE ERASING A PAST AND MEMORIES THAT MAKE EQUESTRIA WHAT IT IS.
IF THERE IS SOME... GREAT DARKNESS, THEN TELL ME! LET ME HELP YOU!
A WEIGHT IS ALWAYS EASIER TO CARRY WHEN YOU DON'T DO IT ALONE.
SO... EITHER I EXPLAIN, OR ELSE YOU'RE GOING TO JUST KEEP POPPING UP LIKE THIS?
WELL... YEAH, PRETTY MUCH.
PLUS, MY FRIENDS MIGHT SWOOP IN AND KICK YOUR HAUNCHES IF YOU TRY ANYTHING FUNNY AGAIN.
HA...
FINE. LET'S TALK.

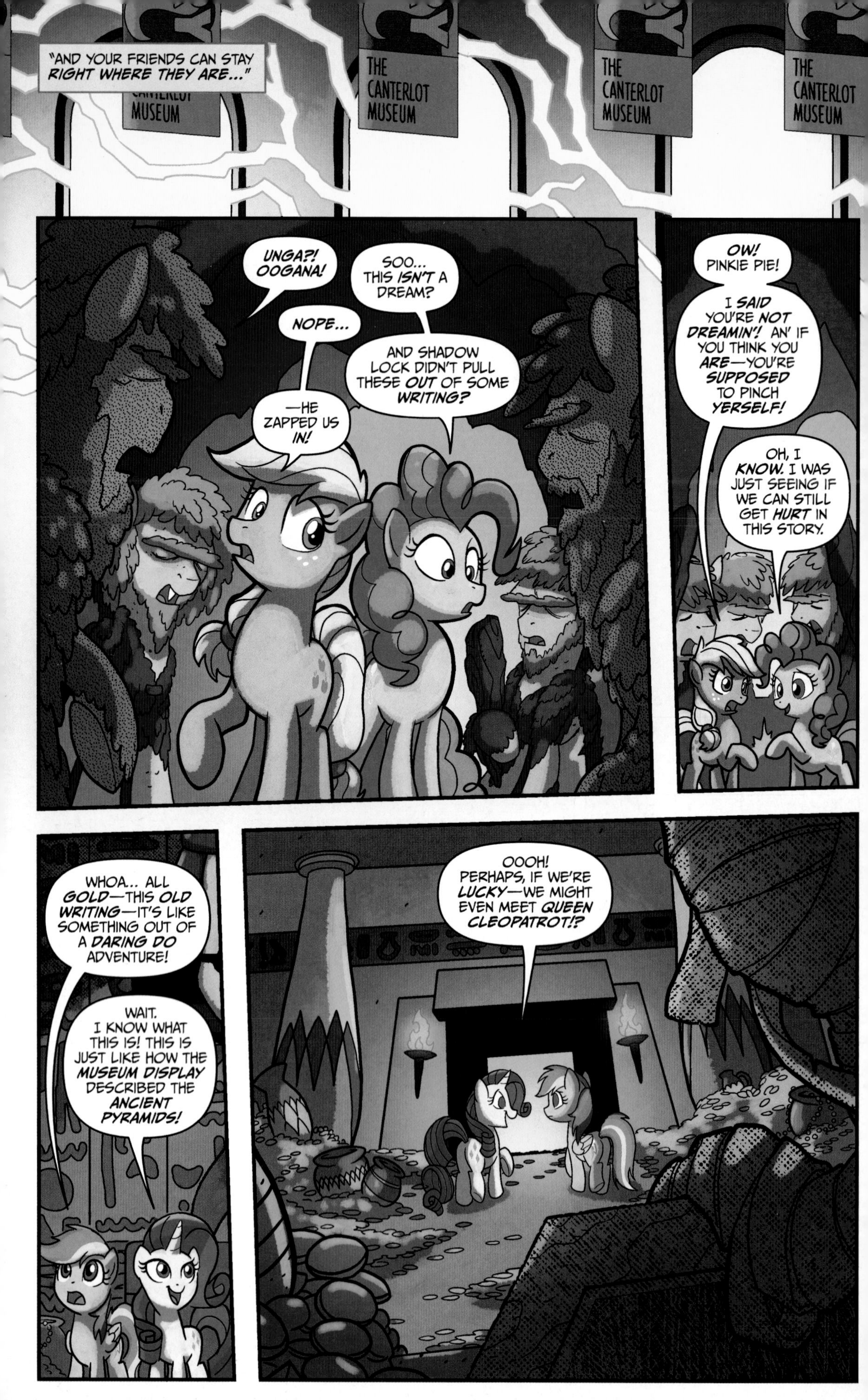
"AND YOUR FRIENDS CAN STAY RIGHT WHERE THEY ARE..."
THE CANTERLOT MUSEUM
THE CANTERLOT MUSEUM
THE CANTERLOT MUSEUM
UNGA?! OOGANA!
SOO... THIS ISN'T A DREAM?
NOPE...
—HE ZAPPED US IN!
AND SHADOW LOCK DIDN'T PULL THESE OUT OF SOME WRITING?
OW! PINKIE PIE!
I SAID YOU'RE NOT DREAMIN'! AN' IF YOU THINK YOU ARE—YOU'RE SUPPOSED TO PINCH YERSELF!
OH, I KNOW. I WAS JUST SEEING IF WE CAN STILL GET HURT IN THIS STORY.
WHOA... ALL GOLD—THIS OLD WRITING—IT'S LIKE SOMETHING OUT OF A DARING DO ADVENTURE!
WAIT. I KNOW WHAT THIS IS! THIS IS JUST LIKE HOW THE MUSEUM DISPLAY DESCRIBED THE ANCIENT PYRAMIDS!
OOOH! PERHAPS, IF WE'RE LUCKY—WE MIGHT EVEN MEET QUEEN CLEOPATROT!?

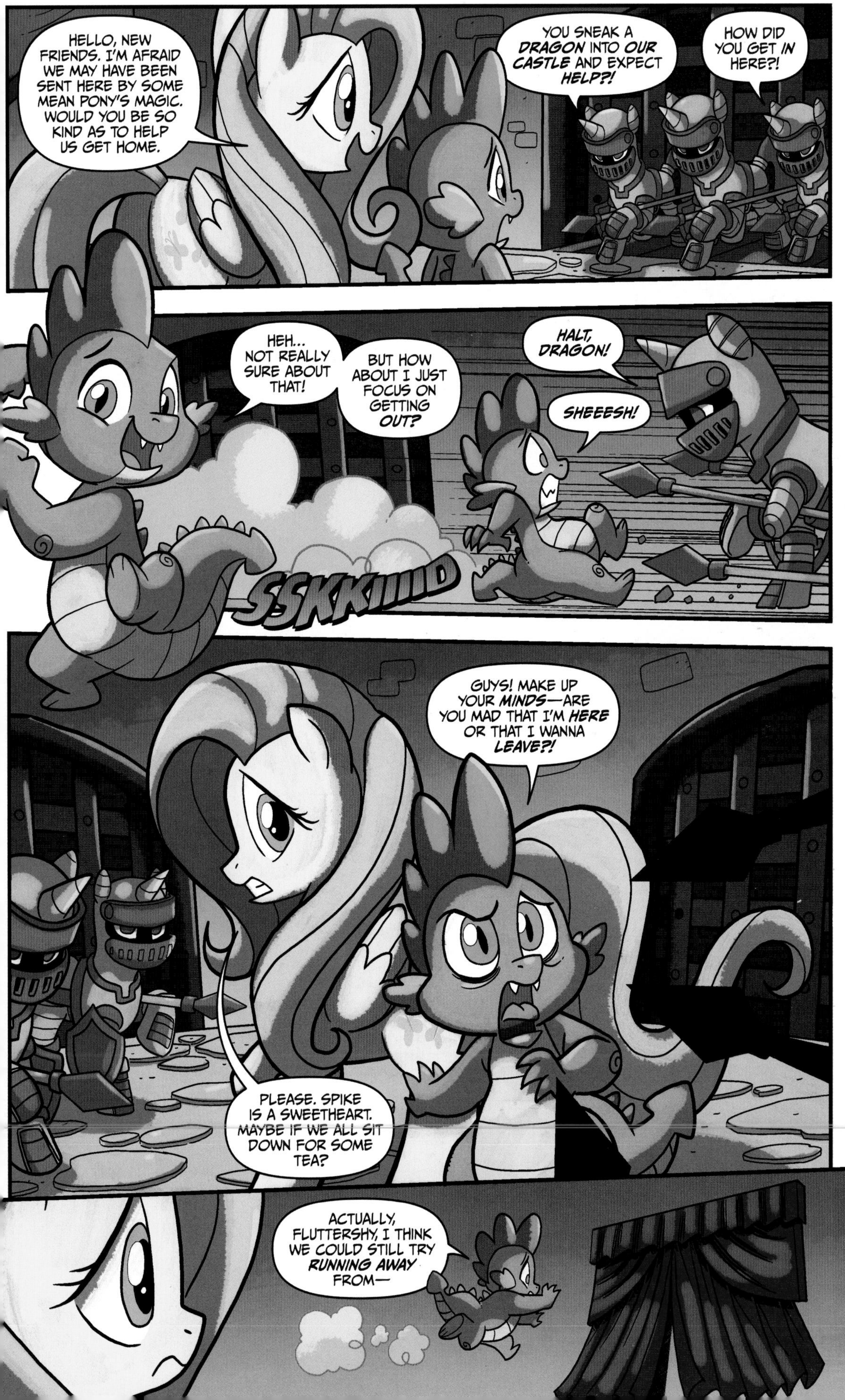

HELLO, NEW FRIENDS. I'M AFRAID WE MAY HAVE BEEN SENT HERE BY SOME MEAN PONY'S MAGIC. WOULD YOU BE SO KIND AS TO HELP US GET HOME.
YOU SNEAK A DRAGON INTO OUR CASTLE AND EXPECT HELP?!
HOW DID YOU GET IN HERE?!
HEH... NOT REALLY SURE ABOUT THAT!
BUT HOW ABOUT I JUST FOCUS ON GETTING OUT?
HALT, DRAGON!
SHEEESH!
SSKKIIIID
GUYS! MAKE UP YOUR MINDS—ARE YOU MAD THAT I'M HERE OR THAT I WANNA LEAVE?!
PLEASE. SPIKE IS A SWEETHEART. MAYBE IF WE ALL SIT DOWN FOR SOME TEA?
ACTUALLY, FLUTTERSHY, I THINK WE COULD STILL TRY RUNNING AWAY FROM—

THWAK!

SPIKE?! ARE YOU OKAY?

I'MMM... GONNA BE JUSS *FINE*, MOM... WHYYYOU *ASK*...?

THE DOOR! THERE ISN'T ONE!

IT'S JUST A... STONE WALL?

I GUESS THAT EXPLAINS WHY THEY WERE SO SURPRISED WE GOT *IN* HERE?

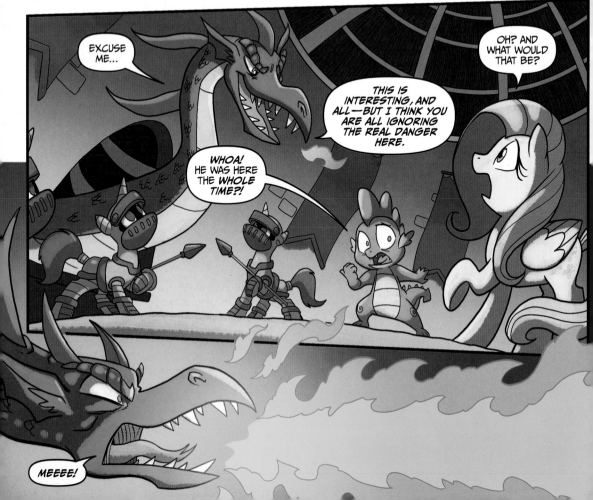

EXCUSE ME...

THIS IS INTERESTING, AND ALL—BUT I THINK YOU ARE ALL IGNORING THE REAL DANGER HERE.

OH? AND WHAT WOULD THAT BE?

WHOA! HE WAS HERE THE *WHOLE* TIME?!

MEEEE!

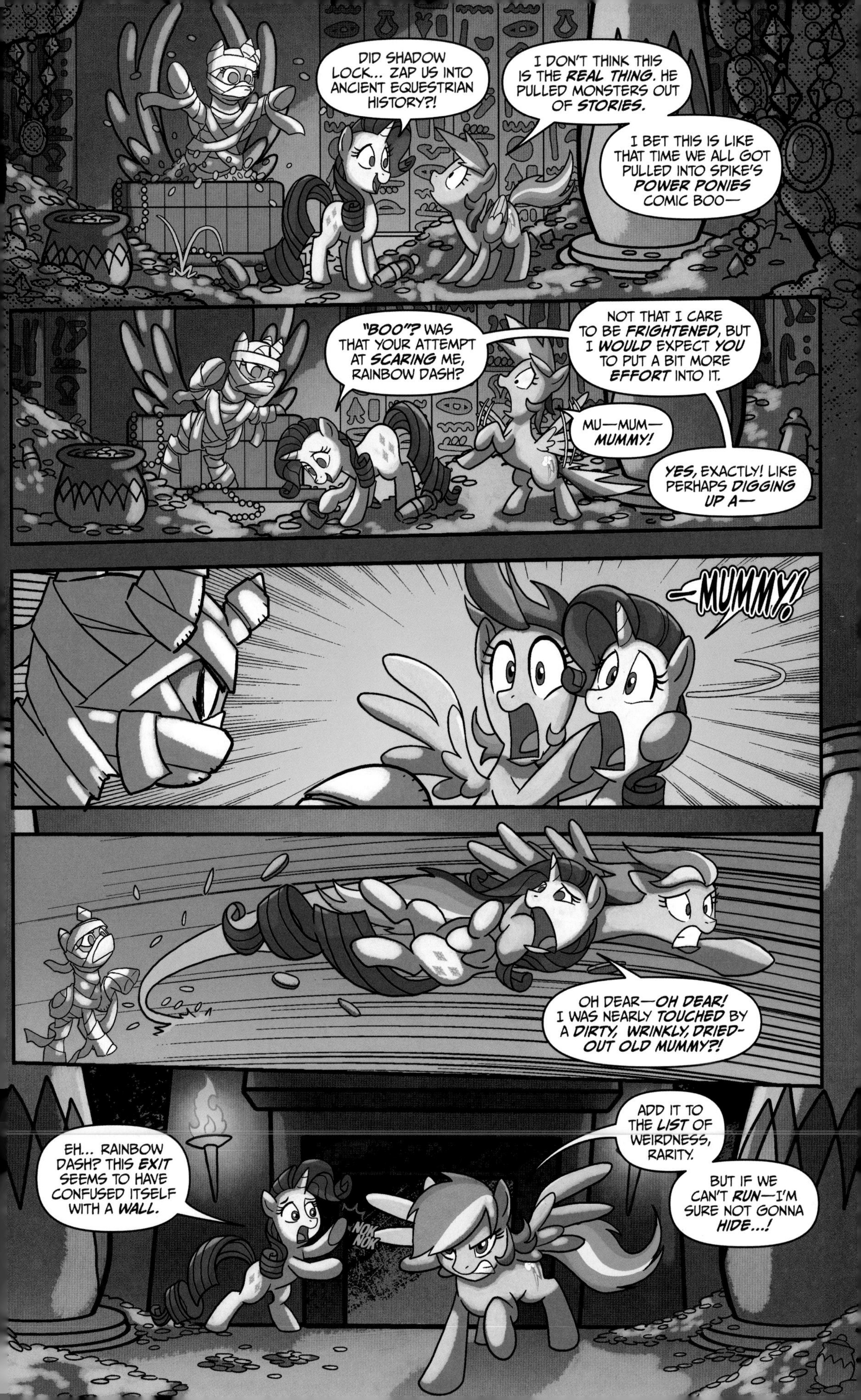
DID SHADOW LOCK... ZAP US INTO ANCIENT EQUESTRIAN HISTORY?!
I DON'T THINK THIS IS THE REAL THING. HE PULLED MONSTERS OUT OF STORIES.
I BET THIS IS LIKE THAT TIME WE ALL GOT PULLED INTO SPIKE'S POWER PONIES COMIC BOO—
"BOO"? WAS THAT YOUR ATTEMPT AT SCARING ME, RAINBOW DASH?
NOT THAT I CARE TO BE FRIGHTENED, BUT I WOULD EXPECT YOU TO PUT A BIT MORE EFFORT INTO IT.
MU—MUM—MUMMY!
YES, EXACTLY! LIKE PERHAPS DIGGING UP A—
—MUMMY!
OH DEAR—OH DEAR! I WAS NEARLY TOUCHED BY A DIRTY, WRINKLY, DRIED-OUT OLD MUMMY?!
EH... RAINBOW DASH? THIS EXIT SEEMS TO HAVE CONFUSED ITSELF WITH A WALL.
NOK NOK
ADD IT TO THE LIST OF WEIRDNESS, RARITY.
BUT IF WE CAN'T RUN—I'M SURE NOT GONNA HIDE...!

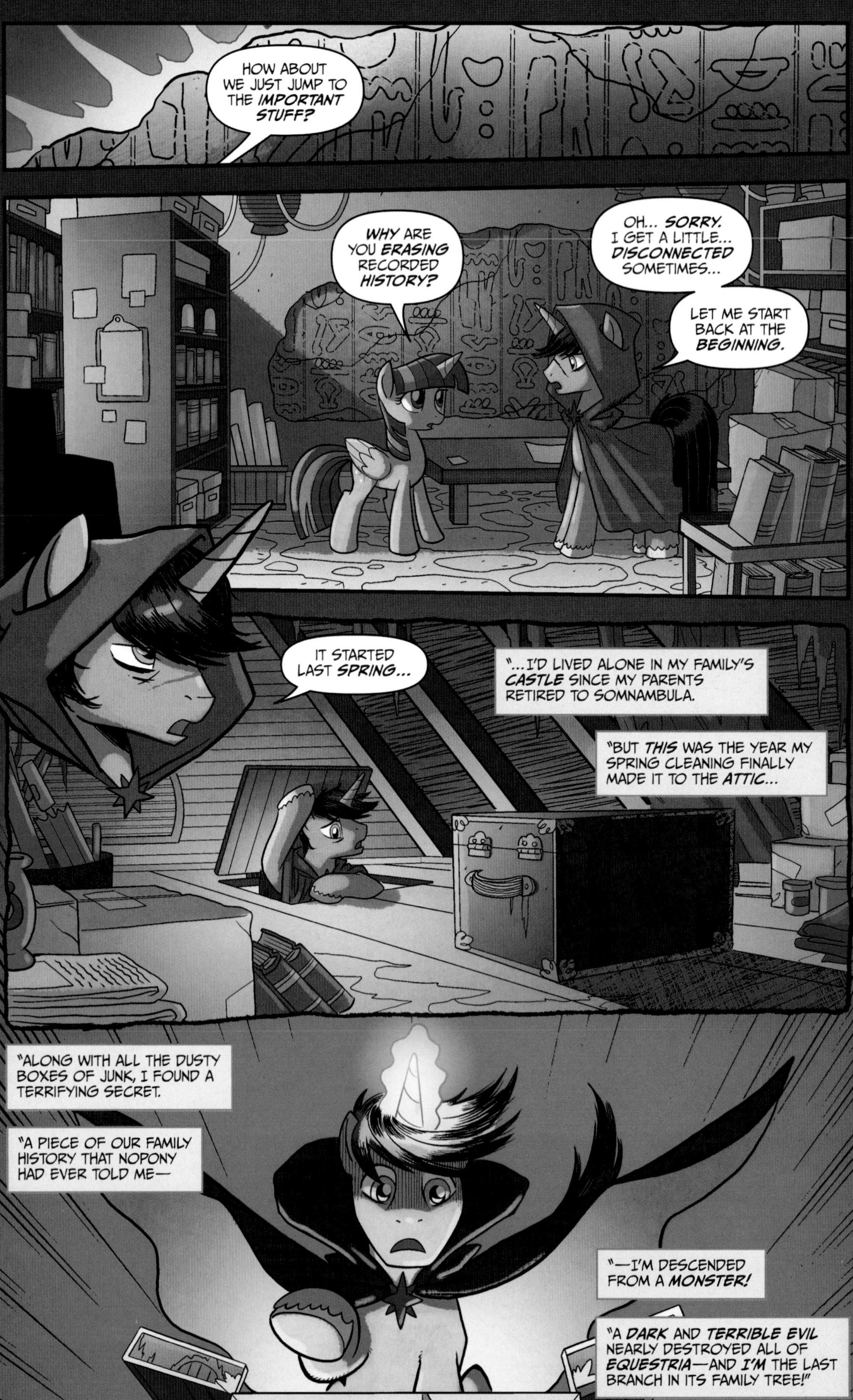
HOW ABOUT WE JUST JUMP TO THE IMPORTANT STUFF?
WHY ARE YOU ERASING RECORDED HISTORY?
OH... SORRY. I GET A LITTLE... DISCONNECTED SOMETIMES...
LET ME START BACK AT THE BEGINNING.
IT STARTED LAST SPRING...
"...I'D LIVED ALONE IN MY FAMILY'S CASTLE SINCE MY PARENTS RETIRED TO SOMNAMBULA.
"BUT THIS WAS THE YEAR MY SPRING CLEANING FINALLY MADE IT TO THE ATTIC...
"ALONG WITH ALL THE DUSTY BOXES OF JUNK, I FOUND A TERRIFYING SECRET.
"A PIECE OF OUR FAMILY HISTORY THAT NOPONY HAD EVER TOLD ME—
"—I'M DESCENDED FROM A MONSTER!
"A DARK AND TERRIBLE EVIL NEARLY DESTROYED ALL OF EQUESTRIA—AND I'M THE LAST BRANCH IN ITS FAMILY TREE!"

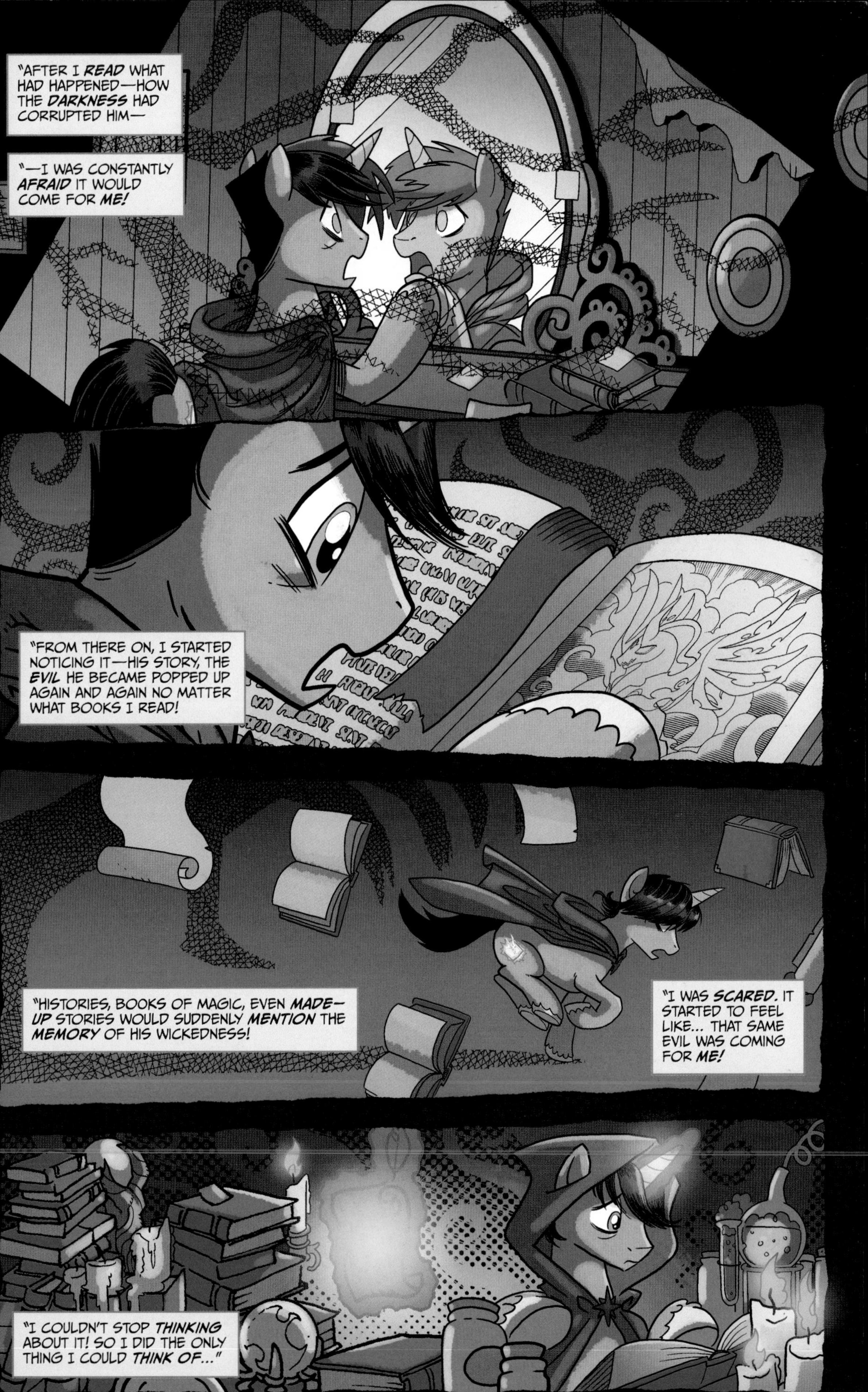
"AFTER I READ WHAT HAD HAPPENED—HOW THE DARKNESS HAD CORRUPTED HIM—
"—I WAS CONSTANTLY AFRAID IT WOULD COME FOR ME!
"FROM THERE ON, I STARTED NOTICING IT—HIS STORY, THE EVIL HE BECAME POPPED UP AGAIN AND AGAIN NO MATTER WHAT BOOKS I READ!
"HISTORIES, BOOKS OF MAGIC, EVEN MADE-UP STORIES WOULD SUDDENLY MENTION THE MEMORY OF HIS WICKEDNESS!
"I WAS SCARED. IT STARTED TO FEEL LIKE... THAT SAME EVIL WAS COMING FOR ME!
"I COULDN'T STOP THINKING ABOUT IT! SO I DID THE ONLY THING I COULD THINK OF..."

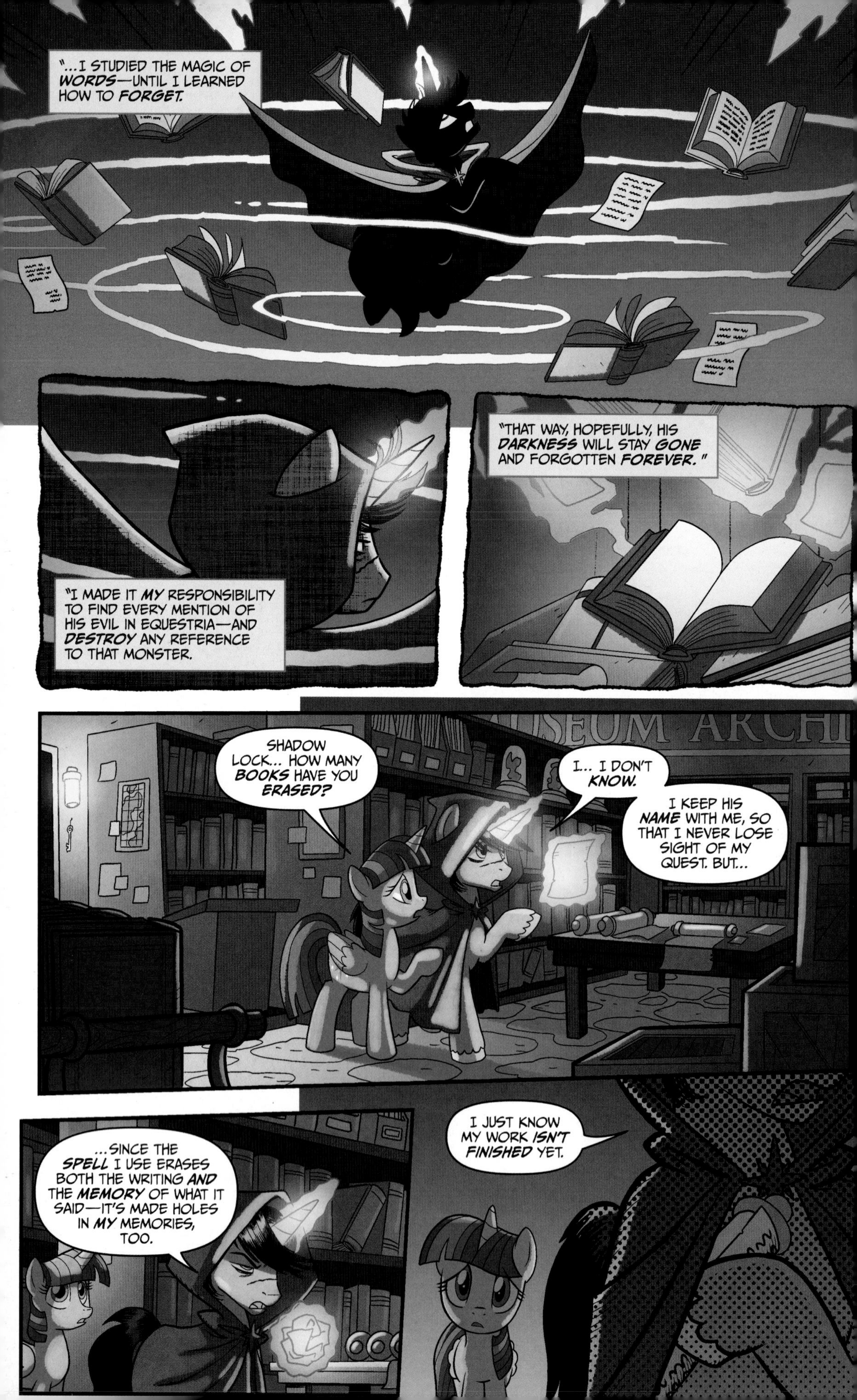
"...I STUDIED THE MAGIC OF WORDS—UNTIL I LEARNED HOW TO FORGET.
"I MADE IT MY RESPONSIBILITY TO FIND EVERY MENTION OF HIS EVIL IN EQUESTRIA—AND DESTROY ANY REFERENCE TO THAT MONSTER.
"THAT WAY, HOPEFULLY, HIS DARKNESS WILL STAY GONE AND FORGOTTEN FOREVER."
SHADOW LOCK... HOW MANY BOOKS HAVE YOU ERASED?
I... I DON'T KNOW.
I KEEP HIS NAME WITH ME, SO THAT I NEVER LOSE SIGHT OF MY QUEST. BUT...
...SINCE THE SPELL I USE ERASES BOTH THE WRITING AND THE MEMORY OF WHAT IT SAID—IT'S MADE HOLES IN MY MEMORIES, TOO.
I JUST KNOW MY WORK ISN'T FINISHED YET.

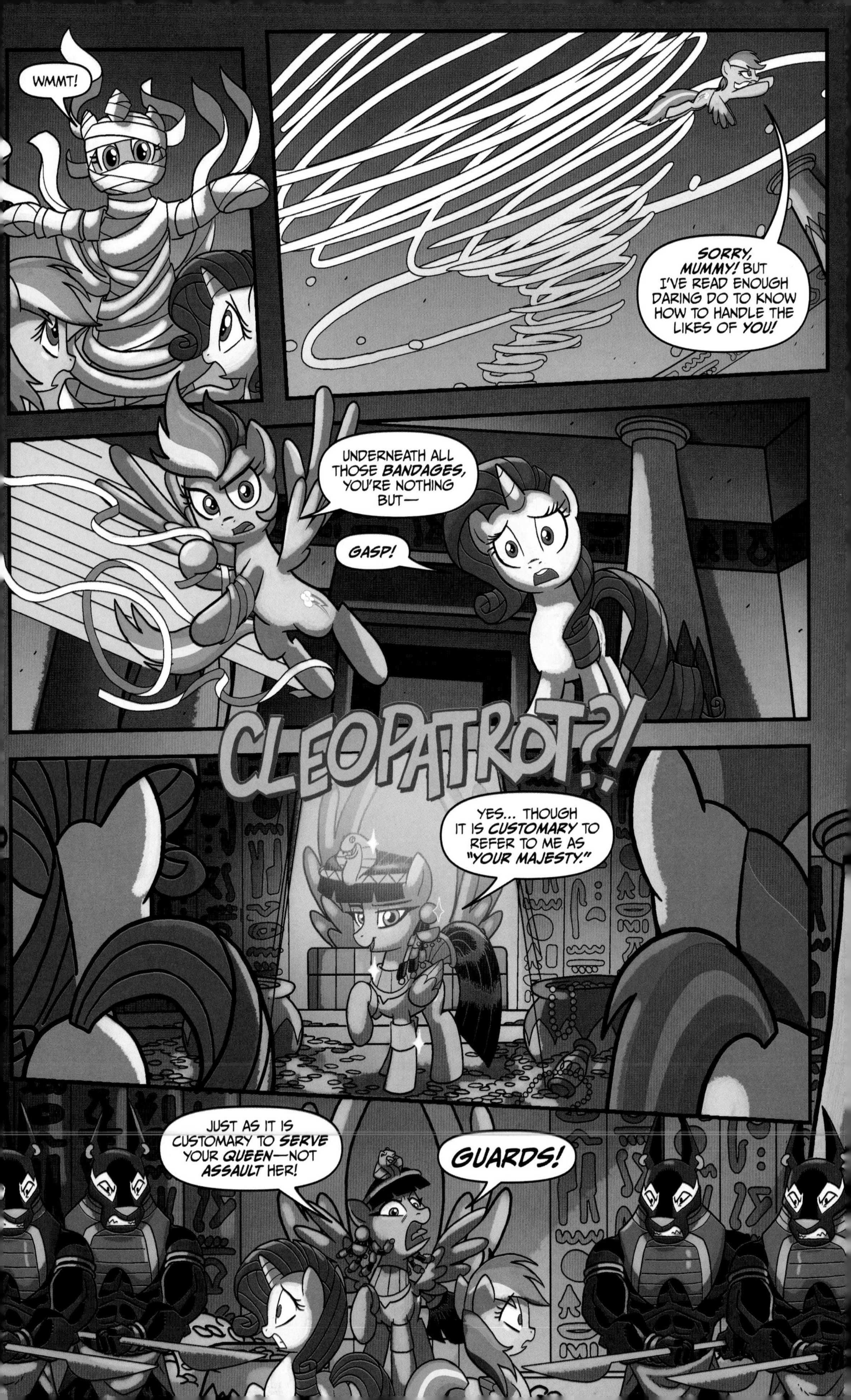
WMMT!
SORRY, MUMMY! BUT I'VE READ ENOUGH DARING DO TO KNOW HOW TO HANDLE THE LIKES OF YOU!
UNDERNEATH ALL THOSE BANDAGES, YOU'RE NOTHING BUT—
GASP!
CLEOPATROT?!
YES... THOUGH IT IS CUSTOMARY TO REFER TO ME AS "YOUR MAJESTY."
JUST AS IT IS CUSTOMARY TO SERVE YOUR QUEEN—NOT ASSAULT HER!
GUARDS!

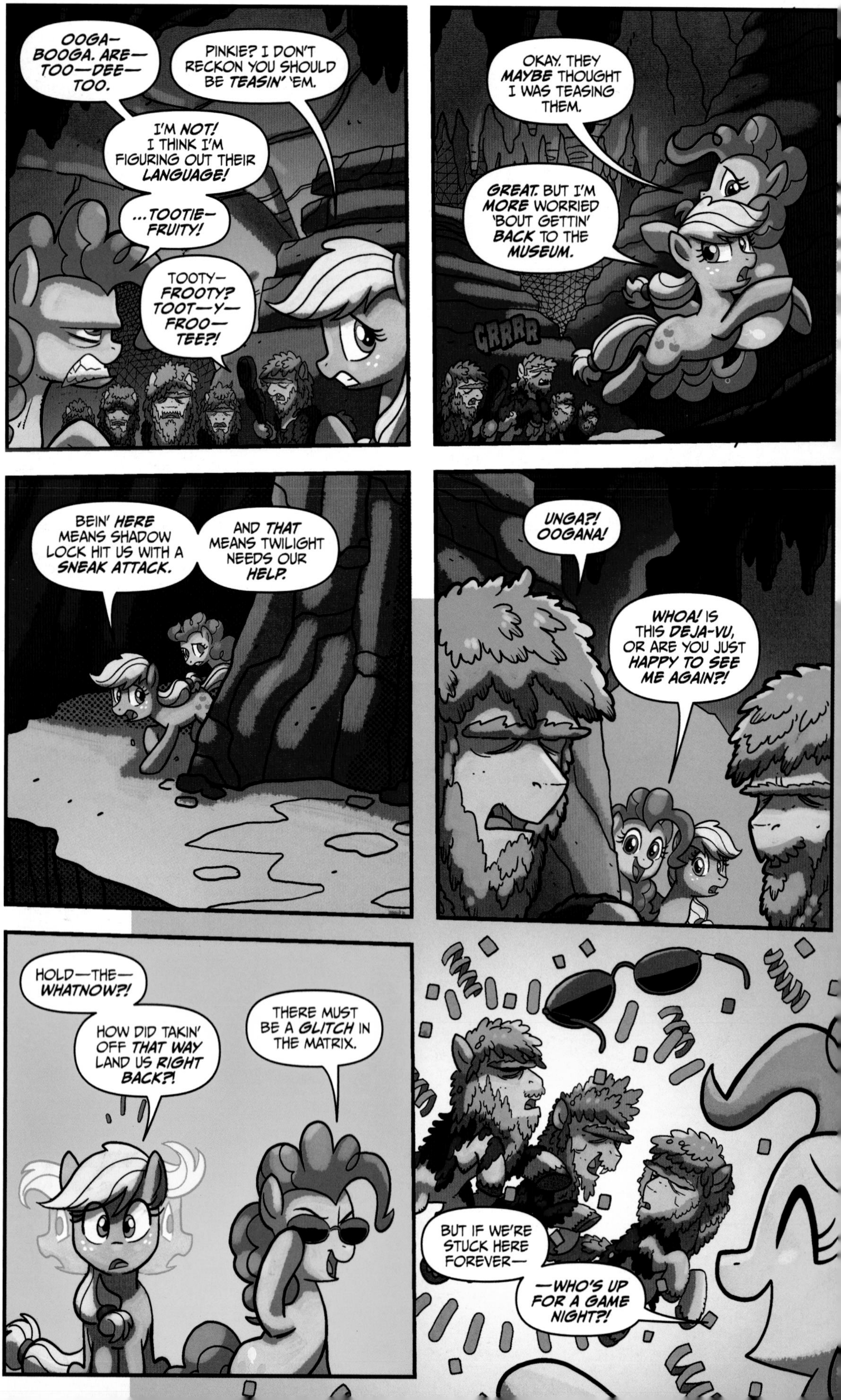

OOGA—BOOGA. ARE—TOO—DEE—TOO.
PINKIE? I DON'T RECKON YOU SHOULD BE TEASIN' 'EM.
I'M NOT! I THINK I'M FIGURING OUT THEIR LANGUAGE!
...TOOTIE—FRUITY!
TOOTY—FROOTY? TOOT—Y—FROO—TEE?!
OKAY. THEY MAYBE THOUGHT I WAS TEASING THEM.
GREAT. BUT I'M MORE WORRIED 'BOUT GETTIN' BACK TO THE MUSEUM.
GRRRR
BEIN' HERE MEANS SHADOW LOCK HIT US WITH A SNEAK ATTACK.
AND THAT MEANS TWILIGHT NEEDS OUR HELP.
UNGA?! OOGANA!
WHOA! IS THIS DEJA-VU, OR ARE YOU JUST HAPPY TO SEE ME AGAIN?!
HOLD—THE—WHATNOW?!
HOW DID TAKIN' OFF THAT WAY LAND US RIGHT BACK?!
THERE MUST BE A GLITCH IN THE MATRIX.
BUT IF WE'RE STUCK HERE FOREVER—
—WHO'S UP FOR A GAME NIGHT?!

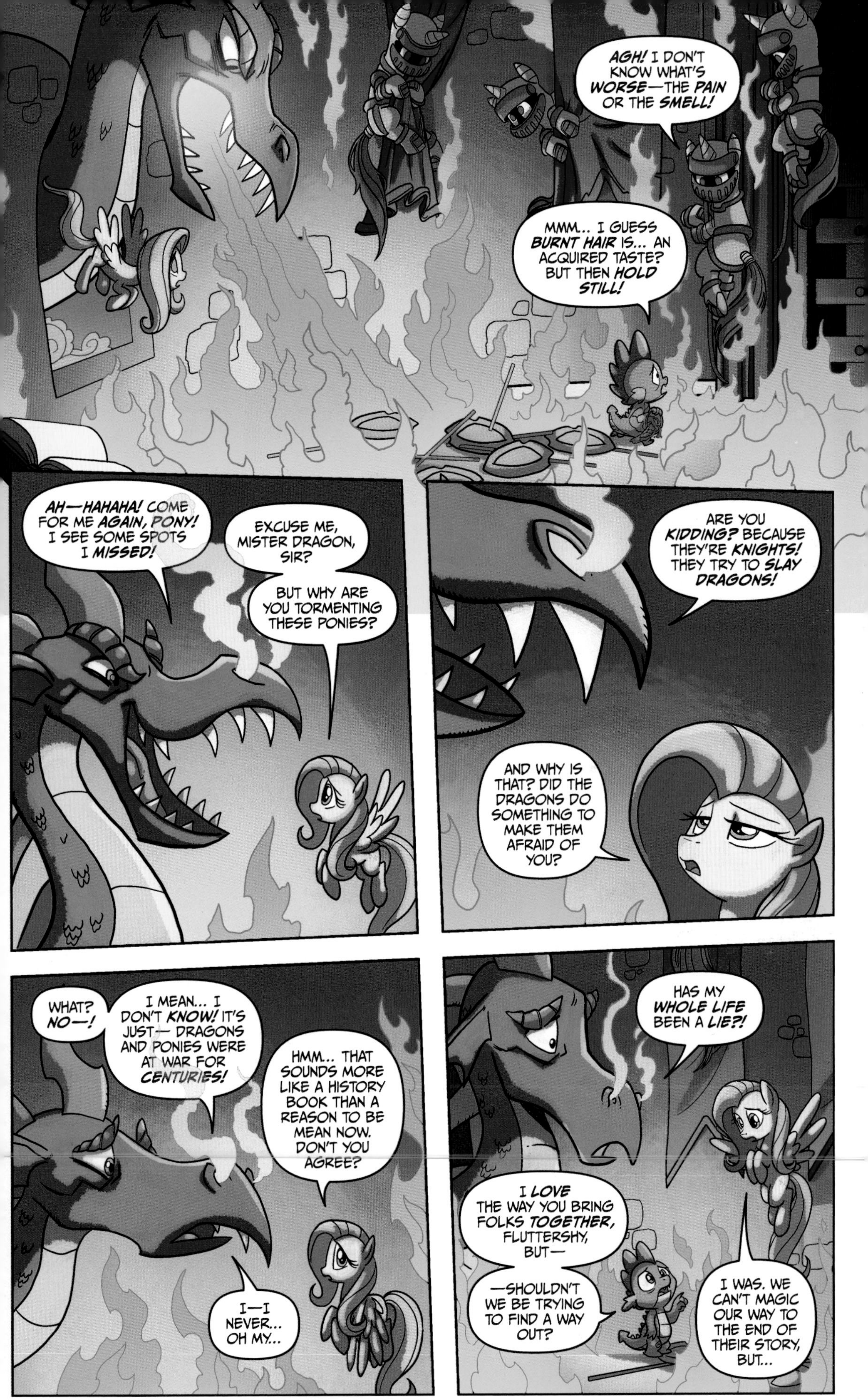
AGH! I DON'T KNOW WHAT'S WORSE—THE PAIN OR THE SMELL!
MMM... I GUESS BURNT HAIR IS... AN ACQUIRED TASTE? BUT THEN HOLD STILL!
AH—HAHAHA! COME FOR ME AGAIN, PONY! I SEE SOME SPOTS I MISSED!
EXCUSE ME, MISTER DRAGON, SIR?
BUT WHY ARE YOU TORMENTING THESE PONIES?
ARE YOU KIDDING? BECAUSE THEY'RE KNIGHTS! THEY TRY TO SLAY DRAGONS!
AND WHY IS THAT? DID THE DRAGONS DO SOMETHING TO MAKE THEM AFRAID OF YOU?
WHAT? NO—!
I MEAN... I DON'T KNOW! IT'S JUST— DRAGONS AND PONIES WERE AT WAR FOR CENTURIES!
HMM... THAT SOUNDS MORE LIKE A HISTORY BOOK THAN A REASON TO BE MEAN NOW. DON'T YOU AGREE?
I—I NEVER... OH MY...
HAS MY WHOLE LIFE BEEN A LIE?!
I LOVE THE WAY YOU BRING FOLKS TOGETHER, FLUTTERSHY, BUT—
—SHOULDN'T WE BE TRYING TO FIND A WAY OUT?
I WAS. WE CAN'T MAGIC OUR WAY TO THE END OF THEIR STORY, BUT...

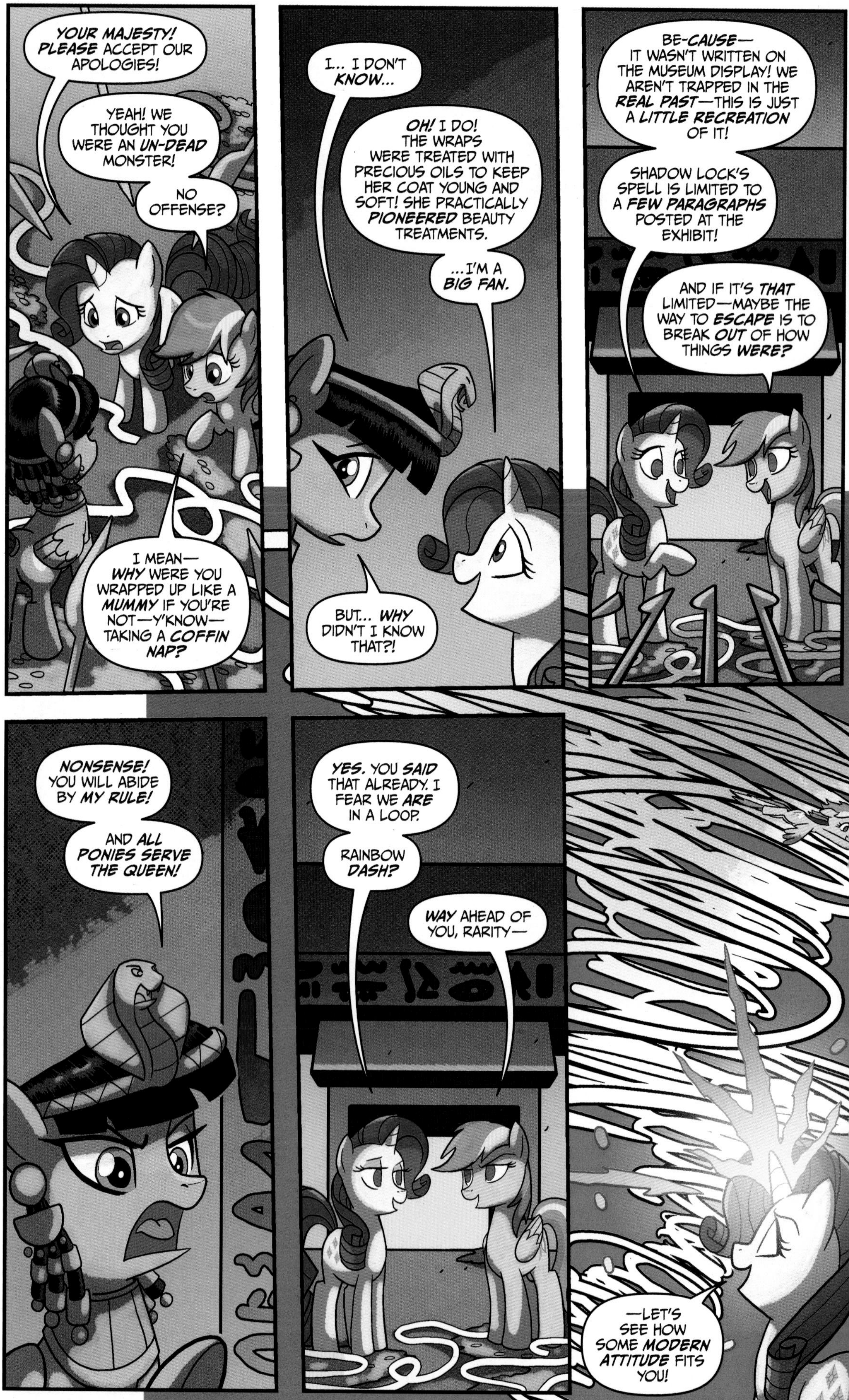
YOUR MAJESTY! PLEASE ACCEPT OUR APOLOGIES!
YEAH! WE THOUGHT YOU WERE AN UN-DEAD MONSTER!
NO OFFENSE?
I MEAN— WHY WERE YOU WRAPPED UP LIKE A MUMMY IF YOU'RE NOT—Y'KNOW— TAKING A COFFIN NAP?
I... I DON'T KNOW...
OH! I DO! THE WRAPS WERE TREATED WITH PRECIOUS OILS TO KEEP HER COAT YOUNG AND SOFT! SHE PRACTICALLY PIONEERED BEAUTY TREATMENTS.
...I'M A BIG FAN.
BUT... WHY DIDN'T I KNOW THAT?!
BE-CAUSE— IT WASN'T WRITTEN ON THE MUSEUM DISPLAY! WE AREN'T TRAPPED IN THE REAL PAST—THIS IS JUST A LITTLE RECREATION OF IT!
SHADOW LOCK'S SPELL IS LIMITED TO A FEW PARAGRAPHS POSTED AT THE EXHIBIT!
AND IF IT'S THAT LIMITED—MAYBE THE WAY TO ESCAPE IS TO BREAK OUT OF HOW THINGS WERE?
NONSENSE! YOU WILL ABIDE BY MY RULE!
AND ALL PONIES SERVE THE QUEEN!
YES. YOU SAID THAT ALREADY. I FEAR WE ARE IN A LOOP.
RAINBOW DASH?
WAY AHEAD OF YOU, RARITY—
—LET'S SEE HOW SOME MODERN ATTITUDE FITS YOU!

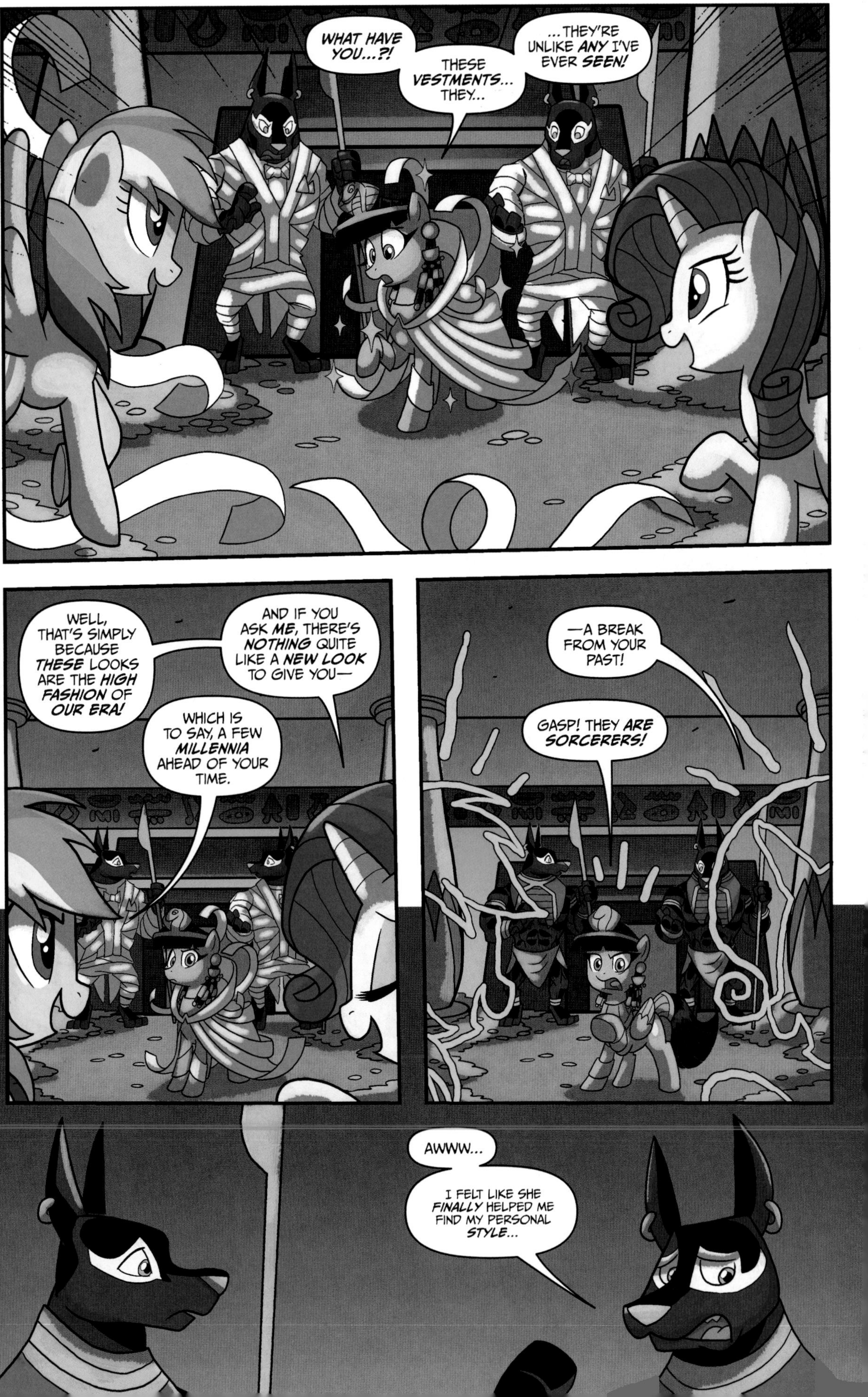
WHAT HAVE YOU...?!
THESE VESTMENTS... THEY...
...THEY'RE UNLIKE ANY I'VE EVER SEEN!
WELL, THAT'S SIMPLY BECAUSE THESE LOOKS ARE THE HIGH FASHION OF OUR ERA!
WHICH IS TO SAY, A FEW MILLENNIA AHEAD OF YOUR TIME.
AND IF YOU ASK ME, THERE'S NOTHING QUITE LIKE A NEW LOOK TO GIVE YOU—
—A BREAK FROM YOUR PAST!
GASP! THEY ARE SORCERERS!
AWWW...
I FELT LIKE SHE FINALLY HELPED ME FIND MY PERSONAL STYLE...

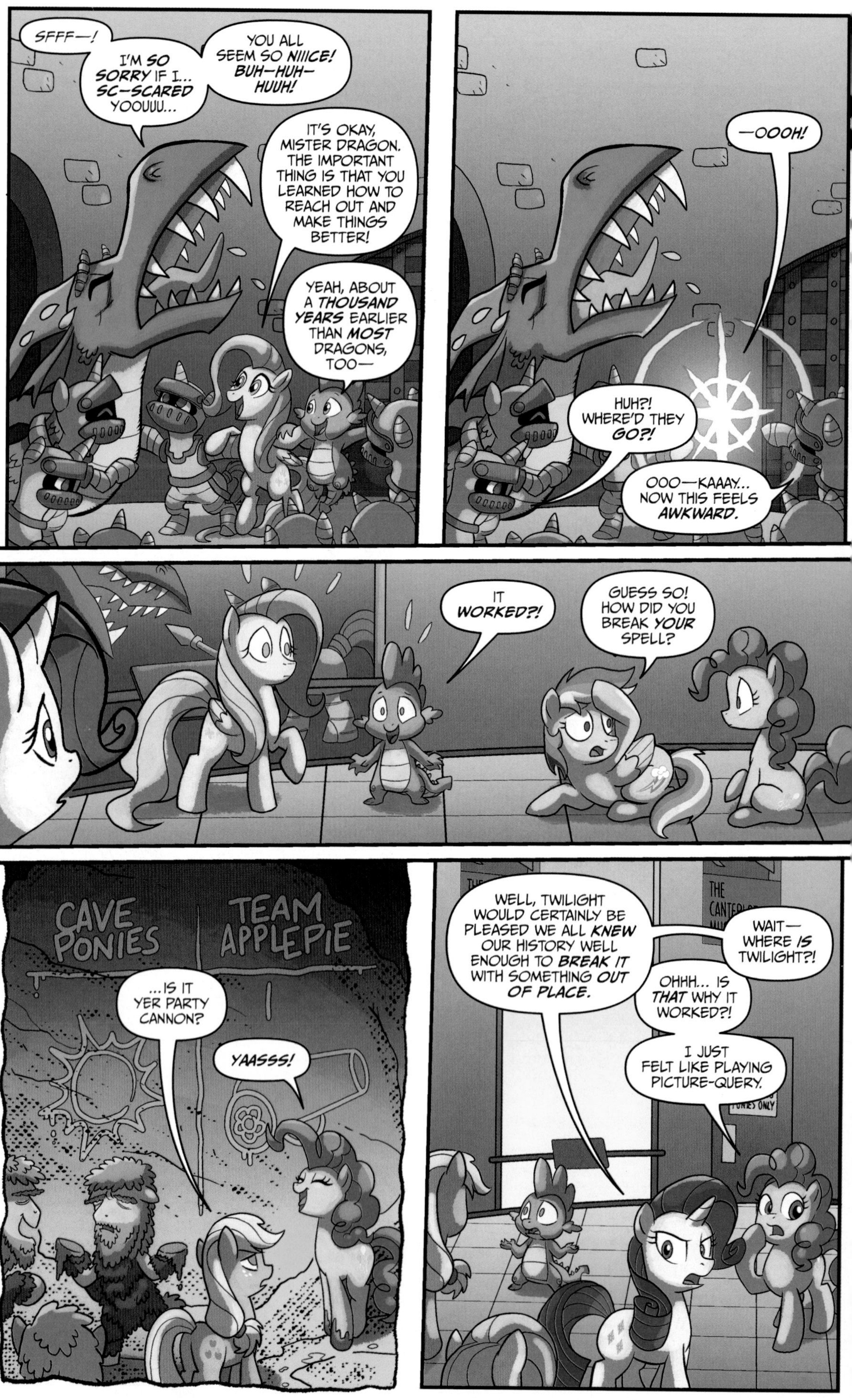
SFFF—!
I'M SO SORRY IF I... SC—SCARED YOOUUU...
YOU ALL SEEM SO NIIICE! BUH—HUH—HUUH!
IT'S OKAY, MISTER DRAGON. THE IMPORTANT THING IS THAT YOU LEARNED HOW TO REACH OUT AND MAKE THINGS BETTER!
YEAH, ABOUT A THOUSAND YEARS EARLIER THAN MOST DRAGONS, TOO—
—OOOH!
HUH?! WHERE'D THEY GO?!
OOO—KAAAY... NOW THIS FEELS AWKWARD.
IT WORKED?!
GUESS SO! HOW DID YOU BREAK YOUR SPELL?
CAVE PONIES
TEAM APPLEPIE
...IS IT YER PARTY CANNON?
YAASSS!
WELL, TWILIGHT WOULD CERTAINLY BE PLEASED WE ALL KNEW OUR HISTORY WELL ENOUGH TO BREAK IT WITH SOMETHING OUT OF PLACE.
WAIT— WHERE IS TWILIGHT?!
OHHH... IS THAT WHY IT WORKED?!
I JUST FELT LIKE PLAYING PICTURE-QUERY.

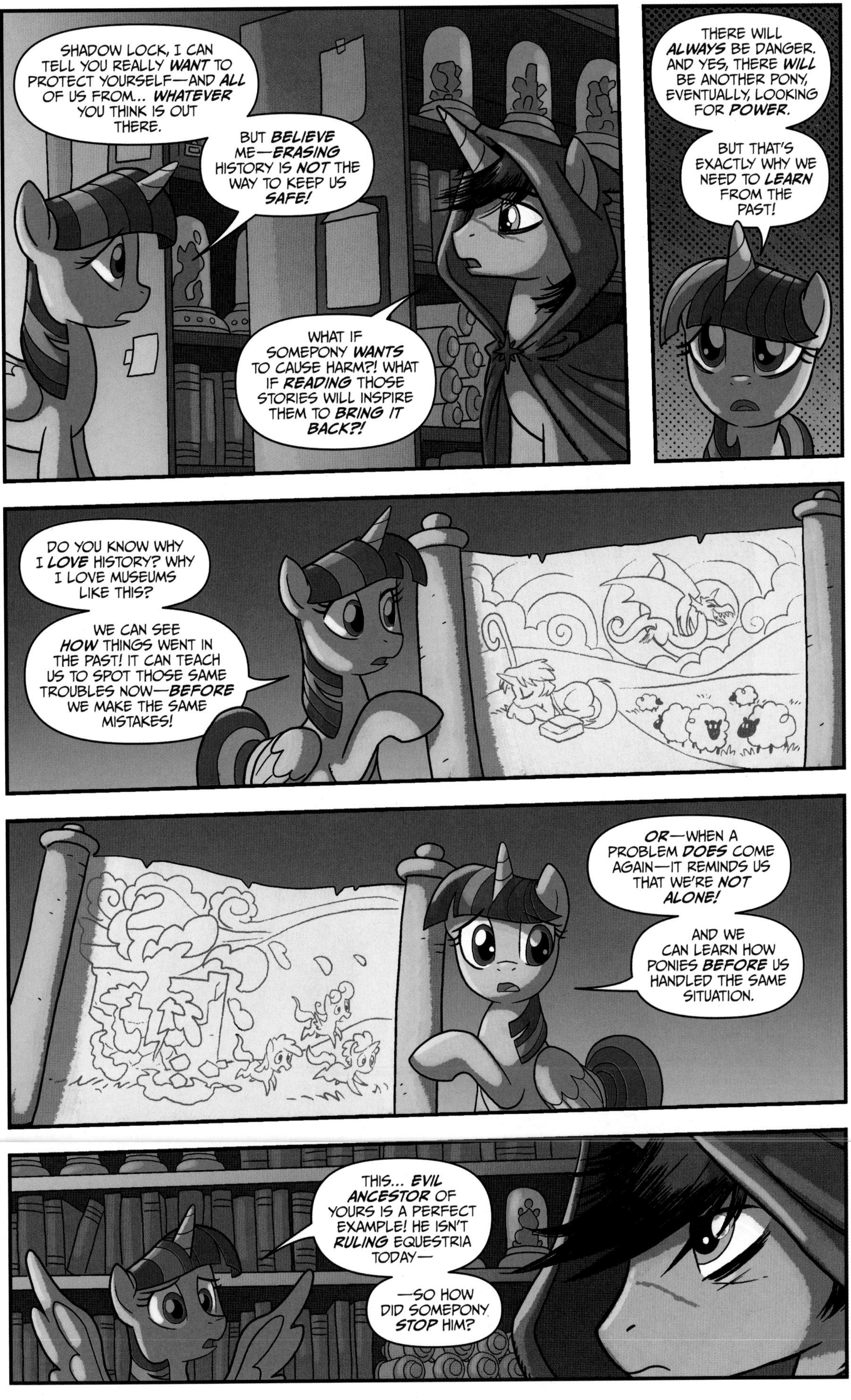
SHADOW LOCK, I CAN TELL YOU REALLY WANT TO PROTECT YOURSELF—AND ALL OF US FROM... WHATEVER YOU THINK IS OUT THERE.
BUT BELIEVE ME—ERASING HISTORY IS NOT THE WAY TO KEEP US SAFE!
WHAT IF SOMEPONY WANTS TO CAUSE HARM?! WHAT IF READING THOSE STORIES WILL INSPIRE THEM TO BRING IT BACK?!
THERE WILL ALWAYS BE DANGER. AND YES, THERE WILL BE ANOTHER PONY, EVENTUALLY, LOOKING FOR POWER.
BUT THAT'S EXACTLY WHY WE NEED TO LEARN FROM THE PAST!
DO YOU KNOW WHY I LOVE HISTORY? WHY I LOVE MUSEUMS LIKE THIS?
WE CAN SEE HOW THINGS WENT IN THE PAST! IT CAN TEACH US TO SPOT THOSE SAME TROUBLES NOW—BEFORE WE MAKE THE SAME MISTAKES!
OR—WHEN A PROBLEM DOES COME AGAIN—IT REMINDS US THAT WE'RE NOT ALONE!
AND WE CAN LEARN HOW PONIES BEFORE US HANDLED THE SAME SITUATION.
THIS... EVIL ANCESTOR OF YOURS IS A PERFECT EXAMPLE! HE ISN'T RULING EQUESTRIA TODAY—
—SO HOW DID SOMEPONY STOP HIM?

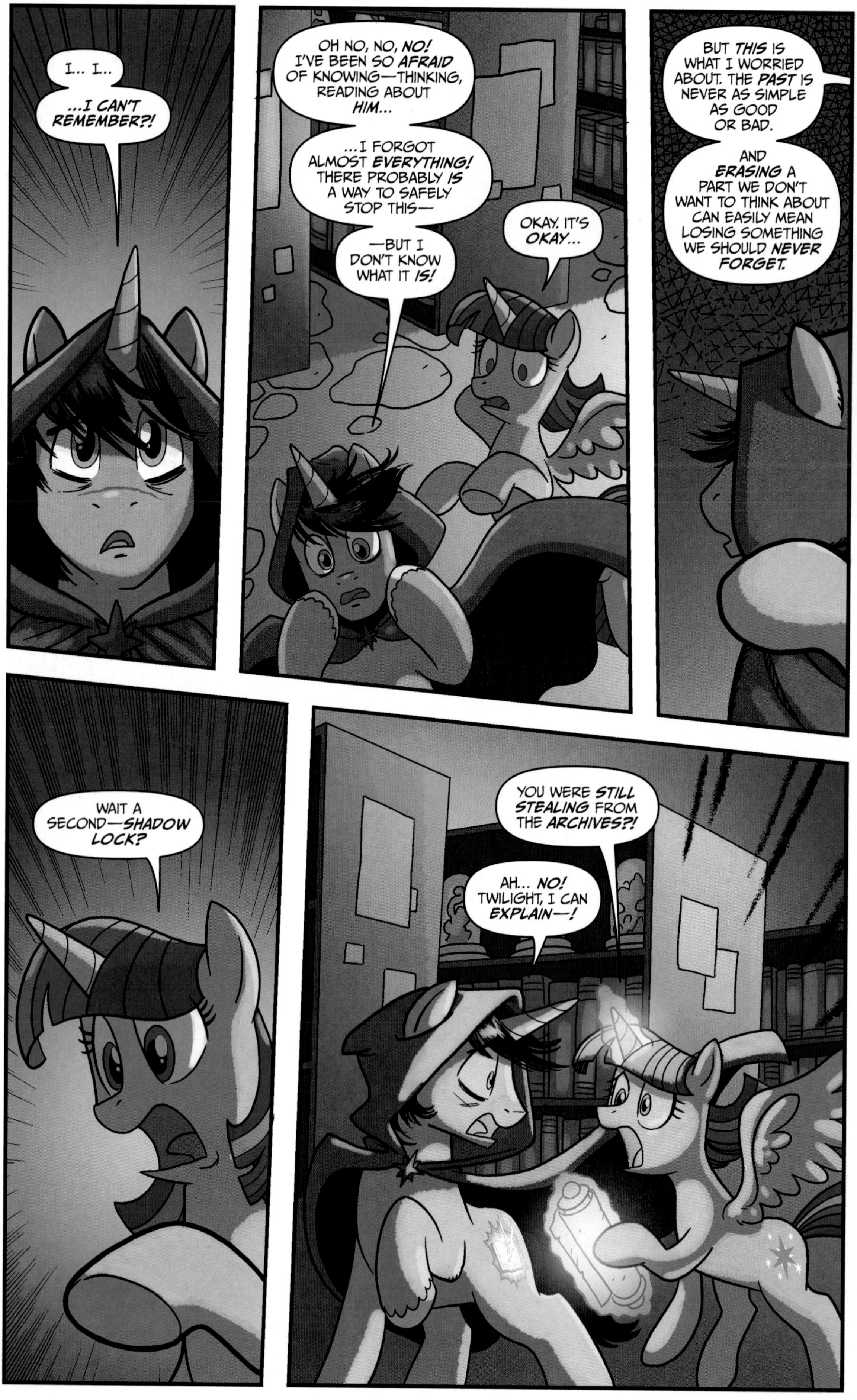
I... I...
...I CAN'T REMEMBER?!
OH NO, NO, NO! I'VE BEEN SO AFRAID OF KNOWING—THINKING, READING ABOUT HIM...
...I FORGOT ALMOST EVERYTHING! THERE PROBABLY IS A WAY TO SAFELY STOP THIS—
—BUT I DON'T KNOW WHAT IT IS!
OKAY. IT'S OKAY...
BUT THIS IS WHAT I WORRIED ABOUT. THE PAST IS NEVER AS SIMPLE AS GOOD OR BAD.
AND ERASING A PART WE DON'T WANT TO THINK ABOUT CAN EASILY MEAN LOSING SOMETHING WE SHOULD NEVER FORGET.
WAIT A SECOND—SHADOW LOCK?
YOU WERE STILL STEALING FROM THE ARCHIVES?!
AH... NO! TWILIGHT, I CAN EXPLAIN—!

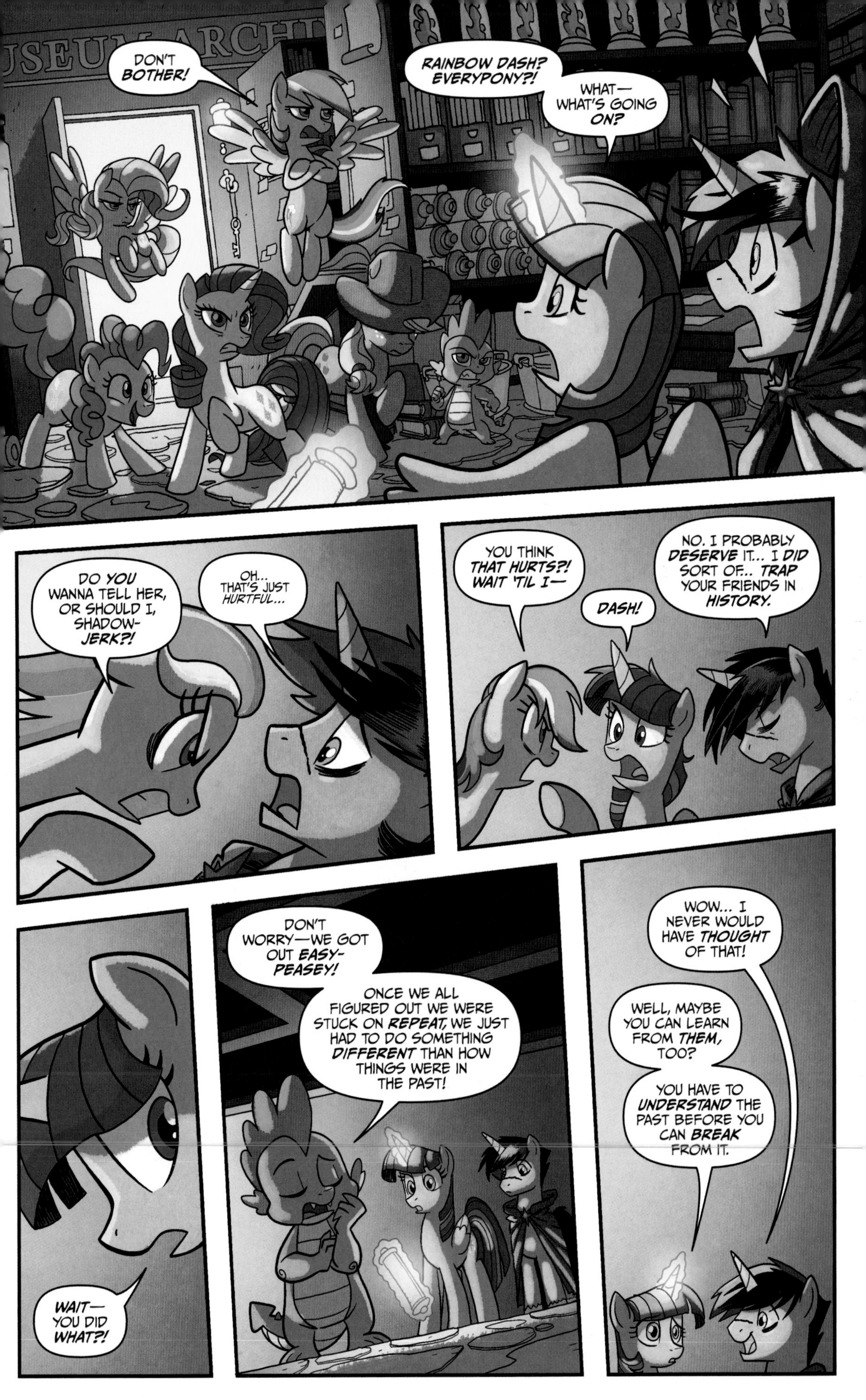
USEUM ARCH
DON'T BOTHER!
RAINBOW DASH? EVERYPONY?!
WHAT— WHAT'S GOING ON?
DO YOU WANNA TELL HER, OR SHOULD I, SHADOW-JERK?!
OH... THAT'S JUST HURTFUL...
YOU THINK THAT HURTS?! WAIT 'TIL I—
DASH!
NO. I PROBABLY DESERVE IT... I DID SORT OF... TRAP YOUR FRIENDS IN HISTORY.
WAIT— YOU DID WHAT?!
DON'T WORRY—WE GOT OUT EASY-PEASEY!
ONCE WE ALL FIGURED OUT WE WERE STUCK ON REPEAT, WE JUST HAD TO DO SOMETHING DIFFERENT THAN HOW THINGS WERE IN THE PAST!
WOW... I NEVER WOULD HAVE THOUGHT OF THAT!
WELL, MAYBE YOU CAN LEARN FROM THEM, TOO?
YOU HAVE TO UNDERSTAND THE PAST BEFORE YOU CAN BREAK FROM IT.

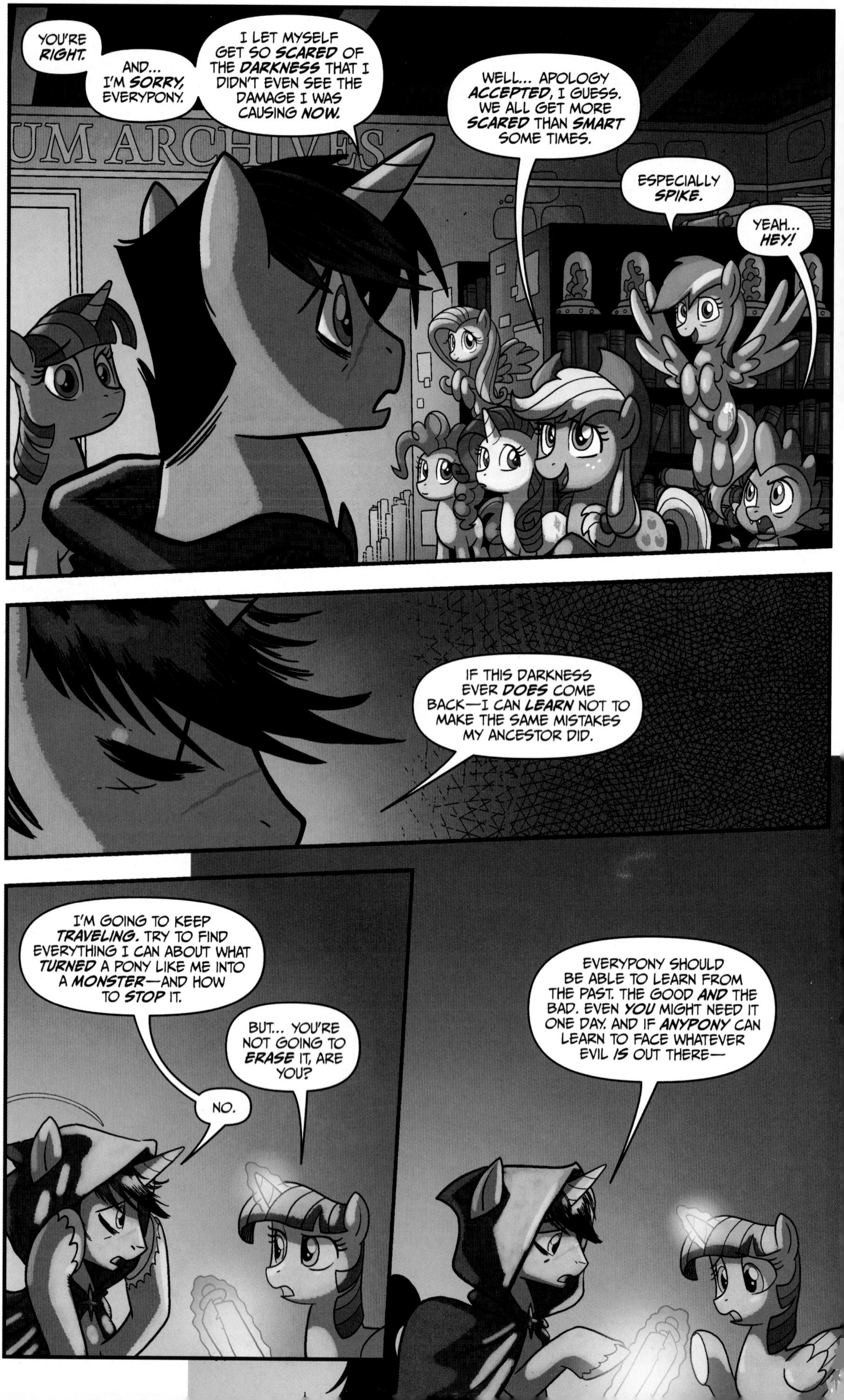
YOU'RE RIGHT.
AND... I'M SORRY, EVERYPONY.
I LET MYSELF GET SO SCARED OF THE DARKNESS THAT I DIDN'T EVEN SEE THE DAMAGE I WAS CAUSING NOW.
UM ARCHIVES
WELL... APOLOGY ACCEPTED, I GUESS. WE ALL GET MORE SCARED THAN SMART SOME TIMES.
ESPECIALLY SPIKE.
YEAH... HEY!
IF THIS DARKNESS EVER DOES COME BACK—I CAN LEARN NOT TO MAKE THE SAME MISTAKES MY ANCESTOR DID.
I'M GOING TO KEEP TRAVELING. TRY TO FIND EVERYTHING I CAN ABOUT WHAT TURNED A PONY LIKE ME INTO A MONSTER—AND HOW TO STOP IT.
BUT... YOU'RE NOT GOING TO ERASE IT, ARE YOU?
NO.
EVERYPONY SHOULD BE ABLE TO LEARN FROM THE PAST. THE GOOD AND THE BAD. EVEN YOU MIGHT NEED IT ONE DAY. AND IF ANYPONY CAN LEARN TO FACE WHATEVER EVIL IS OUT THERE—

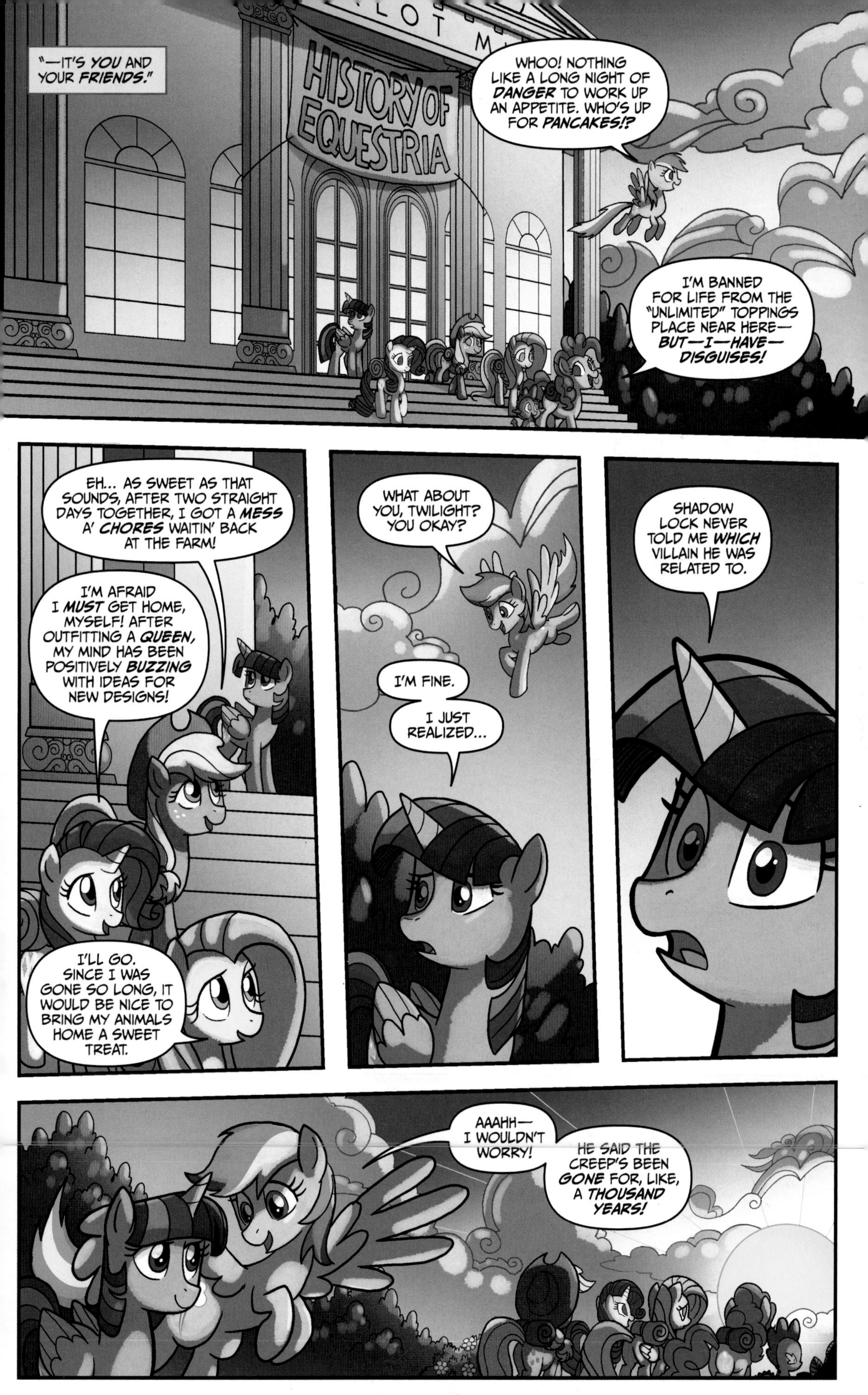
"—IT'S YOU AND YOUR FRIENDS."
HISTORY OF EQUESTRIA
WHOO! NOTHING LIKE A LONG NIGHT OF DANGER TO WORK UP AN APPETITE. WHO'S UP FOR PANCAKES!?
I'M BANNED FOR LIFE FROM THE "UNLIMITED" TOPPINGS PLACE NEAR HERE— BUT—I—HAVE— DISGUISES!
EH... AS SWEET AS THAT SOUNDS, AFTER TWO STRAIGHT DAYS TOGETHER, I GOT A MESS A' CHORES WAITIN' BACK AT THE FARM!
I'M AFRAID I MUST GET HOME, MYSELF! AFTER OUTFITTING A QUEEN, MY MIND HAS BEEN POSITIVELY BUZZING WITH IDEAS FOR NEW DESIGNS!
I'LL GO. SINCE I WAS GONE SO LONG, IT WOULD BE NICE TO BRING MY ANIMALS HOME A SWEET TREAT.
WHAT ABOUT YOU, TWILIGHT? YOU OKAY?
I'M FINE.
I JUST REALIZED...
SHADOW LOCK NEVER TOLD ME WHICH VILLAIN HE WAS RELATED TO.
AAAHH— I WOULDN'T WORRY!
HE SAID THE CREEP'S BEEN GONE FOR, LIKE, A THOUSAND YEARS!

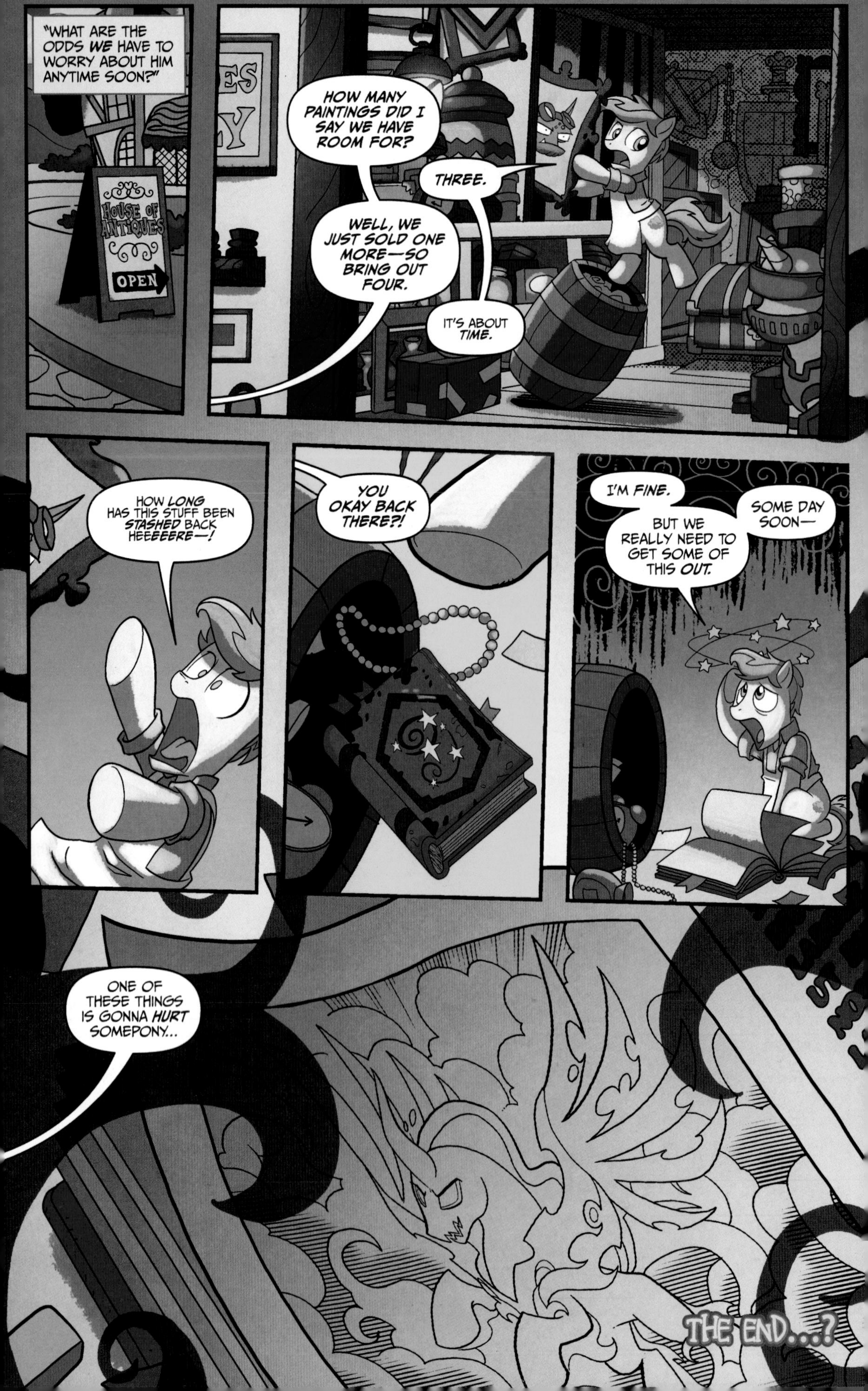
"WHAT ARE THE ODDS WE HAVE TO WORRY ABOUT HIM ANYTIME SOON?"
HOUSE OF ANTIQUES
OPEN
HOW MANY PAINTINGS DID I SAY WE HAVE ROOM FOR?
THREE.
WELL, WE JUST SOLD ONE MORE—SO BRING OUT FOUR.
IT'S ABOUT TIME.
HOW LONG HAS THIS STUFF BEEN STASHED BACK HEEEEERE—!
YOU OKAY BACK THERE?!
I'M FINE.
BUT WE REALLY NEED TO GET SOME OF THIS OUT.
SOME DAY SOON—
ONE OF THESE THINGS IS GONNA HURT SOMEPONY...
THE END...?

my LiTTLE PONY
Friendship is Magic

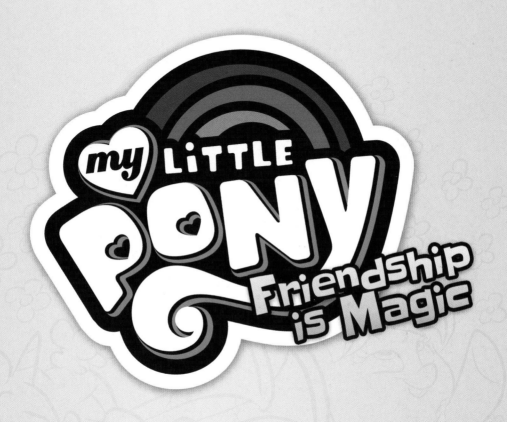

art by Andy Price

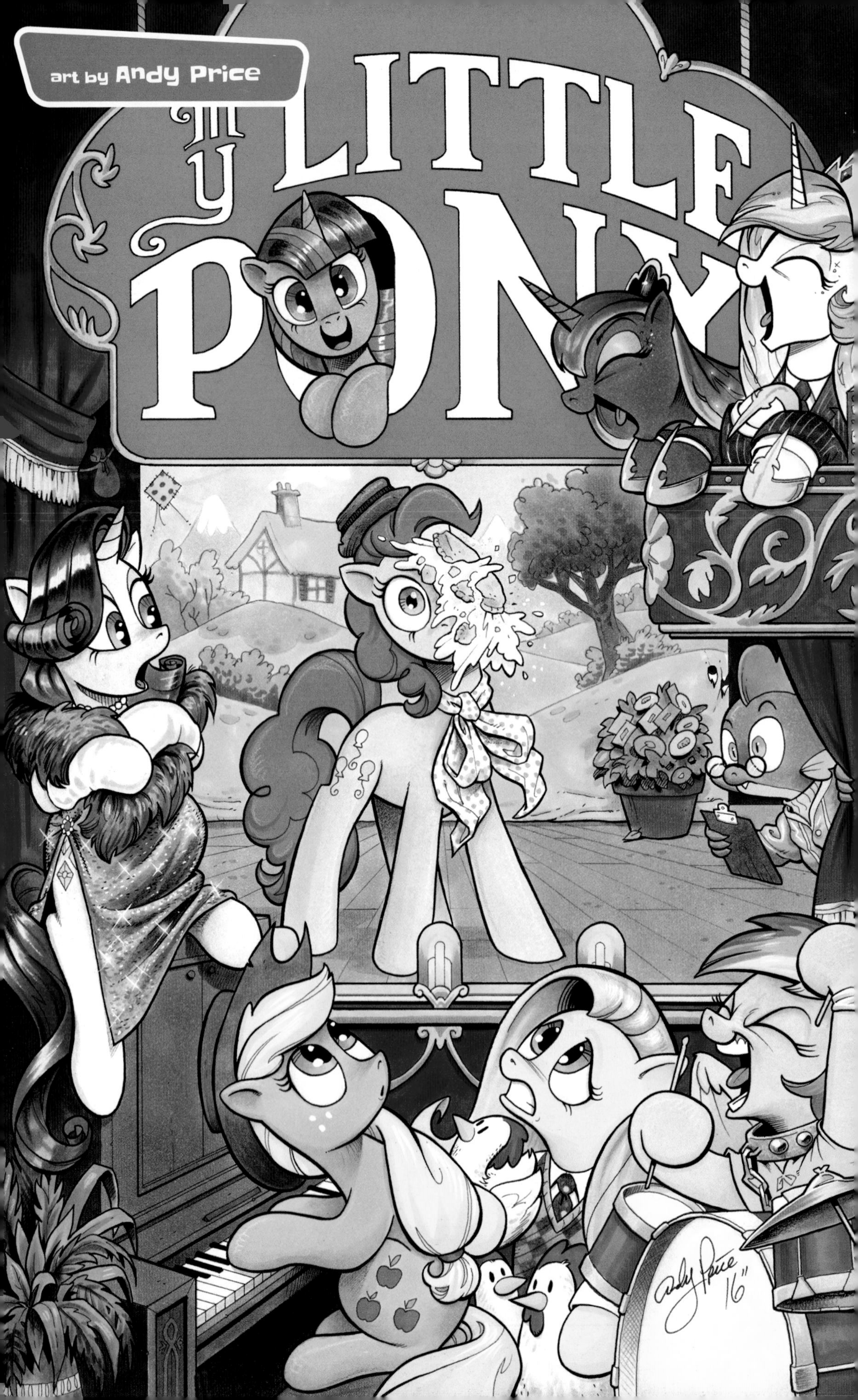
MY LITTLE PONY

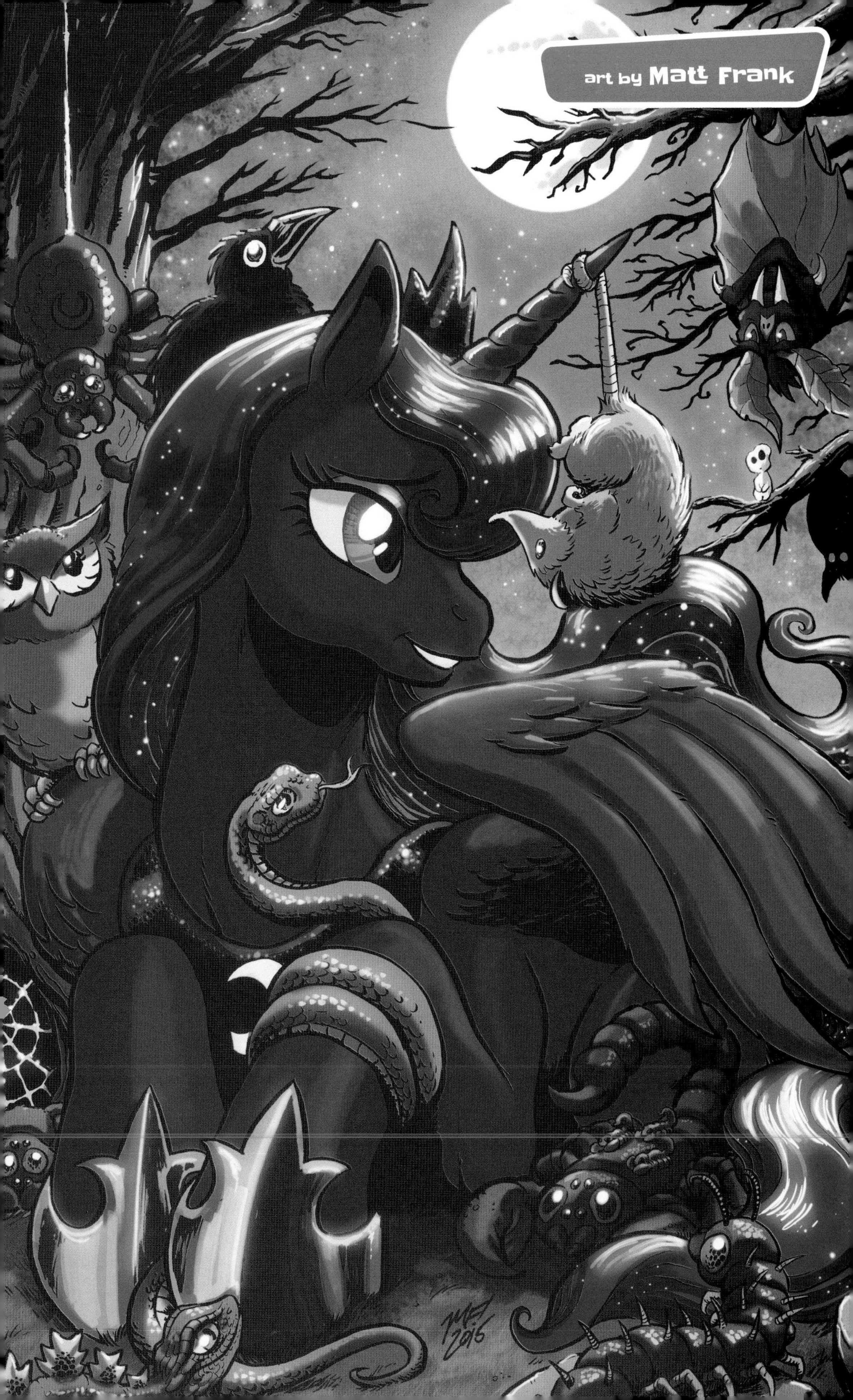
art by Matt Frank

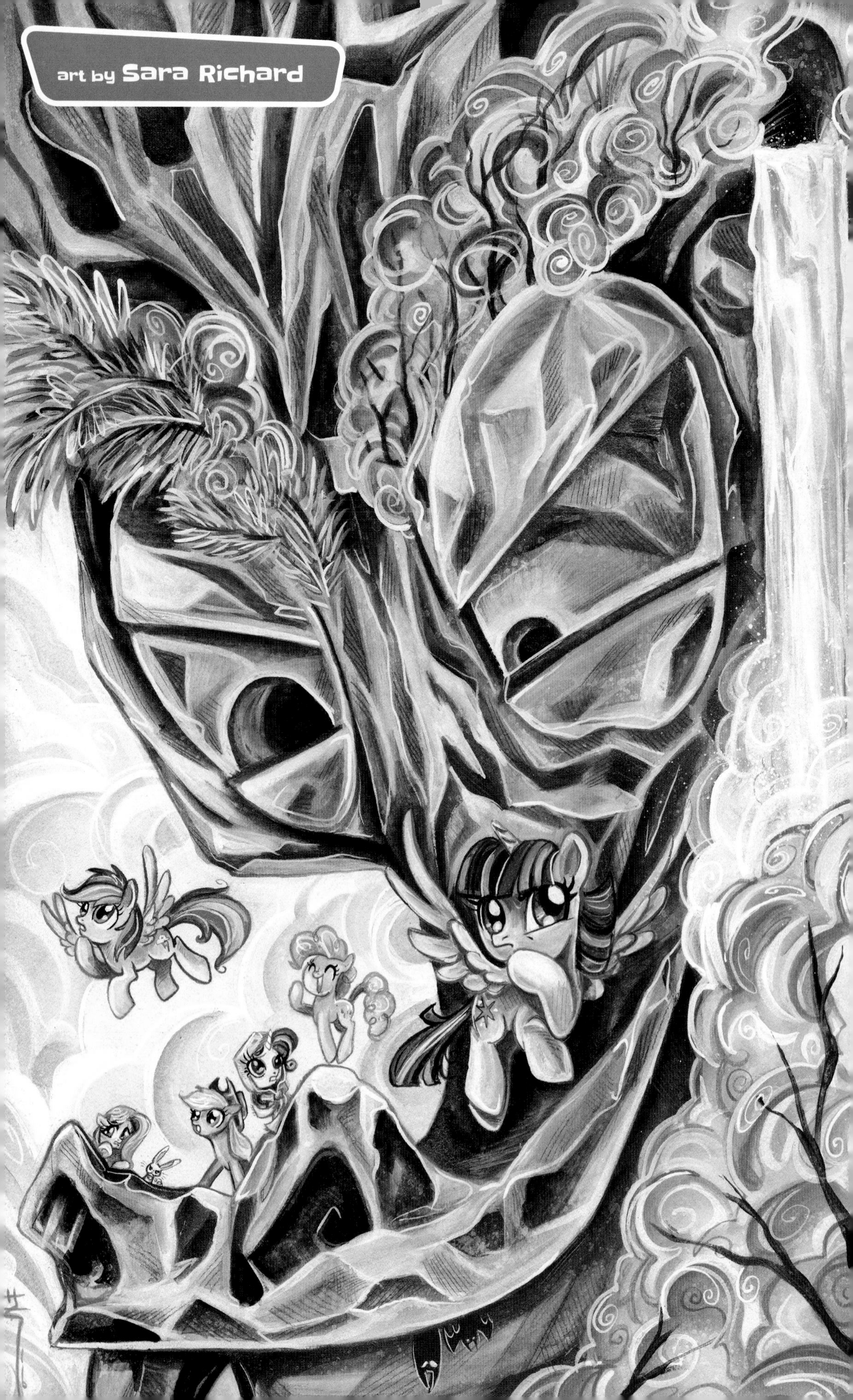

art by Sara Richard

art by Kaori Matsuo

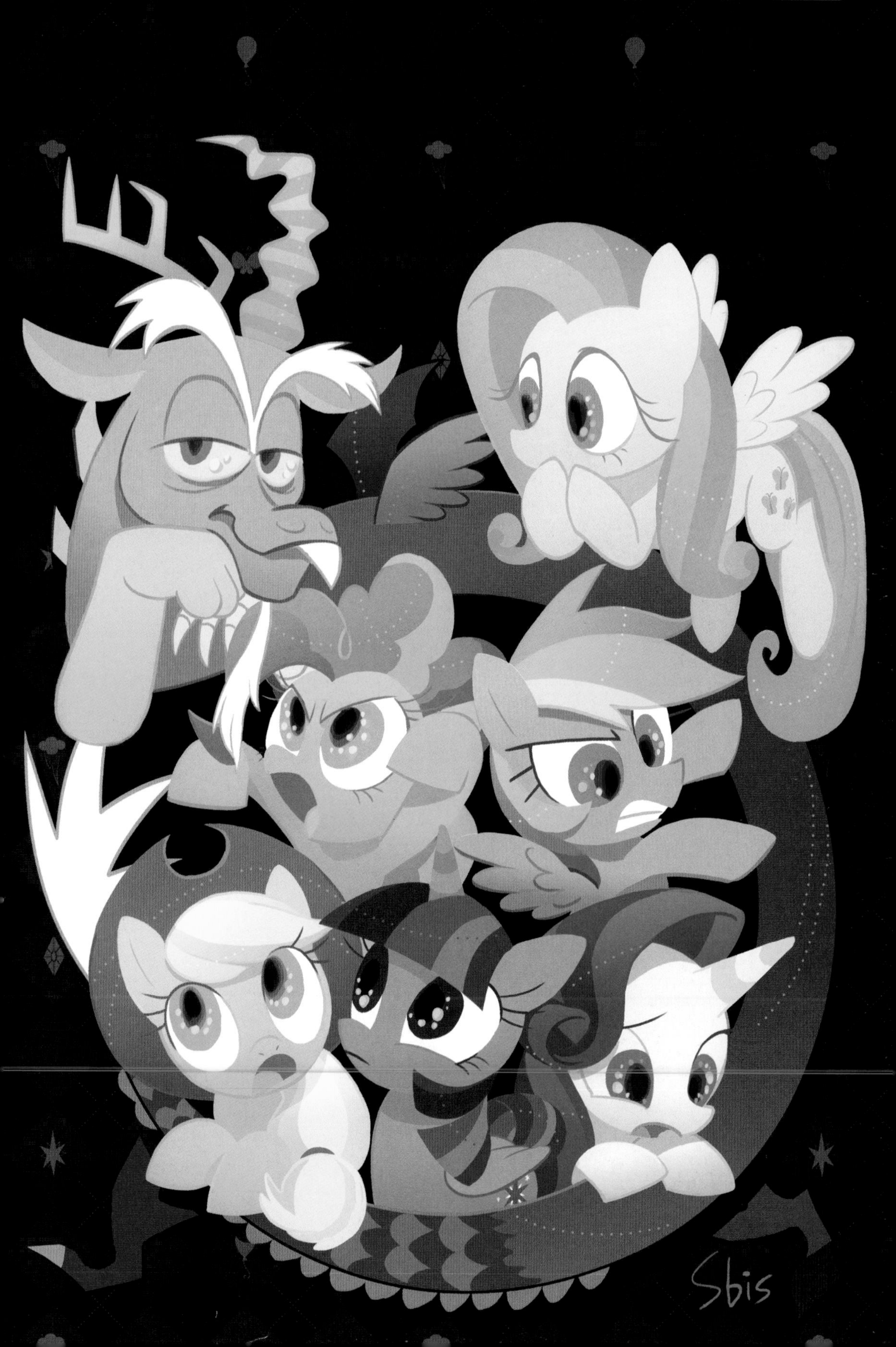
Sbis

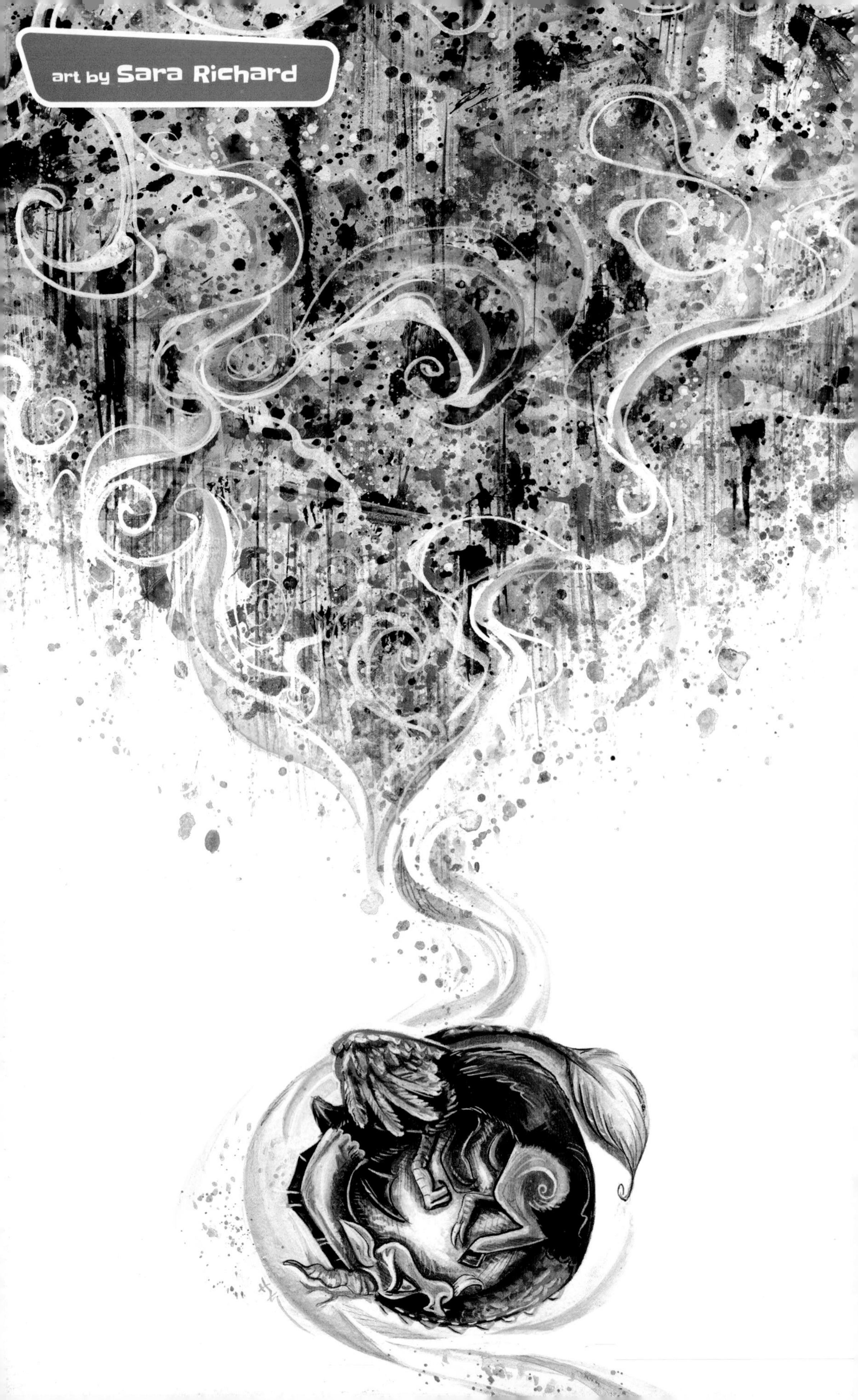

art by Sara Richard

art by Andy Price

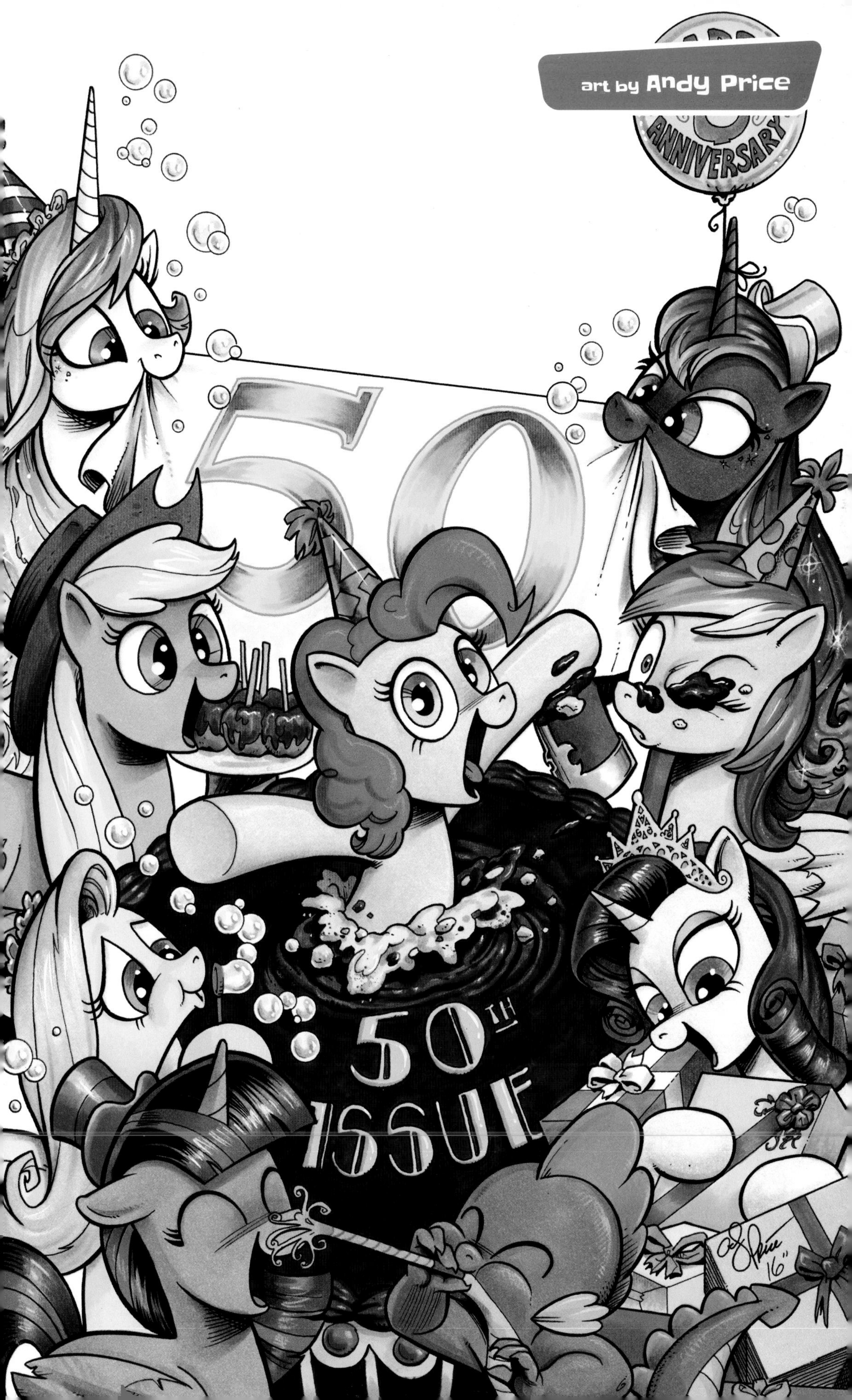
ANNIVERSARY
50
50TH
ISSUE

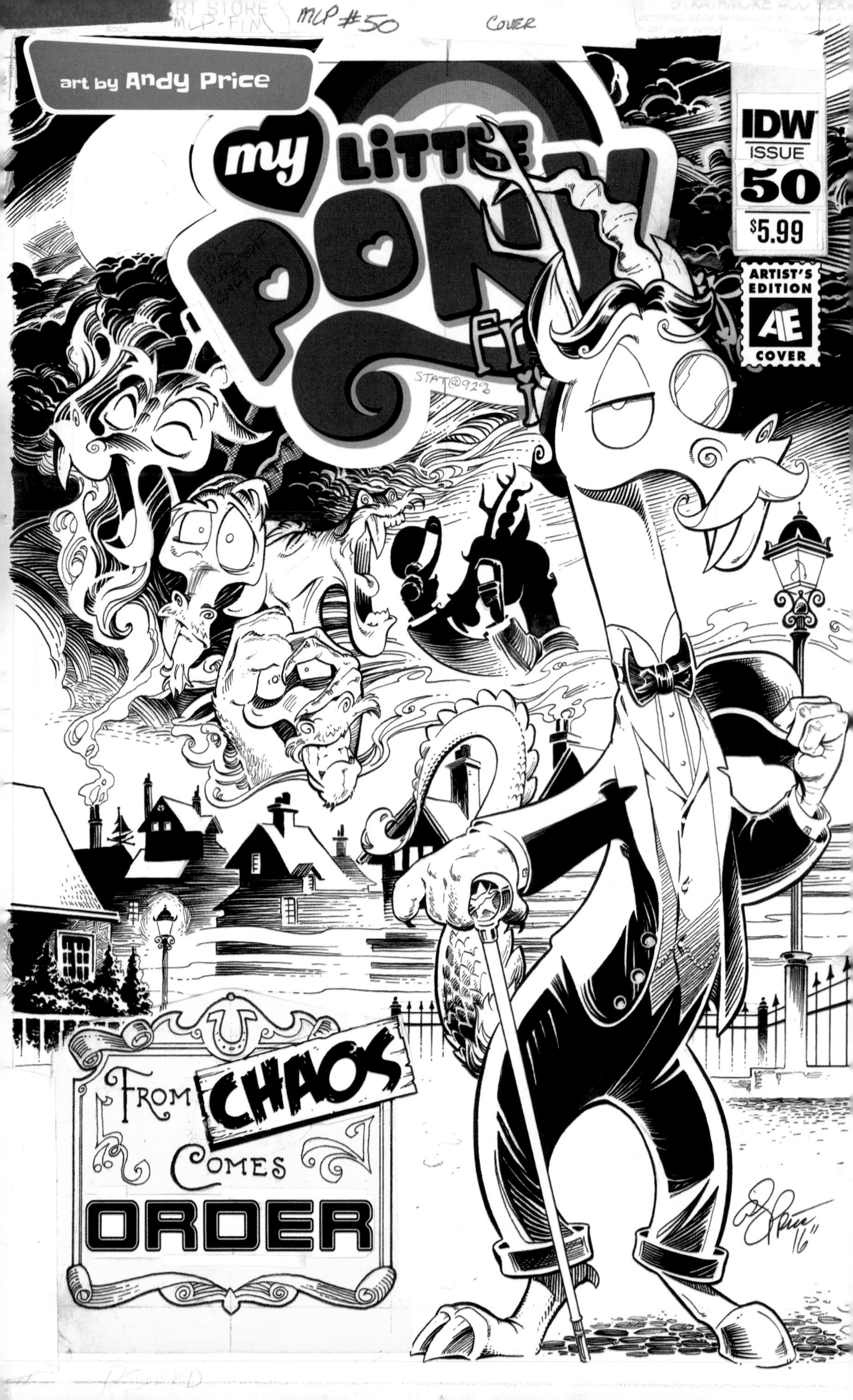
MLP #50
COVER
art by Andy Price
my LITTLE PONY
IDW
ISSUE
50
$5.99
ARTIST'S EDITION
AE
COVER
FROM CHAOS COMES ORDER

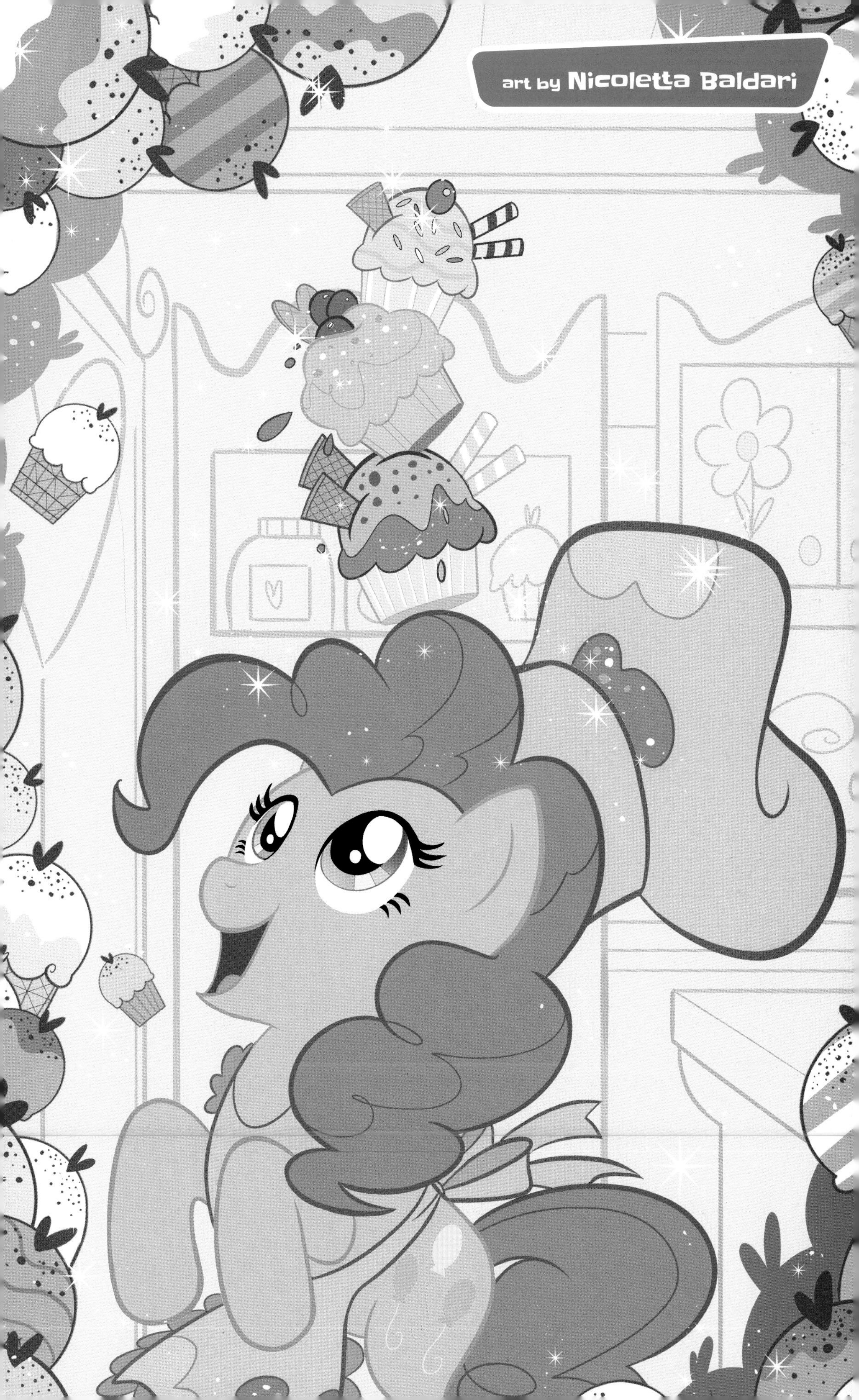
art by Nicoletta Baldari

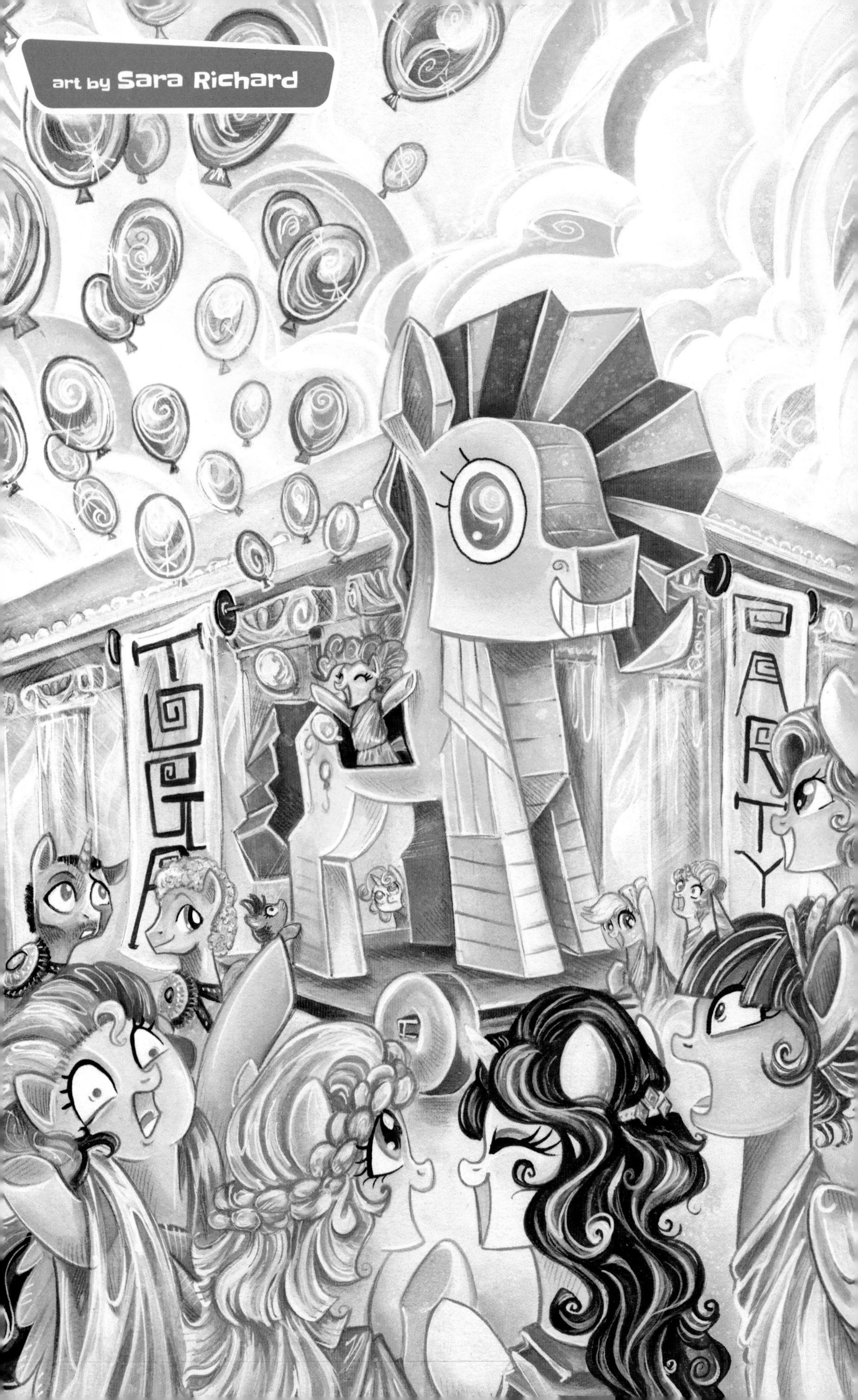
TOGA
PARTY

art by Sara Richard

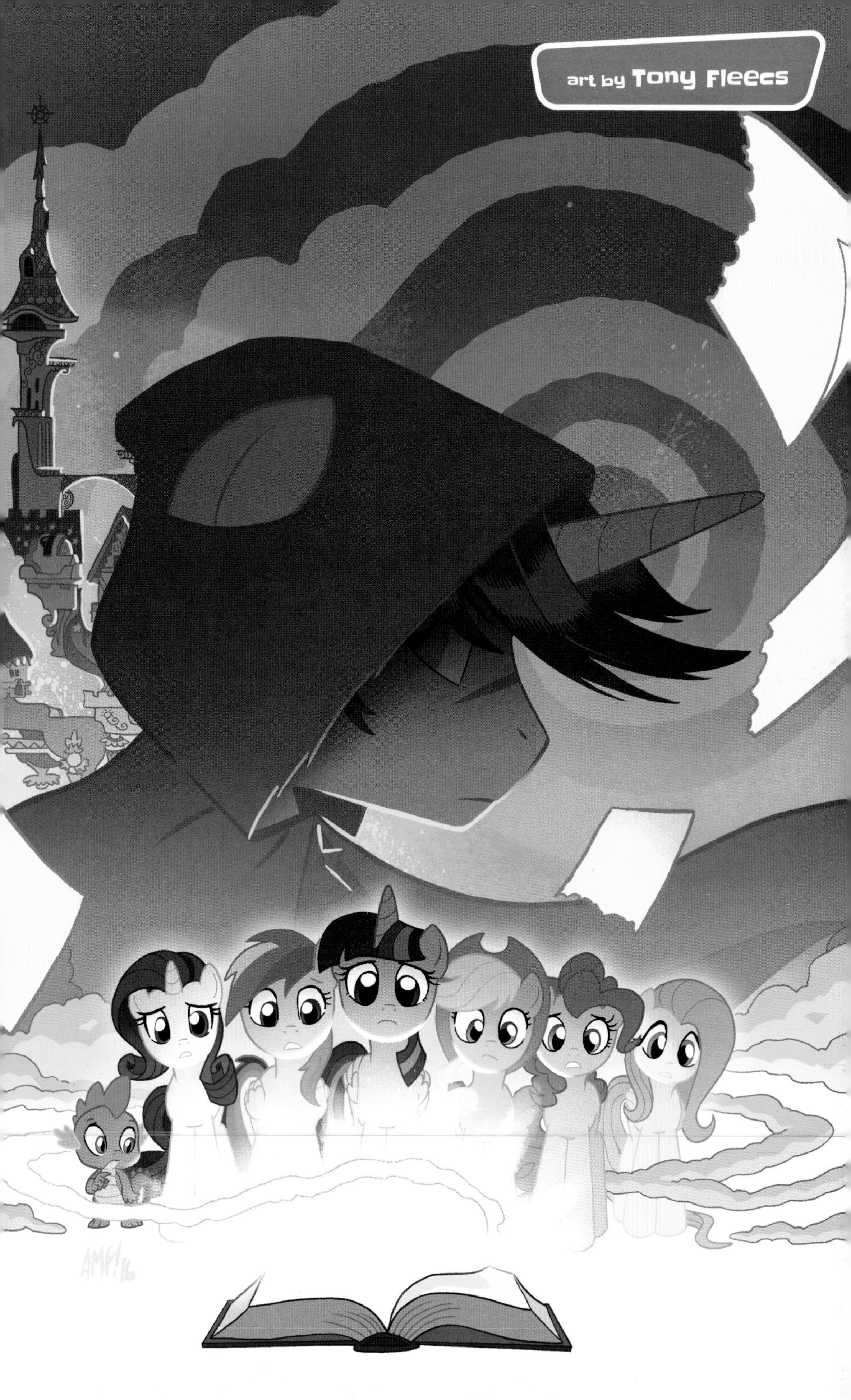
art by Tony Fleecs

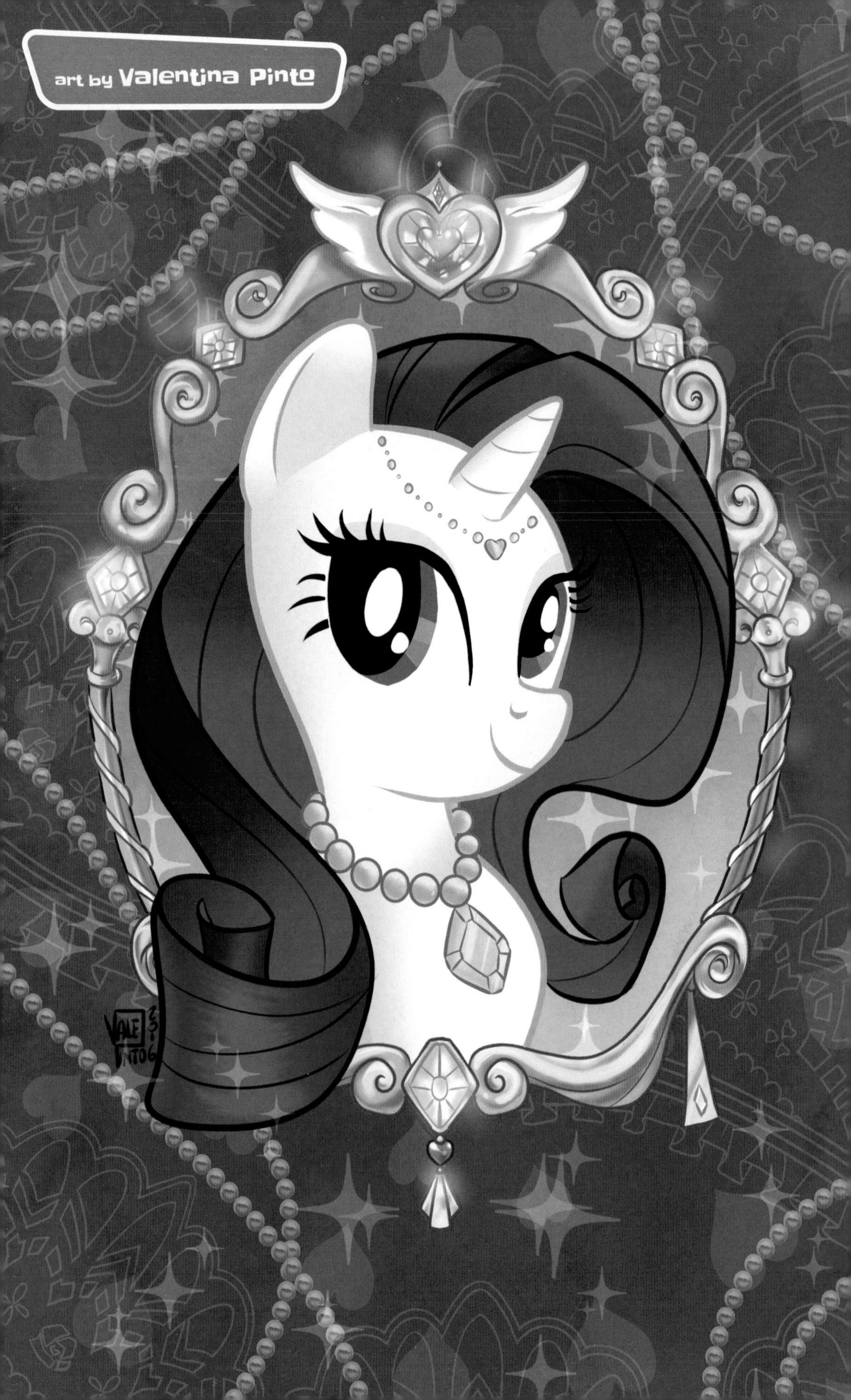

art by Valentina Pinto

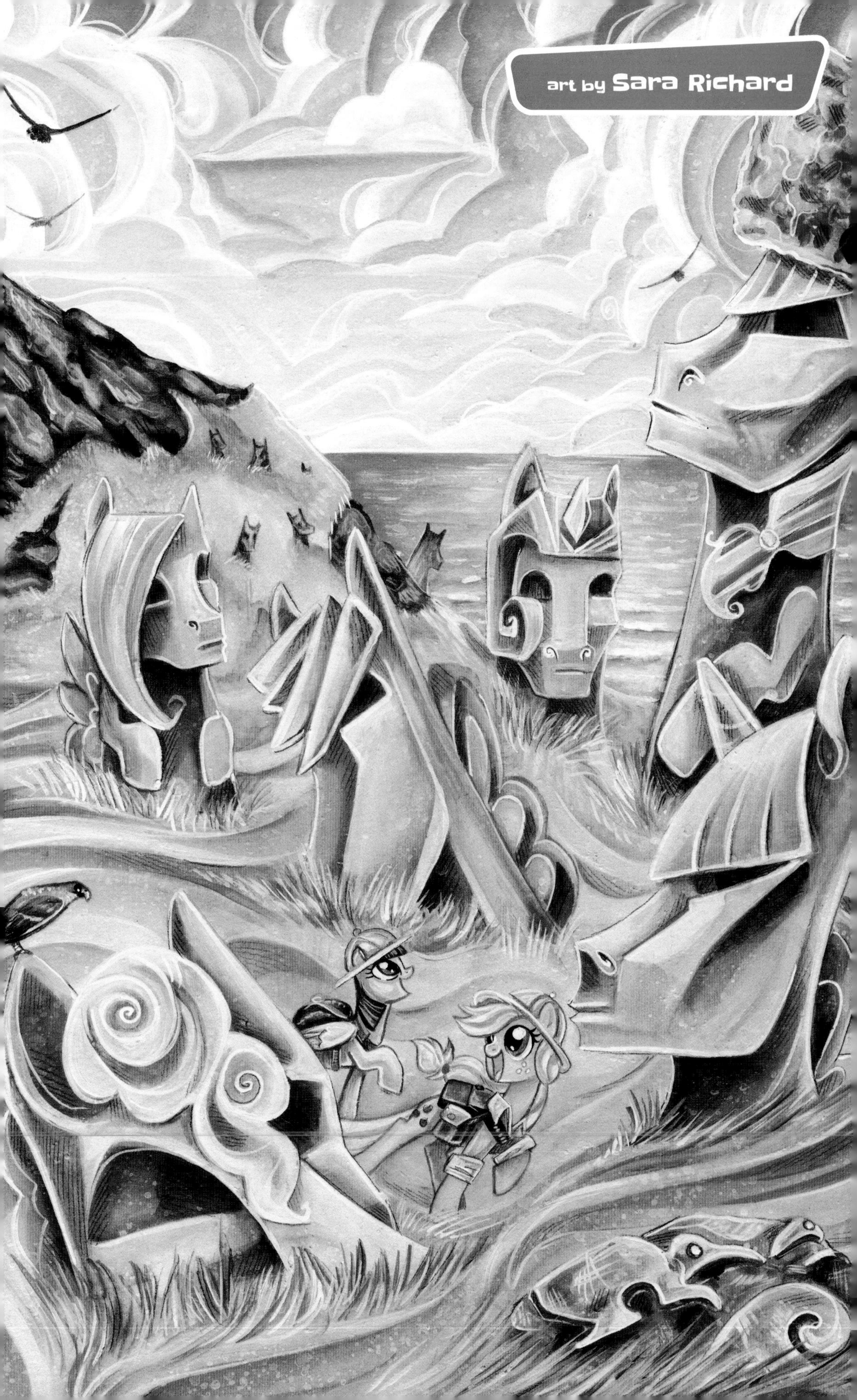
art by Sara Richard

  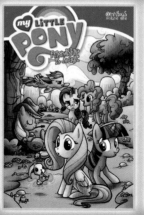